# Praise for Persia Walker's

## *HARLEM REDUX*

"Harlem's fabled 1920s 'Renaissance' provides the dynamic backdrop for Persia Walker's entertaining debut novel. A murder mystery set among the black bourgeoisie, it is also the heady tale of a bygone era…What distinguishes this novel is Walker's attention to the workings and characters of the times, from the club stars to the numbers runners, to prickly class issues between Strivers' Row residents and their working-class neighbors. A Harlem native, Walker understands this community and its history, creating a compelling family intrigue and a full, vibrant portrait of that storied era when Harlem's pulse was the rhythm of black America."—*The Boston Globe*

"McKay emerges as a resolute yet flawed protagonist, trying to restore his family's honor while pursuing an elusive and perhaps nonexistent killer."—*St. Louis Post-Dispatch*

"As much a story of lies, deceit and murder as it is a commentary on race and class, Harlem Redux is filled with colorful characters."—*Chicago Tribune*

"Sexy."—*New York Daily News*

"Walker excels at creating characters that manage to be memorable without being likeable."—*The Washington Post*

"A notable debut. This intriguing page-turner, convincingly set in the heady era of 1920s Harlem, is atmospheric and smart and will keep readers guessing until the very end."—Tananarive Due, author of *The Living Blood* and *The Black Rose*

"A rich, thoroughly enjoyable tale of greed and deceit, passion and betrayal."—April Christofferson, author of *The Protocol* and *Clinical Trial*

W9-CFI-811

# DARKNESS

# &

# the DEVIL BEHIND ME

## A LANIE PRICE MYSTERY

## PERSIA WALKER

Published by Blood Vintage Press 2008

Printed in the United States of America

ISBN-13: 978-0-9792538-2-9
ISBN-10: 0-9792538-2-9

To

*Essie, Tyler and Jordan*

# Acknowledgments

My first words of thanks go to Our Father in Heaven, who has helped me and mine weather many a storm, and without whom I wouldn't dare dream, much less hope that my dreams would come true.

Lots of love to my mother, Essie, and my children, Tyler and Jordan. Without them ... well, I don't even want to think about where I'd be without their loving support and endless patience.

My thanks also go out to Janete Scobie, my former business partner, and John Paine at Paine Literary for their encouragement, wisdom and guidance. Jane Aptaker and Catherine Maiorisi get a special acknowledgment for having done double-duty by repeatedly slogging through this manuscript and offering invaluable humor, insight and commentary. My friend, literary agent Julie Castiglia, also offered incisive last-minute critique for which I'm also grateful. Much appreciation to Michael Henry Adams for sharing his insight and knowledge about Harlem, its history and architecture. Also thanks to Danny Allen for proofreading.

Last, but not least, I have to thank Rodney Shelton, who re-entered my life at just the right time and gave me the strength to make that last mad dash for the finish line.

Thank you one and all. You're a fantastic team and I'm so glad to have you!

# 1.

A task-force investigation is like a fast moving train. Divert it onto the wrong track and it'll derail. At some point, somewhere, it'll slam into a wall or plunge down a hill, and when it goes, it'll take a lot of people with it. It's just a matter of time.

That's what happened to the Goodfellowe investigation—and, by extension, the Todd case.

We may never fully know what happened on the night of December 18, 1923, but what we do know is bitter fact, based on details shared by a grieving family and hard truths that later came to light, and what I can tell you with confidence is this:

It was nearly midnight when Esther Sue Todd hurried out into that blustery night. She was bent against the wind, wrapped tightly in her coat. Her older sister, Ruth, stood just inside the front entrance to Harlem Hospital, under the large Christmas wreath hanging over the lobby door. She watched Esther's thin, buffeted figure until it faded behind a wall of swirling snow. With a sigh, she repressed a sense of fear—*You always thinking the worst, Ruth*—and hurried back to the emergency waiting room to rejoin their friend Beth.

Beth Johnson had claimed a corner of a bench. She sat hunched over, gripping the seat's rounded edge as though she'd pass out any minute. Her olive-toned complexion had taken on an undertone of pearl gray. The flat light of the waiting room added to her pallor, but it wasn't entirely to blame. Bad fish for dinner: That was it.

"Want me to get you a cup of water?" Ruth asked.

Beth shook her head. She sagged and leaned her head back on the bench, but the wood was too hard to be comfortable, so she sat erect again with a groan.

"Why don't you just stretch out?" Ruth asked. "There's plenty of room. I'll just go sit over there." She pointed to one of the nearby benches.

As Ruth would say later, Beth was too weak to argue. She gave a weary nod, drew her feet up and lay down, curling into a tight knot of misery. Ruth took off her coat, rolled it into a ball and put it under Beth's head as a cushion.

Ruth eased down onto a bench and shivered. The waiting room was poorly heated and a cold draft swept through the massive Victorian hall. She blew on her hands, rubbed them together and hugged herself. How, she wondered, had the evening turned out so wrong?

It had started well enough. They were going to see the Christmas Show at the Renaissance Ballroom, a large entertainment center on 138th Street and Seventh Avenue. All kinds of events were held at the Renaissance, everything from basketball games, to dances and musical shows.

It had been snowing off and on all day and the forecast predicted more, but not even warnings of a blizzard could've stopped their plans. The chance to go out was something special, but to have the time—and money—to see the Christmas Show at the Renaissance was extraordinary. Esther, especially, had looked forward to the evening. She'd been talking about it for weeks. Between working, taking care of her young son, and practicing the piano to please Mrs. Goodfellowe, she had little or no time for herself. That night was to have been different. She was going to kick up her heels and have fun.

Ruth glanced up at the huge clock above the door. Was it really only five hours ago that she and Esther had picked up Beth with Mrs. Goodfellowe's car? They'd been so excited as they drove off and more than satisfied with their balcony seats. The performers had the audience laughing and clapping and everyone was having a fine old time. Everything was going swell until about twenty minutes into the show. That's when Esther noticed that Beth was holding her stomach and grimacing.

*You all right?*

Beth could barely answer. She nodded that she was, but she'd broken out into a sweat. Esther touched Beth's forehead. The girl was cold and clammy.

*Maybe I'd better go to the hospital.*

She worsened fast. By the time Ruth and Esther got Beth down the stairs and outside, she was so weak, she could barely stand. Esther put the pedal to the floor and sped to Harlem Hospital on 135th Street and Lenox Avenue, going as fast as the snow would allow. She brought Ruth and Beth to the hospital's front door, and then drove away to find a parking space.

She was gone twenty minutes.

By the time she got back, a doctor had seen Beth. He suspected it was something she'd eaten. Sure enough, Beth said she'd had fish for dinner and that it hadn't smelled right. Beth would be fine, the doctor said. She had upchucked and gotten some medicine. She just needed rest. She could spend the night at the hospital, but she'd have to pay for the bed up front.

Well, they didn't have the money for that. So the doctor said Beth could rest for a while, an hour or so, and then go home.

Esther and Ruth took up watch downstairs in the waiting room. Outside, the wind picked up and the snow fell harder—thick, heavy flakes that quickly accumulated. After two hours, a nurse brought Beth downstairs. She was still weak, but said she felt strong enough to go home.

Ruth and Esther eyed Beth with matching frowns.

"You sure you don't want to rest here a little longer?" Esther asked.

"No, no, I want to go home." Beth rubbed her forehead. Her eyes were bleary and unfocused.

Esther and Ruth exchanged another look.

"I don't like it," Ruth said.

"But we can't force her to stay. Maybe taking her home would be the best thing to do. The doctor said he can't do much more for her. What she needs is to relax. She can't do that here. She can at home."

Ruth was still unhappy, but she relented. "All right."

"I'll go get the car." Esther tightened her coat. "Give me fifteen, twenty minutes."

"Let me walk you out." Ruth turned back to Beth. "You'll be okay?"

Slumped on the bench, Beth nodded and closed her eyes. Ruth gave her a worried look, but decided she'd be all right alone for the five minutes.

"Where'd you park?" she asked Esther as they headed down the corridor.

"Over on 132nd and Madison, right at the corner, in front of the bakery. It's not far, but it's too far for Beth to walk."

They were soon at the entrance. Esther started toward the door.

"Wait a minute," Ruth said. She went past her sister to the door and peered out. The night was as dark as soot; the only light came from the gas lamps that lit Lenox Avenue. It was windy. The snow was coming down hard.

"Maybe I should go with you. I don't like the way it looks out there. I don't see nobody on the street right now and you know, this ain't the best part of town."

"This is a fine part of town." Esther spoke with the pride of a new emigrant. She'd only come up from Virginia seven months earlier. "It's the best part of New York City. Ain't nobody hanging around this hospital who'd do me no harm."

Ruth was unconvinced.

Esther gave her a peck on the cheek. "You stay here with Beth." She swept out the door with a wave. "See you in a few!"

As the minutes crawled by, Ruth began to pace. She tried hard not to check the wall clock. But it was nigh on impossible not to. Beth turned over, trying to get comfortable.

"She's not back yet?" Beth asked. "Just how far did she park that thing?"

Ruth told her not to fret, but she was feeling uneasy herself. More time passed. She headed toward the door.

"Where you going?" Beth asked.

"Just outside to see." Ruth pushed open the door and stepped out into the night. A harsh wind slammed into her and she gasped. The night had turned so very cold. The wind sliced through her coat, as sharp and penetrating as a blade made of ice. The driven snowflakes scratched her face. A gust of wind kicked up her front coat flap. She pushed it down and held it in place with one gloved hand, while holding down her hat with the other.

She gazed to her left, down the way Esther must've gone. Lenox Avenue was a wide boulevard. Some people thought of it as the Fifth Avenue of Harlem, and it was usually brimming with people. But that night, the wind and snow had driven away every living soul. The avenue, poorly lit by street lamps spaced far apart, was an icy blur, shadowed, dark and desolate.

Teeth chattering, she snuggled deeper into her coat. As soon as they got home, she would make herself a hot cup of tea. That sure would be nice.

Esther must've found it hard going in the snow. The wind itself would've pushed her back. Ruth had to lean into it just to take the few steps to the curb. This kind of weather would've made the short walk to Mrs. Goodfellowe's car seem double the distance. No doubt that was why Esther hadn't returned yet. Ruth felt a stab of annoyance. Fighting your way through this weather was crazy. Esther should've come on back to the hospital. The three of them could've waited out the worst of it and then gone on home. A person could catch pneumonia out here.

Ruth pushed her way through the snow and wind to get to the corner of 135th Street. She peered to her left, eastward: nothing but darkness and shadows and more snow.

She stomped her feet to shake off the snow. Like Esther, she was wearing thin shoes, not boots. If her toes were curling at the cold after just two minutes of standing outside, then Esther's feet must be soaked by now—or feeling like ice.

At the thought, Ruth's sense of irritation vanished. She couldn't stay angry with her baby sister for not turning back. Esther wasn't the kind to give up. That's all. She was the kind to set her head against the wind and keep on going.

Again, Ruth shivered. It didn't make sense to stand out here too long. She just prayed that Esther wouldn't come down with pneumonia. It sure wouldn't be good if both she and Esther got sick. She'd better go back inside. She started toward the hospital entrance. She was nearly there, when a car honked, startling her. The sound was brief, harsh and abrupt. She turned in its direction.

With ghostly headlights, Mrs. Goodfellowe's car came barreling around the corner of 135th Street, moving way too fast for the slippery street. The soft snow caught the front tires and sent the Packard into a slow spin. Ruth's heart skipped a beat and her breath caught. For one terrible moment, she thought the car would flip over or crash into a lamppost.

It did neither.

The car swerved to a nerve-rattling halt and rocked on its axle. There was a dull moment when the whole world seemed to stand still. Even the battering wind and swirling snow paused.

In that split second, Ruth heard a terrified sob. She would never forget it, a gut wrenching, cut-off cry so familiar and yet so foreign that it engraved itself on her mind. *I heard her*, she would say. *Impossible*, people would answer, *simply impossible given the distance and the conditions*. After a time, Ruth would stop mentioning it. What others thought was irrelevant. She knew what she'd heard—and still heard every night, year in and year out, as that cry echoed within her, cutting deeper into her soul. But on that night, before grief took over, it was fear she felt, fear and puzzlement. Who was driving Mrs. Goodfellowe's car? It couldn't be Esther. It just couldn't be. Esther didn't drive like that. So, where was she? And who was behind the wheel?

As the driver put the car in reverse, straightened it out and headed up the street, Ruth could see that the driver was indeed Esther—Esther driving with a madwoman's determination, heedless of danger.

Kicking up a spray of white dust, the Packard plowed through the snow with gathering speed. The car's front end wove right and left. It was moving so fast it looked as though it would go on by. But as it approached the hospital entrance, it slowed. Enormously relieved, Ruth stepped off the curb.

The headlights died and the car gunned forward. It sped past Ruth and headed down the street. For a moment, she was too stunned to react. That *was* Mrs. Goodfellowe's car, wasn't it? Sure it was. It had to be. She could still see Esther at the wheel.

Ruth gave a yell and ran out into the street, jumping up and down, waving and calling out. But Esther just kept on going. If anything, she drove faster. Ruth couldn't understand it. Esther must have seen her.

Confused and worried, Ruth stumbled back inside and told Beth what she'd seen.

"Maybe she went to get some gasoline," Beth suggested.

"Where'd she be getting it this time of night? And what's that got to do with her driving right past me?"

"You sure it was her?"

"Of course I am."

Beth fell silent. Ruth paced. Esther was bound to come back. And she'd have a good explanation for driving away like that. They'd just have to wait. Esther would come back. Of course, she would.

She had to.

But it was a while—a long while—before Esther Todd was seen again.

## 2.

I spotted her before she spotted me. It was the first Monday in December and I was at my desk in the city room of the *Harlem Chronicle*. Our newsroom sounded like Farmer John's barnyard with people squawking at each another, telephones jangling and typewriters clacking. Everybody was pounding the keys, working on their year-end roundups.

To be fair, I was making my share of the racket, trying to get out my weekly column. The latest item for *Lanie's World* was supposed to be a glittery Christmas piece, another report on the glamorous life of Harlem's fast set. But I was bored and uninspired, and my copy showed it. It was about as glittery as the bottom of a rusty bucket. The thing is, I actually enjoyed writing that kind of gossipy stuff. At least, most times I did. But doing it full-time was like eating cotton candy twenty-four hours a day. After a constant diet of sugar and nothing but, even the most die-hard sweet tooth will get to yearning for a nice, substantial steak.

I read what I'd written and shook my head. I'd been a good reporter once, covering crime and its consequences. But that was a lifetime ago.

I was about to rip out the page and start over, when someone said my name. The voice was familiar, but I couldn't place it. That's when I looked up and saw her—a split second before George Greene, one of the rookie reporters, pointed her to my desk.

I paused, both surprised and concerned. It had been three years since we'd last spoken, but I could remember that conversation word for word.

*What're you going to do now?*
*I don't know. What can we do?*
*Just don't give up.*

Even then she'd been thin, but now her face was lean and toughened. She was in her mid-thirties, but appeared to be older. Worry and fatigue had etched fine lines in the corners of her eyes. In another life, she could've been beautiful. She had the requisite high cheekbones and dark, liquid eyes, but hard work and tragedy had lent an air of permanent exhaustion and abiding grief. She came over, clutching her battered purse and looking politely apologetic.

"Mrs. Price, you probably don't remember me, but—"

"Of course I do. You're Ruth—Ruth Todd."

Her smile was soft and grateful. She extended her hand and I rose to shake it.

"It's been a long time," I said. "How's the family doing?"

"Not good."

Of course not, given what they'd gone through. I remembered my manners, borrowed a chair from a desk nearby and offered her a seat. She sat down with a thank you.

"None of us has ever forgotten," she said. "We live with it day in and day out, but it's worse at Christmastime. Seems like we've lived with this for such a long time. Can't none of us remember what it was like before ..." She stumbled, still unable to say it, "well, before it happened. We got our faith in Jesus and that helps, but I got to admit, there's been times when I was so low it felt like my heart was scraping the ground." Her hands tensed. "Last year, Daddy died. It was the not knowing that killed him."

"I'm sorry to hear that."

Mr. Todd had been a fine old gentleman. He did better than most with the cards life dealt him. He'd lost his right leg to a railroad accident early on, but still managed to make it North, teach himself to read, and open up a shoe shop that fed him and his family.

"Now Mama's going, too. She's over at Harlem Hospital. The doctors say it's T.B., but I know it's got to do with what happened to Esther. Mama may not even make it to New Year's. I think—I know she'd be able to go more peaceful if she had a—if she just knew something ... anything."

"Yes, I understand." Thoughtful, I picked up a pencil and rolled it between my fingers. "How's Job?"

"He's fine. I took him in, raised him like he's my own."

"He knows about his mother?"

"Sure does—and that's another thing. He's ten now and asking questions. He's a smart kid and I'm a bad liar. Even if I was good at making up tales, he's too quick to believe 'em."

"Lying wouldn't make sense. It never does. Sooner or later, he'd find out the truth."

"The problem is, don't nobody know the truth. Not all of it. Not really. Just which truth is he gonna hear? What the cops say—or what we say? And don't neither truth tell the whole story." She paused. "That's why I'm here."

I tapped the pencil on the desk. "I take it you want me to write about Esther."

She sat forward, on the edge of the chair. "It's time for the real story to be written, Mrs. Price. And if anybody can do it, you can. You the one."

I wished that I shared her confidence—in me or any other columnist I knew. "If I wrote about Esther—and I'm not saying I will—but if I did, just what're you hoping will happen? It's been a long time. People forget."

"You can make 'em remember. People will read your stuff and get to thinking about it."

She wasn't giving me a compliment just to get what she wanted—or maybe she was. But I thought she meant it. The compliment was heartfelt but it was also naïve.

"I write fluff. People don't expect anything serious from me."

She started to object, but I raised a hand to forestall her.

"As a matter of fact, they read my column for just that reason. They want to be entertained. They trust that when they step into *Lanie's World*, they can turn off their brain and never be asked to think."

"You once said you'd do everything you could to help us."

"And I meant it. But letting you get your hopes up just because of my column would be cruel, not kind."

"Cruel?" Her eyebrows shot up. "I'll tell you what's cruel. The things people keep saying about her, the cops and their dirty suspicions. That's cruel. As for disappointing us: Don't even think about it. Can't nobody disappoint us more than we been disappointed already." She was resolute. "Well? What about it? Will you do it, please?"

I leaned back in my chair, reflective. "I'll think about it."

She was disappointed. "Will you really?"

"I promise. I'll let you know."

She thought about that for a minute. With a sigh, she adjusted her cloche hat and rose. Shaking my hand, she thanked me.

"Nothing to thank me for."

She gave a brave smile. "I want to believe there will be."

I watched her leave and exhaled. Every now and then someone would come in with an axe to grind and want to use my column to do it. I usually took the time to listen and I usually had to say no, but it was never easy to turn people away.

Sam Delaney walked up. He was a carefully dressed man in his early forties with handsome features and faint gray circles under dark brown eyes. He was the most eligible bachelor in the newsroom. He was also the most remote. That frustrated a lot of the single women on staff, but it didn't bother me. I'd pretty much lost interest in men since my husband died.

As my boss and the city room editor of the *Harlem Chronicle*, Sam was hard working, dependable and for the most part fair. I sensed he had a kind heart, but what I most often saw was his conservatism and caution. He had both instincts and imagination, but he trusted neither, not in himself or in others, and that did bother me. Sometimes, I wondered if he didn't have too much respect for authority— never too good a trait in a newspaperman. But I couldn't argue with his dedication. His primary concern was to protect the paper. He'd been there less than a year and had already managed to bump up its circulation. He was certainly a welcome relief after our previous editor, an alcoholic who'd harassed the women and belittled the men. Part of Sam's style was to know everything that went on in his newsroom. Now he nodded toward Ruth's departing figure.

"What was that all about?"

"Remember Esther Todd?"

He nodded.

"Well, that was her older sister." I explained what Ruth wanted.

He listened sympathetically, but shook his head. "Wouldn't be a good idea."

"Why not?"

"It's depressing. Especially right now, before Christmas. People want to read something cheerful, upbeat."

Practical and levelheaded, Sam had handed me the perfect reason to give Ruth for refusing her request. I should've been relieved. Instead, I was faintly irritated.

"Upbeat, sure. Cheerful, maybe—but also real. Not fake." I glanced at the page in my Underwood. "Not mindless."

"Trust me on this one. Folks don't want to be reminded of crime and misery. Not at this time of year. Furthermore, that's not what you're paid to write about. You're a society columnist, remember?"

I eyed the stack of unopened party invitations littering my desk. "How could I forget?"

"Well, then."

Those two words were like a key turning. They opened up my heart and made up my mind. Sam wasn't a callous man, but his light dismissal of Ruth's request was a strong reminder of the way police had treated her when she begged for help—and of how I'd made a promise I'd failed to keep. In fact, I must've felt a lingering trace of guilt about the Todd case for years, because a sense of forgotten obligation surged back.

"Sam, I'm going to do the column on Esther."

My sudden resoluteness surprised him. He started to object, but I cut him off. Given my initial reluctance to fulfill Ruth's wish, I felt like a hypocrite, but having committed myself to the idea of helping her, I was going to argue for it.

"Let's be honest. Christmas isn't just about good times. You and I know it can be a time of misery—and not just for a few, but for the many."

"Lanie, what's—"

"There's a whole bunch of people out there bleeding, and the holiday just shoves the knife in deeper."

He lifted a skeptical eyebrow and folded his arms across his chest. His decision made, he was going to let me make my little speech, confident it wouldn't change his mind.

"They're alone. They're sad. And maybe, just like Ruth Todd, they're grieving. Those people deserve to be acknowledged, Sam. We owe them something."

"Lanie," he said with the patience of a saint. "I know there are—"

"If I can write a column that gives someone hope, or brings even one person some peace, then everybody benefits."

"But it's not why people read your column. It's not what they expect."

"All the more reason for me to do it. Our readers will find a story about a family battling grief a hundred times more uplifting than another story about A'Lelia Walker and the shenanigans of people who don't have a care in the world."

He hesitated.

"Let me try, Sam. Just let me give it a shot."

We eyed one another. If it were a matter of who blinked first, it wouldn't be me. Selena Troy walked past, giving each of us a curious glance. She was our obituary writer. Very pretty, very doll-like and very nosey. She had high ambitions—not of being a lowly reporter, but a widely syndicated columnist. Sam sighed, leaned in toward me and spoke in a tense undertone.

"Okay, but keep it light. I'll give the final word on it when you're done. Understand?"

"Thanks, boss."

He grimaced at my plantation humor and I hurried off to catch up to Ruth Todd. She was in the corridor, about to board the elevator. Johnny, the elevator operator, saw me running and held the door.

"I'll do it," I told her and enjoyed her expression of relief. "But on one condition."

Some of the trust in her eyes went away. "You want money."

"No, of course not. What I want is for you to understand that my writing about Esther doesn't guarantee a thing. It's just a shot in the dark, a try that could lead to nowhere."

A sad but determined smile touched Ruth's face.

"I was taught to expect little in life, and I've had to get used to even less. But what I got plenty of is faith. You do what you can and let the Lord do the rest. He's our friend, Mrs. Price. I do believe that. He's on our side."

"You're asking for a miracle. I can't give you one—"

"But He can."

As I watched Ruth Todd step into the elevator, I felt the touch of grace, and I knew that hers was the cause I'd been waiting for.

## 3.

Hours later, I sat cross-legged on my sofa in the front parlor of my house on Strivers' Row. A cup of steaming, hot tea sat within easy reach on a lamp table. A platter by the Creole Jazz Band played on the Victrola. My old notes and newspaper reports on the Todd case were in two piles on the coffee table. The first stack contained my articles; the second comprised work by others.

The collection of reports was less than comprehensive. I'd stopped accumulating them in late January of '24, right after receiving word of my mother's illness. The articles I did have were well written, but they were less detailed than a real police report. So my file was limited, but it was a beginning, the only record of the case I had.

I'd decided to spend the evening culling the articles for names of police officers, neighbors, anyone who'd known Esther or been familiar with the case and been quoted. Although it wasn't likely their memories had improved in the years since her disappearance, there was always the chance they might recall something that hadn't been quoted or they'd considered too insignificant to mention.

I took up the earliest of the clippings and the memories came rushing back.

I met Ruth Todd and Beth Johnson for the first time about two hours after Esther's disappearance. At the time I was a police reporter for the *Harlem Age*. In the early hours of Friday, December 15, someone rang my doorbell, waking me from a sound sleep. I glanced out my bedroom window to see Sleepy Willy standing on my doorstep. He was a janitor at the Harlem Police Station on West 135th Street, and one of my favorite tipsters.

"Esther Todd's sister and a friend of hers, they down at the station raising a ruckus," he said when I got downstairs. "Something about Esther having gotten herself into trouble."

My first reaction was puzzlement. "What kind of trouble would Esther Todd get into? Far as I know, she's a church-going woman."

"Dunno. Just know that something's gone wrong. That sister of hers is about to raise the roof."

"All right. I'll get down there and check it out."

Sleepy Willy got his two bits for the info. I ran upstairs, got dressed and threw some cold water on my face, recalling what I knew about Esther.

She was twenty-four years old and a pianist. She was enjoying—some would say enduring—the strong-arm patronage of Mrs. Katherine Goodfellowe, an immensely wealthy widow. Mrs. G, as Esther called her when speaking to friends, demanded parlor performances every two weeks at her Fifth Avenue salon. The lady always wanted to see *progress* and enjoyed putting Esther's talents on display before her society friends.

Esther was already a minor celebrity in Harlem. If Mrs. Goodfellowe had her way, then Esther would be famous beyond it. Mrs. Goodfellowe was doing everything she could to get Esther's name out there, to make her a known commodity throughout New York City. She'd already gotten Carl Van Vechten, a popular socialite and influential columnist, to write one piece on Esther and she was pushing him to write more.

Esther was also a single mother. She not only had to practice piano every day, but also take care of her seven-year-old son, Job. And despite Mrs. G's patronage, Esther needed the income from a job, so she worked long hours as a laundrywoman.

I'd seen Esther and her son perform at a neighborhood church only the prior Sunday. They were good, real good. I hated to think of anything happening to either one of them.

I dried my face, shimmied into some warm clothes and hurried out. The snow had stopped falling and the temperature had dropped. The city was a ghost town—cold, gray and empty. What kind of trouble, I'd asked. On a night like this, there was a lot to choose from.

No other reporters were at the station when I got there. Ruth and Beth were just leaving. I introduced myself and asked what had happened. Beth, who I learned was one of Mrs. Goodfellowe's maids, appeared to be in shock. Ruth was frightened and angry. Esther, she said, had disappeared. No doubt kidnapped. But the cops weren't taking it seriously. They didn't care and wouldn't let her file a report.

"They think she done run off by herself. Esther wouldn't do that."

"Maybe you'd better start from the beginning."

She told me how the evening had started as a night on the town and ended in sickness at Harlem Hospital.

"Did you actually see anybody in the car with her?"

Ruth thought about it. "No. But that don't mean there weren't nobody in there. He could've been hiding in the back seat. She was getting bad letters, you know. It must've been him who took her."

"Bad letters?"

"Yeah, the mean kind."

"From who?"

"Some man."

She explained that about two weeks earlier Esther said she'd received an unsigned threatening note in her mailbox. A few days earlier, Esther had mentioned another note.

"I never saw the notes—Esther threw 'em away—but she said the guy who wrote 'em knew *all* her business. Just everything. It was like he was looking over her shoulder, from the time she went out for groceries to when she went to pick up Job."

"Did she say who wrote them?"

"She said the handwriting was familiar, but she couldn't place it."

I scribbled all this down in my notepad, and then gestured toward the sergeant, sitting behind his desk. "Did you mention this to—?"

"I tried to. I talked to a detective. I tried to tell him about the notes, but he cut me off."

I glanced at Beth to see if she had something to add, but she averted her gaze. She was pale and obviously ill. I asked Ruth where Esther parked. The corner she described was just three blocks down and two blocks east of the hospital: It didn't sound far, but the blocks over there were long and dim.

"May I contact you later?" I asked Ruth.

She agreed, so I took down her address and got Beth's information, too. Then I helped them into a taxi and returned to the station to find the lawman they'd spoken to. Detective John Reed, a thin, pale man with a superior air and bored expression, confirmed what Ruth had said. He was very disinclined to do anything.

I took a taxi over to where Ruth said they'd parked the car. I could understand Ruth finding it impossible to accept the idea that Esther might've run away. I found it difficult, too, especially after what I'd seen during that church performance. Esther didn't strike me as the kind of woman to run off in the middle of the night and leave her family, especially her son, without warning or explanation, knowing they'd be worried sick about her, no matter what kind of troubles she had.

As we pulled up to the corner, I asked the cabbie, "You got a flashlight I could borrow?"

His gaze met mine in the rearview mirror. "Just what're you planning on doing out there?"

"Nothing you want to know about."

He gave me a suspicious look and cast a nervous glance up and down the deserted street. Maybe he thought I was setting him up. He was a fat man in his mid-fifties; he was soft and had a gut. He'd be no match for a young hustler.

"Don't worry. I'm not gonna take a powder and I'm not stalling so somebody can jump your back. I'll be right back."

Still uneasy, he gave a reluctant nod. "All right." He reached under his seat and came up with a flashlight. "But don't take too long. It's a bitch out here."

"Won't be a minute."

A black Model T stood in the parking space Ruth had described. It was easy to envision the Packard in its place and the laughing young women who'd set out in it only hours earlier.

What about the snow? Had it caught something— footprints, traces of a struggle—anything that would bear testimony to what had happened to Esther? But, no. Whatever traces there might've been were gone.

What was the likelihood that someone had been out there earlier and seen something? It was a frosty night, the kind that drives people indoors. The street was empty as far as the eye could see. The windows of the tenement buildings were dark. Hmmm. Yes … dark now, but they would've been lit earlier. Would an attacker have risked assaulting Esther on the street?

Less than three feet away was an alley. Esther would've passed it on her way to the car. Shadowy doorways, supply entrances to the apartment buildings and businesses lined the alley on either side. The doorways would've offered a kidnapper a choice of perfect covers. All he had to do was step out and confront her. If he'd forced her back into the alley and stood in front of her, he would have both blocked her way of escape and cut her off from view.

Had her kidnapping been a crime of impulse? Was she a random victim, simply in the wrong place at the wrong time? Or was she chosen, her disappearance planned?

I ran the circle of light up and down the sides and along the ground in between. The alley was lined with metal garbage cans. It was neat, as alleys go. None of the cans were knocked over, as might happen in a struggle. The blanket of snow covering the ground was smooth and undisturbed.

Out in the street, the cabbie honked his horn.

I moved the light over the snow, checking every doorway. But there was nothing interesting—nothing I could discern, anyway. I went back out to the street to take another look at where Esther had parked.

"Hey, what're you doing?" the cabbie called. He stuck his head out the window. "I'm freezing my butt off. C'mon!"

He started his taxi and pulled out into the street. He drew up alongside and a little ahead of the Ford. I took one more glance around, but saw nothing out of the ordinary. With a sigh, I turned off the flashlight and walked around the front of the car to get to the taxi. Something caught my eye, something that twinkled. I paused.

"What is it now?" the cabbie whined.

Caught under the curve of the Model T's left front wheel was an item, small, delicate and metallic. I picked it up and stepped back onto the curb to stand under a street lamp. It was an earring with fake diamonds, inexpensive, but pretty. The little wire loop that would pierce the ear was touched with dark red, and something else: dried blood, maybe, and human tissue.

The cabbie honked. I palmed the earring, holding it lightly, and climbed into the taxi.

"Where to now?"

I gave him the address of the newsroom. While he drove, I wrapped the earring in a clean handkerchief.

When you cover death and tragedy for a living, you have a tendency to wall in your emotions, to distance yourself from the victims and their loved ones. It's self-preservation. I had often done it, but in Esther's case I couldn't. I didn't want to. Something about her story gripped me from the beginning. Perhaps, it was the image of a woman walking off into the darkness alone. Or, maybe, just maybe, it was the memory of that concert she'd given.

At one point Esther had done a piano solo. It was incredible. To merely say she was talented would be to insult both her gift and the Lord who gave it to her.

But while Esther's music was great, it was her boy who took my breath away. He was with her that day. He was only seven, but his voice had a maturity that brought tears to your eyes. It certainly brought them to mine. Every now and then he'd throw his mother a glance and she'd return it with a smile. The memory of their silent communication, of him standing strong, singing confidently with the choir behind him and his mother playing alongside him, stayed with me for days afterward. The lyrics sung by his sweet voice echoed in my mind long after the words of Reverend Baldwin's sermon faded from memory. So I thought of Esther's son when I thought of Esther gone, and I couldn't even pretend to be neutral.

Twenty-four hours passed and Esther failed to appear. Early on the morning of December 20, Ruth accepted my offer to return to the police station with her and file a formal report. We were sent to a gray room at the back of the station, a room full of desks pushed too close together, covered with too many forms and papers for the men behind them to keep track of.

Reed received us with barely concealed irritation. He asked Ruth for a description.

"She resembles you?"

"No, she's pretty. Real pretty." Ruth paused. "Except for the scar."

"Scar?" He looked up from his note taking.

"It's a bad one," Ruth said. "Her ex-husband messed her up like that. Esther's real sensitive about it."

I remembered looking at the scar and feeling sickened. Whoever did it must've held her down and taken his time. The scar was vicious and curved, like a snake rippling under Esther's skin. It went from the outer corner of her left eye, across her cheek, down to her chin. It was startling and unsettling, and, no doubt, it had indeed caused Esther not only physical but emotional pain.

After taking down the description, Reed asked a few questions, about Esther's job, her friends, her habits, but he listened with only half an ear. It surprised me that he failed to ask about Esther's husband, the one whose violence disfigured her. So I did.

"This ex-husband of hers ... could he be behind it?"

Ruth shook her head. "No way. Not him."

"What makes you so sure?" Reed asked.

"'Cause he's dead. Been dead half a year now. Got cut down by a train."

Reed grimaced and made a note. "What about boyfriends? Your sister got any? Maybe she ran into one of them and went off with him."

"*One* of them?" Ruth was indignant. "My sister's not like that, and she never would've done nothing like that—run off and leave her boy."

"Yeah, right."

"No. Not her. She's a church-going woman. She don't drink, use drugs or commit no fornication."

Reed was unconvinced, so Ruth brought up the letters, told him what she'd told me.

"Were the threats explicit or just hinted at?"

"Oh, they were clear, all right," Ruth said. "Esther told me that in one note he threatened to skin her alive."

"She was sure it was a man?"

"Of course she was. Wouldn't no woman write a letter like that."

"She might, if Esther was stepping out with her man."

Ruth drew herself up. Her face was tight. "I told you. My sister is a Christian, God-fearing woman. She don't commit no fornication. And she sure don't commit no adultery."

"Well, Ruth, what do you think happened?" I asked, trying to ease the tension.

"If it wasn't that man behind them notes, then it was a thief, somebody who saw her and that rich lady's car. Daddy never did like it when Mrs. Goodfellowe lent Esther that car. He always said it would be the death of her and now I'm scared he's right."

It was Mrs. Goodfellowe who had bought the tickets. In one of the bold gestures of generosity that typified her, she'd also lent the young women her Packard for the evening.

Reed and I exchanged glances. You could see he was skeptical of the car idea. To be honest, I didn't put much store by it either. It didn't feel right, not in light of those notes.

"Then I guess that's all for now," Reed said. He started to put down his pencil.

"Hold it, Detective." I took out the handkerchief holding the earring and handed it to him.

"What's this?"

"Open it up and you'll see."

He put down his pencil and unfolded the cloth, exposing the single earring. At the sight of it, Ruth put both hands to her mouth and stifled a sob. Reed set the handkerchief down on his desk, neatly spreading out the corners, and contemplated the earring.

"It was hers?" he asked Ruth.

Ruth opened her mouth but nothing came out. She tried to swallow and managed a jerk of a nod.

"Where'd you find it?" he asked me.

I told him.

"Did you know it was hers when you saw it?"

"No—just picked it up on the off chance it might be."

"How convenient." His gaze returned to the earring. "I suppose you have a theory about how it got there?"

"I think her kidnapper came up behind her. She tried to fight him off and lost the earring in the struggle. Then he forced her into the driver's seat and lay low."

He rubbed his chin and tried to look thoughtful, but he couldn't maintain the pretense. After a few seconds, he shrugged. "Maybe, you're right, but I don't think so." He raised his right hand and lightly flicked his index finger to signal a patrolman.

Ruth's gaze had been fixed on the earring, but at the annoyed disinterest in Reed's tone, she looked up. "You *will* search for her, won't you?"

"Of course, we will." A patrolman appeared behind us. "This officer will show you out."

"But—"

"We'll be in touch. If we find out anything, we'll let you know."

That was it.

Ruth turned to me, bewildered and worried. I didn't like the way Reed was treating us, either, but I didn't see where we could help Esther by staying any longer. It was time to go.

Two days later, Reed summoned Ruth down to the station. He said he was "ninety-nine percent sure" of what had happened. Ruth called me at the newspaper and asked me to go with her. It wasn't so much that she needed the emotional support, she said. She wanted a reporter there so the story would come out, and "come out right."

Reed met us in the waiting room. His narrow face showed that he was unhappy to see me.

"We usually don't allow the press in during an ongoing investigation."

"Oh, is it ongoing? Well, that's good to know. Where did I get the impression that you guys are ready to shut it down?"

"Miss Todd, do you actually want her here?"

"Yes, I do."

He gave me another evil glance. "Let's get this over with."

He led us down a short hall to a room with a long table with four chairs in the center. He carried a thick folder, which he laid on the desk. He had us sit down, took a seat and opened the folder.

He said he could "assure" us that Esther had not been kidnapped. Speaking in the smooth, oily tones of a con man, he set out to convince Ruth that her sister had "merely" run away from home.

Before Ruth could open her mouth to protest, he explained that "several aspects" of the case pointed toward this conclusion. He ticked off the relevant "facts" on the tip of his long, skeletal fingers. First, she had reported seeing Esther alone in the car as it sped past. Second, no one could report hearing a woman's screams, and, last but not least, they had found no proof that a stalker ever existed. There were no notes in evidence. There was only Ruth's word that Esther had told her about them. In legal terms, that could be considered mere hearsay.

"But—"

"To be blunt, either you or your sister could have made this guy up."

Ruth was taken aback. "Why would we do something like that?"

"Don't know. Why don't you tell me?" He eyeballed her, and when out of fear or confusion, she didn't answer, he told her, "You know, it's a crime to file a false report."

Incredible.

"Are you threatening her?" I asked, my tone low, but my anger rising.

"Of course, not." His eyebrows shot up in an attitude of hurt innocence. "I was just giving you the goods. That's all."

There was a panic in Ruth's eyes and in the way she gripped her purse, her knuckles gleaming.

"What about the earring?" she asked.

"The earring?"

"Yes, the earring," she pressed. "You can't have forgotten. It proves she didn't run off. Somebody got her. He ripped that earring out and—"

"I'm sorry, but it doesn't prove a thing."

Ruth was incredulous. "You mean you think she pulled that earring out herself?"

"I'm saying that one earring doesn't make a kidnapping. Not when considered in balance with the other ... well, lack of evidence."

"So you're giving up." Ruth was bitter.

"There's nothing to pursue. Your sister had her reasons for leaving. You're more aware of them than I am." Reed paused. "Listen, I don't mean to be hard. But the facts speak for themselves. We've got too much going on in this city to spend time on a crime that didn't happen. Adults do run away. And they do come home. When they want to—if they want to. If I were you, I'd simply be grateful for the knowledge that she's all right."

If he was trying to sound compassionate, he missed it by a long shot, so I put my two cents in.

"Detective, would you mind telling me who you talked to?"

"You wouldn't understand our methods."

"Try me."

He gave an exasperated sigh. "All right." Speaking in the tone of a man being put upon, he described how he'd spent a day searching for evidence and interviewing residents of the buildings and businesses near the alleged crime scene. He interviewed Esther's parents and friends, the people who attended church services with her, her son's teachers and her own co-workers at the laundry service. He interviewed Mrs. Goodfellowe and Beth, seeking clues as to the identity of the man who had sent the notes, the man who preferred to see Esther dead rather than lose her. But he found no witnesses who could describe Esther's last walk back to her car, no one in the neighborhood who could recall hearing a woman's cry and no clues as to the phantom writer's identity.

"Last night, me and my superiors went over what we had—or, more to the point, didn't have—and we reached the conclusion I just shared with you."

"Interesting," I said. "Admirable. You managed to interview so many people in so short a time, and all by yourself. You must've moved faster than lightning. I guess that's why so few of them remember seeing you."

Reed's eyes grew colder.

"I talked to a lot of those people in the neighborhood," I said. "Not as many as you did, of course. But I've been going door-to-door—and not a single one of them remember ever having seen you, much less spoken to you. Ruth and I, we spoke to Esther's boss, her pastor and some of her co-workers, to ask them to cooperate when you stopped by. And just before coming here, I checked with her pastor and her boss. They both said you never showed up. Now how do you explain that?"

"I don't have to."

"I know you don't have to. I'm wondering if you can."

He slammed the folder shut and stood up, pushing his chair back. "Look ladies, as far as the department is concerned, this matter is settled. You," he said to me, "are welcome to write what you want. I don't give a damn." He turned to Ruth. "As for you, my advice would be to keep this so-called 'reporter' at a distance. She'll just make an embarrassing situation worse."

He didn't give us a chance to respond, simply picked up the folder and left.

Ruth turned to me. "Do you believe this? He must think we're fools."

"Don't they all?" I stood. "Come on, Ruth, let's go."

The Todds lived in a seven-room apartment on 128th Street and Lenox Avenue. They couldn't afford to pay the rent on their own. Ruth explained that her family used three rooms—she was in one bedroom, her parents in another, and Esther and Job shared a third. The Todds had rented out the two remaining bedrooms, as well as the dining room and tiny maid's room behind the kitchen. All in all, they had five lodgers, all of them young women.

"They go to our church," Ruth said. "They're like family. We decided to take in women 'cause they're the ones need the help. Sometimes, you know, these guys'll send 'em tickets to come up here and the girls promise to work to pay for it. Then they get here, and find out that the guys ain't nothing but pimps. Our church can get 'em away from all that."

She led me into the living room and introduced me to her parents, Diane and Joseph Todd. Mrs. Todd was a tiny woman. Esther had taken after her. Mr. Todd was big and broad-shouldered, but stooped. He'd lost a leg and walked with a cane. Both thanked me for my interest and help. Ruth told them what had happened. They discussed their options and agreed upon their next step.

Job entered the room, rubbing sleep from his eyes. "Is Mama back?"

For years afterward, I could see Ruth's pain as she struggled to give him an adequate answer and his panic and bewilderment upon hearing it.

He searched the eyes of the adults and saw our helplessness. His gaze settled on me, maybe because Ruth had introduced me as "the newspaper paper lady who was trying to help."

"You'll bring her back?" he asked me.

"I'll ..." I hesitated. I wanted to comfort him, but not lie, not make promises I couldn't keep.

"You'll bring her home?" he insisted.

"I'll try. I'll do my best."

"You promise?"

I smiled sadly. "You bet."

That same day, Ruth went to see Katherine Goodfellowe and appealed for help. Mrs. Goodfellowe called Police Chief Dan Berman and expressed her displeasure. He said he was surprised that she was "so excited 'bout the disappearance of a mere Negro." He did note, however, that when Esther vanished, the Packard vanished too, and he could understand her being upset about *that*. Best thing for her to do would be to file a report on stolen goods. The police would tend to it immediately. He could assure her of that. But Mrs. Goodfellowe refused to do it.

Of course, she wouldn't. It would mean that she was accusing Esther of having stolen her car—and that was something Mrs. Goodfellowe wanted to avoid, not only because of the pain it would cause Esther's family, but because of the personal embarrassment it would cause her.

The next day, Katherine Goodfellowe said she could give me five minutes, and that's what she did. We spoke in the second-floor library, the only quiet room in the house. The mansion was in an uproar. Mrs. Goodfellowe was planning a charity auction for the following evening and it was being hailed as the social event of the Christmas season. She'd invited the oldest and snobbiest of New York's millionaire dynasties to put their family jewels up for auction—not for sale, but for loan. Outsiders would bid for the privilege of wearing heirlooms, sometimes legendary jewels.

I hadn't seen Beth since the night of Esther's disappearance, so after interviewing Mrs. Goodfellowe, I made a quick run down to the kitchen. Beth agreed to talk with me, but said it would have to be the next evening. Once the auction was under way, she'd have time.

On the morning of December 23—a Sunday—the Reverend Charles Witherspoon of Christ, the Redeemer, Esther's home church, led the congregation in an emotional prayer for her safe return. Afterward many of his parishioners canvassed 132nd Street, going door-to-door and asking residents if they'd seen or heard anything suspicious on the night of Esther's disappearance. They started out with high hopes, but ended up disappointed. None of them learned anything useful.

That evening, I returned to Goodfellowe House for the interview with Beth, but I never got to conduct it. What happened at the house that night augured a radical change in how police viewed the disappearance of a "mere" Negro.

## 4.

### A MILLION GONE IN BLACK-TIE HEIST
By Lanie Atkins Price
*Harlem Age* Staff Writer

NEW YORK Dec. 24, 1923—Gunmen made off with $1 million in jewels yesterday when they attacked an auction being held at a Park Avenue mansion, police said. Two people were killed in what is being described as the largest robbery of a jewelry collection on private premises in U.S. history.

The incident occurred at the home of Mrs. Katherine Goodfellowe on East 57th Street and Park Avenue shortly before 7 p.m., according to police spokesmen. The jewels, which belonged to some of New York's wealthiest families, were to be auctioned for the benefit of Mercy House for Women. Some 150 guests were in attendance. Their names were withheld.

Nearly 100 shots were fired in a getaway gunfight between security guards and thieves, a police spokesman said.

Killed was Mrs. Mathilda Gray, 69, wife of real estate magnate Malcolm Gray, and Mr. Edward Slocum, 45, a former Bureau of Investigation agent turned security guard.

"It was a wonder more people weren't injured," Detective Jack Ritchie said.

Experts said it was highly unusual to hold an auction of such magnitude in a private residence, but sources say Mrs. Goodfellowe insisted it be held in her home—rather than at the fortified Sotheby's, for example—because she felt that the intimate atmosphere was more conducive to generosity.

The jewelry was not to be sold. What was being auctioned was the right to wear the famed pieces to one social event next year. Many of the jewels were heirlooms that had not been worn in decades, much less been on public display, in part because of security concerns. The items included the famed Hemphill Diamond, the Tilden Ruby and the Star of Tanzania—all stolen.

"To my knowledge, this was the largest theft of a jewelry collection on private premises in U.S. history," said Ritchie. Police have no suspects, but do have clues that should quickly advance the investigation, he said.

Mrs. Goodfellowe refused to comment on the robbery. However, she sent her condolences to the families of those killed.

The auction had just begun when three heavily armed men entered the main salon where the auction was being held, witnesses said. The masked gunmen forced the guards to disarm, then herded both guards and guests into the main salon and locked them in the room. They handcuffed Mrs. Goodfellowe and took her with them. One gunman remained stationed outside the salon, while the other three systematically robbed the safes throughout the house. They touched nothing else. Mrs. Goodfellowe said the thieves apparently had detailed knowledge of her home, including the locations of all the safes. They found each safe without hesitation, forced Mrs. Goodfellowe to open them, and then emptied them of the jewelry up for auction—$1 million worth.

As the gunmen were leaving the house with bags containing the jewels, one of the guards locked inside the salon managed to get the doors open. The gunmen spun around and opened fire, witnesses said.

"It was pandemonium," said a guest who chose to remain anonymous. "Suddenly we weren't on Park Avenue—but Tombstone."

"It was horrid. Being locked in. Not knowing what they were going to do," said a second guest, who also spoke only on condition of anonymity. "I've never experienced anything like it, and I hope to never again."

Security experts had suggested the use of costume imitations during the bidding in order to keep the amount of real jewelry on hand to a minimum. Winners would then have collected the real pieces from the bank vaults where they were being kept. But Mrs. Goodfellowe reportedly insisted that no imitation, no matter how beautiful or well done, would inspire the same largesse as the real items.

"No one is inspired to bid for fakes. No one wants to touch them, wear them," she is quoted as having said. "I want the people to be able to see the jewels up close. This auction is about raising funds for young women. It's about opening your hearts and your wallets, and that can only be done if we open our family vaults."

Sotheby's agreed to handle management of the auction itself, but sources say it was Mrs. Goodfellowe who took responsibility for security. For security purposes, the jewels had been stored in various camouflaged safes throughout the

Goodfellowe mansion. As a further protective measure, the guest list was kept secret and no one not on the list was supposed to have had detailed knowledge of the event.

There was no word on whether the auction was insured against theft.

The whole robbery took no more than twenty minutes, but it felt like an eternity. The sights and smells of that evening were etched in my memory—the pushing and shoving of people in panic, the acrid haze of gun smoke, the stench of cold sweat and hot fear, the screech of wheels outside as the robbers' car sped from the scene and the sudden silence thereafter.

My article conveyed little of the mayhem, none of the sickening terror. To steady my hands while typing it, I'd had to focus on the facts, shutting out the emotions. At the time, I'd been proud of my ability to become detached from the story, of my "wise" decision to protect readers from the shock of those twenty minutes. But in hindsight, I wondered if my detachment had been more of an effort to protect myself. If so, it hadn't worked. The terror I'd felt in those minutes had revisited me in my dreams. It had been months before I could regard sleep as a friend.

Citing undisclosed sources, another article reported that several of the families had urged Mrs. Goodfellowe to allow them to install extra security measures before the auction, but she had refused. She was adamant. Having scads of beefy, threatening men standing around, carrying hefty weapons, would destroy the ambiance.

Three days after the heist, the *Sunday Tribune* wrote that several of the families were thinking about suing Mrs. Goodfellowe. It quoted unidentified legal sources as saying that efforts were being made to reach out-of-court settlements. The article suggested that Mrs. Goodfellowe's vast fortune would certainly receive a dent, but that perhaps even worse for the widow was her precipitate fall from grace. Overnight, she had gone from Brahmin to pariah.

The story concluded with a return to the police probe. It noted that the search for the robbers had expanded to include consideration of Esther's disappearance. It also quoted police experts as saying that the robbers had over extended themselves. It would be difficult to fence such distinctive jewelry, the experts said. Investigators were confident that the thieves would be forced to "bury" the items until they were "cooled off."

> "But it don't matter when they try to fence the gems." Detective Frank Bellamy said. "Now or later, it don't matter. Just let one of them babies hit the street. Those thieves will be like sitting ducks. Their own greed will betray them. With those types, it always does."

Mrs. Goodfellowe had refused to allow the press in to cover the auction, but, as chance would have it, she ended up with a reporter in the house. Beth had let me in by the back servants' entrance and handed me a maid's uniform.

"Here, wear this. I don't want her catching you and firing me. This way, you'll fit in."

I accepted the outfit, understanding Beth's concern and admiring her cleverness. With the house full of extra servants because of the event, I was less likely to be noticed if dressed as one. I still had to avoid Roland, though. If that sharp-eyed butler saw me, he'd no doubt recognize me and show me the door.

The kitchen was a madhouse, with servants rushing back and forth. I'd never seen such a beautiful display of dishes. Food preparation had been going on for two days. Rather than trust a caterer to bring in the food, Mrs. Goodfellowe had hired one of New York's best chefs to prepare it on site. The result was dazzling: pâtés, shrimp and lobster dishes, set off by a huge, glittering ice carving of a swan with raised wings.

The first guests arrived. Soon the hall was buzzing with excited voices. After a short period of cocktails in which the guests sipped champagne and nibbled on appetizers, they were ushered into Mrs. Goodfellowe's second salon, which had been rearranged to suit the evening's purposes. The hubbub in the kitchen quieted down. Beth didn't return. Twenty-five minutes went by. Then thirty. Beth had not appeared, so I went looking for her.

I found her busy setting up for the post-auction reception, another mini-event in itself. She was harried and tired and told me she didn't know when she could talk to me.

I decided not to be irritated. Left on my own, I gave in to my curiosity about the house. The place was enormous. I'd read that it contained eighteen rooms. That included seven master bedrooms, a grand reception hall, a library, three salons and a formal dining room. This was a world of hand-carved moldings, dark wood paneling and trompe l'oeil ceilings, muraled walls, intricately tiled fireplace mantles and stylized gold fixtures.

It was all so very impressive, but after a while, it began to feel oppressive, too. Observing the ostentatious display of wealth, the cold perfection of the Christmas decorations, I had to wonder: Had Esther felt as lost in the place as I did?

I was already mentally framing sentences to describe the place when I followed a set of back stairs and landed at the side entrance to the salon through which the auctioned items would be brought. The gavel fell just as I arrived and the auction began. The first item up was an exquisite pink diamond-and-ruby studded tiara and necklace set.

The guard standing in the doorway had just turned and asked me for a glass of water when a second guard walked up and tapped me on the shoulder.

"Shouldn't you be in the kitchen?" He jerked a thick thumb back toward the stairs. "The caterers have arrived and they need help unloading."

"The caterers?" I asked. "What caterers?"

Two pairs of blue eyes and one pair of brown, all hit by the same thought.

Some people who survive traumatic events say they remember everything as happening in slow motion, as though time stretched out and then snapped together like a rubber band. But it wasn't that way for me. I remembered everything, all right—every detail—but as a series of photographs, individual camera shots all run together to make a jittery film.

From the salon came a mixture of indignant exclamations, startled cries, and the crash of overturned chairs. We all turned just as a white-uniformed figure appeared in the main salon doorway. Everything about his attire was white, except for the thick beige stocking mask distorting his features and the black Tommy gun. He was tall and lanky. I heard a click behind my back and turned to see a second masked white-uniformed figure. He was of medium height and slender build. He too held a submachine gun on us.

The gunmen marched us into the salon to join the others. One other gunman was in the room. Like the two behind them, he also wore a stocking mask and carried a shotgun, a sawed-off Remington. The guests were huddled in the center, their eyes wide, their faces pasty. Mrs. Goodfellowe, wearing an ice pink silk evening dress, still stood on the slightly raised dais that had been installed as a platform from which to hold the auction. Like her guests, she was holding her hands up, but whereas everyone else looked terrified, she looked furious. For a moment there was absolute quiet, as though in their fear the guests had forgotten to breathe.

The one with the Remington produced a satchel. He strode to the podium and reached for the necklace and tiara that had been up for bid. Mrs. Goodfellowe tried to stop him. She grabbed him by the arm and opened her mouth to speak, but he didn't give her the chance. The sound of his gloved hand smacking her smooth cheek clipped the air. He'd backhanded her so fast the action was a blur.

The rifleman snatched the trophy necklace and dropped it into his bag. Then he grabbed Mrs. Goodfellowe by the elbow and hustled her down off the dais, pushing her forward until she stood on the periphery of the circle of guests.

Meanwhile, one of the men with the Tommy gun was securing each of the two other entryways to the salon. He had a key. When he'd locked each door, he joined his comrades at the room's main entryway. The Remington man—he was bigger than the others, and especially broad-shouldered—pointed to Mrs. Goodfellowe and beckoned.

The whole thing was done in silence, like a well-rehearsed ballet. The thieves never said a word, not to the guests, not to one another.

When Mrs. Goodfellowe refused to step forward, the Remington man grabbed her by her crown of steel gray hair. He dragged her to the door, took out handcuffs and clamped them around her wrists.

All three gunmen backed out the door, taking Mrs. Goodfellowe with them. They slammed the door shut behind them and locked it.

Inside the room, there was a moment of fear-induced paralysis, a moment of uncertainty, and then the security guards rushed for the door. From the other side came a volley of gunfire. Bullets punched holes the size of mothballs in the door. Blood spattered the floor. Two of the guards stumbled and fell. I dropped down. The elderly, slightly blue-haired woman standing next to me gave a stunned cry. Her hands still held in the air, she stared at the hole that had erupted in her silk-covered midriff, at the crimson rapidly spreading down her front. I would always remember Mrs. Gray's expression—a mixture of surprise and horror and dismay. Her eyes rolled up and her knees gave way. No doubt, her heart had stopped before she hit the floor.

"Down!" someone yelled. "Everybody take cover!"

Unnecessary words. Everyone *was* down, crawling, scampering, diving behind chairs. Little cover was available. Mrs. Goodfellowe had had all the large furniture removed to make room for dainty scrolled chairs with skimpy legs and padded seats. None of that padding was tough enough to stop a bullet. Several people found cover behind the four faux Ionic columns spaced throughout the room.

We waited but no more shots came.

I peeped out from behind my column. The guards had inched out of their places and approached the door. They exchanged glances. Who would dare? One, braver than the rest, started forward, and then came to an abrupt halt. We'd all heard it, the click of a weapon being cocked for firing. The guard backed down, actually crawled backward, and I was glad to see him do it. Mrs. Gray's face would haunt me for many a nightmare. I could do without any more food for thought of that kind.

Ten minutes went by. No more, maybe less.

A rattling at the door was accompanied by a woman's cry, not plaintive, still resistant: Mrs. Goodfellowe refusing to be bowed. The door opened and she stumbled into the room, propelled by an unseen hand. Her regal coif was tousled. Her left eye was swollen and a dark bruise had begun to appear on the cheek where the gunman had backhanded her. She was a tall, thin, angular woman. Not pretty, but attractive. Normally commanding in appearance. Commanding even then. A queen toppled from her throne by savages. You could still see the fury in her eyes, the burned pride. She tripped over the corpse of the blue-haired woman and fell with a cry.

The rifleman issued a short abrupt laugh. It was the only sound I heard from any of them and it was a peculiar one. It conveyed callousness more frightening than the gunfire.

The gunmen stepped back and pulled the door shut. The guards rushed forward. Some of the guests screamed, "No! Don't!" But the guards didn't listen. They yanked the doors open.

The thieves were already out the front door. The guards pursued them. I slipped from behind the column and followed them. Once in the vestibule, I slid down behind the large Louis XIV wardrobe and peeped around it. Through the open front door, I could see the robbers running toward their getaway car. They'd left a fourth man behind the wheel. The three guards crouched in the doorway and opened fire. The thieves turned and sprayed the guards with gunfire. Two of the guards stumbled backward and fell. The third dived to one side, but then in a heroic, suicidal pitch, jumped up and ran straight at the gunmen. They cut him down before he made three steps.

I slipped back into the salon, found the telephone and rang for help. At first, the operator didn't believe me and when she did, she became hysterical. Precious minutes were wasted while I argued with her, and then calmed her before she put me through to the police.

I hung up and surveyed the scene. These were the kind of people who were so quintessentially self-assured that they couldn't imagine uncertainty—not until today. Quite possibly, they'd never known a moment of fear in their lives and most certainly they'd never been cowed before, but they were cowed now. They huddled behind upended tables, the faux columns and overturned chairs or flat against the floor along the periphery of the room. An auburn-haired woman in a royal blue satin gown stood in one corner, weeping. She leaned on the shoulder of an older gentleman. He was holding her and patting her on the shoulder, but he was about ready to topple over himself. Mrs. Goodfellowe sat slumped in a chair, her midriff stained with Mrs. Gray's blood. Someone had found a white tablecloth and placed it over the dead woman. The cloth was a pristine white, except for the dark red flower soaking its center. The air was heavy with the smell of blood, gun smoke and vomit. A young man leaning on a table surreptitiously wiped his mouth with a handkerchief. He caught me looking at him and turned away.

Violence, I thought, is a grim but efficient social leveler.

## 5.

Detective Jack Ritchie joined Frank Bellamy on the case. Ritchie and Bellamy were in their late fifties and two of the most experienced investigators in the New York Police Department. They were built like football players and liked to say they hit a case like fullbacks. The newspaper reports were confident. The Goodfellowe heist would be solved within a fortnight.

Bellamy and Ritchie wanted to know who was privy to information about Mrs. Goodfellowe's jewels and safes. There were her servants, of course. And there was Esther—Esther, who'd disappeared with Mrs. Goodfellowe's car only days before. A theory quickly developed that Esther had spied on her patron and either sold her knowledge or helped plan the caper outright, then disappeared well in advance of it.

To be sure, the rest of the servants were interviewed, but they'd all been in service in the house for many years. The most recent had joined her staff four years prior. They were beyond reproach.

Esther stood out as an obvious choice.

The suspicions dealt her family a bitter blow. To have lost her and now hear her accused of treachery added salt to an already excruciating wound.

"We're trying to stay hopeful," Ruth told me. "At least the cops are really looking for her now. We keep telling ourselves that it don't matter why they're looking, as long as they look."

Bellamy and Ritchie assembled a task force. They tore into Esther's life, hunting for indications she kept company with thieves. They found none.

On December 30, one week after the robbery, the Todds received a typed letter. It contained three words: I've got her. Esther's family and friends offered it as proof that a maniac had kidnapped her. The police were skeptical. They speculated that Esther herself had sent the note.

Mrs. Goodfellowe offered a standing reward: $2,500 for information on the robbery and/or the whereabouts of Esther Sue Todd. Publicly, she flat-out denied that her protégée's disappearance and the auction heist were in any way connected.

But the wording of the reward implied otherwise.

The Todds now begged the police to investigate Esther's case apart from the inquiry into the robbery. The detectives working the case, the Todds argued, saw Esther only as a perpetrator, not a victim. With that attitude, they would ignore any evidence to the contrary. Bellamy and Ritchie refused, countering that they had an open mind. They said Esther stood a better chance of being found as part of the larger investigation than if investigated on her own. The Todds were unconvinced. They were certain their beloved daughter would have had nothing to do with robbery. Ruth told me in confidence that she almost wished that Esther *had* been a part of it.

"Then at least we'd be sure she was alive. Now we don't know. And we'll never have peace till we do—till we can bring her home, to where she belongs."

A second note followed on January 7. Like the first, it carried the chilling message, "I've got her." It also taunted the Todds with a description of what Esther had been wearing that night. It was specific, right down to the earrings she wore.

The Todds turned this second note over to the police, as they had the first. They felt it bolstered the contention that Esther was being held captive, but it only served to increase police suspicion that she herself was part of a conspiracy.

Events apparently bore out this suspicion three weeks later.

On January 20, Mrs. Goodfellowe's Packard was spotted in Saratoga Springs, in upstate New York. Police stopped the car and interviewed the driver. Geoffrey Coleman, age 74, told police that he'd bought the car for cash two weeks earlier from a young woman. Coleman described the seller as a Negro in her twenties. He said she was of medium height and very pretty, except for a nasty-looking scar that ran from her left eye down across her cheek. The description fit the missing young woman to a T. The police were now certain that Esther Sue Todd was alive and trying to cover her tracks.

City newspapers reported heavily on the new developments. The notes to the Todds stopped. When asked to comment, Bellamy openly speculated that Esther Sue now knew that sending notes would be of no more use in trying to support her alleged innocence. The Negro establishment, which had been proud of Esther and supportive of the Todd family, quietly distanced itself from the grieving relatives. Esther's relatives felt themselves alone and abandoned.

For all intents and purposes, they were.

I too had left them on their own. Personal circumstances had intervened. Only six months earlier, my husband, Hamp, had died of a heart attack. He was just thirty-six and appeared to be in perfect health. The ache over losing him was still so strong it sometimes cut my breath off. But by that December at least I could go whole weeks, instead of days, without seriously contemplating whether to join him. One of the concerns that stayed my hand was my mother. She'd suffered the loss of her husband too, and yet she'd boxed her way through, kept on going, raising me alone. Now, after struggling all those years, she was frail and elderly. I was her only child. Losing me would kill her.

Such thoughts had always drawn me back from the edge. Now it they wouldn't plague me anymore. She wasn't losing me.

I was losing her.

The problems of Esther and her family receded to the background. Sitting at Mama's bedside in Virginia, I was only dimly aware of the events in New York. A fog of fear and grief muffled any news from Gotham, made everything there seem unreal and irrelevant.

My mother lingered for three months and then passed in her sleep. With no brothers or sisters, I felt drained and alone.

When I returned to New York, I was out of a job and nearly out of money. But I did have a house and I had friends, all of whom were kind enough to welcome me back with open arms.

Trying to pick up the threads of my old life, I checked in with the Todds. They told me that Mrs. Goodfellowe's reward still stood. She had yet to receive a single useful response. They also said that no one was investigating the case anymore, and they told me why.

In their time, Bellamy and Ritchie had made touchdown after touchdown in case after case, but they slammed into a wall with this one. As the weeks turned into months, the tenor of the news changed. The reports that had lionized them began to peck at them.

At one point, the two cops did get a lucky break, but they botched it, and what could've been a moment of triumph turned into one of defeat. It was their first and last break on the case. A wave of humiliating publicity followed.

After the uproar died down, they quietly moved on to other assignments. The file remained open formally, and Bellamy still made inquiries when he had time, but basically the case was dead in the water.

Then came the day when Ritchie took a bullet. An escaping prisoner got hold of Ritchie's gun and turned it on him. Bellamy shot the prisoner, but Ritchie was already down. He was DOA at St. Luke's. The next day, Bellamy retired.

"Ritchie and me, we was partners for more than thirty years," Bellamy said in one newspaper report. "I'm too old and too tired to start over again with someone new."

The Todd case had become an obscure footnote to the much larger, sexier riddle of the Goodfellowe heist. Without fresh developments to keep the story alive, the newspapers moved on and both crimes soon slipped to the dark recesses of the public mind. I wished I could've helped the Todds, but I was at a loss. I no longer had the one weapon I could wield in their favor, the power of the press.

While searching for a job, I received a note from John Baltimore, my old boss at the *Harlem Age*. He told me the newspaper had an opening and would be happy to take me back. But it struck me that I didn't want my old beat. I was tired of writing about loss and death.

That June, I joined the *Chronicle* and convinced them to let me write society news. Harlem society was hopping. It was a fun job and I was grateful to have it.

The years went by. My contentment eroded. I became restless. My life had become my job. When my attitude toward it changed, the dissatisfaction went deep. Needless to say, I received little sympathy. I was lucky to have a job at all, associates said, especially such a dream one. I had a nice home, nice clothes. I was young and healthy. No, I didn't have a man, but I didn't want one, not after Hamp.

What did I want, then?

Something ... indefinable. That's what.

I felt like a sleepwalker, distant and detached. It was getting increasingly harder to smile at the inane jokes so prevalent at Strivers' Row gatherings, to gush at the right moment and to the right degree. I was living in a cage and didn't know how to break out of it.

Then Ruth Todd came to see me.

## *6.*

Bellamy lived in a scruffy little house in Bayside, Queens. It was a two-story, with white shingles. Small, but nice. At least it would've been, if it had been kept up. Unfortunately, the exterior showed signs of neglect. The paint was chipped and peeling; the stoop was cracked and needed sweeping. Two large planters held dead plants on either side of the door, and a thin Christmas wreath, less than a foot in diameter, decorated the front door.

It was bright and early and I had an appointment. I checked my watch—saw that I was exactly on time—and went up the steps leading to his front door. I rang the bell and waited. A long minute dragged by. I rang again and another forty seconds crawled past. I glanced at my watch again. This was the time I'd said I'd be there. Maybe, Bellamy had stepped out.

Or maybe, he was inside, watching.

I'd ring one more time. If he didn't answer, I'd leave.

I pressed the button. Again, no answer. I turned to go and felt, rather than heard, the door open behind me.

"Mrs. Price?"

It was a scratchy voice. Not unpleasant. And somehow young, much younger than I would've expected from a cop of retirement age.

I turned to face him.

His watery blue eyes were dark with amusement. I could just about read his thoughts.

Back then, a lot of white folk were taken aback by the very notion of a colored reporter, much less the sight of one. Actually, they were surprised to see black folk at all. We were usually invisible—servants, domestics, cleaning men, laundry women, handymen, and the like. We never spoke and were rarely spoken to. And when we did speak, it was only because we *had* been spoken to. So it was obvious what Bellamy was thinking: what kind of colored woman would have the audacity to think she could question a white man?

He ushered me in with a tobacco-stained grimace that passed for a smile. He had a bulbous nose with prominent veins and used a walking stick. His wild salt-and-pepper eyebrows needed trimming, and so did his gray nose hairs. He had a little paunch and dirty fingernails, but he wasn't totally unkempt. His white shirt was pressed and spotless and so were his gray pants. His wavy silver hair was combed and his black leather shoes were worn but polished. So he'd made some kind of effort—but was it out of respect or merely vanity?

He led me into a small square living room, crowded with lace-draped furniture, surprisingly fussy for a man. He gestured toward a small armchair upholstered in worn green velvet. A red-and-green plaid shawl was folded neatly and thrown over the chair's back.

"Here, take a seat. Never had a spade in here before. Mom would be rolling in her grave if she knew. But I always say, why not? Ain't nothing wrong with you people. Nothing that a little hard work wouldn't cure."

I let the insult slide—it would've been counterproductive to challenge it—but I promised myself to get his information and get out.

"Interesting place," I said, sitting down.

"Oh, you like it?"

The place was neat, outwardly as clean as a whistle. But it stank of stale smoke and it gave off a heavy underlying funk, a mixture of unwashed clothes, hidden dust and hidden memories.

"Looks like you've been here awhile."

"All my life. Took it over when my mom died." He gripped the cane with one hand and made an expansive gesture with the other. "A place like this is hard to come by. See that old buffet?" He pointed to the large piece just outside what appeared to be the entry to his kitchen. "Solid mahogany. Came with Gramps from Ireland. Some people say I should get rid of it. But not me. Why throw that out, then go and get something half as good? I never been a man to waste money. Didn't waste the department's when I was on the force. Don't believe in wasting mine now."

Bellamy eased down in the armchair opposite, a large wingback covered with thinning blue brocade. A worn pack of cigarettes lay on a round wooden table nearby. He leaned forward, folded his hands on the handle of his cane and regarded me with puzzled interest.

"You're really here about the Esther Todd case? You can't be serious."

"But I am."

"That case is ... what? Three, four years old? Nobody's thinking about it anymore."

"I am."

He looked me over and then relaxed back in his chair. "What's your name again?"

A man like Bellamy, someone with thirty years on the force ... he'd started having me checked out the minute we hung up the phone. He knew my name, all right, and a whole lot more. If he wanted to play dumb, I could play along. But if he wanted to annoy me, I wouldn't give him the satisfaction.

"Lanie," I said. "Lanie Atkins Price. I write a column for the *Harlem Chronicle*."

"What's that?"

"A weekly newspaper."

"Never heard of it."

He gave a wicked little smile and a raised eyebrow. He was good at this, the game of provocation. But I was even better at resisting it. I had to be. In those days, for a black person dealing with a cop, even a retired one, knowing when and how to yield was a matter of survival.

"Well," I smiled back, "take my word for it. It exists. Has a good circulation, too. At least 20,000."

"Just among shines, though, huh?"

I worked hard to keep the irritation in check. "Just in Manhattan, some parts of Brooklyn and New Jersey."

"Basically wherever you people are found? I mean, in the New York City area?"

"I guess you could say that."

He tapped his cane on the floor. He had a white canary in a small cage sitting in the window. The bird gave a pretty chirp, spread its little wings and made an attempt to fly. But it hit the top of the cage with a hard thump and fluttered back to the little wood stick that served as a perch. Sad little thing ... Frustrated. I pulled my gaze away, went into my purse and took out my pad and pencil.

"So are you interested in the robbery or the kidnapping?" he asked.

"I'm writing about the kidnapping. But the kidnapping and the heist have been tied together."

"That's right. No way of dealing with one without the other."

"So the police say."

His smile turned cynical and he gave a little nod, as though I'd just confirmed a suspicion.

"What you're here for," he said, "what you're really here for is to do another hatchet job on the department. Or is it just on me?" He touched his chest.

"No. Not at all."

He gave a skeptical grunt.

"You wouldn't be the first one. The papers printed some nasty stuff about us. Me and Ritchie, we were busting our guts and all we got was grief. Everybody took shots at us. At first you colored said we weren't doing enough to find her. Then you said we were doing too much for the wrong reason. As for that Park Avenue crowd … Bah!" He gave a dismissive wave. "I used to tell Ritchie to forget about all of you. I used to say, 'You can't keep one eye on the evidence and the other on the papers.'"

"With a high profile case like that, that's what happens. You either solve it or sink it, before it sinks you."

He didn't like that. We both knew what the case had done to his career.

"All I know is, you guys made a bad situation worse."

The bird in the cage made another attempt to fly. Once more, it thumped against the roof and came down. I've seen birds go crazy like that, banging their heads and beating their wings against bars until they were stark raving mad.

"Why the sudden interest? After all this time? You digging for some Christmas change, the reward money?"

"Let's just say I'm doing a favor for a member of the family."

"Oh," he nodded. "You mean Ruth Todd? She's still around? Yeah, I guess she would be. She's something, isn't she? Man, oh man, was she a pest. But I guess I can understand it. No doubt, I'd be the same way if it was my sister disappeared like that."

"Quite honestly, Detective, you surprise me. At the time of Esther's disappearance, the police showed little empathy for her or her family. All they wanted to do was blame her for the heist."

"Yeah, I know, but ..." he sighed. "Actually, I'm kind of happy to see the case get some attention. It was one of those cases that get a hold of you and don't let go." He paused at my expression. "What? You don't believe me?"

"Like I said, I'm a little surprised. But it's good to know that you welcome my interest."

"Ritchie and me, we tried. Boy did we try. But we couldn't find that one thread that would unravel the knot. We got together a task force. We gave it four months. Full-time, working round the clock. We tracked down just about every contact she had, going up to a year before the robbery. We talked to her pastor, her relatives, friends and co-workers. We checked her mail, her bills, her church donations. We even checked out the books she got from the damn library."

They ended up, he said, with an extraordinary amount of information on a woman who'd apparently led a very ordinary life. None of it contained a clue to the reason behind her disappearance or an answer as to her ultimate fate.

"We could tell you every step she took from birth to that night, but the page stayed blank after she left her sister and friend. She walked into the darkness ... and stayed there."

He did sound as though he cared. For a moment my skepticism weakened. Then I remembered that three years earlier he'd been more intent on jailing Esther than on setting her free. I took a moment to check my notes.

After four months, the only evidence Bellamy and Ritchie had to show for their efforts were the thirty-two bullets and shell casings collected after the shoot-out. Some of this evidence would be helpful in a trial, once they had their suspect collared and cuffed, but none of it was helpful in finding the suspect to begin with.

He shook out a cigarette and offered me one. I declined and he lit his own.

"We wondered if the thieves were foreigners," he said, emitting puffs of smoke. "Everyone noticed how silent they were. Maybe they didn't want to talk 'cause they had accents, and that would've helped nail them."

Then the two cops got a lucky break. Bellamy and Ritchie had circulated a list of the stolen jewels to gem dealers and pawnbrokers likely to carry jewelry of high caliber. Months after the robbery, one of the jewelers called in to report. A man in his late twenties had come in and pawned a sapphire and emerald bracelet that matched the description of an item on the list of stolen goods. Bellamy and Ritchie went to work. The identification and personal information the young man had given turned out to be false. That was no surprise. What *was* a surprise was that the young man apparently knew nothing about fingerprints. He had leaned on the counter and left a perfect set of five. The bracelet itself also yielded partials, some matching the prints taken from the countertop, some not.

"We didn't dare hope the guy's prints would be found downtown. I mean, they got hundreds on file at police headquarters. But there's thousands of crooks." He tapped his cigarette in the ashtray. "My feeling was that if we was gonna find them, then great. If not, we still had a new witness, the pawnbroker. He'd given us a whale of a description. In thirty years of police work, I'd never seen nothing like it. That guy sat down with Jerry, our artist, and what the two of them came up with—it was better than a photograph."

Bellamy scratched his knee.

"So, to make a long story short, we soon had a name to go with the prints. And within two days, we had a body."

"A body?"

"Yeah. A guy by the name of Johnny Knox. A truck hit him. Deader than a bedbug under a fat man's ass. Happened down on 14th and Broadway. We figured it was the others— the thieves, I mean. Maybe they'd told him to lay low till the stones cooled. But Knox couldn't wait. He jumped the gun, so they killed him. The thing is, Knox had a brother. They always worked together. Redheads, both of them. Once we knew it was Johnny, it was easy getting a bead on his brother, Jude. Caught up with him in a pool hall over on East 73rd. Unfortunately, he tried to shoot his way out. He didn't make it."

What followed was a barrage of embarrassing publicity.

"To hear the newspapers tell it, we'd messed up every chance of solving the crime."

The brief hope that had flared up and illuminated the investigation died down. A grim determination set in.

Bellamy ground out his cigarette. "We could've broke this case—if they'd given us time. If they'd just … But the higher-ups decided otherwise. "

Bellamy's task force was disbanded. Each investigator resumed his share of taking on other cases. Bellamy was given to understand that he could work the Todd case on the side, but it was no longer his prime responsibility.

"Ritchie and me, we tried to keep it hot. But there was no way. The cases were coming hard and fast, other cases we'd neglected so we could work on this one. And then..." He shrugged.

Then came the day when a prisoner transport went wrong. I'd found a clipping about the officer shooting in my file. The story was short and to the point.

### ESCAPING PRISONER KILLS COP

NEW YORK August 10 (AP)—Famed Detective Jack Ritchie was killed yesterday during a shoot-out with an escaping prisoner, police officials said. Ritchie was rushed to St. Luke's Hospital but was pronounced dead on arrival. He was 58.

The gunfight erupted during a prisoner transport in Lower Manhattan when convicted murderer Armand Douglas, 32, originally of Bayside, Queens, got hold of Ritchie's gun and shot him with it, police officials said. Ritchie's partner, Detective Frank Bellamy, shot and killed Douglas, who died at the scene.

Normally, a paddy wagon is used for prisoner transport, but Douglas was being transported in a police car. According to Bellamy, Ritchie did not want to wait for the paddy wagon to arrive from the station.

"It was close to the end of the shift," Bellamy said. "He just wanted to be done with it."

Douglas sprang from the backseat, grabbed Ritchie's gun and shot him in the throat, Bellamy said. Sources who prefer anonymity said the prisoner's hands were not cuffed behind his back, a violation of accepted practice.

Ritchie's death drove the last nail into the investigation's coffin. Bellamy buried himself in retirement and any interest in the Todd case went with him.

"What about the people who helped set up the auction?" I asked. "Who knew which jewels would be up for bid? Which families would be invited, how many guards there'd be and where they'd be stationed?"

"I thought you didn't think Esther had anything to do with the robbery."

"I don't believe she did—but I do believe her disappearance did."

"What?"

"I think it was part of a scheme to send the cops looking for a way to place blame where blame was unjustified."

"You people," he said, shaking his head. "You and your conspiracy theories."

"It's quite possible that even one of the guests was behind it. Maybe one of the families had hidden financial trouble."

"No," he said, "No, no, no. We checked all that out. It was the first thing we checked. Those families were in the black, every single one of them."

"All right, then. Maybe there's something else. What about the case files? Did you take them with you when you retired?"

"Thought about it, but I decided not to. I thought some hotshot kid might reopen it. You know, try to break it and make his career."

"But that's a long shot."

"It's better than nothing."

"The files—could you get them?"

The thought amused him. "What if I could? Would you expect me to give them to you?"

"Why not?"

"Think you can just step in and solve it when we couldn't?"

"Not to insult you, but maybe a pair of fresh eyes would—"

"I'm not insulted. I'm just telling you it won't happen."

"Please. I need details, enough new information to reawaken public interest. Maybe even spark a new effort to find her."

"Well, I'm sorry," he said without a trace of regret. "Even if I had them, I wouldn't let you see 'em."

"Department regulations?"

"You said it."

His gaze held mine. A smile played about his lips.

"I thought you said you were glad the case was getting new attention," I said.

"I am. But that don't mean I'm prepared to break the law to make it happen." He gave me a friendly grin full of brown teeth. "You don't need those files anyway. I got it right up here." He tapped his gray-haired temple. "Everything worthwhile, it's all here."

"Is it really?"

"Hm-hmm," he nodded. "And to show you what a right guy I am, I'm gonna give you a tip."

"Out of the goodness of your heart, right?"

He liked that. "Yeah, out of the goodness of my heart, a bit of information that wasn't released to the public. You interested?"

I was skeptical, but curious. "Okay, sure."

"Then listen carefully." He slid forward in his chair, leaned toward me and dropped his voice to a confidential whisper. "You remember hearing about the car being found, right?"

I nodded.

"We got a call after that. As a matter of fact, it came because of all the publicity about the car. You know, the car was, like, proof that Esther 'kidnapped' herself? Well, this guy was real pissed over it. Said he'd yanked her. That she had nothing to do with the heist. And that it was useless to keep looking for her. She was dead, very dead. I remember his words like I heard 'em yesterday. He said he'd warned her and that he'd killed her 'cause she lied to him."

The caller said he'd followed Esther by car from the theater. He'd watched her park and followed her on foot to the hospital. He waited outside the hospital, and then stalked her as she walked back to the Packard. He approached her and asked her about her "cheating ways."

Bellamy winked two fingers to indicate quote marks.

"He told her he had pictures of her loving somebody else. She said he was crazy, so he slapped her. She fought back and things went from there."

The image he painted was chilling. I could see it happening just as he described.

"What makes you think the call was genuine?"

"He knew about the earring."

The match to the one I'd found at the crime scene: Only the kidnapper would know about it.

Bellamy lit himself another smoke. "So yeah, she had a man friend, all right. We just couldn't get a bead on him." He looked regretful. "The fact is, we didn't try. But getting the punk who did Esther was not my job. Getting the guy who did the heist was."

I was amazed, on several levels: by the image he'd conjured, by the magnitude of NYPD's blunder and by his candor. That call had merited serious attention. How could they have ignored it? And that he would tell me....

Bellamy gazed off into the distance, through his room's small window. The canary was quiet for the time being, worn out, I suppose. It would rest until frustration or instinct—or both—drove it to try for freedom once more. The old cop cleared his throat.

"I've had a lot of time to think things over. And I see things differently than I saw 'em back then. I mean ... I hate to say it—and I trust you're not gonna go repeating it—but we went wrong early on."

They fell into the trap of trying to create evidence to match a theory, he said. They couldn't see the importance of details that didn't match their expectations, details like the notes and the phone calls. They weren't overlooked, but their importance was interpreted to fit the theory.

"We talked to all those people—and never once considered the possibility that any one of them might've had a sick fix on her. And that's what bothers me. That's why I'm talking to you. It bothers me that he might've been one of the ones who sat across from us, and talked about what a wonderful person she was, all the time knowing he was the sick fuck who took her, and maybe even still had her, buried in his basement, for all we know."

When I left, he got to his feet, leaning heavily on his cane and accompanied me to the door. I thanked him for having seen me. He shook his head with regret.

"You know that old saying, that there's no such thing as the perfect crime? Well, that's a bunch of malarkey. There's scads of them, murders that weren't even recognized as murders and cases, like this one, where the killer just plain old got away. Take my advice, and write about the boyfriend. If you want a new angle, then he's it."

My initial plan had been to canvas the guest list, to see if any of them might've been tied to the robbery or had unusual contact with Esther. But now I wasn't so sure. Bellamy's reminder of the mysterious admirer gave me pause. His regret about not having followed up on the telephone call struck me as genuine. This business about the phantom admirer was a legitimate trail. It deserved time. I would find out as much about him as I could and put that information into my column. Someone who knew him might come forward. Better yet, he himself might be drawn into the open.

For the first time, in a long time, I felt a tremor of excitement, one that went hand-in-glove with a sense of relief. I hadn't been sure I could find anything that would help me help Ruth. Bellamy had given me a real starting point.

But there was more. Somewhere deep down was a stirring of the hunter's instinct. It had been years since I'd walked the beat, but the drive was still there, the need to ask questions, track down answers and assemble the delicate human puzzle behind every crime. My mind missed the concentrated effort. My guts missed the thrill of the result, and my nature missed the communion with darkness.

This would be the first time I'd used my column in this way. When I joined the *Chronicle*, I was tired of reporting on death and misery. I believed I could achieve good by reporting inspiring, positive news about the doings of Harlem's upper crust, but I'd consistently been reminded that the "light" news often has its dark side, too, and I wasn't doing anyone a favor by ignoring it. My job in life was to tell both the good and the bad. I had no grand ideas about being the catalyst for lasting change, but I did want to be able to look back and say I'd done my bit to keep the record straight.

Mentally, I was coming full circle. Emotionally, I was going home.

# 7.

That afternoon, I caught up with Ruth at Christ, the Redeemer, where she worked as a bookkeeper and taught religious studies in the church's after school program. Ruth sat in a chair, before a semicircle of ten five- to ten-year-olds in the church's basement. She was teaching the story of the Annunciation to Mary. When she saw me, she paused, and then finished reading her paragraph.

"Here Jordan," she handed her Bible to a little round-headed chubby-cheeked boy in the front row. "You read a paragraph, then pass the book to Naomi." She gestured toward a pretty little girl with long, dark curls. "Each of you, take turns. I'll be right back."

She came over, her expression anxious. "What's wrong? Have you changed your mind about doing the column?"

"No, nothing like that. I just wanted to double-check something."

"Yes?" Her frown lessened a little but not much.

"Three years ago, you said Esther didn't have a male friend. Are you sure?"

"Don't tell me you're going to start with that business again."

"No, but I am going back to the threatening notes."

"But those notes ... they didn't necessarily mean that—"

"No, they don't mean that whoever wrote them was her boyfriend. But maybe Esther was in love with somebody and you didn't know about it. Or maybe she simply said hello to the wrong person one day and he got a crush on her. We don't know, but we should try to find out. Don't you agree?"

"Yes, of course, but ... I really don't think she was seeing anybody. I can't imagine her going out with somebody and not telling me. I can't imagine her going out with anybody, period. She was so shy. So scared of being hurt. And that scar—it made her believe that nobody'd ever love her."

"Maybe that was it. She was hungry, so hungry that she took what she needed from the wrong man—and didn't realize it until it was too late."

"God, I hope you're wrong."

A thin, little boy appeared at Ruth's side. His intelligent face was familiar. He tugged at her skirt.

"Oh, Job," she said, glancing down at him.

He nodded to me. "This is the lady, right?" Before she could answer, he turned to me. "You the lady, right? The one said she was gonna bring my mama home?"

Ruth and I exchanged glances. I was so embarrassed, I could've gone through the floor, but I nodded. "Yes, I'm the one."

"You promised. I remember. And then you went away. Why'd you do that?" His face and voice showed more bafflement than anger.

I swallowed. "I ..."

Ruth intervened. "Job, it's not so easy."

He gazed up at her. "But she said it. She promised. You said to always keep a promise."

"Job," I gently touched his shoulder and hunkered down to his eye level. "You're right. I did make a promise and I should've kept it. But something happened in my life."

His eyes were sad. "Something bad?"

"Yeah," I said softly, "something bad." I deliberated whether to tell him, and then decided to. "I lost my mama, too."

His lips formed an O. Ruth started, surprised and upset.

"I didn't know," she said. "I'm so sorry. When we didn't hear from you no more, I should've known something happened. But I just figured—"

"It's okay." I said, and then told the boy, "So Job, I know what it's like to lose your mama. And that's why I'm back. I know it lays a hurting on you like nothing else."

His eyes were large and wet. "So you gonna find my mama now?"

"No," I said, "I can't promise to bring her home. I can only promise to ask questions, push for answers. You understand?"

I heard myself and thought how ridiculous it was to ask a child, or any grieving relative, to hope and not hope at the same time. As far as this little boy was concerned, I'd just promised to bring his mother home. Period.

He nodded. "You won't go away again?"

It hurt to hear him ask that. I smiled to cover my sense of failure and guilt and took his hand to reassure him.

"No, I'm not going anywhere."

His dark brown eyes searched mine, and they struck me as old. Already, he'd learned harsh lessons in disappointment and loss. He was deciding whether to believe me, deciding between skepticism and faith. I was relieved to sense him choose the latter. He put his slender arms around me and gave me a tight hug. I hugged him back, feeling the frail bones beneath the skin. Then Ruth whispered to him to go back to the other children. She'd be with them shortly.

When she turned back to me, her expression was slightly disapproving.

"I'm sorry about your mother, but I wish you hadn't made that promise. It's one thing for me to have hope and maybe be disappointed, but—"

"What was I supposed to do? I did make him a promise and I should've kept it. We both know there's not much I can do, but I'll do everything I can."

That little boy had gotten me to commit myself to a far greater degree than I ever intended to. But was that so bad? I had a gnawing ache to make a difference to someone, to write something that would impact someone's life and, yes, maybe even right a wrong.

Furthermore, it was true, what I'd said. I did know what it was like to lose your mother. I was a grown woman when I lost mine and I still ached from it. How much more must Job have been suffering? He was only a kid.

"I don't mean to criticize," Ruth said. "It's just that—"

"I understand," I said, cutting her off. I wanted to get through this as quickly as possible. There were only so many hours before my next deadline. "Now, I need to know: are you still in contact with Beth Johnson?"

She shook her head. "We sort of had a falling-out after Esther's disappearance."

This was news to me. "About what?"

An embarrassed silence.

"It was my fault, at least partly. I kind of lost my head and blamed her for what happened. Said a lot of stupid things. If she hadn't been ill, then we wouldn't have had to go to the hospital, Esther wouldn't have had to park the car so far away, and she wouldn't have had to go back to fetch it alone. You know, that kind of stuff. Beth might not want to talk to you."

"Well, when I find her, you can apologize—if you want to."

"I wouldn't mind doing that, but that might not be enough. I had the feeling she didn't want to have no more to do with us anyway. Not after the robbery and the cops started talking like Esther had something to do with it. Beth was acting scared, like she was afraid they'd start thinking she had something to do with it, too."

Made sense. I didn't say so, but I could understand Beth's concern.

Back at the newsroom, I went through my notes and found Katherine Goodfellowe's telephone number. I studied it for about two minutes, mulling things over. Then I reached for the telephone.

Esther Todd's disappearance did not signal the end of Mrs. Goodfellowe's benevolent interest in all things colored. Goodfellowe no longer maintained the kind of one-on-one interest in her protégés that she had shown with Esther, but she did continue to make substantial contributions to develop young talent. As a matter of fact, Mrs. Goodfellowe was the second highest contributor to the Agamemnon Awards, after Adrian Snyder, the West Indian numbers king. The pile of invitations on my desk included one to a Christmas awards banquet at which Mrs. Goodfellowe's contributions would be honored. Maybe I could use it to get her to talk to me.

When she came to the phone and I introduced myself, she assumed that I was calling to set up an interview because of the dinner; I did not correct her. I said I was pressed for time and she agreed to let me come down that day.

## 8.

Built on a northeast corner of Park Avenue, set slightly back from the street behind a tall, sturdy wrought-iron gate, Goodfellowe House was one of the most imposing displays of ostentatious architecture in Gotham. Five stories high, it had a conspicuous façade of limestone and redbrick; detailed, decorative moldings; floor-to-ceiling windows; and two curved towers. Since my last visit, something new had been installed: a guard's station, set just outside the front gate. A man dressed in a cowboy hat, heavy gray wool coat, and black lizard-skin boots stepped out to meet me. He was the best-dressed guard I'd ever seen. He was all cowboy, from the slanted hat to the cobbled leather boots. His face was leathery, lined and craggy; his eyes slanted downward at the outer ends, where crow's feet creased the skin. The only thing missing was a bit of straw dipping from one corner of his mouth. For a fleeting moment, something about him seemed familiar.

"Yes?" he asked with a charming smile. His lizard green eyes raked me up and down.

"Lanie Atkins Price. Mrs. Goodfellowe is expecting me."

"She told me. My name's Denver Sutton." He was tall, about six-foot-two, and his handshake was strong. "I'm Mrs. Goodfellowe's private security chief. You got any ID?"

Since when did she have a private security chief?

I showed him my newspaper identification. He actually read it before handing it back to me.

"It looks fine. I'm going to have to pat you down, though." There was a mischievous twinkle in his eye as he said this.

I raised an eyebrow. "You're not serious."

"Oh, but I am."

I expected him to try something, but he didn't. His touch was sparing and professional. Satisfied, he unlocked the gate and escorted me to the front door.

Like Goodfellowe House itself, the huge Christmas wreath that hung on the mansion's front door was grand and meant to impress. It left no doubt that the home and its owner were to be taken seriously.

Sutton rang the doorbell and I felt the sound—not heard it, but felt it—echo deep within the house. A moment later, a tall, slender butler with a bald pate answered the door: Roland.

"Why, hello, Miss Lanie. It's good to see you again."

Five minutes later, I found myself seated in the so-called Red Room. It was called that because it was … well, red: velvet drapes of ruby red, sofas covered with burgundy brocade, a deep Persian carpet of burnt sienna dappled with orange. The room was larger and the ceiling higher than some cathedrals I've seen, but it still managed to be claustrophobic. It was chock full of furniture, with lace doilies draped everywhere; mosaic tiled tables; stain-glass windows and Tiffany lamps. Steuben glass vases filled with dark red roses and small gold-framed photos decked the gleaming black baby grand piano in one corner. A dense, richly green Christmas tree, hung with gold ornaments and miniature porcelain figurines, towered nearby. The room was chilly, despite the huge fire crackling in the fireplace.

A large oil portrait of Solomon Goodfellowe hung over the mantelpiece. The painting itself was traditional and predictable, the kind of thing the nouveau riche have done when they're trying to ascend the social ladder. Like many such works, it was a sophisticated portrait of a very unsophisticated fellow. Solomon Goodfellowe had earned his money as an oil rigger. By all accounts, he was as rough and rowdy as they come. He'd made his first million by the time he was twenty-two and lost most of it in reckless poker games by age thirty-four. Eight years later, he was back on top, older and richer, but not particularly wiser. This time he didn't lose his money; he lost his life. He decided to spend his forty-second birthday in bed with a prostitute. She tried to rob him and ended up shooting him. He died on the spot and she died in prison.

Katherine Goodfellowe took her husband's death in stride. She had his daughter to raise and his remaining investments to manage. Apparently, she was astute at both. A regal woman, she was a Boston Brahmin. Her belief in her infallibility was ingrained in her bones. She did well until fate dealt her another blow. Her daughter, a talented pianist, died of leukemia. The girl was only nineteen.

Mrs. Goodfellowe turned out to be one of those people who are dogged by tragedy. Within four years of her daughter's death she would remarry and less than one year later, again be widowed. This second husband, Eric Alan Powell, was twenty years her junior. Like her first husband, Powell would also end up being shot to death. But in his case, the killer was never found.

Powell's scandalous death in the fall of '23 was a huge emotional and social blow. It rocked Katherine to her blue-blooded core. It was not the blow that would undo her, however. That would come later.

When one pondered that time in Katherine's life, at the risk of getting gothic, it was easy to envisage her roaming the halls of her great mansion, haunted by the images of her lost loved ones. Easy to imagine her desperate to find a way to fill her time, to do something significant, to understand her interest upon learning about Esther.

The social grapevine was strong in those days and white patrons were rushing to find young colored talent. Someone mentioned Esther to Katherine and the next thing Esther knew, she was being invited to Goodfellowe mansion. Mrs. Goodfellowe interviewed her and then offered to cover her expenses while she pursued serious musical studies. Esther was leery at first, Ruth said. Esther had heard how some of these patrons tried to control their artists, but in the end, Esther's family convinced her that Mrs. Goodfellowe's offer was too good to pass up. What future did Esther have? She was a single mother with a young son and few work skills, faced with the ever-present threat of unemployment. Maybe with this rich lady's help, she could climb out of the muck and mire. Maybe she could even reach the stars. Esther had laughed at the thought, Ruth said, smiling sadly at the memory.

"It's our fault she ended up with that woman. We pushed her. Maybe she knew. Sensed something. We just wanted things to be good for her..."

But just as she'd feared, Esther became caught like a fly in a Venus flytrap, lured by the money only to be held under creative control.

For Katherine Goodfellowe, the combination of Esther's disappearance and the subsequent heist formed the proverbial straw that broke the camel's back. It was a period of personal loss and intense embarrassment. She made fewer and fewer appearances and lost her place as the queen of the upper crust. Once the doyenne of New York society, she became its laughingstock. After the spoiled auction, she withdrew, hurt, embarrassed and no longer confident of her ability to judge people. She was now a virtual recluse. There were few recent photos of her, and those few showed her with her lips pressed tightly together in a fine bitter line.

When she first put out the reward, she said she was doing so, not because she believed that Esther had taken part in the robbery, but because she wanted to prove Esther's innocence. But I wondered. In her heart, Mrs. Goodfellowe must've had doubts, especially after the car business.

I admired her for having stood by Esther, but of course I suspected her motives were as much self-preservation as altruism. Even with regard to the heist, my sympathy for her was limited.

Mrs. Goodfellowe had maintained that the auction was set up for purposes of charity, but common sense had always made me doubt it. I didn't know her well, but in the few minutes I'd interviewed her, I'd gotten an impression of a headstrong woman. That auction was as much a matter of social conceit, as it was of philanthropy. It wasn't about the jewels or charity or even trust. It was about showing off. Mrs. Goodfellowe had spent years making a name for herself as a patron of the arts and charitable causes, but she'd played the game according to other people's rules. Now she was going to do it her way, on her territory. Mrs. Goodfellowe called for such an audacious auction because she had the power to do so and wanted the world to know it. If everything had gone according to plan, no one would've dared challenge her place as the head of New York society. It was the bold plan of a bold woman and it might've worked, if it hadn't ended in death and scandal.

I was about to turn away from the mantel when the photograph of a young woman caught my eye. She so resembled early pictures of Katherine that I thought it must be her, but then I saw the signature in the corner, a small elegant script: "To Mommy and Daddy, with love, Elizabeth." So this was Katherine's long lost daughter. Photographs of her were rare, very rare. The photograph showed a woman-child with soft, dark eyes and a gentle, luminous smile. Having recognized Katherine in her, I stepped back to compare her features with those of her father. The resemblance was there, too, but—

"Do you like it?" a dry voice asked behind me.

I turned, surprised at the voice—and its owner.

She had changed far beyond any photo had shown. She sat in a wheelchair, her large frame reduced to skin and bones. The left side of her face was slack and her left hand lay unmoving in her lap. Her right hand rested atop her paralytic left one, gripping a lacy white handkerchief and a little bell. She wore a crocheted red shawl over a gray silk blouse with a large diamond-and-ruby brooch at the collar. A red-and-green plaid wool blanket had been laid across her lap. Roland stood behind her, tuxedoed and proper, his hands clasping the handles of her wheelchair.

"My husband's portrait," she rasped, "do you like it?"

Katherine Goodfellowe did not have the reputation of caring about anyone else's opinion, so why was she asking for mine? Was it a test, perhaps? I chose to be blunt.

"It's pretentious. I don't like pretentious things."

It was outrageous to talk to a white person like that, but sometimes outrageousness paid off. I was gambling that it would this time.

The right side of her lips curled upward. The left side stayed immobile. It was a sour smile, but the best she could do.

She raised her right hand and flicked her index finger. Roland pushed her forward and parked her to one side of the fireplace. The dancing flames cast hellish shadows on her profile. She gazed up at the painting.

"I've always hated it. Pretentious? Yes ... not like him at all."

She had a high forehead, a straight, sharp nose and square-cut chin. Her skin was milky white and had an unhealthy waxy sheen. She wore her gray hair coiled on her head. Roland bent and adjusted the blanket covering her lap, gently lifting her useless left hand. His tenderness was striking. She shooed him away, in the voice of someone who treasures the attention but cannot admit to it.

"My hot chocolate," she told him, and then asked me, "You'd like some, too, I suppose?"

"No, thank you."

She gave him some last instructions and sent him away. Her voice was scratchy and her words slightly slurred. A thin line of spittle trickled from the left corner of her mouth. She dabbed it away with the handkerchief.

"You're here about the dinner?"

"Well, actually, no. I'm here about Esther."

She blinked, dumbstruck. Her mouth opened again, but nothing came out. So I spoke. I told her about Ruth's visit and what she wanted. I told her why I was there and what information I hoped to obtain. By the time I was finished, she'd found her voice again.

"I … No, I don't talk about that—ever. And I think it's rather callous of you to—"

"I'm not writing this story for myself. Esther's family asked me to. They want to know whether she's alive and where she is. They're hoping that someone out there will remember something."

She gave a harsh chuckle. "I think not. No one remembers. Just liars who come here. And reporters who want a story."

I ignored that.

"You must still have some hope," I said. "You're still offering the reward. Twenty-five hundred dollars for information leading to Esther—or the recovery of her body. If you don't believe anyone remembers anything, then why do you keep it out there?"

"Because I'm a fool, a stubborn old fool."

She gazed at the orange flames, her thin frame soaking up their radiant heat.

"All my friends," she whispered. "Supposed friends. They laughed at me. 'How could I have trusted Esther?' 'Why did I tell her about the auction and my safes?' But I didn't tell her. I didn't. And I told them that, but they didn't believe me."

She'd dared to care about someone that society deemed unworthy of the slightest concern. She'd dared to be different and had paid a high price for it. I felt a surge of sympathy for her.

She drew a deep breath. "I guess I can't blame them. First, I marry two men who get themselves shot. Then I practically adopt a Negro and give her free run of the house."

My sympathy evaporated. I could overlook the flash of resentment toward her murdered husbands, but I couldn't ignore how she'd referred to Esther, as though she'd been a pet. Had the insult been intended, or was it simply one of those instances when a self-described forward-thinker accidentally reveals entrenched prejudice, even contempt, for the cause she advocates?

Roland entered with a silver service, laden with delicate porcelain cups and a sterling teapot. He set it down on the mahogany coffee table and poured a cup of chocolate for each of us. He placed one cup and saucer in the upturned palm of Mrs. Goodfellowe's paralyzed hand. Then he handed me a cup and withdrew with a silence deeper than that of a church mouse. As he closed the doors, I wondered if he would stand outside, listening. An unworthy thought, perhaps, but that's what I would've done.

"So, Mrs. Goodfellowe, have you changed your mind about her? Do you now think she was in on the heist?"

She sighed. "No, you can't say that."

"What could I say then?"

"I told you. I don't want to talk about it. Any of it."

I set down my cup. "Please, listen. I'm exploring the possibility– the very strong possibility—that Esther's disappearance really was a kidnapping and that it had nothing to do with the heist. I know the two events have been strung together, but I have new information that they were totally separate, unfortunate events. If I assure you that I'll only ask questions about Esther, will you answer them?"

She used her good hand to raise her cup to her lips and took a sip. A slight look of dissatisfaction flickered across her face. She lowered the cup to the saucer with care. Her right hand had a slight tremor that underscored the utter stillness of her left.

"All those jewels ... gone. All those people, blaming me. But to be honest, I didn't care. At the time, I really didn't care about them. I didn't miss those people's company, either. It was Esther I missed—Esther and her music. All that talent ... wasted."

She was silent, staring into her cup. I waited, hoping she'd say more. A few seconds passed and she shook her head.

"I don't see the point of a new article. I don't want new publicity about that time in my life. It was very painful. What good would it do me?"

"It might prove that you were right. Right to trust Esther, right to believe in her. It might prove that the others were all wrong."

She gave a snort. "What do I care what others think?"

But she did care. It was in her eyes. She cared very much. For a moment, despite her denials, I saw the thoughtful gleam in her eye and was hopeful.

"No," she said. "It's too dangerous for me. I don't want the whole thing raked up again. I want my peace."

"Is this really the kind of peace you want?" I glanced pointedly around the room. "The peace of an expensive mausoleum?"

She gave another paralytic smile. "You're very blunt, aren't you?"

"Listen, you don't have to do this for yourself. You can do it for someone else."

"Like who?"

"Esther's son."

"Don't tell me you care about that child. You're only interested in selling papers."

"That's right. I am. I want to sell papers, lots of them, and I aim to write a fantastic story, one that lots of people will read, and talk about. A story that'll make people remember Esther, and come forward."

She regarded me with pity. "I did everything a person could do. I pushed the police to investigate. Put out a reward. Even hired a private detective. None of it helped. The cops didn't turn up anything. The reward didn't make anyone come forward. And the private investigator found nothing. What makes you think you'll succeed? You're just a columnist at a small Negro newspaper. How many people actually read it? How many who might make a difference?"

That was a slap. I thought of all the donations she'd given to black publications. Was it all a pretense? Had she no faith in the cause she supposedly supported? I guess the Todd case and the heist had really done her in. What would the folks about to grant her an award say if they could hear her now? Or did they already know? Did they even care, as long as they got her money?

"Sometimes, all it takes is one person to start a landslide," I said, "One thread to unravel the Gordian knot."

"Hmph. That's the kind of thing my daughter would've said." Her gaze shifted to Elizabeth's photograph. "They were so similar. Both young and talented and ..." She paused. "Dependable." Her eyes met mine. "Esther never would've stolen from me. Never."

The room was silent, except for the crackling of the flames.

"All right. I'll talk to you—but on one condition: Whatever you learn, you bring it to me first, before you print it."

I'd felt a moment of hope, but at that, I shook my head. "No."

"I think it's reasonable. I've been burned by too many reporters in my time. Why, when I think of that other one, that Carter fellow. The charges he made! The questions! Reporters. When it comes to them, I've learned that trust is wonderful, but control is better."

"I'm not Carter, whoever he is."

"No, you're not. But you are one of them, a reporter."

I put my notepad back into my purse and stood up. I took in her shrunken face and the outline of her withered legs under the blanket and felt sorry for her. In spite of all the grief and agony she'd known—and still knew—she hadn't learned to empathize with the pain of others.

"Mrs. Goodfellowe, only one person gets to look over my shoulder, and that's my editor. However, I will do you the courtesy of telling you this. My column will be about Esther, not you. To the extent that it mentions you at all, it'll state that you refused to comment."

"That's all?"

I nodded. "That's all. Of course, it could also say that you referred to prior bad publicity. That you showed concern—no, fear—that renewed attention to Esther's disappearance would hurt you. Then some readers might infer that you're more concerned about your reputation than Esther's fate. Or that you have something to hide. If I were a certain type of reporter—the kind who wanted to 'burn' you—I would add that. Aren't you lucky that I'm not?"

She stared at me. I stared back. After a while, I got tired of it.

"I'll find my way out." I was in the front entryway when her voice stopped me.

"You're going to write about this whether or not I talk to you, aren't you?"

She sounded weary. I simply nodded.

"All right," she sighed. "What if I did agree to talk? What would you want to know?"

I turned. "Everything. Everything you think you know and more."

## 9.

She made me wait another two seconds, then nodded. I went back, sank down on her sofa, and took out my notepad and a pencil.

"Did you notice whether she had any male admirers?"

At first glance, a daily schedule like Esther's was so packed, so jammed with responsibility, that you'd think it was impenetrable. But when you look at anybody's schedule, really look close, you often find little cracks in time, those moments when the unexpected can slip in. A lot can happen in a crack in time. In Esther's case it might've been crossing paths with a man she normally wouldn't have met. If so, then what started out as an unexpected meeting might've turned into a deadly and secret love affair.

My question surprised her. Apparently, no one had put it to her before.

"No, of course not. She didn't run around like that. She didn't have time. And she wasn't that kind of girl. She was a serious artist."

I was glad to hear her defend Esther so vigorously. I tried to ignore the wicked little inner voice that kept saying that any defense of Esther was a defense of herself.

"You used to give parties, didn't you? Every two weeks. And Esther used to play?"

"Yes. So?"

I tried to think of a tactful manner in which to put it, but I'm not a tactful person.

"So, did any of your guests, male guests in particular, seem to … especially admire Esther's talent?"

"They all admired her talent. She would have been tremendous if this—this thing hadn't happened."

"But none of your guests ever—"

"No. Never. I wouldn't have permitted it." She gave me a stern look. "You said you wanted to help. But you aren't helping her. Not like this."

"I'm not afraid to learn something ugly or impolite about Esther, not if it means bringing her back."

"You're a fierce one, aren't you?"

"I try."

"Your chocolate," she said, "it's getting cold."

She took a sip of her own, tasted it, then took another and frowned down at the cup. "This really needs a kick." She directed me to a writing desk across the room, told me where the key was and instructed me to unlock it. Inside I found a bottle of twenty-year-old Scotch, half-empty. It was Prohibition, but everybody—especially the rich—had a little something on the side.

"Bring it here."

I did so.

"Pour it in." She indicated her cup.

I gave her a generous dollop.

"Don't you want any?" she asked.

"No, thank you." Resuming my seat, I continued. "I'd like the names of everyone who knew the details of the auction. Who took care of the inventory list? The guest list? Most important, who knew where the jewels would be stashed?"

She shook her head. "I can't tell you that."

It took an effort to check my temper. "I could understand why this information was withheld at the time of the heist. But three years have passed."

Again, she shook her head, this time more vigorously. "These families are old. They value their privacy. Right now it's just a matter of speculation as to who lost what. If I confirmed, or even denied, any of those reports … If I, in any way, gave any of them validity, it would be a betrayal on the most intimate level. I cannot and will not disclose that information."

The door opened and Roland entered, carrying a little silver tray. It held a glass of water and a saucer with two little pills.

"Excuse me, Miss Katherine, but it's time for your medicine."

She gave a shaky nod. Her right hand trembled as she put the pills in her mouth using her right hand. Roland held the glass to her lips and she sipped carefully from one side of her mouth. Despite her care, a trickle of water escaped. Roland produced a handkerchief from nowhere and gently dabbed the moisture away.

"Thank you," she whispered in a voice so low I almost didn't hear it. Again, sympathy tugged at my heart. How many members of her class ever thanked a servant for anything?

In a somewhat gentler voice, I picked up where we'd left off.

"What about the private detective?"

"He's dead. If you're thinking about his files, I'm sure they're long gone."

"But—"

She shook her head. "There's no point in looking in that direction."

I drew a deep breath. "Then I'd like to speak with Beth Johnson."

"Beth? Why, she hasn't worked here in ..." She turned to her butler. "How long's it been, Roland?"

"Quite some time, ma'am. You released her two years ago, this past spring. It was in April, if I remember correctly."

"Yes, that's right." She looked at me. "Why in the world would you want to talk to her?"

"I'm hoping she'll remember something from that night."

"Well, I'm sorry, but I can't help you there."

"If you don't mind my asking, why did you ... 'release' her?"

Katherine Goodfellowe actually averted her eyes. With her good hand, she readjusted her shawl around her thin shoulders. Then she gave Roland a pointed glance and he left the room. When he was gone, the doors closed behind him, she cleared her throat.

"I had to send her away."

"She did something wrong?"

Mrs. Goodfellowe drew herself up. "I'm a Christian," she said, her voice quietly strict. "I'm in good standing with my church community and my God. I follow the teachings of the Bible and I expect my servants to do the same."

Interesting. Mrs. Goodfellowe was not known for her religious beliefs.

She fussed with her shawl some more and squirmed in her chair, as much as she could. There was movement in her legs. So, she wasn't paralyzed, just debilitated.

"The silly girl went and got herself in trouble." Mrs. Goodfellowe looked angry just thinking about it.

The news dismayed me. Mrs. Goodfellowe went on, trying to justify her self-righteousness. I half-listened, worrying. Beth, a single mother, and losing her job when she most needed it: Where was she? How was she doing? How would I find her?

"It was such a shame," Mrs. Goodfellowe was saying. "She was an excellent girl, you know. Quiet, obedient. Efficient. Very dependable. I don't know what happened. She tried to keep it from me. If she'd come to me, told me what she'd done, then maybe I'd have ... I could've helped her. I certainly would have tried."

"Tried how?" I was genuinely curious.

"Well, I would've made sure she had a place in one of those homes. You know the ones, where girls like her, girls who've made a mistake, can go and get taken care of. Then later, when it's all over and done, they can come back."

"And you would have taken her back?"

"Perhaps. That depended ..."

"On what?"

She was silent, so I answered my own question.

"On whether she gave up her child?"

She turned her steely eyes on me. Guilt battled self-righteousness.

"Don't you understand? She wasn't married. She couldn't even tell me who the father was."

Couldn't? Why not simply *wouldn't*? Had she assumed that Beth had slept with so many men that she couldn't identify the father? Would Mrs. Goodfellowe have made the same assumption if Beth were white and not poor?

"How far along was she when you, uh … 'released' her?"

"Stop saying it like that. It was the best thing I could've done for her. She wouldn't have fit in, anymore. Everyone would've talked about it."

Yes, of course. That was a consideration.

"How far?"

"Maybe six months, maybe seven. I don't know. I don't remember."

"And you haven't heard from her since?"

"Of course not. She knew better than to come back here. Not without … you know. Now is that all?"

I left her sitting by her fireplace, trying to absorb the heat of the flames. I was tempted to tell her it was a lost cause. Somewhere along the line, a sliver of ice had slipped into her heart. It would take more than nesting by the hearth to melt it.

Roland appeared out of nowhere to return my coat and open the door. The temperature had dropped outside. I had forgotten my gloves at home, so I tucked my purse under one arm and stuffed my hands in my pockets. An unfamiliar piece of paper tickled my fingertips on the right side. I drew out the torn square and squinted at it. Handwriting I didn't recognize, but a name I did.

*Beth Johnson*
*410 St. Nicholas Ave, Apt 59*

I turned back to the house. Roland stood at a ground-floor window, between parted curtains, watching.

"Thank you," I mouthed.

He gave an answering nod, then let the curtain drop and stepped back into the shadows.

## *10.*

I walked over to Lexington Avenue and took the train back up to Harlem. Once at my office, I called Ruth at her church.

"I might've found Beth. I'm going over to see her tonight. You want to come with me?"

"I don't know. She might not want to talk to me."

"How about you wanting to talk to her? Now's your chance to apologize."

A pause and then a nervous decision: "All right."

"Look, if it makes you feel any better, there could be another reason why Beth dropped off the scene." I told her what I'd learned. "Now I don't mean to be spreading the girl's business around, but at least you know she was busy with problems of her own."

"Oh, that's rotten. Did the guy skip out on her?"

"Don't know. Could be."

"Beth must've been feeling real bad." A thoughtful pause. "But she should've called me. I would've understood. She should've known I wouldn't hold nothing like that against her. Sure, I'll go with you, When were you thinking about?"

"This evening."

I offered to pick her up at her apartment at seven.

"Can you make it a little earlier? Say around half past five? I want to stop by and see my mother. If you come with me, then you can see her, too."

I agreed and we hung up.

Ruth Todd had moved to a tenement building over on 140th Street and Eighth Avenue. She was leaving her house as I came up. We headed east, over to Seventh. A stray cat scooted across our path, gray and ragged.

"Where's Job?" I asked.

"Visiting friends. We got some nice neighbors, thank the Lord. They got a boy his age and they let Job sleep over when I got to work late."

"And is work going well?"

She smiled and shrugged. "It's a good job, but maybe a bit much for one person. It'd be great if I could find somebody to help. But you know how it is," she laughed. "Good help ain't easy to find."

The wind cut through my coat like a knife through butter. A thin sheen of ice covered the ground and it was slippery going. I kept my head down and shoulders hunched. My feet hurt from the cold, even though I had boots on. My eyes strayed to Ruth's thin-soled shoes and I decided I had nothing to complain about.

I tried to work the stiff muscles in my face. This was not the best time to be posing questions, but it would have to do.

"Ruth, what kind of man was Esther drawn to?"

She rubbed her face with nervous hands, and then shoved them deep into her pockets.

"Smart guys. She really liked the brainy ones. She felt bad about not having much schooling herself."

I made a mental note of that. "Did you notice any changes in her mood, going back months before the disappearance?"

Ruth looked uncomfortable. "What kind of changes?"

"Like being cheerful, 'cause she'd fallen in love, maybe?"

Ruth inclined her head in thought. "Well, back in September, she did seem real upbeat, hopeful in a way she hadn't been in a long time. It didn't last long, though."

"What do you mean?"

"I'm not sure. I can't exactly put my finger on it. I asked her about it but she wouldn't answer, and the look she gave me … It was so sad I didn't press her." Her expression clouded. "I guess that was a mistake, letting her off like that. I should've asked. Then maybe I would've known."

"You're assuming she would've told you. Maybe she would've. But maybe she wouldn't. You don't know."

Ruth nodded, but the look in her eyes was one of old regret.

I sighed. "Ruth, you've got to learn to lay your burden down. Beating yourself down for what you should've or shouldn't have done isn't going to help your mother or you."

This time she gave a faint smile. She took a deep breath, set her shoulders and blinked back tears.

"It sure is Christmassy out here," she said, making an effort at small talk.

"Yeah, that it is."

Preparations for Christmas were under way at every corner. Fake ivy had been twisted around street lamps. Wreaths hung in storefront windows. Street peddlers sold trees. Others hawked Christmas presents: toys, "hot" dresses and the like.

When I'd woken that morning, the world was silent. Now, it was anything but. Car drivers honked at one another. Children yelled at dogs and mothers yelled at children, and the smells of greasy food, gasoline and garbage thickened the air.

When we turned the corner to Harlem Hospital, all that noise fell away. It was as though a big muffling blanket had been dropped around the place.

I asked Ruth about her mother. "Has her condition worsened?"

"No, but she's not getting any better either."

We took the elevator up. Diane Todd was in a room with three other women, all in their sixties, all of them fragile. The room was square, with two beds on each side. The walls were a pale yellow. In the harsh light it was hard to tell if they'd been painted that color or were simply dingy. Mrs. Todd was in the bed on the left, to the rear. She was a stick figure propped up by two fat pillows. A red and white checked scarf covered her head. Ruth went over and gently kissed her on the forehead. Mrs. Todd smiled weakly up at her daughter, then looked at me. Ruth beckoned me to come closer.

"Mama, you remember Mrs. Price, don't you? She's gonna write about Esther for us."

Diane Todd extended a shaky hand. I gave it a light squeeze. Her hand was as light as a feather, and just as cool. I glanced up at Ruth. Her eyes showed worry, but she put on a smile.

"How you feelin' today, Mama?"

A faint smile was the answer. Mrs. Todd's eyes turned to me. Her thin eyebrows came together in a look of worry. Ruth gave me a pleading look. Give her some good news.

"I've decided to dedicate half of my next two columns to Esther," I said. "That way her story will be in the paper twice and more people will read about her."

Diane Todd's eyes shone with tears. Her lips moved. I leaned closer to hear. *Thank you*, she whispered. She only managed to get out those two words, but they were more than enough.

If I hadn't felt obligated already, I would've felt so then.

## 11.

Beth's place was down on 130th Street, and a few blocks west. It wasn't that far, but the weather was too cold and the evening too dark for me to feel like hoofing it, so I hailed a taxi to take us over.

"Does she know we're coming?" Ruth asked.

"Naw, but it's the middle of the week, so we got a good chance of finding her home."

Ruth was pensive. "I guess her baby'd be about a year old now."

"Sounds about right."

"I wish I'd bought a present."

I gave her a look. "That's all right. I don't think she'd expect one."

Beth Johnson was in her late twenties. She'd once told me she'd come up from one of the Carolinas ten years prior. She only had a grade-school education, but she was knowledgeable about her work. She was conscientious and dependable, but she'd also struck me as kind of bitter. It wasn't always noticeable and it didn't seem to be directed toward anyone in particular. It just seemed to be part of her makeup.

In bringing Ruth along, I hoped the two women would inspire each other to more profound recollections of the night Esther disappeared. I really wanted to know whether Beth knew anything about Esther having been romantically involved with someone. It's not that I distrusted Ruth's information. No doubt, she was telling the truth, as far as she knew it. But the fact is, people often choose to confide in friends rather than family, even when their family ties are as close and loving as the Todds' appeared to be.

The address Roland had given led us to a small red brick tenement. The front door was unlocked. I pushed it open and entered. The lobby appeared to be clean, but it had a latent odor of urine and squalor. There was no elevator, so we took the stairs. We were both breathing heavily when we reached the fifth floor. A long narrow hallway stretched out before us. A dark door stood ajar at the far end. We started down the hall, looking for number 59.

We had gone halfway when heated voices erupted behind the half-open door, a man and woman arguing. Their words were indiscernible. There was a pause in the argument. A rough-looking man in a sleeveless undershirt appeared in the doorway. He gave us an evil-looking glance, and slammed the door.

Ruth and I exchanged looks. What kind of place was Beth living in?

We found her apartment and knocked. A slender woman opened the door. She wore cheap gold earrings, a poison green dress and bold red lipstick.

"Why, I—"

The words died in her throat and her smile, bright and fake, did a fast fade. Ruth looked stunned. I could guess what she was thinking because I was thinking it, too. Where was the straight-laced, conservative-looking young woman she'd known? The quiet, modest girl who'd been Esther's best friend?

"Ruth! What are you doing here?" Beth's gaze went to me and wariness crept into her voice. "And you! Why, you're the—"

"Yes," I said, stepping forward.

From behind the door down the hall came a shriek, and then a crash—a vase perhaps. All three of us looked down the hall.

"Should we call the police?" Ruth asked.

"Don't bother." Beth waved her hand. "They're like that all the time."

"But—" Ruth began.

"It's okay. Since you're here, you might as well come in. It's not good to stand out in the hallway like that."

After a short hallway, the apartment turned into a one-room setup. Windows overlooking St. Nicholas Avenue took up most of one wall. A recessed stove and sink took up much of another. The room itself was small and square, but high ceilinged. A scrawny Christmas tree leaned precariously in a corner near the window. It was decorated, nicely, with thin ribbons. A bed jutted into the middle. It was covered with a fake leopard skin. A chipped wood closet stood next to her bed and a black linen trunk that looked as though it might've once been expensive sat at the foot of the bed. A bright pink chinchilla was draped over the back of a thin wood chair. Other than the bed, the chair was the only place to sit.

There was no sign of a child. No rattles or other toys. No small pieces of clothing. Instead of sturdy wooden blocks, cheap, fragile china figurines dotted a small bookshelf in one corner and adorned the table next to the bed.

Beth gestured for us to take a seat. Three years earlier, her fingernails had been short and broken. Now they were long, sharp and polished a hard red. Ruth hesitated, then nudged the chinchilla aside and sat down on the wood chair. I remained standing. Beth gave the clock on the wall a nervous glance and then gave Ruth a thin smile.

"So, how you doing?" she asked Ruth.

"Been better."

Ruth's face was an open book. Her gaze roamed over the room and by the time she looked back at Beth, her surprise and bewilderment had given way to dismay and disapproval. Beth saw it; I could sense her hackles rise. Beth opened her mouth to say something heated and I stepped in to intervene.

"Looks like you're doing well, Beth. I heard you had a baby."

She cut her eyes at me, still full of resentment and suspicion. Her lips curled.

"So you been talking to Roland." A sudden thought. "But he didn't know my address, or did he?"

"He says hello," I said. "And the baby?"

"What about it?'

"A boy? A girl?"

"A boy."

"He's not here?"

"Down South, with my mother."

"I wish you'd told me," Ruth said. "Maybe I could've helped—"

"You couldna done nothing." Beth snapped. She looked from Ruth to me. "So what can I do for you? I, ah, ... have a friend coming." Another glance at the wall clock. "He'll be here in ten minutes. So maybe you can tell me what you want and—"

"What's going on here?" Ruth asked.

Beth's mouth tightened. She put her hands on her hips. "What d'you think?"

"I don't want to say what I'm thinking. Girl, I can't believe you let yourself go down like this. You could've—"

"Don't you go judging me! *Don't you dare!*"

"But couldn't you find something else? Something respectable? You could've gone to the church and gotten help—"

"The church? Which one?"

Ruth spread her hands. "Why, any of them!"

"Is that right? Well, let me tell you something. I did go to a church. The one out there on the corner." She pointed her finger at the window facing the southwest corner. "That fine big ol' stone one, with the fine upstanding congregation and the minister preaching every Sunday. You want to know what happened?"

Ruth opened her mouth. Beth interrupted her.

"I'll tell you what. The minister thought he could get some poontang. That I don't mind. But that motherfucker thought he could get it for free."

"I don't bel—"

"I don't give a damn whether you believe me or not. You think I care? Hell, I got to make a living—and this is the best way to do it."

"But Beth—"

"But Beth nothing." She folded her arms across her chest. "What do you two want?"

Quickly, I explained my plan to write about Esther and my hope that she could give me fresh information for it.

"Are you serious?" Beth asked.

"Yes, I am."

She turned to Ruth. "She got you paying her to do this?"

"Beth, I want you to help her," Ruth said. "I need you to tell her whatever you remember."

"Well, you know I don't remember nothing. I was sick that night, remember?"

"That's all fine and true," I said, "but even if you can't tell us anything new about that night, then maybe you can come up with something about the days and nights before that."

"What're you talking about?"

Ruth explained. "Mrs. Price here wants to know if Esther was seeing somebody. You know, a fellow? I told her she wasn't, but—"

"But you want her to hear it from me." Beth gave Ruth a pitying look. "You got some nerve, coming in here and judging me, and then saying you need my help."

"Beth," Ruth said, "We're not judging you. We're just surprised is all. Things are ..." She hesitated, glanced around, and then brought her gaze back to Beth, "so different, you know. Your living here and ... it's not how I expected."

Beth clucked her tongue and put a hand on her hip. "You're such a hypocrite. If you only knew. That sweet little sister of yours? She wasn't all that holy neither."

"What does that mean?" Ruth asked.

"It means ..." Beth hesitated. She looked at me.

"Yes?" Ruth snapped.

"You don't want to hear it," Beth snapped back.

"Tell me!"

Beth's expression hardened. "All right. You asked for it. Esther was getting it, getting all she could. And loving every minute of it."

"You're lying."

"No, I'm not. And deep down, you know it. You must've. You had to."

"But she was saved! She weren't no sinner."

"No, she weren't—no more'n I am. You people tried to make a saint out of her. You wouldn't let her breathe. But she was just a normal woman. Wanted to live, have fun, just like everybody else."

"But she would've never—"

"Yes, she would, too. She would and she did."

"Beth Johnson, you're a liar!" Ruth cried.

"I am not. And she was so proud, too. The way she carried on about that man—"

"*Carried on?* She never said nothing to me."

Beth arched an eyebrow. "Well, that says something about you, don't it?"

I intervened. "Beth, don't you care about Esther? You were supposed to be her best friend. Help us."

A look of embarrassment flickered across her face.

I pressed her. "What did she say about this man?"

She took a deep breath and another glance at the clock. "Nothing much."

"But you said she was carrying on about him."

Beth shook her head. "No, that was … a little bit—"

"Maybe, she said his name?"

"Sexton."

"Last name?"

"Don't remember."

"Something else? What he did for a living?"

"Had a job with the government. Something to do with taxes."

Unease touched me. I knew of a man named Sexton who did taxes for the government. "Do you know where she met him?"

Beth regarded us unhappily. She swallowed and took a moment. "He was at Mrs. Goodfellowe's, at one of them damned parties."

"You mean he was white?" Ruth said with quiet surprise.

Beth glanced at her with derision. "He was as black as coal. As a matter-of-fact, Esther used to make fun of him—not him, but his name. Said it was as far away from describing him as a name could be."

The sense of unease deepened. The description clearly fit one man in particular, Sexton Whitefie—

"So there," Beth said. "It was nice talking to you, but my friend's gonna walk through that door any minute and I—"

"Did it ever go bad between them?" I asked.

Beth folded her arms across her chest again and looked stubborn. "I need you to leave."

"Not until you tell us what we need to know."

She gritted her teeth. "All right," she said in a tight voice. "But then you gotta get out."

"Deal."

She licked her lips. "Esther didn't never really say much about him. I think he told her not to. Didn't matter." She looked at Ruth. "Them with eyes to see could've seen she was happy. And them with eyes would've known when it went all wrong."

Ruth bristled. "You should've told me—"

"I didn't *have* to tell you nothing. You should've asked. I wasn't her sister. *You* were." Beth swung back to me. "I kept after her. What was wrong? What the hell was going on? She broke down. Told me she was scared. She thought she was being followed."

"Oh, God," Ruth moaned.

"When was this?"

"I don't remember. It's been too long. But it was a while before she got kidnapped. A couple of months maybe."

"That would've put it in October," Ruth said. "All that time and she didn't say nothing to me." She spoke in a whisper, more to herself than to either of us.

"So," Beth gave us an expectant look. "Now that I've told y'all—"

Ruth got to her feet. She advanced on Beth, her face tight with anger.

"Why didn't you tell the police all this when Esther disappeared? It was just me talking and they didn't believe me. I could've used your help."

"There you go, blaming me again. I didn't say nothing 'cause I didn't think Esther would've wanted me to."

"You thought what?"

"Look, she never acted scared of him, not to me—"

"But you just said she thought he was following her."

"I said she thought she was being followed. She didn't say it was him. And she sure didn't say nothing more about it—but she did make it a big deal about keeping him a secret."

Ruth nearly slapped her. Her hand was moving—but at the last second, she caught herself, closed her eyes and took a deep, shuddering breath. Her lips moved. I think she was praying. When she opened her eyes, the hot anger had cooled, but the look she gave Beth was still sharper than a skewer.

Beth fell back a step. "Listen," she said in a guilty, resentful rush, "for all I know she might've gone off with him. Could be she did run away. Ruth, don't you know how tired she was? Tired of doing for everybody else. She needed to do for Esther. So maybe her being kidnapped weren't no kidnapping at all. It was just her making a beeline for freedom."

Ruth's answer was an accusatory silence.

At her wits' end, Beth pointed to the door. "Get out. Y'all can't be here no more."

She marched down the hall. Ruth and I exchanged glances, and then followed her. Beth yanked open the door and stood waiting for us to leave. Ruth was ahead of me. She started out, but then paused. Looking dazed, she turned back to Beth.

"I just don't understand. Why'd she do it?"

"Do what?"

"Tell you all this and not tell me?"

"You know the answer as well as I do." Beth looked at Ruth's tired face and relented somewhat. "I told you," she added with a touch of sympathy. "She was scared of what you'd say, you and your mama and daddy. And it's not like she wanted to talk to me about it. I made her. I saw her looking sad and I made her tell me why."

Ruth thought about that. Then she asked, "Did she tell you about the threatening notes, too?"

"What notes? I don't know nothing about no notes. She just told me she was scared. Now go. Please. He won't like it if he comes and finds you here." Beth looked at me. "Especially, you, Miss Lanie."

I smiled slowly. "Someone I'd recognize?"

Beth was not amused. "Just go, please."

I gave Beth my telephone numbers and asked her to call if she thought of anything else. She said she would, but the way she slammed the door made me doubt it.

Ruth was pensive as we walked back toward her house.

"Do you believe her?" she finally asked.

"Yeah. Don't you?"

"Yeah. I'm just ..."

"You regret asking me to do this?"

She came to a stop, tears in her eyes. "I got a lot of regrets, but asking for your help ain't one of them. I'm just wondering why I waited so long."

I said good-bye to Ruth at the corner of 139th Street and turned down the block toward home. Ruth was upset at the unpleasantness of the news. I was happy that there was any news at all. As I'd told Mrs. Goodfellowe, I wasn't scared to learn something about Esther if it meant bringing her back. Beth's information bore out the wisdom of Bellamy's advice. Now, I just had to confirm the secret lover's identity.

And I had to wonder how many other secrets Esther Todd had kept.

## 12.

Trouble was brewing. When I entered the newsroom the next morning, the clatter paused. Eyes followed me as I went to my desk.

What had I done now?

Amid the mess of my desk, five personalized, expensive envelopes were stacked in a neat pile next to slips bearing telephone messages. I sat down and shouldered off my coat.

Working quickly, I sorted the invites. A'Lelia wanted me to attend the opening of some new nightclub. Several people were throwing supper parties. The James Weldon Johnsons were inviting me to their next literary afternoon. There were also invitations from Charles Johnson, Enrique Cachemailles and the Rev. Frederick A. Cullen, Countee Cullen's adoptive father. Last, but by no means the least, was a little note from the Walter Whites.

The Whites—Gladys was elegance personified and Walter, a gregarious intellectual—issued some of the most treasured invitations in New York City. Much of Harlem loved Walter, even if just as much of it wondered why this blond-haired, blue-eyed man with edgy Wall Street mannerisms said he was colored. But Nordic-looking blacks weren't unusual among the upper crust of Atlanta, which was White's hometown. He was a founding member of the civil rights movement, and had risked life and limb in the battle against lynching, so no one doubted his commitment to the cause. I'd met White on several occasions but this was the first time he'd invited me to his home.

I was just reading the invitation's opening lines—"We would love the pleasure of your company at …"—when a shadow fell across my desk. I looked up to see Selena. She bent down and spoke in a loud stage whisper meant to carry.

"Sam wants to see you. In his office. Now."

Selena had been with the paper for three months. She had a sharp nose, both literally and figuratively. She was also a woman of definite goals, one of them being my column. Not long after arriving, she'd made it clear that she wanted it and would do anything to get it. She'd been making regular plays for Sam, too, but whether it was because she really wanted him—or just saw him as a means to an end—was anyone's guess.

If bad news was headed my way, Selena made sure she was the one to bring it. She gave me a theatrical look of concern. "Good luck. You're gonna need it."

I ignored her, took a deep breath and cut across the newsroom to reach Sam's office, aware of another wave of glances.

Sam's office smelled of his cologne—clean and woodsy—but it also held the scratchy trace of newspaper dust. The odor wasn't as strong in here as in the main room, but it was just as noticeable because of the confined space. Sam was at his battered desk, wearing a dark gray vest over a white shirt. His sleeves were rolled up, revealing lean, but muscular forearms. He was editing articles, but put them aside and stood as I came in.

"Close the door and sit down."

He gestured toward the chair in front of his desk. I eased down in it and he sat again, too.

"You went to see Mrs. Goodfellowe yesterday."

"Is that a statement or a question?"

He gave me an exasperated look. "Do you know who just called?"

"Let me guess. She called Ramsey and Ramsey called you." 'She' being Mrs. Goodfellowe, and 'Ramsey,' George Ramsey, the newspaper's executive editor.

"No. I had Canfield himself on the phone."

Byron Canfield? The head of the Movement, the umbrella group for black civil rights efforts? Impressive.

"What happened? Did she threaten to cancel a donation?"

"Actually, she did mention a certain award and the Movement's magazine, all of which she sponsors."

"And they let her get away with it?"

Sam's dark brown eyes looked tired. "Mrs. Goodfellowe is an important patron. The Movement needs people like her."

"She's just the kind it doesn't need: people who put their own interests first."

"You're exaggerating."

"Am I? People like her undermine the Movement with her money. We're nothing but puppets on a string for her."

"There's always a trade-off for support."

"And you think that's right?"

"Lanie." He put up a hand. "I will not argue with you."

"Don't you even want to hear why I went to see her? Aren't you even curious about why she's so upset? The real reason?"

"I know why you went to see her. And I don't need to guess why she's upset. That's pretty damn clear."

"But—"

"Look, I respect what you're trying to do. But I cannot let you irritate the powers-that-be. Stay away from Katherine Goodfellowe. And when you write that column, make sure you leave her out of it. Got me?"

I didn't trust myself to answer politely.

"Lanie? Tell me you've understood."

"How can you give in so easily? Why don't you fight? Believe in something?"

"I do believe in something. I believe in this paper. I believe in protecting it."

"You call this protecting it? Letting Canfield tell you what to do? He might choose to listen to that woman, but you don't have to."

His voice took on an edge. "Don't tell me how to do my job."

"And don't you tell me how to do mine."

I stood up and walked out.

"Lanie!"

I went to my desk and grabbed up my coat. Answering invitations could wait. I had to get out of there.

"Lanie!"

The whole newsroom jumped. He came up behind me, grabbed me by the elbow and hustled me out to the corridor. I wrenched my arm away. He spoke in a tense, angry whisper.

"Don't you ever do that again, walk out when I'm talking to you."

He paused, took a deep breath and counted to three, making a visible effort to control his anger.

"You're the only one who can upset me this way, the only one. I'm asking you, don't ever do it in there." He nodded toward the newsroom. "That's my workplace, Lanie. Yours and mine. We don't want to mess it up ... for either of us."

His words surprised me into silence. Marcus Hobbs, our sports writer, was passing by and gave us a curious glance. Sam gave him a curt nod that clearly said, "Mind your business," and Hobbs went away.

Sam looked at me. "Well?"

The hard knot of anger that had formed in my gut softened. I gave a little nod.

"Good," he said, relieved. "I know you're fearless. But these are not the kind of people you mess with. The success of your column depends on their favor."

That comment made me angry all over again. What he said was news to me and I let him know it. He looked at me as though I was missing the obvious, and to him, I guess I was.

"Lanie, who do you think sends you those invitations?"

"I know who and I know why. They send them because they need coverage, because they want to impress their friends, and being in my column helps them do it."

"They help us sell papers—"

"And we make them look good. Tit-for-tat. I don't tell them who to invite and they shouldn't be telling me what to write."

I was pushing hard—I knew that—but I've always been that way. Push me and I push back. At the same time, I realized that my anger was not meant for him.

"Lanie, you're not making my job easier." He sounded weary.

I felt a pang of sympathy. I didn't want to complicate his life. I respected him, and liked him. Furthermore, I understood his dilemma. The problem was, he wasn't understanding mine: I had a promise to keep and I meant to do it.

"Are you going to forbid the column on Esther?"

"I'm close to it."

I searched his gaze, not wanting to believe it. "Don't."

I laid a light hand on his forearm. I hadn't planned to, but I did, and just like that, the connection between us changed. I felt it and he did, too. I saw it in his eyes.

I sensed the newsroom door open behind us. A feminine voice said, "Sam, could you come in here for a moment, please? We have a problem."

It was Selena.

His eyes slid from mine to a point over my shoulder. "I'll be right there."

There was a pause, the sensation of jealous eyes on my back and then the soft thud of the door closing.

Sam's gaze returned to me. He spoke in a low voice. "Maybe we could continue this conversation later?"

I hesitated.

"Sam?" Selena was back in the doorway.

"Dinner? Tonight?" he asked me. "Around seven, at the Bamboo Inn?"

I surprised myself. "Monday would be better."

"Okay," he said. "I'll be there."

## *13.*

The *Chronicle* kept copies of its old issues stacked in a basement room. An old woman named Ethel Cane zealously guarded this room. You didn't dare go near it, much less enter it, without Ethel's permission. Most people said she'd been here before the building was built—that it was actually built around her. That could've been true. Ethel might've well been one of the people whose homes were torn down in the name of progress. Not long after I joined the paper, she told me, "Honey, this is my spot and I ain't gonna leave it."

I took her some coffee. "How ya doin' Mrs. Cane? I brought a little joe for you."

She accepted the cup with a suspicious eye. "What d'you want? You don't never come down here if it ain't for something."

"Course not. I wouldn't waste your time—or mine."

She chuckled and sipped. "Well, I got to say, you sure do know how to make this nasty brew taste like something. What kind of something, I ain't gonna say."

I ignored that. "So Mrs. Cane, I need to look up a party that happened back in '23."

"Now why would you want to do that?" She was nothing if not nosey. "You 'bout to rock somebody's boat, huh? 'Bout to do a Lanie-Lanie on them."

She'd come up with that term and for the life of me I couldn't figure out what it meant.

"Just doing my job," I said, "asking questions."

"Honey, you got a twinkle in your eyes that's brighter than Broadway, and it says you're on to something. Whoever you're after, they'd better start running."

I repressed a smile.

She took another sip. "So tell me again, who can I help you Lanie-Lanie today?"

Not twenty minutes later I had confirmation of what Beth said. Back in '23, the *Chronicle* didn't do full coverage of black society or its parties, but it did run small pieces once or twice a week, especially when the story involved meetings between the socially or politically significant. Such was the case in September of '23. Katherine Goodfellowe and Eric Alan Powell had indeed thrown a party and one of their guests was a man named Sexton—Sexton A. Whitefield.

Whitefield was a prominent Republican, but not just any prominent Republican. He was the Collector of Internal

Revenue for the Third District of New York County and that made him very prominent indeed.

The sixtyish Whitefield was also self-educated and self-made. He had an impressive history of appointments, from private secretary of New York State's Treasurer, to Chief Clerk in the State Treasury to Supervisor of Accounts for the New York Racing Commission. He was on a first name basis with religious leaders, judges, the mayor's staff and Mayor Jimmy Walker himself. He had "friends" everywhere.

Whitefield had certainly used his influence to achieve a lot of good. Thanks to his direct intervention, more colored had been appointed to better-paying city and federal positions than ever before. If you needed coal in the winter, medicine for a Harlem clinic or books for a classroom, Whitefield was the man to see.

But if you crossed him, or criticized one of his allies, you were dead meat. A master of Machiavellian maneuvers, Whitefield moved silently and struck swiftly. He deserved his reputation as being cool, calculating and occasionally vindictive.

People were still talking about the Hamilton incident, five years after the fact. Edward H. Hamilton was a militant socialist and leading Negro nationalist. Back in '21, he had a humble job as a clerk at the post office. He wrote a couple of letters to the *New York Sun* criticizing conservative civil rights leader Booker T. Washington. Whitefield owed his start to Booker T. and was fiercely loyal, so when he saw the letters he was furious. Whitefield picked up the phone and by the time he hung up, Hamilton was out of a job. Apparently, the postmaster general was one of Whitefield's many "friends."

He was a powerhouse, all right. Not good looking by any stretch of the imagination, but impressively clever, urbane and discerning.

I'd met him at one of Carl Van Vechten's infamously smart dinner parties. Whitefield knew about international affairs, and could speak with eloquence and enlightenment on a wide range of matters. But his attitude toward women was primitive. Upon learning what I did for a living—and that no, I wasn't interested in dating him—he lectured me on how women belong in the kitchen, that American women don't know how to appreciate their men and that the so-called 'modern woman' is simply a woman who has lost her soul. A woman, he said, is meant to be taken care of, to be cosseted, coddled and protected—as long as she remembers her place. The moment she forgets it, he said, she must be reminded.

Could an accomplished man of his position really think that way? At the time, I couldn't believe it, but now I had to wonder.

Whitefield wouldn't have been interested in a woman who saw him for what he was, but what about someone like Esther? She was poor and struggling. By all accounts, she was trusting, often naive. He might've found her an easy target. What had he promised her? Help or rescue? Maybe even love? Had he promised her anything? Would he have even had to? Maybe she had simply hoped.

Dear, sweet Esther. The vicious scar that marred her face showed that she'd already once fallen prey to the charms of an abuser. If Whitefield had targeted her for seduction, where would she have found the strength to resist him?

At some point, however, she must've realized that she'd stepped into a trap. She'd tried to walk away. Had he refused to let her? Could he, a man of his high station, have been involved in something so despicable as making her disappear?

## 14.

Back in the newsroom, I contacted Ruth. Had the family retained any of Esther's belongings?

"All of them," she said. "Mama and daddy couldn't never bring themselves to throw nothing away. Neither can I. Dumb, huh?"

"Not at all. Would you mind if I went through them?"

A surprised pause, and then: "Sure, okay."

Ruth had packed Esther's belongings into a trunk and shoved it into a closet. That evening, we dragged it into the living room. Then Ruth headed to the kitchen to prepare supper, leaving Job and I sitting cross-legged on the floor, the trunk before us. We lifted the heavy lid, releasing a sharp smell. Ruth had been generous with the mothballs.

For about three seconds, Job and I just sat surveying the trunk's contents. A stranger would've seen a typical assortment of clothing, books and bills, receipts and odd papers. But I saw much more, and glancing at Job, I was sure he did, too.

I reached for one of the books. It turned out to be a journal. My heartbeat picked up a notch. Maybe Esther had written something about her mysterious beau.

But no, there was only one entry, dated December 18, 1923. It was about her excitement at going out that evening, and a promise to write more on the morrow, a promise she was unable to keep.

I laid the journal aside and started to reach into the trunk, but stopped. It struck me that Job hadn't moved to touch anything. He was sitting quite still, holding himself back. His eyes glittered wetly.

"Job, honey? Are you okay?"

"I didn't know," he said in a small voice.

"Know what?" I leaned closer to hear him.

"That my mama's stuff was in there." He gestured to the trunk.

"What do you mean, you didn't know?"

He spoke in a halting voice. "I been asking Auntie Ruth about that trunk. I done asked her again and again. She always said it was just some old stuff. She didn't tell me..." His tone was bitter. "She didn't say nothing."

"Oh, Job." My heart broke for him. I took him in my arms and hugged him. "Your Auntie Ruth wanted to protect you. That's all. She wants to make sure you never get hurt again. I guess she thought ... well, she must've thought it was better if you didn't know."

He raised his big, brown eyes to me. "But, how could she—?"

"Listen. Today, she let you stay in here with me. So I guess she thinks it's time."

He thought about that and nodded. "She's always telling me how I'm a big boy, now."

"Yeah," I said softly. "You're a big boy."

My gaze went to the trunk, hoping it held answers. "Whatever we find in there, we have to be very careful with it."

"You mean 'cause Mama might want it when she comes back?"

I didn't know how to answer.

He bit down on his lower lip, nodded and sighed. "That's all right, Miss Lanie. I know my mama's never coming back. I know she gone for good. I just want to know why."

"That's what we all want to know, honey." I eyed the neatly folded stack of clothes and papers. *And that's what I'm going to find out.*

After that, I expected Job to dive into the trunk with the excitement of a treasure hunter. Instead, he approached it with the reverence of an acolyte. The first item he took out was a folded white cotton blouse. He held it in his hand for a moment, his face a mixture of joy and sorrow. Then he pressed his mother's poor garment to his face, burying his nose in it, and inhaled deeply.

"It still smells like her," he said with wonder, smiling through his tears. "Even with the mothballs and everything, it still smells like her."

I thought about how after Hamp died, I gave away most of his things, but there were a couple of items I couldn't part with. It wasn't just his tool set, but one of his shirts, too. His favorite shirt. It still hung in our closet. Every now and then, I'd brushed my fingertips over the shoulders and down the sleeves. I'd hold the material to my face, inhaling him and remembering.

Finally, Job laid the shirt to one side and reached into the trunk again. And so it went. Every time he lifted out an item—a book, a belt, a necklace of fake pearls—he held it up with wonder. At one point, he exclaimed with pure pleasure.

"It's her music! See, see!" He grabbed up several sheets of paper covered with musical notations and shook them at me. "I remember. We used to sing together and we were working on a song together. This is all of it!"

He was so happy. Then it was all too much. His face crumpled. He bent his head and sobbed. I wrapped my arms around him and rocked him. Ruth came to the door, a wooden mixing stick in one hand, eyebrows drawn together in a worried look.

"What's the matter?"

"He found some of his mother's music."

She shook her head. "I knew I shouldn't have let him go through that stuff with you." She straightened. "Job, honey, come here. Let Miss Lanie get on with her work and you help me in the kitchen."

"He's no bother," I patted him on the back. His sobs had slowed to sniffles, but he was still curled into a tight ball pressed against me.

"No, he's had enough." She came in and gently tapped him on the shoulder. "Come on, baby."

With a last gulp, Job lifted his face and wiped his eyes with the heel of his hand. He got to his feet, his eyes red. Clutching his mother's songs, he looked down at me.

"Thank you, Miss Lanie."

"Thank *you*," I said, "for keeping me company." *And for believing that I can do this, when I'm not sure I believe it myself.*

Ruth gave his shoulders a squeeze, then ushered him from the room. I could hear her talking softly to him as they walked down the short hall to the kitchen.

As Job had done earlier, I too now sat quite still and took stock. The suitcase was packed more tightly than I'd realized. Job and I had gotten through just under half of its contents. Which was good. It left plenty of room for hope.

The problem was I wasn't sure what I was looking for. I could only hope that I'd recognized it when I saw it. In an ideal world, it would pop out at me—something that proved that Esther and Sexton Whitefield had been seeing each other. But men like him, men with a lot to lose and afraid of scandal, tended to be careful. My best chances lay in the fact that every once in a while, those very same men got too sure of themselves, especially if they weren't worried about a wife finding out anything. Sometimes, they'd let a little something slip: a note, perhaps.

But another forty-five minutes of looking yielded nothing but disappointment. Whoever this cat was, he walked softly and kept to the shadows.

## 15.

They were predicting rain and warmer temperatures, but when I set out the next morning, it was as cold as a mother-in-law's kiss. The wind howled at my back as I sloshed through wet snow ankle-deep, headed for the subway entrance at 137th Street and St. Nicholas Avenue. My teeth were chattering, my toes ached, and I was wondering whether it was really necessary to go downtown—at least that day. Why not wait until tomorrow, when it was supposed to be warmer?

The train came fast. In way too short a time, it reached Columbus Circle and 59th Street, and I was back out in the cold. After another miserable five minutes by foot, I'd reached 250 West 57th Street, the massive building housing Whitefield's office. Resting on a white stone base, reddish-tan building was twenty-six stories high. It ran the length of the block between Eighth Avenue and Broadway. I took a deep breath, squared my shoulders and entered.

The elevator opened onto a long beige hallway. A sign pointed to the office of the Collector. To the left and right were military gray office doors, and the muffled din of typists hard at work.

Whitefield's office was depressingly institutional: pale gray-green walls, uneven overhead lighting and brown-carpeted floor. The waiting room furnishings were spare: just a low-slung coffee table and four austere wood chairs. To one side was a small desk, its expanse covered with forms and thick stacks of gray-green folders. To the rear stood the door to Whitefield's office, and guarding it was a young woman behind another desk. She was in her twenties, late twenties I'd say. She was quite pretty, but had a no-nonsense look—trim and proper. The sign on the desk said her name was Hilda Coleman and she was coolly polite when she told me that her boss was not in.

"When will he be back?"

She started to say, but reconsidered. Caution deepened in her eyes. "Who's asking and why?"

"My name's Lanie. Lanie Atkins Price. I write for the *Chronicle*."

"I thought you looked familiar. You write that society column."

From her tone and expression, it wasn't clear whether she thought that was good or not. However, her intelligent eyes became curious.

"Are you here to write about Mr. Whitefield?"

"Maybe. Could be I'm considering a column on Harlem's sexiest politicians."

That got a raised eyebrow and a faint, cynical smile. Whitefield was short and fat.

"So this is one of those, 'How wonderful he is,' kind of pieces?"

"Maybe. I print what I find."

"Oh, really?"

"Really."

Her gaze switched to a point behind me and I turned to see a young man enter. He was tall, light-skinned and in his late thirties, dressed in a charcoal gray cashmere coat and homburg hat. The coat hung open to reveal a crisp white shirt and black vested suit. He had a military bearing.

"Miss Coleman ..." He paused. His gaze skimmed over me with a fast touch, measuring and dismissing me, all in one glance. His irises were very pale, very light, and coldly professional.

Whoever he was, he had a chilling effect on Hilda Coleman. She tensed perceptibly.

"Good morning, Mr. Echo," she said.

"Morning."

He shouldered out of his coat and hung it up on the heavy wood rack next to the door. Then he went to the desk and sat down. It was hard to believe that his long limbs fit comfortably behind that desk. I watched as he made himself small to accommodate it. His knees must've touched the underside of the desk. He took in the piles of folders on his desk and a look of determination crossed his face.

"Looks like I'm going to have a very busy day."

"Yes, Mr. Echo," she said, carefully neutral. "Would you like me to get your coffee now, sir?"

I felt an eyebrow rise. *Sir?*

"Thank you, Miss Coleman. You know how I like it." He glanced up after saying this and gave her an odd fleeting smile. Then he took down a folder from the stack and flipped it open.

She gave him a look of utter loathing, then turned back to me. Her voice took on a note of bright falsity.

"The ladies room is down the hall, miss. You take a right and then a left and you'll be right there. Oh, but why don't I just show you?" Her eyes asked me to play along.

"Thank you so much," I said.

She grabbed a key out of her desk, led me out of the office and down the corridor. We didn't speak until we were inside the bathroom with the door closed behind us.

"Now what—" I started.

She shushed me and checked each of the bathroom stalls. They were empty. Even so, she kept her voice low. "So why are you really sniffing around Mr. Whitefield?"

"I told you—"

"That sexy politician business? Please. I've got a feeling you're aiming for the jugular."

"Okay," I said slowly.

Pumping people for information is a tough game. It's like playing poker. You've got to know when to bluff, when to draw and when to spread them. There are no hard and fast rules, except one: You've got to look for the tell, the indication of what the other guy's thinking. Hilda Coleman's question was a tell. That little scene in her office said she was less than sympathetic to her boss's assistant. Now, her question said she was probably less than sympathetic toward her boss, too. I decided to take a risk and play it straight.

"You ever heard of a woman named Esther Todd?"

Her eyes narrowed as she tried to recall. "What about her?"

I told her the story.

The light of shock hit her eyes and understanding sank in like pearls penetrating two wells of black oil. "You telling me he had something to do with it?"

"I'm saying no such thing, just asking around."

Her dark eyes searched mine. Esther's story had affected her. It meant something to her. Something real.

She touched my forearm with fingertips turned cold. "Are you really on the up and up? 'Cause if I'm caught spilling to you, I could lose my job."

"Understood."

"You'll keep my name out of this?"

"No problem."

"All right. I'm not a trusting person, but I'm going to trust you. But if you double-cross me and say I talked, I'll deny every word."

"Deal."

She glanced at her wristwatch. "You know Jimmy Dee's, up near Columbia?"

I did. It was a bit of a distance, but that's probably why she chose it. She wouldn't run into anyone who knew her.

"At noon?"

Jimmy Dee's was a little place on the corner of 114th and Amsterdam. It was popular with the domestic help that worked in the fine apartment buildings on Morningside Heights. The place smelled of coffee and grease. A glass-top counter stood to the left and cracked dark brown leather booths lined the wall to the right.

Coleman joined me in a corner booth. I ordered coffee and a bowl of vegetable soup. She took tea and a thick sandwich of pastrami on rye. She was the neatest eater I'd ever seen, and the fastest. She cut her sandwich into perfect squares. They looked like thick petit fours. She speared a piece with a fork and popped it into her mouth.

"Mr. Whitefield is grade-A sleaze. You ever met him?"

I nodded. "He's very charming. Very distinguished."

"He's charming, all right—ugly as sin, but charming as they come. And he knows it. Knows it and uses it."

"He use it on you?"

She stopped eating. "No." She sounded bitter. "Sometimes, I'm cold. Sometimes, I'm hungry. And I *always* got bills to pay. So I can't say I haven't been tempted, but I don't like his ways."

"What ways?"

She started to answer, but hesitated. She wanted to talk, but for all her bravado, she was scared. She put down her fork and dabbed at her mouth with a napkin. "Maybe this wasn't such a good idea."

"I think it was."

She studied me. "Do you have any idea who he is—really is? People don't mess with Sexton Whitefield and survive. He won't kill you outright, but he'll make your life so miserable you'd wish he had. And don't think that working for a newspaper will protect you. Sexton's got a long reach. There's always somebody, somewhere who owes him a favor."

"Well, the paper has a couple of friends, too."

"Friends who'll take on the Internal Revenue? Remember, he's the taxman. He can mess you up in ways you can't imagine—you *and* your paper.."

She was right. Nevertheless, I said, "No one's undefeatable."

"You know what he did to Edward H. Hamilton?"

I nodded.

"And you still want to hear what I've got to say?"

"I'm here, aren't I?"

"All right, then." She licked her dry lips and took a sip of water. "He's got a hand problem."

My gut tightened. "Does that mean what I think it means?"

"I've seen some of his handiwork, seen it on a friend of mine."

I was dying to get out my notepad, but I had a feeling she would clam up if I did. "Tell me more."

As long as she'd been at the office, she said, she'd heard of his affairs and seen his ego at work.

"You'd think he'd be more careful," I said. "Scandal's no good for a man in his position."

"He's not worried. The women are too scared to say anything. One of the bookkeepers, a girl named Mabel, she did try to break it off with him, but she said he wouldn't let her."

I set my spoon aside and gave her my full attention. "What happened?"

"She didn't come to work one day. I was a little worried. She was one of them to-the-minute types, you know? Never came late. Never missed a day. Well, an hour goes by, and then two, and I get a phone call. It's the lady who runs the rooming house where Mabel's living. There's been trouble. Mabel gave her the number. So I run over to see what's what. Mabel's in bed. All busted up. Broken nose, broken wrist. I had to take her to the hospital."

"She say who did it?"

"Not at first. But later, she said it was Whitefield. He picked her up after work. She said she didn't want to go with him, but he made her. Took her home. Went upstairs with her. And got to work."

"She talked to the cops?"

Coleman shook her head. "Too scared."

I shoved my soup aside. My appetite was gone. "You know of anybody else?"

"Nope. There's probably others. I just don't know about them."

"Where's Mabel now?"

"She got a little place over on Lenox. She's lost her job. Whitefield made sure of that. I don't know what she's doing now."

"You don't talk to her anymore?"

"More like, she don't talk to me. I think ... well, maybe she's embarrassed that I know how far it went."

"You think she'd talk to me?"

"Don't know, but I think you should try. Here." She reached under the table and slipped me a folded square of paper. She hadn't written a thing while we were sitting there eating. So she'd brought the paper with her. She'd come prepared to give it to me.

"Tell her I sent you. And say..." She paused. "Tell her I miss her."

I paid the check. Just as we were about to leave, she stopped me.

"There's one last thing I'd better warn you about."

"Yes?"

"You remember that guy who walked in today?"

"Mr. Echo?"

"That's all the name he goes by. He's more than just an accountant. He says he's Mr. Whitefield's assistant for special projects. I can't say what that means, but I do know that he's very loyal. And I got a feeling he does things for Mr. Whitefield, hurtful things that Mr. Whitefield doesn't have the nerve to do himself."

She gazed at me to see how I digested that bit of news.

I digested it, all right. Within seconds, I was wondering if Whitefield had gotten Echo to take care of Esther.

## *16.*

Dinner was a simple plate of buttered toast and scrambled eggs. Breakfast food, I know. But I love eating breakfast foods at night and dinner foods in the morning. Many's the time I've eaten hamburgers for breakfast. It used to drive Hamp crazy. When we first got married, I tried to 'eat normally,' as Hamp put it. But I couldn't keep it up. Habits ingrained since college, now some ten years hence, just didn't fade that easily. After a while Hamp gave up and accepted me the way I was. That he could do that was one of the many good things about him, the real good things.

As often happened when I sat in the kitchen, my gaze went to the wall cabinet. It was a big family kitchen, just the kind Hamp and I wanted and hoped we'd need for all the children we planned to have. The house was only about thirty years old and basically in excellent condition. But for some reason, the kitchen had only one cabinet. It was wide and deep, but tilted. The nails holding it at the top had worked loose or maybe they were never well drilled to begin with. As a result, the top of the cabinet leaned forward. I could put dishes and glasses to the very back of the shelves, but I couldn't take a chance on putting in much and certainly nothing expensive, including the fine china Hamp's mother left us.

Hamp had promised to fix the cabinet and to put up more. I know he would've done it, if he hadn't died. It wasn't a promise he broke, but one he couldn't keep. His leather tool kit still lay open on the countertop under the cabinet, just the way he left it. I'd never put it away. Someday, I was going to fix that cabinet myself.

Someday.

## 17.

The Lenox Avenue address Hilda Coleman had given me turned out to be a rundown boarding house on an otherwise nice block. Despair permeated the building. Resignation crept through its gloomy hallways and defeat roamed its dirty stairwell.

Mabel Dean Henry's room was a wonderful contrast. She'd hung inexpensive bright curtains at the windows. She'd started her own little garden in flowerpots. Small plants, with thin delicate leaves, were inching their way out of the soil.

Mabel herself was small-built, in her late twenties, with prematurely gray hair. She was unemployed and deaf in one ear, from a beating she said Whitefield gave her. In short sentences, she told me about their brief, brutal affair.

"It's not like I went in not knowing nothing. The other girls warned me about him. But I didn't care. He was too important to say no to. I just wanted to have some fun, you know?"

She reflected. "And yeah, maybe I thought that I'd be the one, you know? The woman he finally decided to stay with." She ground out her cigarette. "Boy, was I wrong."

She offered me a glass of water. I declined and she poured herself one. "He was really nice at the beginning. I didn't even mind doing those crazy things he wanted me to."

"What things?"

She was embarrassed. "Look, it's the kind of stuff you don't mind doing at the time, but you can't believe you did later, okay? I didn't enjoy it. But I went along 'cause it turned him on and I really liked that, you know, the idea that I could turn on such an important man."

"Look, Mabel. I know what a woman will do to please a man—and I know how he can make you feel afterward. So you won't be getting any criticism from me. Now tell me, what did he ask for?"

She chewed on her lower lip. "It could make a difference with you looking for this girl you told me about?"

"Maybe."

She thought about it. "Let's just say that he ... he liked doing things that hurt."

"Hurt bad?"

She nodded.

"And you never talked to anyone else about this?"

Her jaw hardened. "Suppose I had? Then what? It would've been my word against his. He would've said he didn't have nothing to do with me, and everybody would've believed him."

I nodded. "You're probably right."

"You damn tootin', I am." She took a sip of water. "You sure you don't want nothing? If you don't like water, I got something stronger."

"Okay, thanks. But water will be fine."

Mabel had put up a brave effort to resist the despair of her environment. At first I thought she was succeeding, but the longer I sat with her and the more I listened, the more I worried. As young as she was, Mabel looked about ready to give up.

"I been looking for work," she said.

"For how long?"

"Too long." She looked out her window, at the hookers on the corner, and spoke in a rush of bitterness. "My friends say I was stupid to be giving it away. 'Specially to a big muckety-muck like Sexton. If I got to be beat and suck his sausage, then I should've gotten paid for it." She looked at me. "You think I'm a nasty girl for saying that?"

"No. But it doesn't matter what I think."

She looked away, but not in time to hide her tears. "He broke something inside me. Every time he …" She bit down her lip. "Every time he took his fists and …" Silent tears slipped from her eyes.

I handed her a handkerchief. She wiped her eyes and sniffed.

"How long did it go on?" I asked.

"He was nice for 'bout two weeks. I was stone cold in love with him. The things I let him do—and that I did." She swallowed. "Two weeks, and then …" A little shake of the head. "And then I don't know. He wasn't never the same man no more."

"You decided to stop seeing him?"

"I went with him for about two months in all. Two sickening months." She hugged herself, cleared her throat. "One day he asked me to do something. It was so scary, I wouldn't do it."

"Do what?"

"He wanted me to … to string him up, you know? With a rope. Hang him—I mean, really hang him. Can you imagine? And he was gonna put on my underwear and make me …" She shuddered, waved her words away, and didn't finish.

"It's okay. It's all right."

Some kids went by outside, chasing a ball and yelling happily at one another.

"Was that when you said—"

"Yeah, I—I couldn't go on like that. And man, oh, man was he angry. The funny thing is, I don't think it was 'cause he was hurt 'bout me wanting to leave 'im. It was more like, how dare I? That day, the day I tried to leave him, he beat me, beat me bad. There'd been other times, but never like that."

"Was it him—or this Mr. Echo?"

"So Hilda told you about him, too?"

"Warned me."

"He and Sexton belong together, two evil peas in a pod. But Sexton never let Echo touch me. He said he wanted to save that for himself. Beating the shit out of me was his own special pleasure." She gave a little grunt. "He actually said that. And I was dumb enough to think it was a compliment."

"And you told no one."

"Hell, no. I was so ashamed. And scared. He made me promise, at the very beginning, not to tell nobody. If I wanted to be with him, then that's what I had to do. But I didn't mind. That kinda made it more fun. I thought." She gave a weak little grin. "Wasn't I the fool?"

"Tell me about that last day."

She drew a deep breath. "I went to work. I knew he'd been following me home, but I thought he'd stop. So I went out with some friends after work. Afterward, we split up. I was about a block away from the house when I looked down and there he was, in the car, telling me to get in. I told him I didn't want to. He said he was sorry he'd hurt me, that he wouldn't ask me to do stuff like that no more. I said I didn't believe him. Then he said that if I didn't get in, and give him what he wanted, he'd make sure I lost my job. So I got in."

She blinked back her tears. "The funny thing is, I let him fuck me and beat me and he took my job, anyway."

She wasn't going to get any criticism from me.

"Mabel, will you go on the record?"

She thought about it and shook her head. "I don't think so. I'm not ready to do that."

"Why not? What have you got left to lose?"

"My life." Her eyes were somber.

"Do you really think …?"

"Oh, yeah." She nodded. "You don't know. You just don't know." She reached out to me. "So please don't let him know I been talking to you. Please don't say a word."

I promised, thinking how lucky I'd been to have had Hamp, and how I couldn't leave her like this, not without trying to do something to help. Then it came to me.

"Mabel," I said, "I have an idea."

## 18.

*"I'll always love you."* Hamp's voice. His warmth. My eyes snapped open. I blinked and looked to my right, where Hamp had always slept. His place was empty. Of course it was. His pillow was in disarray, but only because I had hugged it in my sleep.

Still half asleep, I rose up on my elbows and looked around our bedroom with groggy eyes, half aware of the early morning street sounds outside. His presence had been so real—for a moment, more real than my surroundings.

I flopped back down with a sigh and stared at the ceiling. Which was the dream? This empty house and empty bed, or the loving words and comforting closeness? Three and a half years since Hamp's death and still his voice came to me. Three and a half long years …

Turning on my side, I curled up and drew the blankets to my chin. Hamp's photo gazed back at me from my bedside table. Childhood sweethearts, we'd known each other all our lives. The strong thread of Hamp's life was interwoven with mine as far back as I could remember. When his thread snapped on that hot July night, I felt as though the entire fabric of my life would unravel.

"I miss you, babe," I whispered. "I miss you so much." Briefly, I closed my eyes, and said a prayer, then forced myself to get up.

It was a quiet Sunday. After washing and setting my hair, I wrote Christmas cards, mailed them off and settled in for several peaceful hours of reading *The Amsterdam News and New York Times*. The *Times* was full of talk about the Allies ending arms control over Germany and Britain's plans for China. I skimmed those articles but read every word of a lengthy piece by Edward Smith on crime and chemistry. The report said that new laboratory techniques were an "often uncanny means" of furnishing detectives with evidence of guilt. I paused, wondering. If the techniques had been available when Esther disappeared, would they have made a difference? Hard to say, but I had a feeling that good old horse sense was the key to Esther's case.

It was an article about a war widow that finally made me put the paper aside. This woman's husband had never returned from the war, but as long as she didn't know what had happened to him, as long as he was still listed as 'missing,' she couldn't give up hope. Hope, she said, had become a curse, one that caused her to live in an endless limbo. That reminded me of Mrs. Todd, lying in her bed of pain.

"If only I knew," she'd whispered. "Please, God, if I only knew."

On Monday, back in the newsroom, I dialed COLumbus-8284, the Collector's office. I expected Hilda Coleman to come on the line, but Whitefield himself picked up. I identified myself, reminded him that we'd met before and exchanged pleasantries.

"I'm calling about Esther," I said. "Esther Todd."

"Esther ..." he repeated with surprise.

"You do you remember her?"

"Well, actually, no." He gave an uneasy chuckle. "But of course, I meet so many people. Who was she?"

Not who is she? But who *was* she?

"I have a newspaper story here, describing a dinner party at Katherine Goodfellowe's house in September of '23. Esther Todd entertained the guests by playing the piano. They story says you were there. There weren't that many people. You must've met her."

"Maybe I did, but I don't remember her. Why are you asking?"

It was hard to believe him. Even if he didn't remember Esther from the party, he should've remembered her name because of the heist and its notoriety. I reminded him of the case and explained my interest in it.

"There's a new theory," I said, "that her disappearance was related to a secret admirer."

"How interesting. But what has this got to do with me?"

When I explained, he reverted to a flat denial. "I told you. I never met her—and whoever told you anything different is lying."

"I should tell you that I *will* keep digging. I will find out if—"

"Look, I'm sorry to hear what happened to Miss Todd, but I can't help you. My sympathies go to her family. I wish them God's blessings. Did you get all that down?"

"Every blessed word."

"Good."

He sounded relieved. But I wasn't about to let him off so easily.

"There's another matter you should know about. I've spoken to someone who says she was your paramour. She's told me that ..."

I filled him in. He was apoplectic.

"Lies! All damnable lies! I know who you're talking about. Yes, she was fired. She couldn't do her job. She was crazy. Told everyone that she was my—my mistress. I had to let her go. I couldn't afford to have someone like her around me, around this office."

I made notes. "So you deny hitting her?"

"I've never hit anyone."

"You deny forcing her to perform intimate acts with you?"

"My God! I don't believe this. Mrs. Price, I thought you were better than this—that we were friends. I—"

"I'm nobody's friend, not when they stand between me and the truth."

There was an icy pause. Then came a question, thick with rage: "Are you threatening me?"

"I'm giving you a chance to clarify matters."

Whitefield drew a deep breath. "I've never committed violence against her or anyone else. Anyone who says anything to the contrary is a liar. I won't have my reputation sullied by some stupid, silly woman. I won't have my name associated with crime or dirtied by innuendo. You print a word of what she says and I'll sue you and your paper so fast you won't know what hit you. Got that?"

Before I could answer, I heard a click. He was gone. His reaction was more or less what I'd expected. I put the receiver on its cradle and the phone jangled. It was Bellamy.

"Oh, hello," I said, surprised.

"I was wondering how your investigation is going."

"I'm not investigating anything, just trying to find new material."

"Fine. I won't argue. So, did you find out anything?"

"Maybe." Cradling the phone between head and shoulder, I reached for a blank sheet of paper and slid it into the Underwood.

"Come on, tell me."

"I'm afraid you're going to have to wait, just like everybody else."

"I'm not everybody."

I didn't answer. Just started typing. Loudly. He muttered an oath.

"Wow! You sound like a Tommy gun."

"Really? I'm sorry," I said, and pounded the keys harder.

"Just tell me one thing."

"What?"

"Did you get anywhere with the boyfriend angle? I mean, I know it's not likely but ..."

I stopped typing and took the phone in my hand. "Look, I've got to pull my notes together and I can't do that if I'm on the phone with you."

"So answer my question and I'll get lost."

I thought about it. "Okay, I'll tell you this: I've got a line on a man who might've been Esther's friend. I won't give you his name—"

"Why not? Maybe I know him."

That was something to consider. It went against gut instinct to share information before it went to print, but what was I worried about? He wasn't likely to tip off another reporter—and suppose he had another piece of the puzzle?

"Sexton Whitefield. The name mean anything to you?"

A pause, then the answer, a bit mystified. "Can't say it does. Who is he?"

I told him Whitefield's title.

"You mean she was dating a white guy?"

"Not at all." I could feel his surprise at the thought that a colored man held such a high position.

"You've talked to him?" he asked. "Learned a lot?"

"A number of things. But nothing concrete."

"You going to write about him?"

"Maybe. There're some angles I want to check out."

"Like what?"

I glanced at the clock. It was getting late and I had work to do. "Sorry, detective, but I gotta go. Tell you what? Why don't read the column when it comes out?"

"I sure will," he said and hung up.

## 19.

It took another hour to write a first draft of the column. It led with a section on Esther, followed by a second section on the film festival, with Evelyn's quotes, and a few lines on the party at the Walter Whites. I wrote the second half in under ten minutes. It was the first part, the paragraphs on Esther where I took my time.

How far should I go in identifying Whitefield and describing his role in Esther's life? I could present a convincing case for Esther having been kidnapped by a jealous admirer. Did I dare hint at Whitefield as "an admirer?" I knew I dared not label him as her intimate associate or imply that he was behind her disappearance. I had innuendo and gossip, but nothing concrete.

Maybe, I would talk to Sam about it over dinner.

I got to the Bamboo Inn at six o'clock on the dot and waved at the large tuxedo-dressed bouncer at the door.

"Hi Henry."

"How you doin', Miss Lanie?"

Big Henry had a soft voice and gentle Southern accent, beefy arms and broad shoulders. He had a sweet nature, but he'd deck you in a second if you got smart with him.

"Mr. Delaney here yet?"

"He's upstairs. Got a nice table, too." Henry gave me an amused smile, revealing a large gap between his two front teeth. He was such a romantic. "You have a good night, now."

"Thank you, Henry." I slipped past him with a nod. "Merry Christmas."

"You, too, Miss Lanie."

The Bamboo Inn was lovely and popular, with balcony booths overlooking a spacious dance floor, but it was more than just a pretty face. It offered some of the best Chinese food in Harlem, at decent prices, too. And live music with no cover charge. Henri Saporo's Orchestra played nightly and the club was a great place to hear jazz improv.

If you wanted to see "high Harlem," or aspired to be a part of it, then this was one of the places to go. The guests weren't necessarily highbrow, but definitely a cut above the rest. Debutantes booked the place for cotillions. College kids took their girls on a spin around the dance floor. The diners were well-dressed men with high-tone women. There were lots of models from *Vanity Fair*, lots of beautiful people from different races, some as black as jet, others as pale as alabaster and lots of sepia and mahogany in between: lawyers, architects, doctors, councilmen, the Astors and their darlings, Asian men who brought their porcelain dolls to mingle with Harlem's "better set." The crowd included a few gangsters, but they too were well-mannered, well-dressed, well-shod. A few were carrying, but the guns and hip flasks were tucked away. The laughter was well-bred, genuine but muted.

I'd been to the Bamboo many times, but mostly on business, to do the kind of one-on-one I couldn't do at parties. The thought that I was there to have dinner with my boss took getting used to. I wasn't sure what he expected or wanted. He wasn't like our old boss. That was clear. But in a way, that made matters worse. Because if Sam was interested, then he was really interested. Only I didn't know what to do with a man's interest. It had been so very long …

I decided to be neutral and businesslike. And see what happened.

A waiter showed me to Sam. Just as Henry said, Sam had managed to get one the prized booths in a balcony. He was studying the other diners. His grooming was perfect. From the close cut salt and pepper hair to the buffed fingernails and tailored suit and tie, Sam was clean. He always made a good presentation in his business clothes, but for tonight's appearance he'd taken extra care to fix himself up nice. The result was … well, I had to admit it: Sam Delaney was one fine-looking sheik. There was strength in his shoulders and honesty in his eyes. He was kind and, beneath his caution, compassionate: a solid combination. Any woman in her right mind couldn't help but be aware of it. And most women would respond to it. But I wasn't "most women." I didn't want to respond to it. I didn't remember how, and I wasn't sure I wanted to.

A nervous smile flitted across his face when he saw me. He gave me a polite kiss on the cheek and helped me out of my coat.

"Glad you made it," he said.

"Did you think I wouldn't?"

He deliberated, choosing his words. "I would say that at the moment, you have a lot on your mind. And maybe dinner with me isn't at the top of your list."

His humility surprised me. I didn't know how to answer. A waiter coming to take our order saved me from having to. Neither of us looked at the menu. We'd each been to the Bamboo Inn so often we knew the bill of fare by heart. I ordered beef with broccoli and Sam had prawns. The waiter took the menus, leaving us alone and feeling awkward.

"Lanie," he began, "one reasons I invited you here was to repair our relationship. I have the feeling that somewhere along the line, we got off on the wrong foot."

"No—"

He held a hand up. "Please. I thought if we talked, met outside the office, we might … oh, I don't know, get to know one another better. Find some common approach."

"Well," I shrugged, "Sure. Where do you want to begin?" Before he could answer, I said, "Why don't you tell me something about yourself? You're a big mystery to everyone on staff."

"There's nothing mysterious about me. I'm just a regular guy."

Despite my general disinterest in men, I did sometimes wonder about Sam. He was even more close-mouthed than I about personal history. So now, I listened carefully.

He'd grown up in Washington, DC, he said, attended Howard. Had fought in the war. Never married.

"Never wanted to?"

Wistfulness touched his voice. "Oh, I wanted to all right. Just never made it that far."

"What happened?"

He shrugged. "I don't know."

"We're talking about someone specific?"

"The day before the wedding, she called it off."

"Why?"

"Doubts, she said. Hers—not mine."

"Was there somebody else?"

"Maybe. I don't know." Sam was silent for a moment, away with his thoughts. Then he came back and gave me a warm smile. "Enough about me. I want to hear about you."

"No, you don't."

"Why not?"

"Because I'm not interesting."

But Sam persisted. I tried to tell just the bare outlines, but he wanted more. So I mentioned how my husband died and I found my way to the paper.

"When I first started at the *Chronicle*, it didn't have a social column. The column was my idea. But the powers-that-be didn't want to hear about it. They wanted the paper to be taken seriously and, for them, that meant hard news."

"How'd you get them to change their mind?"

"I told them there was already too much focus on crime, on the bad things happening in our community. We should write about the professionals who're doing well. We should write about the dignity of our people."

"And that got 'em?"

I laughed. "Well, it helped when circulation started going up. It proved that we could compete with the *Tattler* and the *Amsterdam News*. People could buy the *Chronicle* and get both hard news and soft features for the price of one."

"Smart move."

The waiter arrived with our food. I requested chopsticks and Sam looked surprised.

"I'd starve if I had to use those things."

"They're easy, if you know what you're doing."

I got chopsticks for Sam, too, and tried to show him how to use them. That result was hilarious, with very little food making it to his mouth. Sam finally declared that he just wasn't a chopsticks kind of guy. He took up his knife and fork with relief.

Conversation paused while we ate. I hadn't realized how hungry I was. We both came up for air at about the same time. After a moment, he laid aside his fork and fingered his glass.

"Lanie," he said, "I want to apologize."

"What for?"

He sighed. "For coming down so hard on you. It's just that I'm worried. These are not always nice people. They could hurt you."

"I understand. But I'll be fine."

He obviously didn't think so. His eyes told me as much.

"Tell me, why're you so fixed on this Esther Todd thing?"

"Why shouldn't I be?"

"You didn't even know her. You weren't related to her."

"But I don't know any of the people I write about. Not really. And yet I'm expected to write about them with feeling. The difference is that they're famous and Esther wasn't."

"It's not that simple."

"It is to me. Why should I care more about the partying of a rich woman than the disappearance of a poor one? Who do you think I most identify with?"

"But it's not a matter of who you most identify with. It's not even about whom your readers identify with. That's never what your column's been about."

"Then what is it about?"

"Fantasy, entertainment, escape. Places like this, where people can forget about day-to-day reality." He gestured toward our elegant surroundings.

He was right. Absolutely, totally right.

"Then it's too little," I said. "Way too little."

"You don't like your job, anymore."

"I do. At least, most of the time I do. But sometimes … sometimes I get so sick of listening to people whine about nothing. And I get so angry with myself for just focusing on the superficial. Everybody's talking about the Renaissance that's come to Harlem. It's great, yes it is. But there's another Harlem, some would say the greater part, and the people who live in it are struggling to survive."

"That's not your concern."

"It is. Esther was one of those people. Maybe the folks outside of Harlem don't care about her—why should they? They've got cares of their own. But we should care. She was one of us."

"Lanie, it sounds great in theory, but—"

"Theory? All right, how about something that's not a theory: I gave Esther's family—her son—my word. I promised that little boy that I'd do everything I could to bring his mother home."

Sam drew a deep breath. "But nobody expects--"

"He does. Or did." I remembered the look on Job's face when I last saw him, the battle against losing hope, the skepticism and cynicism. A young face grown old.

Sam looked worried. "Lanie, I'll let you in on a little secret: I agree with you one hundred percent. However," he held a hand up, "the job you have, at this paper, at this time, does not permit you to go on a personal crusade for justice."

"I'm just trying to find out the truth."

"I heard that you talked to Bellamy."

"You mean you got a call on that, too?"

"These things get around." Care lines had cut furrows in his forehead. "I'm concerned about you doing too much work on this. And not the right kind of work. Talking to ex-cops and old witnesses isn't quite what I want my society reporter to be up to."

"I'm trying to do a thorough job."

"You're a perfectionist. I commend that. It's one of the things I admire about you. But this job requires superficiality.

The column's supposed to be light and bright. But sometimes you overthink things; you lose track of the forest."

"What does that mean?"

"That you're learning more than you need to know. And that could mean trouble."

"For you or for me?"

"Both. I told you, our readers don't want a sad story for Christmas—and I don't want my reporters going out on a limb."

"But that's what I do. Take chances. It's part of my job."

"No it's not. You're not an investigator. You write gossip. That's what you're paid to do. Write light-hearted gossip."

"I don't see it that way."

He put down his fork and studied me. "For a while now, I've wondered: What's a smart reporter like you doing writing a column about people partying all night?"

"I told you—"

"I know what you said, about your husband and all. But that was then. Maybe you've healed and maybe it's time for you to move on."

"Move on? How?"

"Write something else."

I had a sudden suspicion. "Is that what this was all about? So you could fire me? Do it in public so I wouldn't make a scene?"

"No, of course not."

His denial went right past me.

"Your job is to protect the paper. Instead you're ..." I was so hurt, I couldn't find the words.

"I'm what? Yes, my job is to protect the paper. It's to make sure it makes money and gets funding."

"And you do that by kissing up to rich people and big shots?"

"I do it by not alienating the very people who support us."

"That sounds fine and good, but it's like they say: a man can't serve two masters."

"Lanie, you and I have different responsibilities. I have to see the whole picture. I don't have the luxury of concentrating on just your column. *Lanie's World* might be your world. But it's not mine. And I can't afford to let it be."

His words hit like a hammer. A bolt of pain shot through my head. His eyes reflected instant regret, but the damage was done. A crevice had opened between us. A few minutes ago, we'd stood shoulder to shoulder. Now, we were on opposite sides of a divide.

"We'd better call it a night." I grabbed my purse, pushed my chair back and stood up, not just hurt but angry and disappointed. And suddenly, very very tired.

He was on his feet in an instant. "I'm sorry. It seems like tonight, I do nothing but apologize."

"That's okay. I appreciate your honesty."

"Let me take you home."

I shook my head, wanting only to get back to the sanctuary of solitude. "I'll take a taxi."

## *20.*

*You should've known better*, an inner voice scolded. In the informal atmosphere of the restaurant, I'd let my guard down, something I never would've done at the office. I'd allowed myself to forget that he was my boss. I'd let myself get seduced into seeing him as a man, and into enjoying his company as such. At home, as I climbed the stairs to the second floor, I vowed to never make that mistake again.

Midway up the stairs, the upstairs hallway light went out. If it hadn't been for the pale moonlight shining the skylight over the stairwell, I would've been in utter darkness. As it was, the moon lit the way to the landing. I felt for the light switch on the wall and flipped it. Nothing happened. Darn. No way was I going to replace a blown fuse or light bulb at that time of night.

Holding onto the stairway railing, I made my way down the short dark corridor to my bedroom door. As I put my hand on the knob, the point of a something hard and sharp was pressed against my lower back. I froze.

"Go on inside," said a muffled male voice. "Go on."

"Who are you? What do you want? If it's money, I—"

"Bitch, open the door and get inside."

I swallowed hard and took a deep breath. "No."

"What?"

"No!"

I raised my right foot and slammed it down on where I hoped his instep would be, but I hit the hardwood floor instead. He swung me around and slapped me so hard I fell back against the wall. I had a brief impression of bright, pale eyes—Echo's eyes—before he punched me in my side. I cried out and buckled over in pain. He shoved me to the floor, face down, and dropped down on top of me. He was lithe, agile and strong. Straddling me, he clamped a large, leather-clad hand around the back of my neck and pressed the tip of a blade against the right side of my throat.

"Don't worry," he said. "If I meant to kill you, you'd be dead by now. If I wanted to fuck you, I would've done that, too." He paused. "As a matter of fact, I still might."

"What do you want?"

"For you to mind your own business. If you don't, then what happened to Esther Todd will happen to you."

Terror stabbed my heart.

"Tell Whitefield," I said through clenched teeth, "that I am not afraid. I—"

"You stupid, stupid *bitch!*" He grabbed my hair and slammed my face against the floor. "You think this is some kind of fucking game?" Splinters of pain radiated across my cheek and through my head.

"If it was up to me," he hissed, "I'd do you right here, right now and get it over with, but Mr. Whitefield wants to give you a second chance. Just step out of line again, and I'll be back. And next time, I'll make sure it's worth my time." He licked the side of my face. "You got me?"

Nauseated, I gave a shuddering nod.

"Good."

The next instant, he was gone. I looked up in time to see a black shadow deeper than darkness move swiftly down the stairs. Seconds later came the sound of the front door closing.

Trembling, I pushed myself to my feet. My head throbbed and I felt sick to my stomach. With shaking hands I pushed open my bedroom door and slipped inside. I closed the door and sagged against it, letting my purse slide to the floor. I was trembling so badly I could barely stand. Nausea hit me. I clamped my hand over my mouth and scrambled down the hall to the bathroom, making it just in time.

After rinsing my mouth and dousing my face with cool water, I leaned on the washbasin. For a couple of minutes, I had to grip the wash sink. I'd expected Whitefield to retaliate, but not like that. Given Hilda Coleman's warnings, maybe I should've. But I hadn't expected him to choose violence. Not as his first recourse.

Then again, maybe he'd thought he had no choice. He must've figured out that I was writing under deadline. He didn't have time for niceties.

Should I call the police? But what would that bring? I'd say Whitefield was behind it; he would deny it. It would be his word against mine. I decided not to call the police. I would fight with the one weapon I had.

My column.

## 21.

A newsroom can be an eerie place at night. After the constant din of thirty typewriters going during the day, the silence of an empty newsroom can be deafening.

But I was grateful for it.

I thanked my lucky stars that I worked at a weekly. If the *Chronicle* had been a daily, those typewriters would've been clacking twenty-four hours a day, seven days a week. As it was, the *Chronicle* was put to bed every Wednesday night to appear bright and fresh on newsstands every Thursday morning. Staff could afford to go home in the evenings.

Except for those like me. Who couldn't sleep. Who had work to be done.

With the icy weather outside and the lack of busy human bodies inside, the newsroom had grown cold. I made myself a cup of coffee with lots of cream and sugar, then sat at my desk and took out the draft column I'd written earlier. I reread it, and laid it aside. This soft version would not do. I meant to pin Whitefield to the wall, but faced the same issues as earlier. Just what did I have in terms of information and evidence? And, most importantly, how far could I go with it?

My hands absorbed the soothing warmth of the cup. I took a deep breath. Good writing, effective writing required a passionate heart and a rational head.

Mabel Dean's account was a strong point, but it could not be used in its entirety or even in detail. Her name could not be used at all. Without her, I had only Hilda Coleman's assertion of Whitefield's cruelty—but that was basically rumor—and Beth's statement about his affair with Esther—again, secondhand information, hearsay.

I set my cup aside, took out the typed notes I'd made that afternoon and reread them. Then I selected a fresh sheet of typing paper, rolled it into the machine and set to work. I wrote about the night Esther disappeared, how she started the evening with so much anticipation, only to end it absorbed by the darkness. I wrote about the boyfriend and how my investigation had turned up information that Esther was indeed involved with a man who had a reputation for violence. I put down everything I knew about him, but did not give him a name. Whitefield would certainly recognize himself, as would those who knew him. But even those in his intimate circle might hesitate to acknowledge that he fit the picture of the monster portrayed. I needed to flush him out, to provoke him into striking out at me again and making a mistake—one that would cost him.

After I finished writing, I felt emptied. I read through the column one last time and made my last changes. I put the copy in the middle of my desk and was about to put the dust cover on my Underwood when the door opened. Sam walked in, looking puzzled and concerned. Seeing me, his expression changed to one of surprise.

"Weren't you going home?"

"How'd you know I was here?"

"I didn't. I only live about a block away. I went out for cigarettes and saw the light. What're you doing here?"

I couldn't tell him what had happened. He might blame himself and it wasn't his fault. Worse, he might give me an I-told-you-so. He'd warned me that I was treading on dangerous water, although I thought he had no idea the danger would turn physical. If he found out that I'd been attacked, he might fully block me.

"Lanie, are you okay?"

"Sure? Why?"

"Because you're sitting here working when you should be at home asleep. And you're whiter than one of my grandmother's bleached sheets. Now what's going on?"

I shrugged. "Couldn't sleep. Decided to come back and write my column. Want to see it?"

"Of course."

I handed it to him. He sat at a neighboring desk and started to read it. After about a minute, he looked up with a worried frown.

"Are you talking about Sexton Whitefield? *The* Sexton Whitefield?"

"Yup," I said, tensing for his reaction.

He took a deep breath, held it for a moment and let it out slowly.

"You sure about this, Lanie?"

"More than you'll ever know."

"What does that mean?"

"It means I'm sure. That's all. I'm sure."

Sam read further, the furrow between his brows deepening. "Do you have any idea how big this man is?"

I nodded.

"You've spoken to him?"

"He denied everything." I tapped the pages. "It's all in there."

Sam finished reading the draft. He reflected. "You've done a lot. No doubt about it. You've covered more ground in a couple of days than the cops did in weeks. But you're heading into deep water. And you don't have the evidence to back it up, do you?"

I bit my lip. "I don't name him."

"Thank God for small favors." He heaved another deep sigh. "I'd like you to choose another topic."

"Sam—"

"We need something upbeat."

"We've been through all that."

"For goodness' sakes, it's Christmastime. Nobody wants to read about a kidnapping case that's three years old. And, if we write about this one, then we'll have a stream of people standing at the door, wondering why we don't write about their lost relatives, too."

"It's a good question."

"What?"

"You heard me. Why aren't we writing about the things that matter?"

Sam blinked as if he hadn't heard right. I wanted to reach out and smooth his worry lines away. But I couldn't. I was the cause of them. He laid my copy aside and drew his chair close to mine, very close.

"Look," he said in an intimate voice of puzzled concern. "You've told me how you fought for this social column. Now tell me why you're willing to throw it all away."

"I'm not."

"Remember what you said. You told me you told the paper that too much attention was being paid to the bad things happening in our community, that more should be written about the dignity of our people."

"And I still believe that. Esther Todd was a dignified and talented woman. If crime hadn't intervened, she might've well developed into one of those professionals I write about. Her story could be the story of any one of our people. But Sam, we've already been over this. If we're going to disagree, let it be over how I write the topic—not the topic itself. You gave me the go-ahead. Twice."

"God help me, I sure did. But I also said I'd reserve final approval upon review of your copy." He gestured to the typewritten sheets of paper. "This could get us into some deep shit."

"Exactly. But since when have you been afraid of stepping in shit? Good reporters don't mind getting covered in it."

"That's fine when you're a foot soldier in the trenches."

"Oh, but when you're the general, you want to stay clean—"

"You don't waste ammunition—and you don't send in troops where angels fear to tread."

"What troops? It's just me."

"If this baby misfires, it's the whole battalion. On something this big, we stand or die alone."

"Sam, it's a good story and you know it."

He drew a deep breath, grabbed up the copy and quickly read it through again. By the time he was finished, he was shaking his head. "You can't back this stuff up."

"I have sources—"

"But none of them would climb out on a limb for you, right? Not a single one of them would speak up if necessary."

"No," I conceded. "They wouldn't."

He sighed and tossed the sheets down. Leaning back, he rubbed his eyes. The circles under his eyes were pronounced. He was about to spike this story, all because he didn't want to rock the boat. In a flash of skepticism, I spoke quickly.

"Look at it this way: If nothing else, the story will increase sales."

He sat up straight with a jolt. I'd just wanted to prick his pride, but the look he gave me said I'd gone too far.

"Is that all you think I care about?"

"I think it's one of your concerns. Yes."

He looked frustrated, perhaps even bitter.

I started to apologize. "Sam, I—"

"It's okay, Lanie. I know where you're coming from. I've been there myself."

His eyes reflected an old pain. I felt a twinge of guilt. My comment about him, while containing some truth, had been unfair. Worse, it had tapped a wound, one that apparently went deep. I knew so little about him. At that moment, it struck me how little.

Taking a deep breath, he picked up the pages and eyed them, but his thoughts seemed elsewhere. His expression became distant, as though he was remembering something, something bad maybe, an experience that went well beyond the facile description of his life he'd given at the Bamboo Inn.

"Lanie, I want you to know something." He paused. "I love working at this paper, so don't take me wrong, but the fact is … I took this job because it was all I could get." His eyes searched mine. "Do you understand?"

"I …" No, I didn't understand. In fact, I was stunned. A man of Sam's talents taking a position because it was the only thing offered? At the same time, his job at the *Chronicle* wasn't all that bad. What other jobs or opportunities had he lost that would seem so much better?

"I'm attracted to you," he continued, "because I understand you. Believe it or not, I used to be just like you—impulsive, determined to uncover the truth at all costs, indifferent to the power of those who could hurt me—but I paid a high price for it."

I started to ask how, but he raised a hand to ward off a question.

"I won't go into the details. Now's not the time. But this much I can tell you. You don't want to go where I've been. You don't want to crawl so far out on a limb that you make it easy—*easy*, do you hear?—for your enemies to cut it out from under you. Understand?"

I nodded.

He tapped my printed pages. "If we print this, we're in for a rough ride. Are you ready for it?"

My gaze flicked to the papers, then went back to him. "Without a doubt."

Another moment of consideration, then he blew out his breath and gave me a grim smile.

"Well, okay then. Let's do it."

## 22.

Sam took me home. I told him he didn't have to, but it was nearly two in the morning and he insisted. I have to admit his protective presence made me feel better.

"Listen," he said, as we drove, "I have some tickets to the Savoy. Actually, I got 'em for a friend of mine, for him and his wife, but now he says they can't go. I just wondered, you know, whether, uh …"

"When?" Where was that promise I'd made myself earlier?

"Tonight."

Talk about short notice.

"Well?" he asked.

"Okay."

"Swell." His smile was nice to see. "Show's at eight. I'll pick you up at half-past seven?"

I gave a little nod.

Still smiling, he pulled up to my house. I wanted to smile, too, but seeing my house again gave me the willies.

Sam escorted me up the stairs, ready to say good-bye at my front door, but then he saw how I fumbled with my keys. He gave me a curious look and said, "Let me." I handed him the keys and pointed out which two opened the outer and inner doors. He unlocked both easily and handed me my keys. "You sleep tight, now. I'll see y—"

"Want to come in for a moment?"

He blinked, obviously puzzled and surprised. "Okay."

"Go on in."

He gave me another uncertain glance, then stepped inside and flicked on the vestibule light.

"Wow," he said, looking around. "This is lovely." He turned to see me hesitating on the threshold. "Are you all right?"

The stairway I'd so loved now appeared to be menacing. Esther's kidnapper had climbed those stairs and waited for me. He'd broken into my home, my sanctuary. Had he gone through the house, touched my belongings? A shiver ran through me. Would I ever feel safe here again?

"Lanie?"

"Oh, yes, of course."

I forced myself to step inside. My skin prickled with fear. Everything looked calm and clear, but that's how it had looked before.

The locks would have to be changed.

It struck me that whoever broke in had done an excellent job of picking the lock. I hadn't noticed any scratches or damage. When I'd slipped in the key, I'd felt no misalignment that might've tipped me off and Sam hadn't noticed anything either. Thinking about it, I nearly turned back to double-check it, but caught myself.

Sam was watching.

I put on a bright smile. "Thanks for bringing me home."

"No problem."

He flashed a smile too, but his eyes said he suspected that something was wrong. "Lanie, are you all right?"

"Yeah, everything's jake. Would you like a cup of tea or hot chocolate?" I couldn't stand the thought of being alone in the house, not then.

He shook his head and I felt disappointed.

"But I'd appreciate a glass of water."

"Okay," I said with relief.

I showed him in to the parlor.

"No Christmas tree?" he asked.

I shook my head.

He gave the parlor an admiring look. "It's nice, though. Real nice. You and your husband, you bought it together?"

I nodded.

"Could I use your bathroom?"

"It's downstairs in the back. Follow me." I led the way and showed him to the bathroom door. "I'll be in the kitchen."

I went to get a glass from the leaning cabinet. My gaze touched Hamp's open leather tool kit.

*"I'll fix it for you, hon. Make a start tonight."*

*"Not tonight, Hamp. It's late and I don't want noise and a whole lot of mess."*

*"I'm not going to be making a lot of noise. And I sure won't be making no mess. You worried about a mess? You just put a whole lot of glasses or china in there and watch it all fall out."*

"Lanie?"

I jumped at the sound of Sam's voice and turned to find him standing in the doorway. Seeing him there was a shock. He was the first man to enter my kitchen in years.

"You sure you're all right?" he asked.

"I'm fine. Why?"

He shrugged. "I don't know. You just had this faraway look in your eyes. Daydreaming?"

I took the glass down, closed the cabinet door. "Sort of." Then I went to the sink, turned on the cold water to let it run. He came and stood next to me. For several seconds, he studied my profile, then his gaze shifted to the cabinet.

"What happened there? Looks like it's going to fall down any minute."

"It was like that when we bought the house."

He gestured toward Hamp's tool kit. "Nice set. You got somebody fixing the cabinet for you?"

"I'm going to fix it myself. The tools were my husband's. He started to fix the cabinet, but he, uh ..." My throat tightened. "He went out to buy some nails and he ..."

"That's when he had the heart attack?"

I nodded, holding his glass under the faucet.

"Out on the street?" Sam asked.

I handed him the glass. "People thought he was drunk. They stepped right over him." There'd been a bruise on his stomach. Someone had even kicked him.

Sam touched me on the elbow. His fingertips were warm and their light touch incredibly intimate. I could feel part of me waking to him, a part that had been asleep for a long time, three years to be exact.

He walked over to the tilted cabinet and eyed it. I picked up his glass and followed him. He accepted his drink, thanked me and took a sip. He nodded at the cabinet.

"Do you mind?"

I shook my head.

He opened the cabinet door, looked at the shelves, then closed it and peered at the cabinet from the side, studying the loose nails.

"One of these days, this thing's going to come crashing down. Those nails don't look like they've got another week in them."

"They've been like that for three years. More, actually."

He raised an eyebrow, not wanting to argue. He was right, but I didn't want to agree with him. His glance fell on the tools and he reached for them. Without thinking, I stuck my hand out, covering them. It was rude and childish, and at his expression, I felt ashamed.

"Sorry."

"No, no. It's okay," he said. "I should've known better."

But I felt terrible at the look in his eyes.

He took a step back. "If you want, I could fix the cabinet for you. Build you some more."

"No, that's okay."

"It wouldn't be a problem. I'm good with my hands." He paused a beat. "And I'd bring my own tools."

I averted my eyes and shook my head, no.

"All right, Lanie." He sounded tired. He went back to the sink and set his glass down. "Good night." He started out, up the stairs to the parlor floor.

I ran after him. "Sam!"

He continued up the stairs and went to the front door, where he paused with a hand on the doorknob.

"Please, don't be angry," I said.

He gave me one of his gentle smiles. "I'm not. It would take more than that to anger me." He cupped my chin. "Now you take care. And lock up. I'll see you in the morning." He kissed me lightly on the lips and was gone.

For several long seconds, I stood in the doorway, watching his car drive away. Finally, I closed the door and turned to face the house.

It had never seemed so empty. Not since the night Hamp died.

Once more, my gaze traveled up the stairway. I wouldn't go up there. Not that night.

That night, I would sleep on the sofa.

## 23.

The next morning, at five minutes after nine, the phone on my desk rang. I was bleary-eyed and bone-tired after a night of nightmares on the sofa, so I wasn't at my sharpest when I reached for the receiver. But the mental fog cleared fast when the caller identified himself.

"The name's Echo," he said. "*Mister* Echo. Special Assistant to Mr. Whitefield, of the Internal Revenue."

I felt the shock of fear. What did he want now?

He continued blithely. "This call is to inform you that we will be examining your returns for the last four years."

I was so stunned, I couldn't answer. Last night, he'd attacked me in my own home. He'd put a knife to my throat. Now, he was calling me at work and in the most civilized voice, threatening me with an audit. Scared or not, I had to speak up.

"How dare you. After what you did last night, how da—"

"Madam, Mr. Echo hasn't the faintest idea what you're talking about. This is a courtesy call."

*Courtesy?* I almost laughed out loud. Not that there was anything funny about this. It was insane and cruel. It clarified what Hilda and Mabel had warned me about—and what Esther had tried to escape.

"Mrs. Price? You do understand what I'm saying?"

Oh, I understood all right. "You can tell your boss that—"

"We want to see everything you have from 1922 onward," the silken voice said. "For now, of course, it's just a review."

"This will not work. This will not stop me—"

"Now, a review could be all—or nothing. It depends on what we find. The decision to audit, to dig deeper, if you will—that would come from *him*."

To hear his tone, you'd think he was referring to God.

He got downright chummy. "You know, he only has Mr. Echo make these kinds of calls on cases he really cares about."

"Put him on the line."

"No can do. He's very busy." The sound of papers being rifled came down the line. "You're a journalist?"

"You know I am."

"That's nice. Got a column to write? Your deadline is today?"

"As a matter-of-fact, it is." No need to mention that the column was already filed.

"Well, you're going to have to miss it. We need your bills, receipts, checks, salary statements, etc. And we need it all today. We're especially interested in your 1923 returns."

Why '23? I wondered. Then it hit me. They would've been filed in '24. That was the year I'd been so preoccupied, first with my mother's illness and death and then the struggle to find a new job.

Had I even filed returns for '23? Probably not, if they were asking for them. That meant they'd already done some checking. They'd gone looking for something to use against me, and thought they'd found it.

He was waiting for my response, for me to beg for more time, if not outright mercy. Realizing that I wasn't about to give him the pleasure, he continued, his tone less silken and much more spiteful.

"Mr. Echo suggests you forget about that deadline. Do you hear? If you don't, you'll have to forget about your column, period."

He had some nerve.

"Would you deliver a message?" I asked.

"Why, of course." He sounded surprised at the civility of my tone. To be honest, so was I.

"Tell your boss that your call confirms my opinion of him. Tell him that it's the early bird who catches the worm—and that this time, he wasn't early enough."

Before he could respond, I hung up. For a moment, I sat staring at my hands. They were trembling, the result of both fear and anger. I balled them into fists and took another shaky breath.

I couldn't believe it: I was actually more afraid of the tax threat than the physical one. Maybe Whitefield's strategy of attack made more sense than I realized.

Keep thinking. *Think*. Had I or had I not filed those returns? I was at my mother's bedside in Virginia. The world had seemed so far away. What had I done? Filed them? Forgotten them? I couldn't recall.

In the normal course of things, not filing was no great sin. One could always file later. But given Whitefield's aptitude for spite …

I shivered.

It was time to remind myself that this was about Esther, and about Job. It was time to remember that Whitefield was no good. Of course, he was going to strike back. *Buck up. Stiffen your spine.*

It was quite simple, really: If I was determined to go out and slay dragons, then I'd better be prepared to get scorched.

I was tempted to call Whitefield, to tell him that threatening me with an audit was useless, and that the column was being typeset at that very moment. But why bother? He would find out soon enough.

So, I went to the staff kitchen to get some coffee instead. Sam was there, pouring himself a fresh cup.

"Want some?" he asked.

I rubbed my temple and nodded. He set down his cup, took another from the cabinet and filled it. He added milk and sugar, in the right amounts, without asking. I'd once told him in passing how I liked my coffee. That had been months ago, but he remembered.

"I hope you have lots of energy," he said, handing me the cup.

"What for?"

"For tonight, of course—Lanie, you do remember?"

A blank moment and then it came to me. "Oh yes, the Savoy."

"Look, if you don't want to go …"

"Seven-thirty. Of course, I want to go."

"Can I go too?" said a third voice from the doorway.

The scent of a musky perfume hit the air. I turned to see Selena standing in the doorway. She slinked in and slid between Sam and me, brushing her bosom against his arm, and held her cup out to him.

"Would you fill me up?" she asked, with a perfectly innocent expression. "Please?"

"Sure." He took her cup.

When he offered it to her, filled with coffee, she said, "Oh, but you know how I like it, Sam. Sweet. Very sweet. And hot. So I can suck it down. Slowly."

She was so obvious. I just wanted to shake my head, but Sam apparently thought otherwise. He was giving her an appraising look.

Men, I wondered. Are they really that simple?

"Time for me to go," I said. "I have an appointment to keep."

"Lanie," he said. "You *will* remember, won't you?"

I paused, tempted to break the date. But that would've been childish—and it would've been playing right into Selena's hands.

"Sure." I gave them both a wave. "Bye."

"Bye-ee," Selena cooed.

I started out, but couldn't resist a backward glance. He was handing her back her cup and she was placing her hand over his. I turned away.

Men, I decided, were beyond simple.

Not all, of course. Not my Hamp. But he was one in a million.

And he was gone.

I phoned Ruth at her church. She sounded tired when she came to the telephone, but she perked up fast when I told her what I'd learned.

"It'll all be in my column."

"But shouldn't you go to the police with it first?"

"I have no proof, just bits and pieces."

"But don't you think—"

"There's still time to go to the cops. Actually, the cops might even go see Whitefield themselves. The column could serve as a wake-up notice."

"I hope you're right. I hope he don't try to run off."

"That's not likely. He's got too much to protect. And he's not the running-away kind. Too self-confident."

I went home early to dig around in my home files. After three hours, I gave up. There was no sign of my 1923 return. I was worried despite my determination not to be, and not because I had anything to hide, but because like most Americans, I'd been taught to fear the Bureau of Internal Revenue.

Whitefield's intimidation tactics were working, indeed.

## 24.

It was champagne pink with little glass beads, a very pretty little dress, but I hadn't worn it in years. I'd thought I'd feel strange wearing it—as though I was betraying Hamp—but I didn't. I did feel a renewed sense of his presence, but in a good way, almost protective.

What would he have thought of Sam? What did *I* think of him?

Seeing him with Selena had made me jealous. I'd never considered myself a jealous person, so sensing it now, especially after so many years of disinterest in men, was a surprise. But maybe that's why I was so easily provoked, because I'd been alone so long.

Jealousy—or any emotion like it—was the last thing I needed. Being alone wasn't fun, but it was simple. My life was uncomplicated and I wanted to keep it that way. Whatever was developing between Sam and me, I had to nip it in the bud.

Having decided, I quashed the pleasurable little thump my heart gave when the doorbell rang. I looked through my window to see him standing outside and told myself it didn't matter what he thought about my appearance.

But I checked myself in the hallway mirror just the same.

The Savoy was uptown's answer to downtown's Roseland Ballroom. It had opened that March and become known as the "Home of Happy Feet." The place was big. It took up the whole block between 140th and 141th Streets on Lenox Avenue and it held around four thousand people. But it wasn't all that much to look at—not from the outside and not during the day. But at night, it was really something. You could see the bright, glowing lights of the marquee blocks away. It attracted all the majors: Cab Calloway, Fess Williams, Louis Armstrong, Duke Ellington, and King Oliver—they all played there.

It was nice inside, too. Had a real elegant lobby and the stairway to the ballroom was made of marble. Can't get much nicer than that. The main room had a huge maple wood dance floor and twin bandstands. The bands swapped sets and the music never stopped.

That night, Fess Williams and his Royal Flush Orchestra were on one stage, Cab and his boys on the other. Fess was on at the moment, wearing a diamond and-ruby-studded suit and blowing his clarinet.

Sam had reserved one of the round-topped tables a step up from the dance floor, so we had a perfect view of the showstoppers. They used to call Saturday night at the Savoy "Square's Night" because the place was packed with downtowners. The Saturday crowd was pretty ritzy all right, but Sunday's had the real eye-catchers. On Sunday, Hollywood came to Harlem and the international jet set stopped by for a landing. It was a work night, and not so glamorous as the weekend, but the place was packed. Seeing all those folks out there, determined to have fun, I made a firm decision to put my worries about Whitefield's threats aside.

"It's a good crowd," Sam said with a practiced eye. Between us, we spotted Emily Vanderbilt, Princess Violet Murat, Peggy Hopkins Joyce, Osbert Sitwell, and Richard Bartholomew. We had a little contest to see who could spot the most high-hatters. Sam did well, but I did better.

With a smile, he said, "You do like your job, don't you?"

"'Course, I do. The glitter, the glitz—I love it—and the dirt underneath it doesn't scare me."

He raised reassuring hand. "Hey, it's okay. I didn't bring you here to probe your motives or try to get you to change jobs."

"All right, then why did you ask me here?"

"Because I like you."

He paused to see how I took such a blunt statement. I took it pretty well. Hid it well, I mean. Deep down, my stomach was doing the butterfly shake. I waited to see if there was more.

There was.

"Look. I know what went on before, with the last editor, how he ..." He shifted uncomfortably. "Anyway, what I want to say is that I'm not like that."

"I know."

He looked relieved. "Good."

"Why'd you feel the need to tell me that?"

"Well, I sensed you weren't too happy about me giving Selena that cup of coffee."

"She likes you."

"Selena likes herself. No," he reconsidered. "She *loves* herself."

We chuckled. The waiter arrived with our drinks. Sam waited until the waiter left, then picked up where he'd left off.

"Selena's got nothing that interests me. At the most, she's entertaining."

"And you like that kind of entertainment?"

"I'm a red-blooded male. What do you think?"

"I like men who know what they want ... and who don't dabble along the way."

"Is that what you think might happen between Selena and me?"

"It's none of my business."

"Of course it is." He paused. "At least, I'd like it to be."

He saved me from my embarrassment and an awkward silence by saying, "Look, why don't we stop talking and start shaking?"

"Oh, I don't know. I—"

"C'mon."

"Well, I ... okay. But ..." I cast a doubtful glance at a teenage girl and her boyfriend doing the shimmy on the dance floor. "I don't think I can shake it quite as fast as she does."

The Savoy attracted incredible dancers. In many ways it was better than a Broadway show, because it was improvised and ever changing and right up close. People cut loose, moving from pinwheel spins and breakneck turns to lifts and dips that made me dizzy just looking at them. It had been years since I cut the rug, so I knew I was rusty. But Sam turned out to be a good partner. He whipped off his tie and put it in his pocket. Before I knew it, we were laughing and working together to hit that downbeat.

When we dropped back into our seats, we were exhausted but grinning. The waiter had held our order while we were on the floor and now he brought it straightaway. Sam and I finished our drinks quickly and he ordered more.

Conversation was light, just chitchat about the band and the dancers and Oscar Micheaux's latest film.

It was good to talk about and think about something besides the Todd case. But the minute I realized we weren't talking about it, I started thinking about it again.

"A penny for your thoughts," Sam said.

"Oh, I'm sorry," I said, realizing that I'd drifted off.

"Thinking about Esther Todd?"

I shook my head, hoping he'd drop the subject.

The band had slowed down the tempo and now swung into a soft, romantic tune.

"Let's dance," he said. He pushed back his chair, stood up and offered his hand.

I hesitated.

"C'mon," he said gently. "Trust me."

I looked up at him, and put my hand in his.

Only couples were on the dance floor now: men and women—some men and men and a few women with women—moving closely together as they swayed in place. Sam led me to a small circle of space at the heart of the floor. He guided me into a two-step and I rested my hand on his shoulder. He tried to draw me into his embrace, but I held myself away.

"Lanie, what is it? What are you so afraid of?"

I forced a little laugh. "According to you, I'm not afraid of anything. Aren't you always telling me that I'm fearless?"

"You're afraid all right. Of letting someone get close."

I swallowed hard, but said nothing. With a gentle pressure in the small of my back, he urged me closer. "Relax, I'm not going to bite you." He looked down and added mischievously, "Not yet, anyway."

"Very funny."

"There's nothing funny about it. I'm quite serious."

I decided to play along. "You bite women?"

"Only the sweet ones. It's taking all my strength not to take a nibble off of you."

"You wouldn't dare."

"Try me." He smiled. "Now, come on, relax."

His pressed my head against his chest. His shirt was damp with perspiration, but it was warm from his heat and his breast felt both strong and soft. He was the perfect height for me. My gaze traveled up to his throat. It was a strong pillar glistening with moisture. Then I caught myself dwelling on his lips and lowered my gaze again. This moment ... was wonderful. Closing my eyes, I relaxed against him. He hugged me close and softly kissed me on the top of my head.

Two songs went by, two slow ones, before we sat down again. Unlike the last time, we weren't giddy with laughter, but quiet and happy and maybe even relieved. Baby steps. That's what we were taking. Baby steps. I swung an eye over the room of laughing couples, admiring how easy they found it to interact. I'd never dated before. With Hamp at my side, I'd never had to. Now, here I was, so ill at ease with what these kids took for granted. Then again, they didn't know what was at stake, but I did and so did Sam.

The waiter appeared and asked if we'd like desert. I had a sudden yen for chocolate and Sam indulged me. He ordered a slice of chocolate cake for me, but nothing for himself.

"Can't we share?" I asked.

He shook his head. "I'm fine. I'm getting all the pleasure I need from watching you."

"Sam Delaney, I didn't know you could be such a flirt."

He shrugged. "Like I said, you should get to know me." He offered me a cigarette, then lit himself one. We smoked quietly, our eyes on the swaying bodies on the dance floor, but conscious of each other. After a time, he got up. "Would you excuse me for a minute?"

"Sure."

He disappeared into the crowd.

Watching him go, I realized that, baby steps or not, the sensations Sam inspired were unsettling. What had happened to my resolve to nip everything in the bud? And what was I thinking of, going out with my boss? Suppose things went wrong? I'd be out of a job. I stopped picking at my cake and laid down the fork, having managed to kill my appetite.

When he returned, I gazed up at him and knew he wasn't the kind of man to fire me if something happened. But I was the kind of woman who might not want to stay. I couldn't risk my job. It was all I had.

One look at my face and he said, "What's the matter?"

"I've been thinking ..."

"Lord help us," he said. "My mother used to say that and whenever she did, my daddy knew he was in for it. What did I do wrong? Good grief, woman, I was only gone for a minute."

It was hard not to smile. "Don't make me laugh. This is serious."

"I can tell. Now let me see. I've been gone exactly three minutes, just long enough for you to start worrying. Am I right?"

I nodded.

He continued. "What you want to say probably goes something like this: Maybe it wouldn't be too smart for us to start something, because 'A'..." He held up a hand and ticked off the points on his fingers. "I'm your boss and I might take it out on you if the relationship sours; 'B': I'm your boss and you're thinking that even if I didn't make you quit, you'd want to if the relationship sours; and 'C': It's too soon after your husband's death. Three years is just too soon. Thirty might be all right, but three is just out of the question."

"All right. You've made your point. You must be a mind reader. I refuse to believe I'm that predictable."

"You, predictable? You're one of the most mysterious women I know, and if we were together for a million years, you'd still find ways to surprise me."

It was hard not to feel touched. "But my concerns, they're legitimate, aren't they?"

"Sure they are. To be honest, they're mine, too. And I'm not saying we should ignore them. I'm just saying we shouldn't let fear be our guide. Now am I right?"

He was making me feel incredibly immature. He waited for my answer and I nodded. I had to agree with him.

"Let's dance," he said. He swung me out onto the dance floor and the magic took hold. This man knew how to move and my body moved along with him. All my fearful thoughts and sad memories faded in a whirl of motion. And when the music slowed, he spun me into his arms for a gentle swaying rhythm around the floor.

Thoughts of Esther Todd receded. But when I went home that evening, it wasn't thoughts of Sam or of even Hamp that I took to bed. Nor was it their image that walked with me in my dreams.

It was Esther I saw, Esther and the dark shadow of a figure that stalked her.

## *25.*

Ruth showed up in the newsroom early the next morning. She threw a copy of the paper down on my desk, furious.

"Why didn't you *name* him?"

"I couldn't, Ruth. It wouldn't have been fair."

"Fair? How can you talk about being fair to the man who took Esther?"

"I couldn't name him with what I had. Understand? It would've blown up in our faces."

*And still might*, I wanted to add.

She stared at me, and I saw understanding sink in. She dropped down in the chair next to my desk, like a balloon drained of air.

"I'm sorry," she whispered. "I … I just want it settled. For once and for all, I want it over and done with. That's all. It's been so long."

"I know, but there was no way I could name this man. No way that was defensable."

She sighed, closed her eyes and nodded.

"How's Job?" I asked.

"He asks about you. Wants to know if you've found her yet."

"I'm sorry about that. I didn't mean to make it worse."

"Well, just find her then," she blurted out. "Make this man tell us what he did to her. That's all you have to do." Immediately, she apologized. "Oh, God. I hear myself and know I sound like a nut case. It's just that ... this really is driving us crazy."

"How's your mother?"

"Better. I showed her what you wrote. Read it to her. It made her real happy."

"I'm glad to hear it."

"I hope this'll make a difference," she said. "But suppose he runs away?"

I shook my head. "This guy's not the running kind."

"Well, that's something, then, isn't it?" She got up to go, then paused. "Oh, and I wanted to thank you."

"For what?"

"Recommending Mabel Dean. My reverend likes her and I like her, too. I think she's going to be a lot of help."

"Glad to hear it. Mabel deserves a break."

"We'll take good care of her."

Ruth started away and turned back. "It would've made a difference, wouldn't it, if you'd found something, something real, that showed what was going on between Esther and this guy?"

"Of course. But ..." I shrugged. "I didn't find anything."

Ruth nodded to herself, crestfallen, and walked away. She was barely out the door when Selena sidled up and tapped me on the shoulder.

I turned. "Yes?"

"Sam wants to see you." Selena's slanted eyes were as green as brown eyes can be. "I think you over reached yourself this time." She pointed to Sam's office. With a nasty jolt, I saw that the big cheese himself, Mr. Byron Canfield, was in there.

"You'd better hop to it," she said.

"Selena, you know what? You can kiss my muffins."

Her mouth dropped open. I stifled an urge to put my fist through it and walked away.

The two men stood as I entered. I gave them both a courteous smile, and then addressed the visitor. "Good morning, Mr. Canfield."

The Movement's most senior official granted me a nod. He was a tall man of aristocratic bearing. He wore a long dark gray coat, carried his hat and gloves in one hand, his walking stick in the other. We'd spoken briefly at Movement events and I'd seen him in court while attending the McKay murder trial, but this would be the first professional meeting.

His dedication to the Movement was unassailable. It was his life's work and he'd do anything to defend it—partly because he viewed it as his own personal empire, but mostly because he was truly committed to improving the lives of his people. He waged his battle with pen and paper, but he was as courageous and single-minded as any soldier wielding a gun or grenade. No doubt about it, he was a brave man.

Unfortunately, he was also a high hat. His Oxford education and extraordinary intellect had imparted an almost dogmatic belief in his own infallibility. To a degree, his intellect had curtailed his ability to feel empathy, much less show compassion. His writings were intellectually sound, but often emotionally empty. His opinions were brilliant but lacked elemental human understanding. As a result, many of people admired him but didn't like him.

"Mrs. Price, please take a seat," Sam said. He did not look happy.

"Thanks, but I prefer to stand."

Sam gestured toward Canfield with a pencil. His voice was carefully neutral. "He has some concerns he'd like to share with us."

Canfield cleared his throat. "Your article, Lanie—May I call you that?"

"No, you may not."

Canfield smiled grimly, like a cat enjoying the prospect of torturing a frisky mouse. "I have a message from Sexton Whitefield. What he tells me is very upsetting."

"If I were him, I'd be upset, too."

"I think you should reconsider writing this particular column—"

"Too late. It's already out."

Canfield looked from me to Sam. Sam nodded, refusing to say more than he had to. Was he going to back me up or not? Canfield cleared his throat.

"Whitefield's message came in late yesterday. I was out of the office. Mrs. Price, isn't this the same matter about which you bothered Mrs. Goodfellowe?"

"It is related to the Esther Todd case, yes."

"Didn't you understand that you were to drop this subject? This could cost us."

"Cost who?"

"Well, us." He made an open-handed gestured that could've meant just us three in the room or the world beyond us. "We colored," he said. "The Movement and everything we've worked so hard for."

"If that's what you're talking about, then it's already cost us."

"Excuse me?"

"What's the price of looking the other way? What's the return on letting down one of your own?"

"I have no idea what you're referring to."

"I think you do."

Sam intervened. "Mrs. Price—"

"Look, I was told not to write about Mrs. Goodfellowe and I didn't. No one said anything about not writing about Esther."

"You're exposing a great man to suspicion and—"

"I want him exposed."

Canfield cocked his head as though he couldn't believe what he was hearing. He turned to Sam. "Is she crazy?"

Sam glanced at me. "Well ..." His lips twitched with a smile.

I arched an eyebrow and gave him a severe look. This was no time to be facetious.

"Actually," Sam continued, appropriately serious again, his gaze returning to Canfield. "She's one of the sanest people I know."

Canfield sure didn't expect that answer. His dark eyes darted back and forth between us, suspicious.

"Mr. Delaney," he said, "I would warn you against letting any personal feelings contaminate your sense of judgment."

*Contaminate?*

Sam's eyes grew cold. "Thank you, but you needn't worry."

"Good," Canfield said and turned to me. "Mr. Delaney and I have been talking. We agree that there's another reporter in this newsroom who deserves a column. Selena Troy. You know her, of course?"

"Quite well."

"What do you think of her?"

I glanced at Sam. Was he actually going along with this?

"She's one of a kind," I said evenly.

"Well, I think she'd make a one-of-a-kind society columnist, too. What do you say to that?"

"I say it's for me to decide," Sam said.

Canfield did a double-take. "But you said—"

"You asked me if Miss Troy was talented. I said she was. You asked me if she deserves a column. I said yes, she does. However, I did not say that she deserves Mrs. Price's."

Canfield went from stunned to furious. Sam was not being as malleable as he'd expected him to be. I gave Sam a look of thanks, which he pointedly ignored. Canfield gave Sam a look of smoldering anger.

"So you stand behind Mrs. Price and her actions?"

"I do."

Canfield was disgusted. "You just don't care, do you? Either of you. Certainly not about the Movement."

Sam cleared his throat. "Mrs. Price here is one of our most gifted—and loyal—writers. Her support of the Movement need never be questioned."

"She's showing blatant disregard for our concerns—specifically, the need to stand up and defend our men of achievement."

"What about our women?" I said.

"Excuse me?"

"Our women. What about defending them? Or don't they deserve your respect and attention?"

Canfield sputtered. "Well, them too. But Mrs. Todd's talent can't be compared to—"

"How would you know? Did you ever hear her play? I did. She was unique. I could argue that her talent was—would've been—as great as his. I could also argue that when it comes to the value of human life and equality before God, it doesn't matter whether a person is male or female, talented or untalented, prominent or unknown. They're worthy of consideration. Don't you agree?"

"Mrs. Price," Sam said.

"No," said Canfield. "Let her continue. I love sparring with intelligent women. And your Mrs. Price is indeed intelligent—just misdirected."

"Oh, and I suppose you think you're man enough to straighten me out—"

"Your passion is admirable, but you're missing a basic point."

"And that would be?"

"The need for a cohesive front."

"The need to hide our dirty laundry, you mean?"

"I wouldn't have used such colloquial terms, but yes."

He was such a stuffed shirt.

"You know what? I'm not interested in hiding dirty laundry. Not yours, mine or anybody else's. Not when it means letting a man like Whitefield go free."

"But you should be interested," Canfield said. "Why must we colored always turn on our own? Why can't we retain for ourselves that sense of reserve and dignity that is necessary for progress? The enemy loves it when we destroy ourselves, when we trumpet our weaknesses. You're an intelligent woman. Why can't you understand that?"

"I understand more than you realize. Sure, we can present a united front, but let's do so with our best and brightest. Does Whitefield really meet those criteria? Not in my book—not by a long shot. Are we, as a people, so desperate for heroes that we'll condone the vilest behavior? Yes, the man's a mental giant, but he's a monster of a human being."

"That's not proven—"

"Why don't you step on down to Mabel Dean's house and tell her that? The woman is deaf in one ear and broken in places you can't even see because of what he did to her." I'd used her name, but I was so angry, I didn't care. "He beat her to a pulp and she's too scared to say a word about it."

"That's what she told you," Canfield said.

"And thank God she did."

"But you have only her word for it."

"Yes, I do. I have her word. And I have it because I took the time to hear it. You haven't even done that. And it doesn't look like you're willing to."

"Mrs. Price, calm down," Sam said. "This isn't helping."

"You know what would? It would help if Mr. Canfield here thought about how the Movement jumped ship when things got a little hot and heavy with Esther's family. It would help if he thought about the united front the Movement showed back then. If he thought about who might be the better role model: a single mother struggling to raise her child and develop her talent—or a violent egomaniac who abuses the power of his position."

Two red spots appeared in Canfield's pale cheeks.

"Mrs. Price, I'm not about to waste my time bantering with you. The fact is Esther Todd could've been the role model you describe. But she isn't. And that's because she chose not to be. She chose to bite the hand that fed her. She chose to help thieves, to commit a crime, and then pretend she was a victim to cover up for it. That's behavior we can neither forgive nor condone—much less defend. This is your last warning. Stop harassing Sexton Whitefield. And drop this case. Move on. Crusade for better garbage pickup in the neighborhood. I don't care! Just don't write another word about this matter."

He turned to Sam. "As for you, I most strongly suggest you convince her to cooperate. It would be in the best interest of the paper."

"Is that a threat?" Sam asked.

"Take it as good advice. From a lawyer."

It was the wrong thing to say.

"Well," Sam said with a cold smile of his own, "we most certainly know what to do with advice like that."

Canfield's expression froze. "How dare you."

"I dare," Sam said, "because, as the head of this newsroom, I have every right to."

Canfield was beside himself. "This will cause repercussions."

"I should hope so," Sam said tranquilly.

The Movement leader glared at him. "All right. You want repercussions? Then that's what you'll get." He gave Sam a tight little nod and yanked open the office door.

The din of typewriters clattering and people calling to one another across the newsroom paused. For a split second, everyone out there halted. Canfield paused on the threshold.

He appeared to want to say something, but then bit his tongue and stalked out, letting the door slam behind him. Sam and I were left alone in an uneasy quiet. He gave me an assessing look.

"We are on solid ground with this, aren't we?"

"Yes, we are."

"Ramsey's on my back, too."

"I know."

"But he's nothing compared to this character."

He motioned toward Canfield's departing figure, which we could still see through glass walls. I started out.

"Lanie?" His voice came from behind, soft and heavy with emotion.

I paused with my hand on the doorknob. "Yes?"

"You worried?"

A split second passed. Without turning around, I gave a little nod. He sighed.

"Good to know I'm not alone. I got your back, Lanie. Just don't let me down. Not on this one."

"I never have, Sam. And I won't now."

Ruth needn't have worried. By mid-morning, my telephone was ringing off the hook and everybody, but everybody, had an idea of who the mystery man was. Any number guessed that it was Whitefield and it didn't matter that I refused to confirm or deny it. They knew what they knew and that was that. Quite a few wouldn't give their names, but said they'd seen Esther and Whitefield together. Would they get a reward if they provided the details?

I wasn't the only one getting calls. Around noon, Hilda Coleman called from a pay phone at Jimmy Dee's.

"They've been coming in all morning. From all over. The switchboard's going crazy. *The Harlem Age*, *the Amsterdam News*. It ain't just the Harlem papers either. I'm talking about *the Chicago Defender*, *the Pittsburgh Courier*.

Those kinds of papers. They're big papers, aren't they? I mean, not to insult you, but bigger than yours?"

They were big all right. The story was getting play. Lots of play. Of course, the reason wasn't so much interest in Esther as it was in Whitefield. He'd hurt at least as many people as he'd helped and now his enemies smelled blood. Hilda said he'd issued blanket denials. He'd met Esther Todd once, in passing, and that was that.

I can't say I expected a word of congratulations from Sam. Hoped for it, maybe, but not expected it.

"Aren't you happy, Sam?"

"Sure I am, but I've got to think ahead. Think about it. We didn't name names, but we drew a bead that everybody's followed. You think he's going to sit back and take it? We fired a shot over his bow. I've got to figure out how we're going to protect ourselves from the return cannon fire.'

I didn't tell Sam that Whitefield had already shot his best shot. That he'd already threatened me. And that I'd already prepared a counteroffensive. If Whitefield went after me via my tax returns, then I'd go after him. I'd show that he was not only abusing women, but taxpayers who crossed him. I'd convinced myself that as long as the *Chronicle* backed me, I could deal with Whitefield. And if the paper didn't back me … well, I'd find one that would.

That afternoon brought an early Christmas present.

"Miss Lanie?"

I looked up from my desk to see Ruth. She shuffled her feet nervously and gripped the handles of her handbag, a rather large one. She looked upset.

"What's the matter?" I rose to greet her.

"I want to apologize," she said. "For coming in here like that this morning. But most of all, I want to apologize for this." She opened her bag, took out a package wrapped in brown paper and handed it to me.

"What's this?" I asked.

"It was Esther's. I took it out of the trunk before letting you go through it."

I was stunned. "But why?"

"I was ashamed." She averted her eyes. "I didn't mean to block you, to make it for hard to help us. I just..." She sighed. "I was just so ashamed—for my sister's sake."

"Ashamed?" I turned the package over. It was square and heavy, like a brick.

Ruth nodded at it. "What you'll find in there could ruin Esther's memory. Please don't use it unless you have to."

"But—"

"Please."

I nodded. "All right."

Ruth drew a deep breath and let it out. She smiled weakly. "I feel better now, knowing that I've done all I can."

"You hiding anything else?" I scolded her gently.

"No."

"Good."

Her smile brightened a bit. Then her gaze returned to the package and her smile disappeared. She bit her lip, raised her hand to me in good-bye and moved on.

I plopped back down at my desk and ripped open the package. I found a simple wood box, and inside the box, a Bible, thick and heavy. I don't know what I expected—maybe a box of jewels with signed receipts—but a Bible? What could a Bible have that a church-going sister like Ruth would find shameful?

Two seconds later I found out.

It was a letter, tucked between the pages, and written in a bold scrawl. The date: September 13, 1923. That was right around the time Esther tried to end it with her secret beau. The letter consisted of three pages of thick, elegant vellum.

> 'Love of my life, come be with me again. I can hardly wait to see you, to plunge my spear into your most precious sheath. But first, we will play our special game, the kind that fulfills this fierce need that neither you

nor I can deny. Soon, you will be on your knees before me, exposed and hungry. Merciful as I am, I won't keep you waiting. I will teach you obedience, my love. I will fill you with my—'

I took a deep breath. I'm not a prude, but I found this letter disgusting. How had Esther become involved with this … this—I couldn't think of a word to describe him. I could understand Ruth's feelings, although I felt no shame for Esther's sake. Only rage.

Sickened, I skimmed the rest, reading just enough to learn the rules of his 'special game.' He derived pleasure from a woman's pain and exulted in her degradation. He reveled in Esther's sorrow and shame. He wrote of her tears and even had the nerve to promise that in due time she'd not only get used to his 'games,' but come to love them. That like him, she too would become *addicted*.

I was so angry for her, so disgusted, that my hands trembled. I wanted to rip the letter to shreds. Instead, I blessed it. This was the weapon I'd be able to wield against Whitefield.

When I reached the last page, my eyes jumped down to the closing words, and the signature.

'Until the appointed hour, I remain,

'Your servant in love,

'Antilles.'

That last made me ponder. *Antilles*. Who in the world was that?

Of course, if this was from Whitefield, as I expected—no, *hoped*—then one wouldn't expect him to sign his real name. He'd most likely use a code name or pseudonym, wouldn't he? But could I even be sure that the letter *was* from Whitefield? Mightn't it be one of the notes Esther told Ruth about? Ruth said Esther claimed to have destroyed them, but maybe she hadn't. Maybe …

But no, I frowned.

Esther hadn't known the author of those notes. But she sure knew the author of this one.

I took a good, long look at that signature. *Antilles*. A thought, light as a feather, teased the edges of my mind, but I couldn't quite grab it.

The letter had surprised me on so many levels that it set off several trains of thought. It wasn't just the matter of the letter's content. There was the place I'd found it. Why would Esther have hidden something so lewd in her *Bible*, of all places? Unless …

Unless she was seeking strength in her faith to deal with it.

I glanced back at the pages where I'd found it, in the book of Jude. I might've taken it as accidental or inconsequential, but she'd underlined the passage Jude 1:7. Reading it, I saw that there was nothing accidental or inconsequential about it.

*Even as Sodom and Gomorrha, and the cities about them in like manner, giving themselves over to fornication, and going after strange flesh, are set forth for an example, suffering the vengeance of eternal fire.*

So Esther had been worried about spiritual damnation, and why? Because she'd been having sex, abusive sex, the kind that was meant to make her feel cheap and dirty and sinful. I had to believe that she had indeed known the author of the letter, that she had indeed had a liaison with him, and that she had indeed regretted it.

I frowned at the name.

*Antilles.*

Hmmm. The thought that had danced away earlier had now floated home.

Sexton A. Whitefield. I was willing to bet dimes to dollars that Antilles was his middle name.

# 26.

The story of Whitefield's possible ties to the woman suspected in the Goodfellowe heist traveled like wildfire. Who would've thought that a small paper like the *Chronicle* would carry such clout? But that's how it worked. One paper carried an item and ten others picked it up. Within days the other papers would put out the story, too, but because of publishing schedules, the first one appeared the next day in the *Tattler*, our main competitor. Geraldyn hit the story high and hard in her weekly column:

> "What big shot is under the loop in a query into the three-year-old disappearance of beautiful Esther Todd? Word on the street is that he and the young pianist had an *affaire d'amour*. But Mr. Tax Man isn't talking. Come on, Mr. Tax Man. Share your secret. People want to know."

Sam was in his element. He could hardly wait for the "return cannon fire." When I showed him the letter, his eyes twinkled. We even discussed putting out a special edition. The important thing was to stay ahead of the competition. We had the advantage and we had to keep it.

Whitefield's fans were furious—they were burning up the newspaper's switchboard, calling me every name in the book—but his enemies were eating it up.

It was mid-morning when Hilda called and said Whitefield had gotten a call from his higher-ups in D.C. "They didn't want to know details of the mess. They just said he'd better clean it up."

Fifteen minutes later, my phone rang again and I had a feeling I knew who it was. Even the ring sounded angry. I grabbed up the receiver and heard a male voice, tight with fury.

"You have a hell of a lot of nerve," he said.

I glanced around the newsroom to make sure no one was watching and lowered my voice.

"Hello to you, too, Mr. Whitefield."

"How dare you!"

He sounded just like Canfield.

"You had every opportunity to comment," I said. "I even included the few words you did say."

"You twisted them. Made them sound mocking and callous."

"I wrote it straight. It was what you said, the way you said it."

"I demand an opportunity to set the record straight."

"Of course. When?"

"In an hour. My office."

"Fine. I'll be there."

## 27.

Hilda was out, but Echo was in. He was sitting at that tiny desk of his, working with an adding machine, his left hand busily filling in columns of numbers. Seeing me, his eyes filled with resentment.

"You can tell Mr. Whitefield I'm here," I said. "He's expecting me."

He glanced at my small purse. "You didn't bring your papers? You should've been here with them yesterday."

"Go inside and tell him I'm here."

"In a moment."

My stomach tightened. He went back to his numbers.

"I'll give you thirty seconds," I said.

His jaw tightened, but he didn't look up and he kept on writing in that ledger.

"One, two, three ..." I began.

"Sit down," he said.

Instead, I stood over him. "Ten, eleven, twelve——"

"All right." He put down his pen and closed the ledger. For a moment, he sat there, fuming. Then he appeared to make a decision. He looked up at me, pasted on an artificial smile and stood up.

"Perhaps, Mr. Echo was a bit overzealous in the prosecution of his duties," he said. "If so, he would like to offer his heartfelt apologies."

He extended his hand, but I didn't extend mine in return. So he took it. He actually took my hand, raised it to his lips and gave it a kiss.

"Do you like stories?" he said, still holding my hand. "Let Mr. Echo tell you one."

I tried to pull my hand away, but he held fast, his hold tightening.

"Once upon a time, there was a boy. He had no money or connections, but he had ambitions, plans. He served in the war, served with distinction, and then he came back. He searched for work. He found none, and so he searched harder.

"Days turned into weeks, weeks into months. By then our hero was practically living in the street, one step away from selling his ass for his bread and butter." He cast his narrow eyes at me. "But then, he met a man who took an interest in him."

"I can guess the rest," I said. "This man picked our young hero up, stood him on his feet and gave him an education—"

"Our hero already had an education—from a fine school, Tuskegee. What he didn't have was a job."

"So this man gave him one."

"Not just any job. A *real* job. With responsibilities, and a future. And yes," he saw the look in my eyes, "this job came with a price. Extra duties, you might say."

"Enforcement duties?"

He cracked a smile. "The kind of duties every soldier understands."

He paused to let his meaning sink in. His eyes were dead cold and filthy gray, like the Hudson River on a winter's day. He stroked my hand.

"You're very bright, Mrs. Price. Too bright to be making anymore stupid decisions."

"I could say the same about Mr. Whitefield ... or maybe even about you."

His eyes lit with flash with anger. "Let's speak plainly. When you threaten Mr. Whitefield, you threaten Mr. Echo, too." His grip on my hand switched to my middle finger. He lifted it, pressed it upward. "Mr. Echo has worked hard to attain his position. He will protect it." He forced my finger backward. I tried to pull free but couldn't. Pain shot through my hand. "Do you understand?" He pressed.

Soon, my finger would snap. I kicked him. My hard-toed boot got him in the ankle, got him good. He let go, his eyes registering surprise and pain. I rubbed my hand, shaking with anger. "Don't you ever touch me again."

He didn't say a word, just pressed his lips into a bitter, angry line. Massaging my hand, I started toward Whitefield's office. Echo came at me from behind. He grabbed me by the elbow and whispered in my ear, "We aren't finished yet."

I wrenched myself away. Despite my outer bravado, I was unnerved. But I was also determined. Taking a deep breath, I opened Whitefield's door and stepped across the threshold.

The tax collector's picture could've been in the dictionary next to the definition of 'fat cat.' His face was sleek and smooth, his belly round. His hair was softly waved and graying at the temples, his moustache perfectly clipped. He looked so very professional and assured, framed by a huge desk and shelves of tax tomes, the soft gray winter light filtering in through the window on either side.

He was examining legal documents, marking them with his left hand. He wore a monocle. He rose, leaned over his desk and shook my hand. His handshake was weak, the skin soft. But his eyes were hard, like black pearls. He kept his voice calm and modulated.

"The early bird, huh?" He chuckled. It was a rumble, deep inside his chest. He gestured toward the chair, "Take a seat."

But before my backside could touch the seat, he launched into his little speech. It was more or less what I'd expected.

"I expect a full retraction. That column was nothing but lies and innuendos. I want it made clear that the figure you've slandered in the present column is clear of blame in the next. Get it?"

I made myself comfortable. "Sure, I do. But I don't think you do. You see, I didn't mention you by name. If I wrote a retraction, I'd have to. Your name, your title: I'd have to put it all out there. I'd be confirming what people still only suspect. After all, a retraction's no good if no one knows whom it refers to."

His nostrils flared. "I know what you're trying to do. It won't work."

"Won't it?"

"I have friends ..."

"Yes, you do. But we both know they're the kind who fade when the dirt starts to fly."

"Your returns ..."

"Are in perfect order. And we both know it." I bluffed without blinking an eyelash. Did he actually think I'd come down here just to let myself get whipped into submission? If so, I had surprise for him.

I took out a folded sheet of paper out of my purse. The page contained three paragraphs—about as much as I could stand to copy of the letter. I'd also included the signature and underscored the name. I unfolded the page, laid it on his desk and slid it toward him.

"What's this?"

"Read it and you'll see."

Like an animal suspecting a trap, he regarded the page but wouldn't touch it. Fooled by the fact that it was my handwriting, he was shocked to recognize his own words. And recognize them he did. I could see it in his eyes. For a second there, he looked sick. Then he pulled himself together. He sat up and gave me a severe look.

"I hope you aren't trying to say that I wrote this piece of filth. It's not my penmanship and it's certainly not my signature."

I just shook my head. "Don't even try it. I have the original. Trust me, I do. And the original *is* in your handwriting."

A trip downstairs to Mrs. Cane had confirmed my suspicions about Whitefield's middle name. She'd remembered an interview from 1920, when he was first appointed as tax collector. The reporter had complimented Whitefield on being such an ardent supporter of the common man. Whitefield had told a story about his father. His father, he said, had been strong willed and determined. His father always told him that he expected him to do well and travel far, but that no matter how well he did or how far he traveled, he also expected him to remember his roots. To that end, he'd named him after the place of his birth: Antilles.

Whitefield deliberated his response. I didn't expect him to cave in, of course. People like him don't get where they are without developing skins as thick as animal hide. But I hoped that—

"You're wrong," he said. "Dead wrong. Except for that brief meeting at Mrs. Goodfellowe's house, I didn't—"

"You did and the letter proves it."

"This letter, this letter!" He balled up the page and threw it into the garbage. "It has nothing to do me. For all I know, you wrote it yourself."

"You wrote it and you signed it using your middle name. It was easy to confirm that it's your name. It'll be even easier to prove that the handwriting is yours. Some people say that men like you want to be caught. I don't believe that, but I do believe that vanity induces stupidity."

"You'd do well to remember who I am."

"Oh, I know who you are all right—and what you are. I also know that if you weren't worried, then I wouldn't be here."

He leaned back and formed a teepee with his manicured fingertips. "How much? How much for the letter and to make you forget about this whole thing?"

"A lot. A whole lot—of information."

"I won't—"

"You can't afford to refuse. Not only do I have this letter, but the will and the means to make sure that everybody reads it."

His nostrils flared. "All right, all right. But I want the letter, the original, or else—"

"I can't do that. It's not mine to give."

Understanding dawned. "I see. Ruth has it."

"Ruth? You say you never met Esther, but you know her sister's name?"

He realized his error. His voice was tight. "Fine. I had something to do with her."

"An affair—"

"Yes, but I had nothing to do with her disappearance."

"When did you first meet her?"

"Sometime that September." He let it out a ragged breath, resentment poisoning every word. "Esther was sweet, but she wasn't right for me. She was, you know...."

"What?"

He shrugged. "Talented ... but ignorant."

"And when did you decide that? Before or after?"

The look on his face just about made my day. "I really don't give a damn what you think."

"No, but your superiors do. So who ended it?"

"I did."

That didn't fit.

"When?"

"Late that October."

"How did she take it?"

"She was upset, naturally."

"*Naturally*," I repeated.

His sour expression said he didn't appreciate my sarcasm.

"So what's your alibi for the night she disappeared?" I asked.

"I don't remember what day that was."

I told him.

"I was busy," he said.

"Not good enough."

"It'll have to be."

No, no, no. "Let's get something straight. Your name, your position—they mean nothing to me. As far as I'm concerned, you're just another man who grew up twisted."

His lips curled. "I'll sue you if you ever print another word about me. I swear it."

His arrogance was infuriating—and so naïve.

"Where were you on the night Esther disappeared?"

"Here, damn it. I was probably here. Working like a damn dog."

"Probably?"

"I was *here*."

This interview was over. I got up to go, but then paused. "That was a dumb play," I said, "having your man attack me like that."

"What?"

"Why deny it?"

He stood and planted his fists on his desk. "Madam, you obviously have a very wild imagination. I don't know what you're talking about."

"Good day, Mr. Whitefield."

As I reached the door, his voice stopped me.

"Mrs. Price?"

"Yes?" Something in his tone made me stiffen.

"Forget about Hilda Coleman spying for you. I've fired her. As for that woman, that Miss Henry, I wouldn't expect her future cooperation either. I really wouldn't."

## 28.

A crowd was gathered outside of Mabel's rooming house and an ambulance was parked at the curb. I pushed my way through and ran upstairs. Mabel's landlady stood at the entrance to her room, weeping. I slipped past her and came to a halt. The room had been destroyed. Every piece of furniture had been smashed. Mabel lay amidst the ruins, bloodied, battered and eyes closed. Hilda knelt by her side as an ambulance attendant tried to administer first aide. Hilda glanced up at me, and then returned her gaze to Mabel.

"He had her beaten. Maybe a concussion, two ribs broken and three fingers snapped."

"It was Echo?"

She gave a dazed nod. "He came after me, too, but I dodged him, and then I came over here." She gently brushed Mabel's hair back from her face. "I could kill Mr. Whitefield for what he did to her. Just shoot him dead."

Mabel groaned. Her eyes were crusted with blood and swollen shut. She grimaced in pain. "Hilda?" she whispered.

Hilda took Mabel's hand, the one that wasn't injured. "I'm here, honey."

A second ambulance attendant arrived, carrying a stout wood stretcher. "How's she doing?"

"We'd better get her moved," the first attendant said.

I started to ask, "Should I—"

"Get out," Hilda said quietly. She wouldn't even look at me. "I trusted you. You said you'd protect her, but you nearly got her killed. So please, just go. Go away."

Sick with guilt, I returned to the newsroom and busied myself for an hour, but after that I couldn't stay away. I headed over to Harlem Hospital. They'd put Mabel in a room with five other women. She was awake and in pain. The facial swelling was terrible. She could barely see and it must've hurt her to breathe.

Hilda sat at Mabel's bedside, reading from the New Testament. Embarrassment and shame flitted across her face at the sight of me.

"How's she doing?" I asked.

Hilda returned her gaze to the Bible in her lap. "It'll take a while for her ribs and hand to heal, but they will. The doctors said she's got to take it easy, though, because of her head."

I drew a chair up to Mabel's bed. Hilda's eyes followed me. Eyes lowered, she spoke in a low voice.

"I'm sorry. It was wrong what I said."

"It's okay. Maybe you were right."

She looked up and a small smile crossed her face. "Aren't we the two?"

"Yeah." I gave a little laugh.

"Miss Lanie?" It was Mabel, her voice thick and words slurred.

I placed a light hand on her forearm. "I'm here."

A single tear spilled from her right eye. "Look at me. Just look what he done to me."

I took a deep breath. It was time to get to the reason for my visit. "Mabel, you should press charges."

"No."

"Yes," I said firmly. "Don't let him get away with this."

Hilda was at my side. "The police tried already. She's not gonna talk. She can't. That would be dangerous. Don't you think it would be safer if—"

"No, I don't." My gaze stayed on Mabel. "I don't think she should cower in a corner and let him go free."

Mabel's tear-filled terrified eyes moved to Hilda, asking for direction. Hilda looked at me and I looked at Hilda.

"You talking about charges against Mr. Echo or Mr. Whitefield?"

"Both."

Hilda thought about it. Then she licked her lips. "Mabel, Miss Lanie's right. Maybe, it's time you took a stand. Otherwise, he'll just come back and maybe do it again."

"But—"

"If you press charges," I said, "I'll be able to write about it in the paper. And once that happens, they won't be able to hide anymore." I gripped the metal rail of her bed. "I won't lie to you, Mabel. You'd still be in danger, but Whitefield would think twice before messing with you—not with the whole world watching."

Mabel's swollen eyes stayed on Hilda, and Hilda told her to go ahead and do it. "Press charges, honey. I'll be right beside you. I'll tell him that he went after me, too. Only I was lucky and saw him coming."

More tears squeezed from between Mabel's crusted eyelids and slid down her face. She gave a painful nod and the glimmers of a brave smile lit her bruised face.

## 29.

I phoned the station house from the hospital and spoke to a detective named Blackie. He and I knew each other from way back, when I was covering the crime beat. I explained what was up and he said he himself would come by to take Mabel's statement.

Then I phoned Sam. He knew about Mabel and Echo and the beating—I'd told him earlier. Now, I gave him an update.

"You know what you're doing, Lanie?"

"Yup. Using a mouse to whip an elephant."

Next I phoned Whitefield. "You went too far," I said. "The mouse has learned to roar."

"What are you talking about?"

"Mabel Dean. She'll be pressing charges. A detective's on his way to talk to her right now."

"About what?"

"About you and your lieutenant, and how you had him beat her to keep her quiet. My paper will be running the story: the charges, his arrest and who he works for."

An angry silence, then a stubborn denial: "I certainly had no knowledge of his alleged activities."

"That's not good enough."

"You're a perfect example of why the Negro race is where it is today: jealousy, envy, the need to destroy our own. I have fought people like you all my life. All you want to do is find a good man and take him down."

"Save it."

He was furious, but stuck and he knew it. He couldn't afford any more bad publicity.

"All right," he sighed. "What do you want?"

"A meeting, in one hour."

## *30.*

The chatter and hubbub of the newsroom quieted when Whitefield and Canfield walked in. From the fishbowl of Sam's office, I couldn't hear the sudden drop in volume, but I could sense it. That clamor and the vibrations it produced paused noticeably when two of the most influential colored men in America strode across the floor.

I glanced at Sam. "You ready?"

"Like a pie coming out of grandma's oven."

I repressed a smile and made a mental note of Sam's habit of referring to his grandmother. I'd have to ask him about her one day.

Whitefield had called Canfield as soon as he got off the phone with me and Canfield had called Sam.

"We want this vendetta stopped," Canfield had said.

Sam told me he ended the phone call quickly. It was an attempt to bargain behind my back and he wasn't about to do that. He told Canfield that the meeting was set and any negotiating to be done would have to be done there.

Meanwhile, Blackie had called me. "No charges against Whitefield, at least not yet. The charge will be against Echo and it'll be attempted murder. That'll give us some room to negotiate. That's if we ever catch him."

"You mean he's on the lam?"

"Some little birdie put a whistle in his ear and he took off."

I felt guilty about that. As usual, I'd been in too much in a hurry. It should've occurred to me that Whitefield would warn Echo.

"The thing is, Lanie, we don't have the manpower to search for him."

"Don't worry. I'll dig something up."

Our visitors entered Sam's office, Canfield in the lead.

"Mr. Canfield, Mr. Whitefield," I said. "Glad to see you."

"I assure you, it isn't mutual," Whitefield said.

"Now, now, fellows," Sam scolded. "Let's be civilized, or pretend to be." He gestured toward the coat rack. "Make yourselves comfortable and take a seat."

As he hung up his coat, Whitefield looked around with barely concealed contempt.

"It's chilly in here," he complained, taking a seat.

"Would you like some coffee to warm you up?" I asked.

"We're not here for idle chitchat," Canfield said.

"I'm not offering you any."

Canfield gave me his most intimidating glare; it had about as much effect as a feather against stone. We all knew why they were there, and that it was nothing for him to be proud of.

"We need to settle this. Now." Canfield looked to Sam and spoke about me as if I weren't there. "Will she stop the vendetta against Whitefield if he proves his innocence concerning Esther Todd?"

"Prove it and we'll see."

What Canfield didn't know, but should have anticipated, is that Sam and I had had our own short, but thorough pow-wow. He and I agreed: I would run the show. He would step in only if necessary. I addressed the tax collector.

"Got your accountants busy at work, Mr. Whitefield, trying to create a problem with my returns?"

"We don't 'create' problems."

"That's good to know. 'Cause I'm sure certain people would be very interested in a news story about a certain tax collector who uses his office to intimidate his enemies."

Whitefield and I dead-eyed each other for two long seconds. Then he grunted and looked away. With that point made, it was time to get down to the nitty-gritty.

"So are you proud of your henchman's work?" I asked.

Whitefield's visage hardened with resentment. His eyes flicked to Canfield, who remained stony-faced.

"It's very unfortunate, what happened to Miss Dean," Whitefield said. "I will offer her a formal apology, on behalf of Mr. Echo."

"That's a start."

"Mr. Echo can no longer work for me. That is clear. And I'll make sure he never works again in any other government office."

"How thorough of you."

His face tightened. He started to respond, but Canfield stepped in.

"You demanded our presence here. Why?"

Wonderful. Not only had Canfield acknowledged me, but he was actually asking what I wanted.

"My demands are modest. I want clear answers about Esther Todd: where you were when she disappeared, you *and* your lieutenant. I also want information on Mr. Echo's whereabouts right now."

"I don't know—"

"Sure you do. If you don't, find out. I want you to pay Mabel Dean's hospital bills, get her a nice little apartment, pay two years rent in advance, and give her at least five thousand dollars in cash. And last, but not least, I want you people to stop messing with my tax returns."

Whitefield shook his head. "What you're asking for, the public, even my superiors, could misconstrue as an admission of guilt."

"Well, misconstrue this." I said. "We're the least of your troubles. As soon as this story hits the stands, reporters will be camping outside your door. You'll have a beehive after you. And it won't be just the colored press either. When a man of your standing takes a fall, even the *New York Times* comes a'calling. So don't think about me. Think about *that*. About losing your job, your career, your reputation."

A heavy silence followed. Whitefield's eyes moved from me to Sam, and then took in the office, like he was already fitting himself for a prison cell. His eyes were certainly those of a man trapped, but they also reflected a determination to find a way out.

"If I comply with your demands, then I want that letter back. You know which one I'm talking about. And I demand that your paper print a clarification attesting to my innocence. You will state clearly that I had nothing to do with the Todd woman's disappearance. And your article on the charges against Mr. Echo will make it clear that I had nothing to do with Miss Dean's injuries. I want it out there. Stated flatly."

"Mr. Whitefield," Sam said. "You have to understand something. That clarification, as you call it, might simply fan the flames. Now, that your assistant is being charged with attempted murder—"

"*Murder?*" Whitefield looked genuinely shocked. So did Canfield.

"Yes," Sam said. "So imagine how it'll appear. In one column we'll have your assistant accused of having tried to murder one of your former lovers after she spoke unfavorably about you. In the next, we'll have you denying any involvement in the attack on her and the mysterious disappearance of another woman, also one of your lovers. Many a reader might wonder—unless you're going to blame Echo for the Todd woman, too. Otherwise, that so-called clarification, Mr. Whitefield, might do you more harm than good."

Whitefield exchanged troubled glances with Canfield. Several seconds passed.

Canfield answered. "We want the clarification, anyway. We can't let that kind of implied accusation stand."

"We agree to print your comments," Sam said. "We will not print a conclusion of innocence or guilt." He waited for both men to indicate that they understood. When they nodded, he continued. "You have to understand that this won't fully wash away the stink—"

"No," Canfield said, "But Mrs. Price's *suggestion*," he placed a faint emphasis on his substitution of the word 'suggestion' for 'demand,' "that we help Miss Dean might actually take care of that."

"But—" Whitefield objected.

"Don't worry, Sexton. We'll bury anyone who questions your motives."

At this flash of open viciousness, Sam just shook his head.

"All right," Whitefield said testily. "I don't like it, Byron, but if you say it's okay, then I'll go along."

"So, it's agreed," Canfield told Sam. "Your paper will print a clarification. We expect it to appear in a special edition. We can't afford to wait for the regular issue."

Sam and I concurred.

"But first," I said, "The information regarding Esther. And then the arrangements for Mabel."

Whitefield glanced at Canfield. Apparently they'd agreed that Canfield would speak for him on this matter.

Canfield regarded me with open contempt. "Whitefield couldn't have been the one who kidnapped Esther Todd."

"You know where he was that night, don't you?"

"You'll have to leave the room."

Sam's anger was instant but controlled: "Get this straight: This is my office, my newsroom. I determine who goes and who stays."

"She's dangerous," Canfield insisted.

"She's not leaving."

Canfield didn't like it, but Sam wasn't about to budge.

"All right." Canfield's gaze took in both of us. "But you two have to give us your word that nothing we tell you will leave this room."

Sam and I glanced at one another. He nodded. "Done."

The story Canfield told was brief. What it boiled down to was this: On the night of Esther's disappearance, the esteemed Whitefield was in jail in Brooklyn on a drunk and disorderly. He'd been in a bar, out with a white woman. Somebody said the wrong thing and Whitefield reacted. He called Canfield to help him out. Canfield managed to keep the story under wraps.

Whitefield stayed quiet, allowing Canfield to speak for him. After hearing this story, I remained skeptical. I glanced at Whitefield.

"Suppose you had Mr. Echo kidnap Esther for you?"

"I wouldn't have done such a thing. Furthermore, he wasn't working for me back then."

"Then you could've had someone else do it."

Canfield sighed impatiently. "C'mon, Mrs. Price. That kind of thinking gets us nowhere. No matter what he says, you could always raise that objection."

I had to admit he was right. "Fine. But remember: The clarification will state simply that you were elsewhere when Esther Todd disappeared. It will not be a statement of innocence. It'll be what it is, nothing more, nothing less."

Whitefield's nostrils flared, but he pressed his lips together. Canfield reiterated that the clarification would run alongside the report on Echo and that the article on Echo would contain Whitefield's reaction—including the announcement of Echo's immediate dismissal.

"Now," I said. "What about Mr. Echo's whereabouts?"

Whitefield phoned Blackie from our office. The conversation was short and succinct. Sam sent for Rose, our newsroom secretary, to take a dictation by Canfield. The attorney composed a simple agreement outlining the settlement: in exchange for consideration, Mabel Dean Henry would drop all claims or charges against Sexton A. Whitefield, who in entering into this agreement admitted no guilt or responsibility for her injuries. By the time the agreement was typed and ready, Whitefield had phoned a real estate agent and instructed him to find a one-bedroom apartment for Mabel. Whitefield signed the agreement and wrote three checks: to cover the agent's fee, two years' rent and monetary compensation.

Handing the contract and checks over to Sam, Whitefield said. "Now, my side of the deal is done. I expect you to do yours."

"Don't worry," Sam said. "We will."

Sam's phone rang. He picked it up. Most of the conversation took place on the other end. He nodded once and hung up. He looked at Whitefield.

"That was Blackie. They got him."

Soon afterward, Whitefield and Canfield left. By then most of the newsroom had cleared out. I returned to my desk, wrote up the two articles, and brought them to Sam, pacing back and forth as he proofed them. He looked up at me.

"You feel good about this?"

"No."

"You still think he had something to do with Esther's disappearance?"

"I don't know. I suppose not. Otherwise, I wouldn't have agreed to this so-called 'clarification.'" I flopped down in the chair.

Sam frowned. "What's bothering you? Is there something you're not telling me?"

Sure there was. My thoughts kept returning to the night I'd been assaulted in my own home. I couldn't get the attacker's words out of my head: *If it was up to me, I'd do you right here, right now and get it over with, but Mr. Whitefield wants to give you a second chance.*

Those words bothered me. If only I could figure out why. I wanted to discuss it with Sam. But I was afraid to because I hadn't told him about the attack to begin with. He'd be furious if I did now.

I forced a bleak smile. "I'm just worried that we're back to square one. If Whitefield didn't take Esther, and he didn't have Echo do it, then who did?"

## 31.

That evening, I attended a Christmas concert by Paul Robeson to benefit the Negro Orphan League. The event at the Harlem Symphony was crowded but not packed. And the attendees were certainly 'select.' They included Langston Hughes, as well as Mrs. Eugene O'Neil and her sisters. Of course, my recollection would be lacking if it failed to mention one other attendee: Selena Troy. In the lobby after the show, we spoke or, rather, she spoke to me.

"You're a smart one, Lanie. I have to hand it to you. You have these dicties eating out of your hand."

"You're not doing so bad yourself."

"Oh, I'm not in your league—not yet. I've got to admit you're pulling a slick one with this Esther Todd business. Handle it right and the sky's the limit."

I inclined my head. "I don't follow you."

"Get off your high horse. You don't care about the case any more than I do. It's the story you're after, the Big One that every reporter dreams about."

"Selena—"

"C'mon, I know what you see when you close your eyes at night. Headlines: 'Negro Reporter Breaks Case that Stymied Police,' 'Lanie Price Solves Historic Heist.'"

"You're—"

"You see the *Times* coming to your door. You see yourself at the *Nation* maybe, or the *Courier*. You see yourself at a real paper, not this rag."

"You're wrong, Selena. All wrong."

"Well, if I am, then you're a fool. Nobody sticks their neck out for someone they didn't know. Not unless there's something in it for them. Maybe I'm wrong about the job, but I'm right about everything else. You're in it for yourself, Lanie Price. And you'd be better off admitting it."

She flounced off. Within a few minutes, she was talking to Louis Squire, the conductor. I just looked after her and shook my head. Where was the humanity? I wondered.

Everyone headed for the Sugar Cane Club. The folks had a rousing good time there, but it was simply the first stop in a party that went until nine o'clock in the morning, when Mrs. O'Neil invited us all to breakfast at Eddie's.

The winter sun was peaking over the horizon when I got home. I kicked off my shoes and fell into bed, fully dressed. When I woke up hours later, I had a mouth full of nasty cotton and an evil pounding in my head. I rubbed my temples, annoyed with myself—and even more annoyed at the politicians who'd pushed for Prohibition. That law hadn't done a damn thing about stopping the flow of liquor. It just made criminals out of ordinary citizens. You were either a bootlegger making cheap liquor or a sucker drinking it.

I made a pot of hot chocolate with a dash of mint, Hamp's recipe for a hangover. Then I ran a hot bath and sweated it out. Another hour or so was spent working on my face and hair, repairing the damage.

At around one o'clock I dragged myself to the newsroom. Along the way, I paused at a newsstand to take a quick look at the special edition of the *Chronicle*. The two pieces were there, just as promised, right above the fold. It was strange seeing them, strange seeing my name attached to anything but fluff. Strange, but nice.

I should've phoned Ruth, warned her. She would be calling the paper, seeking an explanation. It would've been smart to phone Hilda and Mabel, too. Ruth needed assurance and Mabel would be happy to hear about the money.

I resolved to make those phone calls immediately, but the minute I walked in, George Greene dashed over.

His news gave the Todd case a whole new spin.

Reporters were camped out in front of 250 West 57th Street. Uniformed cops had set up barriers to keep the area in front of the building free. A wagon from the medical examiner's office was parked at the curb, along with several police cars. It took a while, but I convinced one of the cops to call upstairs to Whitefield's office. The cop escorted me to the elevator and then returned to his post at the front door.

Upstairs, office workers buzzed about the outer office door, with one guard holding them back. He let me in, but the guard just outside Whitefield's door needed extra convincing. I was fussing at him when the door behind him opened and the words died on my lips.

Whitefield's office was lousy with people—uniformed cops, a photographer, a medical examiner and a plainclothes detective. A flash bulb threw the whole group into a merciless bright light. Everything was black and white and shades of gray, with a frozen tableau of men dancing around a dead guy in a three-piece suit.

Whitefield sat upright in that huge chair of his, his head slumped to the left, his eyes open. His left arm hung over the armrest; his right rested in his lap. Blood spattered the right side of his face. It had run down from his nostrils and dripped into his open mouth. Blood had also soaked the left side of his collar. The ME, a bony man named Cory, was examining him.

I started forward. The cop put a restraining hand on my elbow.

"Let her in," a voice called.

The patrolman glanced over his shoulder, saw who'd given the order and stepped aside.

Blackie had caught the case. He was an all-right guy in his mid-forties, with thick, beetle black eyebrows and muddy brown eyes. He stood next to Whitefield's desk, smoking a thin cigar. Blackie had a weakness for expensive smokes. He nodded at Whitefield.

"Not a pretty sight, but I've seen worse."

Whitefield's right eye was swollen and bruised, but that wasn't the worst of it. A bullet had opened up his right ear. The edges of the wound were star-shaped and blackened. The fingers in his lap were loosely curled around the handle of a Colt .45.

Cory lifted Whitefield's head. "Entrance through right ear, exit through lower left jaw."

I started to ask a question, but Blackie laid a light hand on my forearm, looked past me and spoke to Cory, who was busy scribbling on a form.

"So doc, how long's he been dead?"

Cory answered without looking up. "At least twelve hours."

"So you'd say around midnight?"

"Thereabouts."

"Suicide?"

"I'd say so. Gunpowder traces on his hand."

Blackie turned to me. "Seems like your column did the trick. You should be proud of yourself."

I'd never been accused of driving a man to suicide before. Blackie made it sound like a compliment.

"Would you be?"

He shrugged. "Maybe. Maybe not."

A fly darted around Whitefield's open mouth. Where'd a fly come from in the middle of winter?

"You talk to him yesterday?" Blackie asked.

"Around three."

"How was he?"

"As you'd expect. Angry."

"You're lucky he didn't shoot you, instead of shooting himself."

The fly crawled inside Whitefield's mouth. I wondered, idiotically, if it would get stuck in there, in the thickened blood. I turned away, having seen enough.

"Lanie, you don't need to be here."

"No, that's okay. I ... I wanted to ask—was there a note?"

Blackie nodded. "He mentioned your column." He watched me to see how I took that bit of news. "You ain't got nothing to feel bad about."

"Who says I feel bad?"

"Aw nuts, Lanie. We go back a long way. I remember how you were when the Todd case first broke. You sank your teeth into it and you were never gonna let go. Then that thing happened with your mother and, well ... I know what the case means to you. I talked to Bellamy and I know that—" He caught himself.

"Know what?"

His mouth turned hard. "I know that without your column, this guy would've walked. I remember when Bellamy and Ritchie had their little talk with him."

Shocked, I said, "When they what?"

"I wasn't in on it, just heard about it. They found about his connection to the Todd girl, came down here and had a little chat. Everything was on the QT, given who he was and all." At my expression, he said, "Didn't you know?"

"I had no idea." I'd asked Bellamy, asked him directly about the tax collector, and he'd lied to me. Why?

"So what happened?" I asked Blackie.

"Whitefield buttoned up tight. Wouldn't say a word about the night Todd disappeared."

"So you guys never knew if he had a legitimate alibi?"

"Nope."

My gaze went back to the gun. "The Colt. It's definitely his?"

"Don't know yet."

"Who found him?"

"The secretary in the next office over. About an hour ago. She dropped by to chat with Whitefield's secretary, but she wasn't here. So the girl knocked on his office door. It swung open and she found him."

I'd forgotten about Hilda. *I could kill him,* she'd said. *Just shoot him dead.* Had she done just that? I wanted to believe that she was at home, checking the job ads—or at the hospital, watching over Mabel.

"You've met her?" Blackie asked.

"Who?"

"The secretary?"

"Oh, yeah."

Blackie read something in my eyes. "Look Lanie, this was definitely a suicide and, despite what Whitefield told you, he was definitely guilty."

Something in his tone said he wasn't operating on general suspicion.

"What do you mean?"

He reached into a pocket and pulled out a folded handkerchief. He laid it in his palm and opened it. I suspected what he was about to show me.

"We found this with the note."

Esther's long-lost earring: It lay sparkling in his hand.

## 32.

I stopped at a payphone and started to call Hilda, but then decided against it. If she had anything to do with Whitefield's death, then I was doing the investigation a disservice by warning her. The news about Whitefield's reparations toward Mabel would have to wait.

I made another call, one that wouldn't hinder Blackie's inquiry—and was definitely necessary for mine.

"Blackie already called," Bellamy said. "I got to say, you did a mighty fine job."

"Think so?"

"Don't you?"

"Why'd you tell me you'd never heard of him? Why did you lie like that?"

Bellamy was quiet. Ragtime played softly in the background. "Look, we tried. We watched him. Tailed him. But we just couldn't chase him down."

"So you figured fresh pressure would—"

"It was a win-win situation. If Whitefield was the perp, then he got exposed. If he wasn't then ..."

"Then what?"

Now, my stomach wasn't just uneasy. It was churning.

"Then he made good bait. The letter writer, remember? He said she was cheating on him. Maybe Whitefield was the guy this creep thought she was cheating with. So even if we were wrong about Whitefield, we could be right about the writer. He's still out there. And this column of yours could draw him out. But we weren't wrong about Whitefield, were we?"

I hung up, feeling ill. Maybe Bellamy honestly thought he was making me feel better. But he'd made me feel worse. I'd set up Whitefield as a target. The only good thing about that notion was that it offered an alternative to the idea that Hilda Coleman shot him. Either way, Whitefield was dead and my column had set in motion the forces that killed him.

I went to see Ruth. She already knew. Had heard the news on the radio. Guilt washed over me at the look on her face. She took me into the kitchen, away from Job. Her hands balled into fists around her handkerchief. Her face was tear-stained, her voice bitter.

"Ruth, I'm sorry."

"I begged you. Begged you! Go to the police, I said. They could've arrested him. Made him tell what he did with Esther. Now we'll never know. There's no way we ever gonna find out."

"I didn't—"

"I asked you to help. But you just made things worse. I have to see Mama at the hospital. I don't think I can tell her. And you, you stay away from her. Stay away from us both."

I returned to the newsroom. Sam waved me into his office. He was eating a sandwich. The smell said tuna. He chewed rapidly and swallowed.

"Thank goodness we formulated that so-called 'clarification' as carefully as we did. He nearly hoodwinked us."

"I'm not so sure."

About to take another bite, he stopped. "Sure about what?"

"His guilt."

He looked as though he didn't believe his ears. "But the note. The earring."

"They were planted."

He put the sandwich down and wiped his hands on a napkin. Folding his arms across his chest, he gave me his full attention. "Talk to me."

My throat was tight and I felt faintly nauseous.

"Lanie, what is it?"

Choosing my words, I began. "The night I wrote the column, I was attacked."

"You were what?"

I explained.

His face grew paler with every word. "I can't believe this. That son-of-a-bi—Why didn't you tell me? Why'd you keep it to yourself?"

"Is it important? Do we have to discuss it right now?"

"Yes."

"My not telling you has nothing to do with Whitefield."

"It has everything to do with you going it alone. You could've been killed."

"Sam—" I raised a hand. "Please, listen. The man who attacked me, I thought he was Echo. I mean, he actually said that he wanted to kill me, but that Whitefield wanted me to have a second chance. So I thought Whitefield had sent him. But then, I started to wonder. And now I don't think it was Echo at all."

"Why not?"

"It was the way he spoke. Echo has this odd habit. He refers to himself in the third person. This guy didn't."

"That's it?"

"No. The attacker was right-handed. He had me face down, so I couldn't see him. But when he put the knife to my throat, it was to the right side." I brushed my fingertips over the spot. "And I'm pretty sure Echo's a lefty." I paused. "And their build was different. Everything ... was different."

As the meaning sunk in, his expression changed. It went from hot anger to cold calculation, and caution. "You sure about this?"

"Yes."

"There's no way it could've been the same guy?"

"I don't think so. No."

Sam drew a deep breath and let it out slowly. "I should've never let you go after this." A muscle in his jaw worked. I'd never seen him so angry. From the street outside came the sound of a fire engine screaming as it sped to the rescue. Sam cleared his throat. "Is there more?"

"The gun was in Whitefield's right hand."

"Are you telling me he's a lefty, too?"

"I saw him marking up documents. He was using his left hand."

Doubt flickered in his eyes. "Maybe he was ambidextrous."

"Maybe. But I saw his body, Sam. I saw the way he was holding that gun. It was all wrong. I've seen suicides before. Their hands sort of freeze, real tight around the handle. His fingers were curled around it. Just like someone had placed them there. And then there was the way he was shot. The bullet went in through his ear and traveled down and came out the other side of his jaw. He would've had to hold his arm up at some weird angle to shoot himself like that. I've been trying to imagine it and … well, it just doesn't sit right."

Mentally, I was back in Whitefield's office. "Somebody shot him, Sam. They stood on his right side, slightly behind him, and pulled the trigger."

Sam licked his lips.

I took a deep breath. A sick knot of anxiety was making it hard for me to breathe. "I got a man killed today."

"Lanie, don't—"

"Do you honestly think Whitefield would kill himself after going through everything we put him through yesterday?"

"I don't know. Maybe."

I slid forward on the chair. "Whitefield was shot last night. Whoever did it didn't know about the articles coming out. They didn't know that he'd decided to fight rather than fold."

I told Sam about Bellamy's theory, and he got angry all over again.

"So Bellamy used you. He used this paper. Shit." He muttered under his breath. Then he looked at me. "This guy who sent Esther the letters … you think he's the one who attacked you?"

"It makes sense."

Sam pushed the sandwich away, leaned on the desk and wiped his face with his hands. "But why would the letter writer kill Whitefield? After all these years, why now?"

"Because he's still jealous. He didn't know the identity of Esther's lover, but when my column came out, he did."

"So you're telling me we painted a bull's-eye on Whitefield's forehead."

"Not you," I said quietly. "Me."

A pause, and then: "Have you told the police any of this?"

Before I could answer, Sam's office door opened and Canfield barged in, carrying a copy of the paper. He slammed the door behind him. His face was ashen. His eyes flashed with anger.

"So, are you two satisfied?"

"Please sit down," Sam said.

"I don't want to sit down," Canfield snapped. "I want to make you understand what you've done. Who cares if he had troubles with women? The fact is, he did more good for our community than you two combined. Do you know how many men can feed their families because Sexton Whitefield got them jobs, made a phone call? Do you even care?"

"Mr. Canfield," Sam started.

"You're to blame," he told Sam. "You could've stopped this whole business, stopped it before it got started. Now look what's happened."

He held up the newspaper. "As for this—this clarification you promised us—not only was it too late, too little. It's the worst piece of muckraking I've ever seen."

Sam stiffened. "We wrote it straight."

"The hell you did. It leaves more questions than answers."

"I warned you. I told you how it would look."

Canfield twisted his lips into a bitter line. "You lied is what you did. You tricked him."

"He tricked himself. He knew the risks. You both did."

Canfield yanked the door open. He paused on the threshold. "You'll answer for this, the both of you. I'll make sure of it." He flung the newspaper on the floor and marched out.

In the abrupt silence that followed, I shut the door and leaned on it. "He's right, you know. To some degree." I looked at Sam. "We need to go see Blackie."

He nodded. "I'm going with you."

Over at the station, I told Blackie what I'd told Sam, that I didn't think Whitefield's death was a suicide and why.

"But Cory found evidence on Whitefield's hands that he shot himself," the detective said.

"Did Cory find any other injury?" Sam asked. "A bruise maybe to indicate that he was knocked out?"

"He had a swelling around his eye," I said.

"You mean someone could've put the gun in his hands," Blackie said.

"And then pulled the trigger," Sam said.

Blackie reached for the phone. In a few seconds, he had the ME on the line. The conversation was short. When Blackie hung up, his expression was grim.

"Cory says there was a bruise, a swelling actually, but it was near the wound: too close for him to say it wasn't caused by the shot. As for the angle of trajectory, he says it's consistent with a self-inflected wound. So he's sticking by his decision. Officially, it's a suicide."

And unofficially, I was to blame.

## 33.

The next day, Canfield had the Movement declare me persona non-gratis. By then, word had gotten out that in his supposed suicide note, Whitefield not only confessed to having kidnapped and killed Esther, but accused me of having hounded him to death. Many people applauded my having 'uncovered him and his crime,' but many more maintained that he was innocent and had been framed. The great irony was that I agreed with them.

Whitefield's supporters turned on me with a fury. Many of the invitations on my desk were withdrawn. Angry calls came in—some from Whitefield's fans, the rest from people who wanted it known that they disliked the press in general and now me in particular. At some point, I told the operator to stop putting calls through. She could take messages and I'd phone people back. But most of the messages weren't worth taking and most callers didn't leave numbers. There was one caller who was different. I got the message and called right back.

"Hello Hilda," I said. "How are you?

"I'm fine. I—"

"And Mabel?"

"She's getting better. They let her out this morning, and now she's staying with me. Listen, I just wanted thank you. Thank you for destroying that man."

I didn't say what I wanted to say. I told her about the arrangements Whitefield had made for Mabel. I gave her the name and phone number of Phil Payton, the real estate agent he'd contacted, and told her to stop by to pick up the contract. She had to return it with Mabel's signature before we could give them the checks. She was thrilled. She couldn't stop thanking the paper and me. Then I asked her the question that had been hovering at the back of my mind.

"Where were you the night Whitefield was killed?"

There was a stunned silence. When she answered, all the warmth in her voice had cooled.

"I told the police and now I'm telling you: I was at the hospital, with Mabel. I wish I'd had the nerve to kill him. Then I wouldn't have had to wait for somebody like you to come along."

"It's just that, the other day, when Mabel was beaten, you said—"

"I said what I wanted to do. That doesn't mean I did it. Anyway, why are you asking? It was a suicide." She didn't wait for an answer. "You sure know how to ruin things. I'm sorry I called." She hung up.

Hating myself, I telephoned the nurse's station at Harlem Hospital and lucked up. One of the late shift nurses had come in early. She confirmed that, Yes, Miss Coleman had been there, all that night. She had slept in a chair by Miss Dean's bedside.

As I replaced the receiver, it occurred to me that Hilda still could've done it: Unaware that Whitefield had given up Echo and made reparations to Mabel, she could've snuck out and shot him, but to be honest, I didn't think so.

The phone jangled under my hand. I was surprised and annoyed. After all, I'd told the operator to take messages. I started not to answer, but was glad I did. It was Mabel.

"Hi," I said, surprised. "I'm so glad to hear from you. How're you feeling?"

"I'm fine. Just got a little pain is all. But I had to call and thank you. Hilda just told me what you and the paper did for me. God bless you."

"Thank you."

"I can't believe it. I'll have my own place! And Miss Lanie? Hilda told me what you asked her. She was angry and I told her to stop being silly. Look at all you've done for me. And you don't really believe she shot Sexton, do you?"

"No," I said, feeling guilty about the call to the nurse's station.

"See, Hilda," she said, turning away from the phone and speaking to her friend in the background. "Miss Lanie's just doing her job is all. She's a smart lady and smart people ask questions."

She spoke into the phone again. "Miss Lanie, I know you having a hard time. But don't you pay people no mind. They can be so ignorant. I know Miss Ruth is angry, real angry. But whatever she said, she didn't mean it. And well ... I just wanted to thank you, and to say I know you didn't do no wrong. Sexton was no good. Whatever you did, you didn't do nothing wrong."

## 34.

As I hung up, a shadow fell across my desk. It was Selena.

"Oh, Lanie," she cooed. "This is terrible."

"Don't worry, I'll survive."

"Of course you will. But what about your column?"

"Excuse me?"

"Well, really, it's clear, isn't it? What you should do—for the sake of the paper?"

I have to admit my tongue failed me. Hours later, in hindsight, I thought of a million things I could've, should've, said. But at the moment, nothing occurred to me.

"Don't worry," she said. "It doesn't matter if you don't have the guts to make the right decision. Someone else already has."

She pointed to the glass fishtank of Sam's office. He was on the telephone, listening tensely. He started to argue, apparently got cut off and gritted his teeth. The speaker must've paused because Sam jumped in, his hand movements emphatic.

"That's George Ramsey on the line. He's ripping Sam a new one. It doesn't take much to figure out why, does it?"

Her enjoyment of Sam's predicament surprised me even more than her vulgarity. But then I realized it shouldn't have.

Sam's conversation ended. He dropped the receiver onto the phone cradle and let his hand rest on it. His other hand balled into a fist. He looked up through the glass walls and his gaze locked onto mine.

"Uh-oh," Selena said. "I guess your time has come."

I nearly told her that if she didn't get away from me, hers would, too. Instead, I mentally shoved her aside and walked past the desks to Sam's office. He stood when I entered and ran a nervous hand over his head.

"Was that who I think it was?" I asked, closing the door.

He gestured for me to sit down. I didn't want to, but he said please, so I did.

"Lanie, I've asked you this before. You did answer me, but I feel I have to ask it once more."

I waited. When he hesitated, I prompted him. "Well, what is it?"

"Are you happy here? Are you happy in your job and happy at this paper?"

It wasn't what I expected. "Ramsey told you to ask me that?"

"No, he thinks he knows the answer. It's me who's asking."

I nodded. "I see. Does it matter what I say?"

"Yes, it does."

I believed him. Still I was wary. "I don't like games, Sam. If Ramsey gave you a message for me, then please just deliver it."

"It's no game. And I'm no messenger boy."

"I'm sorry. I didn't mean it that way."

He tapped his pen on his desk. "I'm going to have to suggest that you take some time off to rethink your affiliation with the paper."

"Is that a pretty way of asking me to quit?"

"It's a way of asking you to think."

His words hurt.

"You know, I didn't expect much from Ramsey, but from you I ... I thought—"

"I did my best. But Canfield's pulling some mighty strings. Ramsey wanted me to fire you. He wanted your scalp and he wanted it now. And I'm on his shit list for having run the initial column to begin with. You wrote it, but the decision to print it was mine. So he thought about getting rid of both of us."

"What stopped him?"

Sam shook his head. "I don't know. But I did tell him he'd regret it if he made a quick decision. Finally, he agreed to you just taking time off."

"So I'm suspended?"

"Don't think of it that way."

"And I could still be fired?"

"We both could be. At any time. But what I want you to think about is whether you really want this job to begin with. Seems to me, you want to do something else entirely."

"I'm quite hap—"

He held a hand up. "Let's not discuss it now. Take the time. You need it."

"All right then. I'll go immediately." I stood to go.

"Don't leave angry."

"I have a right to be angry, Sam. But not at you."

"Lanie—"

He spoke to my back. I was already on my way out.

## 35.

The phone on my desk *brrng-brnnggged* as I walked past it. I ignored it and headed for the door. George Greene ran after me.

"Lanie, you should get that."

"Why?" I said, not slowing down.

"It's probably Blackie. He's been calling for the past five minutes. Says it's urgent."

That stopped me. "Did he say what it was about?"

"Nah. Just for you to please call him back."

With an irritated sigh, I went back to my desk, snatched up the phone and called the station house. I was put through to Blackie immediately.

"Ah, Lanie. I'm glad I got you." He had a thick brogue when he was upset, and it was thick now. "They've gone and let the devil out of the dog house."

His meaning took a moment to register.

"You mean Echo?"

"Aye, He's free."

I sank down in my chair and pressed the phone to my face. "How did that happen?"

"It was Mabel Dean. She dropped the charges."

He kept on talking, but I'd stopped listening. Why would Mabel lose her nerve? Why now, when Whitefield was dead and Echo had been jailed? And why didn't she tell me?

"It happened about an hour ago," Blackie was saying. "I just came in and found out, or I would've phoned sooner."

"That's all right. I …" My voice trailed away. I didn't know what to say.

Blackie cursed under his breath. "A mess it is, a royal mess. What are we going to do? I'm afraid he'll come after you." His use of the word 'we' touched me.

"*We* are not going to do anything. *I'm* just going to go on with my … my life." I'd started to say 'my job.'

"You can't just continue as though nothing's happened. The guy's out there."

"I know. And I'll be careful. Don't worry. I'll be fine."

I think I hung up on him. He was in the middle of saying something, warning me again, when I put the receiver down, just simply put it down. *You should've known*, my little inner voice said. *You've should've expected this.*

In a daze, I called Hilda's phone number. Mabel answered.

I didn't even bother to identify myself. I just said, "Why?"

"You've heard," she said, her voice full of guilt.

"You and I, we were just talking. Why didn't you tell me?"

"I couldn't." Silence. "Miss Lanie, I'm so ashamed."

I closed my eyes and leaned on the desk. "He got to you. How?"

"It wasn't just him. It was all of them. I couldn't take it any more."

She'd been getting death threats, she said. Terrifying letters sent to the hospital, anonymous phones calls from Whitefield's supporters. Some newspaper report had carried her name and somebody in Hilda's house had recognized her and told other people. Now it was horrible, terrible.

"These people are crazy. What they're saying and writing. You can't imagine."

Oh, but I could. Hadn't I been getting the same treatment? I should've known that she would be in for it, too. "It's okay, Mabel. I understand."

"I didn't want to, Miss Lanie, but—"

"No, it's okay." I paused. "I take it you're not scared he'll come after you?"

"Well … yes, I am. But he only went after me that one time, and he did it 'cause Sexton told him to. Without Sexton, I don't think he'll bother, especially now, with the newspaper report and everything."

She was probably right. She was safe—as safe as anyone could be under the circumstances.

I thought about my house. I'd overcome memories of the attack to again feel good there, and seconds ago, I'd been looking forward to returning home. Almost out of a job, that house was the only refuge I had left. But now, once again, fear surged at the very thought of entering it.

Would he be waiting for me?

## 36.

I didn't tell Sam about Blackie's phone call. I did phone a locksmith, though, and I called Blackie back to ask him to meet me at my front door. Inside the house, the telephone was ringing when I arrived. It had taken on a very shrill, insistent tone—one that I'd come to associate with shrill, insistent reporters. It was ironic to have become the prey of my own species. I ignored it.

Blackie went through the house with me, both to make sure Echo wasn't lurking somewhere and to offer suggestions as to where to add locks or bolt doors. Before leaving, Blackie talked to the locksmith, and then stepped back inside to talk to me.

"It's going to be all right. The guy knows what he's doing. He'll set you up real nice."

"Thanks, Blackie."

"I wish I could do more."

"You've done enough."

I saw him out. For a few minutes, I watched the locksmith at work, and then I returned to the living room. Exhausted, I sank down on the sofa, kicked off my shoes, leaned back and closed my eyes. I was exhausted, but too tense to relax. I sat up again and rubbed my eyes. When the phone rang, I picked it up without thinking.

"Mrs. Price," the silky voice said. "Mr. Echo knows the truth. You killed him. You made him betray his brother and then you killed him. The gun was in his hand, but you put it there."

Fear stabbed me.

"Mr. Echo will make you pay. That is a promise. Mr. Echo will make you *pay*."

I slammed down the receiver and unplugged the phone. He'd gotten my phone number. No doubt, he knew where I lived. I hugged myself, feeling cold and dirtied, as if a snake had crawled over me. I wrapped myself in a blanket and sat on the couch, shivering.

I couldn't let this guy get to me like this. I couldn't and I wouldn't.

I shook myself free of the blanket and went upstairs, to my bedroom, and the night table next to Hamp's side of the bed. The drawer slid open. The gun was still in there, wrapped in an oil rag, untouched since the day Hamp put it there. How I'd argued with him.

*Don't you be bringing death into our house.*

*We need this, Lanie. The way things are, every home should have one.*

I checked the weapon. It was loaded. Hamp had taken me out to the gun range and forced me to practice. Practice. Practice. Until the gun no longer sickened me. Until it actually began to feel normal in my hand. And I sensed a certain pride in marksmanship.

I rewrapped the gun and returned it to the drawer, feeling calm and determined.

The locksmith called out to me. He was done. I fetched some bills from my purse and paid him. He told me the money was too much and tried to give some back. I pressed the bills into his hand, curled his fingers over them and told him to keep the change.

When the door was shut the door behind him, I flipped the new locks adorning my door. They were heavy and ugly and I hated what they stood for.

In stocking feet, I went down stairs to the kitchen. My gaze found Hamp's leather tool kit. Whenever I entered the kitchen, it was always the first thing I saw. Three years, those tools had lain there. Three years. Right after his death, I couldn't bear to touch them. As time went by, I'd told myself it didn't make sense to put them away because I was going to fix the cabinet myself. One day, I'd do it.

But I never had.

I could've called in a carpenter to do the job, or asked any one of a number of friends to do it. But again, I never had. And to be honest, I probably never would.

My hands shook as I reached into the cabinet for my favorite cup—a dark blue chipped one that Hamp had made for me in a pottery class when he was in college. The cabinet was a bit too high for me, so I stood on tiptoe and leaned on the door in order to reach inside. I'd always been careful not to put too much weight on the door, but I guess that day I put on one ounce too many.

The cabinet shifted—like a picture off balance—and Hamp's cup slid out. I tried to catch it, but fumbled it—the way I was fumbling everything that day. The cup slipped from my hand, fell to the counter top, and rolled off it. It hit the floor and shattered. It landed so hard it actually seemed to explode.

Frozen, I stared at the scattered bits and pieces. Even if I could find all of them, I wouldn't be able to glue them back together again. I could never make the mug whole. Somewhere, somehow there'd be a place for liquid to bleed through.

I stood back and stared at the cabinet. This thing had somehow come to house so many of my memories, my yearning for my man's return. It had been the focal point of my refusal to see the future, and allowed me to hold on to the past. It wasn't irreparably broken, but the only man I wanted to fix it lay six feet under. How silly to have thought I could fix it myself.

How dangerous.

It was my determination to go it alone that had made me think I could handle the Todd case all by myself, and that determination that had played right into the hands of a killer.

I attacked the cabinet, hating it. All the grief-stricken rage I'd been carrying around since Hamp's death roiled up, all the frustration at struggling to make it on my own, to take care of myself emotionally as well as financially, to not just be alone but proud and alone when everyone else I knew was part of a couple—all those bottled up feelings spilled free.

I grabbed hold of the cabinet door and pulled down on it with all my might. But the cabinet didn't come crashing down, as I thought it would, as in all those years I'd feared it would. It stayed stubbornly in place, only now so dangerously tilted forward that all the dishes in it had skidded toward the edge.

I wanted to clear them away with a sweep of my arm, to let them fall to the floor and shatter, too. Instead, with deliberate calm, I removed the remaining four dishes and cups and stacked them on the table. It took less a minute.

Then I went to work.

Taking firm hold of the door, I brought my entire weight to bear. There was a tearing sound as one nail wrenched free. After fifteen seconds, the final nail holding the cabinet in place gave way. The whole thing tore away from the wall with a shudder and tumbled to the floor.

I stood over it, breathing heavily. It looked like a poor man's coffin. A dead box and a box for the dead. A box too tilted and off-center to securely contain anything so precious as hope or life. I kicked it. The wood was so thin it cracked. So I kicked it again, and this time, my boot put a hole in it. I kicked it and kicked it until the battered box collapsed. Finally, I grabbed up the panels and whacked them against the floor. New scars appeared in the wooden floorboards. I didn't care. I beat the panels until they splintered.

My rage expended, my guilt over Whitefield weighing me down, I sagged to my knees. Covering my face with my hands, I wept. I cried harder than I'd cried in years. At some point, I must've curled up and fallen asleep. I don't know how much time when by. But the next thing I knew, it was dark outside, and I was on the floor shivering. Pushing myself into a half-sitting position, I surveyed the damage. It was the first time in my life, I'd ever let go like that and I was tired beyond words. My muscles felt stiff and cramped. My eyes hurt and my face felt swollen. I stood up and began clearing up.

I thought about taking the wood into the backyard. Later, I could chop it up and burn it in the fireplace. But I knew I'd never do that. It would haunt me out there. I'd never find the time or nerves to turn it into kindling. So I marched up and down the stairs, taking the pieces to the garbage can out front. Someone would find them and make good use of them.

When the cabinet's remains were removed, I returned the kitchen to make that cup of java. Instead, I paused in the doorway and leaned against the doorframe. Across the room, on the other side of the table, Hamp's leather took kit still lay open on the counter.

Without the cabinet above it, the kit looked abandoned.

I took a deep breath and crossed the room to the countertop. I reached out for the kit, but hesitated. There would be pain ... I took a deep breath and lowered my hand to the leather.

There was a rush of sorrow, but it was only a ghostly echo of the old grief. More than that was the comfort of putting my hands where his had been. My fingertips traced the initials he'd carved into the tools' scarred handles and my lungs released a slow exhalation. It was time now. Past time.

I rolled up the kit, just as I'd so often seen him do, and put it to my lips for one brief kiss.

Then I stowed it away.

## *37.*

Upstairs, with a cup of strong java, I went to the front parlor and put on a record by the Duke. *Mood Indigo*. As the somber notes filled the room, I pulled off my boots and stretched out on the sofa. For a few minutes, I let my mind drift. Naturally, it returned to the newspaper wanting me to disappear. I felt angry all over again, angry with myself as well as the paper. The one person I couldn't be angry with was Sam. Recalling his phone conversation with Ramsey, I knew he'd fought the best battle he could.

I set the coffee down on the table and went to the back parlor. Hamp had a stash in a shoebox behind a dictionary on the bookshelves. The bottle was half-empty—or half-full, depending on how you looked at it. I took it back to the parlor and poured a shot into my coffee. Then I sank back on the sofa and sipped.

I needed advice. Hamp had never told me what to do, even when I asked him to. He'd always said, "Lanie, you don't need me to solve it for you. You just need me to listen." And he was a good listener. He never made fun of even my wildest thoughts.

Of course, if I were fair I'd admit that Sam was a good listener, too, or would be if I gave him half a chance. I'd never understood women who emotionally buried themselves when they saw their husbands lowered into the grave. But here I was, one of them.

Sam had questioned my column but printed it anyway. He believed in me—and cared. He cared in a way that no one had bothered to care in many a year. Now, he might lose his job over it.

Then, there was that little boy over on 140th Street. He'd dared put his trust in a stranger. Not once, but twice. And I'd messed up both times.

I had to figure a way out of this.

Sexton Whitefield.

An image of him slumped over the armrest filled my mental movie screen. I closed my eyes, as if that could stop me from seeing it.

Deep in my head, a vein throbbed. Alcohol was the worst thing to drink when I had a headache.

Being stubborn, I took another sip.

Question number one: Who had an interest in killing Whitefield and making it look like suicide?

Whoever kidnapped Esther, of course, and that would be the phantom lover. He was the man who'd attacked me. He'd been angry at me for stirring up a hornet's nest. Then he'd read my column and realized that I hadn't fingered him, but actually helped him by identifying his nemesis.

I took a deep breath and leaned back, nursing the cup and feeling deeply disappointed in myself.

Why had I been so quick to assume that the attacker was Whitefield's henchman?

I let the question float through my mind, more as a self-criticism than an angle of inquiry. But then it hit me that the question might be worth serious consideration.

Had he misled me intentionally? Had he wanted me to believe Whitefield sent him? Or had I made that stupid assumption all on my own, with the timing of the attack and my focus on Whitefield simply coincidental? Was there any way to tell?

Well … for him to have wanted me to believe he was Echo, he had to have known about my interest in Whitefield *before* the column came out. But how could that be? Who knew of my specific interest in the tax collector? Who, other than Sam?

Only one name came to mind.

I thought about it for a while. Then I remembered something. During the attack, I'd used Whitefield's name. I'd spoken it aloud. But, when? Before or after the attacker had issued his warning? I couldn't be sure.

If the killer hadn't been aware of Whitefield before attacking me, then my mentioning the tax collector would've been enough to alert him, wouldn't it? The last name, plus the details that appeared in the column would've been more than enough to give the killer Whitefield's identity. The column alone had been enough for many.

Dear Lord, what had I done?

I added more kick to my coffee and took a swig. I went over it again and again: the sequence of events, the words the assaulter used. Whether the attacker wanted me to believe he was from Whitefield or whether I'd made the assumption on my own: there was no way to tell and it was an important point.

I grabbed up my bag, dug out my notebook and found Bellamy's number. The instant I plugged in the phone, it started ringing. I frowned at the thought of another call from one of my colleagues. Of course, it could've been Sam and so perhaps I should've answered, but I couldn't take the chance.

Finally, the phone stopped ringing. I grabbed it up and dialed. Bellamy answered on the third ring.

"I been meaning to call you," he said. "You're getting a bum rap."

"I'll be all right. Been doing a lot of thinking."

"About Whitefield?"

"About him and something else." I popped the question: "Did you tell anyone about our conversation, Detective?"

"Which conversation?"

"The one in which I mentioned Whitefield's name. Did you share that information?"

"I talked to the guys down at the station about it, about getting you to do an article on him. So they knew, yeah."

That was an unpleasant bit of news. Not only had he used my paper and me, he'd made sure his fellow cops knew about it.

"What about to somebody else?"

"No, of course not. What is this?"

"The night before he was killed, somebody waylaid me—"

"They *what?*"

"Got into my house and waited in the hallway. When I came upstairs, the guy put a knife to my back. Mentioned my column and Esther."

"You think it was this Echo guy?"

"I did. I don't anymore."

A pause. "And why's that?"

"Trust me. I've got good reason."

"What—"

"I've got to go, Detective. Thanks for your help."

I hung up, wondering. If Bellamy hadn't let Whitefield's name slip, then—

The telephone jangled under my hand. Annoyed, I snatched it up, ready to give one of my pesky colleagues a piece of my mind.

But it was Sam's voice that came down the line.

"You actually answered," he said, surprised. "I just heard about Echo. Blackie called. Said he had a feeling you hadn't told me."

"I—"

"You have got to stop trying to go it alone. Let me help you."

"I'm fine," I rubbed my forehead. "I've gotten new locks on the doors, and ..." I was too tired to finish the sentence. I flopped down on the sofa, picked up a pillow and hugged it. "I'd be okay, if I could just ... think this thing through."

"What's to think about? A maniac is on the loose, and he could be after you."

"I need to know who shot Whitefield."

He gave a sigh of exasperation. "The cops say it was a suicide. The case is closed."

"For them, not for me."

He paused. "All right. Let's think this thing through. Assuming it was murder, not suicide, then we'd have to conclude that the person who was crazy about Esther, who attacked you and killed Whitefield were all one and the same."

"Yes," I paused. "And no."

*Lanie ...*

"I've been going over what that guy said when he attacked me, and I'm wondering if he already knew about Whitefield before the column hit the stands. Maybe it's just wishful thinking, but if this guy did know, then I want to know how he found out and when."

Silence as Sam thought it over. "Did you mention Whitefield to someone—someone outside the paper?"

"Bellamy. He's the only one—and he says he didn't mention it to anyone."

"You believe him?"

"I don't know." I paused. "There's more and it's about the killing itself. I keep wondering: Would this crazy lover have taken the trouble to stage a suicide?"

"Sure. Why not?"

"This guy liked publicity. He was the type who wanted credit for his actions. That phone call Bellamy told me about: Somebody who'd make a call like that—claiming credit when the case was hot and cops were swarming all over it—who'd take a chance like that?"

"He didn't risk anything. They didn't follow up."

"But he didn't know they wouldn't. I'm telling you: This guy wouldn't have made Whitefield's death look like suicide. He would've made it about *him*."

The other end was silent for two seconds. Then Sam cleared his throat.

"So, let me get this straight. You're saying you believe that Esther's crazy admirer attacked you, but you don't believe he killed Whitefield?"

"I'm saying that this guy's behavior—even according to his own crazy logic—just doesn't make sense."

"But you could be wrong."

"Yeah," I said. "I could be. It's been known to happen."

## 38.

Sam and I chatted for a couple more minutes. Then he started worrying and fretting about Echo and how the house could be made safer. Maybe I should just move out, he said, temporarily. No way, I said, and reminded him that Blackie had come and gone over security with me. Furthermore, I wasn't about to let Echo chase me out of my own house. Brave words, but the moment I hung up, I went to the door and double-checked the locks.

A deep pain pulsated behind my left eye. In the bathroom, I washed my hands and splashed warm water on my face. Then I changed into some worn flannel pajamas, but I didn't go to bed. I couldn't afford to. I returned to the living room and tried to pick up my deliberations where I'd left off.

After thirty seconds of impatient reflection, I fetched a couple of sheets of typing paper from my writing desk, grabbed up a copy of *Opportunity* magazine to use for backing, and curled up on the sofa.

Many detectives will tell you that most people are killed or victimized by people they know or at least have met. It seemed to be true for Esther. Was it true for Whitefield?

I wrote down his name and drew a circle around it. Then I added Esther's name, encircled it and connected the two names with a short line. On impulse, I added Beth and Ruth, linked them to one another and linked them to Esther. A little farther up, I wrote Mrs. Goodfellowe's name. She got strokes for her relationships with Esther and Beth. I added the butler, Roland, to Mrs. G's links, too. I paused and looked at what the sketch showed. Everyone had multiple links but Sexton Whitefield. His sole link was to Esther.

But was he so isolated from the others involved in this case?

Whitefield had met Esther at a party at Goodfellowe House. Obviously he was there at Katherine's invitation, not Esther's. I drew another line, directly linking him to Mrs. Goodfellowe herself.

Again, I studied the diagram. To one side, I wrote, "All roads lead to Goodfellowe House." After some reflection, I added Eric Alan Powell's name and hooked it up with Mrs. Goodfellowe's. It's true that Powell was dead and buried when Esther disappeared, but he was alive and in the house when she and Whitefield met. It was a small detail, but it helped flesh out my understanding of who was in and around the place when their affair began.

Who else was there to watch the drama unfold?

The first person who came to mind was Mrs. Goodfellowe herself. She had denied the affair, but I had to wonder. Was she lying or simply unaware? Had she really noticed nothing? Had her husband? If so, had he mentioned it to anyone?

Mrs. Goodfellowe and her husband, however, weren't the only ones who could've known about Esther and Whitefield.

What about Beth? She'd been there. And Roland? Had he noticed it? Probably. I had the feeling that Roland missed nothing of what went on in that house. But did either Beth or Roland tell anyone about it? I'd have to ask them.

It was nearly three in the morning. I walked around the room two times to stretch my arms and legs and sat down again. I studied the sketched diagram of who knew whom and reread the little notes I'd jotted at odd places on the page. When all was said and done, one sentence jumped out.

*All roads lead to Goodfellowe House.*

I stretched out on the sofa and let my eye dance over the diagram. My eyes hurt and I was exhausted. There was a pattern in the diagram, a hidden image I could sense but not see.

My eyelids drooped.

## 39.

*All roads lead to Goodfellowe House.*

That was my last thought before sleeping and my first upon waking. It was dark and I was still on the sofa, feeling cramped and uncomfortable. The diagram was a crumpled sheet beneath me, its sharp edges poking me in the back. The clock on the mantel said it was three o'clock in the morning. I dragged myself up the stairs, planning to fall into bed and then sleep, sleep, sleep. In the morning, all the mental cobwebs would be gone and I'd be able to think.

I pushed open my bedroom door. The room was lit only by the filtered light of a streetlamp. As groggy as I was, I registered the open night table drawer, the discarded oilcloth. Then an arm was around my throat, swinging me around and slamming me against the wall. The blow sent shards of white light through my head. A man jammed the cold barrel of a pistol hard up against my ribs.

Echo.

He put his face close to mine. "Did you honestly think Mr. Echo would let you destroy his life, and do nothing?"

"I—"

"Shut up."

He yanked me away from the wall and pushed me out the door. "Up the stairs. We're going to the roof."

I stumbled forward, alternately shoved and jabbed by the gun in my back.

Moonlight poured through the skylight over the stairway, bathing us in a cold blue light, lending us the complexion of the dead. He gave me another shove and I tripped across the top stair to the third-floor landing. My legs shot out from under me and I went flat on my stomach. He was so close behind me that he tripped over my feet and fell to one side with a grunt. His finger depressed the gun trigger. The weapon fired and the bullet hit the skylight. The thick pane exploded, releasing a rain of shattered glass.

We both cringed, covering our faces, but I recovered first. Acting on instinct, I snatched up a shard and stabbed blindly at Echo's face. I didn't even feel the pain as the glass sliced through my palm. He screamed and dropped the gun as the shard plunged through the soft bubble of his eye.

Shaking, I grabbed the gun, backed down two steps and held the weapon on him. I tried to hold the gun in my right hand, but my palm was slippery with blood. I switched the gun to my left and steadied it with my right.

Blood coursed from his ruptured left eye. The shard had gone in about an inch deep—far enough to do damage, but not enough to kill. With a quivering hand, he started to pull out the glass.

"I wouldn't do that if I were you. The glass will cut on the way out, like it did on the way in. It'll turn your eye into chop liver."

His hand froze.

I backed down another step. "Now get up. And don't do anything to make me shoot you. Because I will." The firmness of my voice surprised me. I was terrified.

He grabbed hold of the railing and got to his feet. I backed down the steps to the second floor. There I waited and kept trained the gun on him as made his way down, gingerly, step by step. From downstairs, came the sound of heavy fists pounding the front door.

"Police! Open up!"

I was tempted to run down and let them in, but I didn't trust Echo. Even though I was armed and he was disabled, I was taking no chances.

"Hurry up," I told him.

By the time we got downstairs, the cops were ready to break down the door.

"Lanie! It's Blackie! Are you okay? Somebody reported shots." More pounding. "Answer the damned door, Lanie, or we're coming in! NOW!"

I ran to the door and undid all the locks. A bunch of uniformed officers surged in, shoving me aside, their guns drawn. Blackie took one look at Echo and disgust flashed across his face.

"Grab him," he barked. "And get a doc!"

He turned back to me and his gaze caught the gun. His tone became gentle, even though his eyes stayed watchful.

"You can let go of it now. You won't need it anymore."

He extended his hand and, with a sob, I placed the gun in it.

## *40.*

Blackie took me to Harlem Hospital, where the doctors stitched and bandaged my hand. Blackie had just finished taking a statement when Sam showed up. He'd been monitoring the police band, he said, hoping to hear of Echo's capture, when he caught word of a gunshot heard on Strivers'

Row. He'd rushed over to my house, and was then directed here. He wrapped his arms around me and hugged me tight.

"Good God, if anything had happened to you ..."

"She'll be okay," Blackie said.

Sam took in the bandaged hand.

"I'm fine. Really," I said.

"Where's Echo?" he asked.

"You needn't worry about him," Blackie said. "You should be proud of her. She did a right fine job."

"I'm sure she did," Sam said.

Blackie left us alone and I gave Sam an abbreviated version of the events. I hoped he'd let me write the story myself, but that was wishful thinking.

"I can't let you write the main piece. You know that. You're part of the story. I'll have to pass it on. I just need to think of the right guy."

"Not Selena."

He chuckled. "No, not her."

"How about George Greene?"

"He's just a rookie."

"He's talented, Sam. He deserves a chance."

"Okay, then he'll get one."

Sam drove me home. He wanted to see me inside, but I wouldn't let him. He'd only heard about the gunshots. He didn't know about the skylight. He'd never let me stay inside the house if he did. He'd insist that I stay away, or that he stay with me, until it was fixed. I didn't want that. I needed to be home. And I needed to be alone.

Sitting in the car, he eyed my house and said, "You shouldn't have to come back here tonight."

"But I feel good here."

"Even after being attacked in it—twice?"

"This is my home."

He drew a deep breath and sighed.

"It's okay, Sam. No one will bother me now."

I kissed him goodnight and got out of the car before he could say anything more. I felt his worried concern as I climbed the stairs, so after unlocking my door, I put on a brave smile, turned around and waved to him. He waved back with a forced smile and reluctantly drove away. I closed my eyes, exhaled and let my shoulders drop.

Once inside, I took the broom and swept up all the glass. Still wearing my coat, I made myself a pot of tea, dragged the blankets off my bed and returned to the parlor, where I closed the doors and built a fire.

I slept like a stone. Maybe it was the relief of knowing that Echo was no longer a problem. Maybe it was the satisfaction of having beaten him. Whatever it was, I woke up bright-eyed, and while not exactly bushy-tailed, I did feel more light-hearted than the day before.

I threw back the blankets, sat up and gave in to a good head-to-toe shiver. The place was freezing. Of course, it was. The fire had gone out and icy air was pouring in through the roof. I'd have to get that skylight taken care of soon.

My hand throbbed. The doctors said the cut was relatively superficial, but it was still deep enough to cause some serious hurting.

From outside came the dull sound of metallic scraping. I went to the front window and saw that a thick layer of snow, ankle deep, had fallen overnight. People were busy scraping off their cars. Others were out with shovels, clearing their front steps. I'd have to do the same and do it before the snow hardened. I went out to the hallway and saw that the runners were all wet and small pools of water covered the stairs.

I sensed the beginnings of a headache. Downstairs in the kitchen, I set on a pot of water for coffee and threw a hamburger in the frying pan. After eating, I returned to the parlor and built another fire in the fireplace. The telephone rang. Instinct told me it was Sam and it was.

"How're you feeling this morning?"

"Better than before."

"Why didn't you tell me about the skylight?"

I bit my lip. "Who told you?"

"It's an open secret, as open as your roof. That's why you didn't want me to see you in last night."

"I didn't want you to worry."

"Don't you get it? It's your keeping me in the dark that makes me worry. Now, I'm sending a guy to fix your roof. The paper will spring for it."

"Thank you."

"And what do you say I come over and clear your steps? That snow's pretty heavy."

That made me smile. "No, Sam, I can do it myself."

"I know you can. The point is, you don't have to."

My smile faded. I thought about the cabinet and wondered. *When will I learn to—*

"Never mind," he said. "I'll just send the repairman. So, don't worry. I'm not going to invite myself over. Not as long as you promise me that if you need anything—anything at all—you'll call me."

"I will."

He started to hang up.

"Sam?" I said.

"Yes?"

"Thank you."

I felt very alone after we hung up. Maybe that's why I started to put on some Duke Ellington, but then I looked at the coffee table, still strewn with my notes from the night before and realized that I couldn't afford distractions, especially anything sweet and sexy that would evoke memories of other late mornings spent lazing in bed with the man I loved, of afternoons spent picking out a Christmas tree, taking out decorations and hiding presents.

My home was so bare of anything resembling Christmas now. I hadn't realized how bare until Sam walked in and asked about a tree. Maybe this year I'd try for one. But I said that every year, didn't I?

I returned to the sofa and for several minutes, just sat there, holding the cup, warming my hands, and reviewing my notes.

*All roads lead to Goodfellowe House.*

I took a sip and set the cup aside. The telephone rang. I glanced at it, sensing that it wasn't Sam, and willed it to be silent. When it kept on jangling, I ignored it. I picked up a pencil, flipped the notepad to a blank sheet and began to do something I should've done earlier—set down a timeline. I started with the two most prominent dates, those of Esther's kidnapping and the subsequent Goodfellowe heist. It was a good way of getting a handle on the case.

| | |
|---|---|
| December 19 | (Just past midnight) Esther is kidnapped |
| December 23 | Goodfellowe mansion robbed |

After due consideration, I added the approximate dates of Esther's relationship with Whitefield. Then I set the notepad aside. Having finally decided to sit down and do this, I figured I might as well be thorough. I fetched the file containing my old notes and the newspapers clippings on Esther's case.

The telephone rang. I ignored it. Half an hour later, it rang again. Once more, I ignored it. For the next couple of hours, it rang on and off. Finally, I took the receiver off the hook. In the meantime, everything got reread—every jotting, every comment, every article. I made some educated guesses and added new approximate dates to the ones I already had. Then I rewrote the dates, in order.

| | |
|---|---|
| September 1 (Approx.) | Esther meets Sexton Whitefield at a party in early September |
| October 1 (Approx.) | Something goes wrong in relationship with Whitefield in early October |
| 1st week of December | Esther gets first threatening note |
| 2nd week of December | Esther gets second note |

| December 18 | (Just past midnight) Esther disappears |
| December 20 | Police accept report |
| December 22 | Det. John Reed decides that she ran away |
| December 23 | (5 days after disappearance) Goodfellowe mansion robbed |
| December 30 | (1 week after heist) Esther's family receives 1st note |
| January 7 | (1 week later) Esther's family receives 2nd note |
| January 20 | (3 weeks later) Katherine's car is spotted |

I studied the list of dates and something stirred. I sat quite still, letting the ideas float and dance and gently bounce off one another.

Esther's affair and her disappearance. Her disappearance and the Goodfellowe heist. What were the connecting threads? How had the information been passed along?

I padded downstairs to the kitchen and poured another cup of java. I didn't want it, but needed the movement. Actually what I needed was to put on warmer clothes. Fifteen minutes later, snug in a heavy sweater, thick stockings and a long wool skirt, I returned to the parlor to study my timetable. Minutes slipped by. I frowned.

A date was missing.

I flipped back through the notes I'd prepared before going to see Katherine Goodfellowe. Not seeing what I was looking for, I turned the pages forward again. There it was, the date I sought. I added it to the list and drew a line to indicate where it belonged.

| October 6, 1923 | Eric Alan Powell found shot to death |

I sat back, considering. Mrs. Goodfellowe's husband murdered, her favorite protégée kidnapped and her house robbed in a multimillion-dollar heist that was based on inside information, all taking place within months of each other.

Was it just a streak of incredibly bad luck or was there more to it?

It was late afternoon when I put my notes away and put the telephone receiver back on its cradle. I had just enough time to get to the library.

## *41.*

New York booklovers are a hardy lot. They refuse to be daunted by Mother Nature. Their footsteps had already flattened the snow on the steps to the main entrance of the New York Public Library at 42nd Street. Given the weather, no one was loitering about, as was the habit in summer, but children were throwing snowballs at Lady Astor and Lord Lenox, the giant marble lions guarding the main entrance.

Once inside, I clomped down the hall to the Periodicals Room. There I asked a librarian for copies of the *Times,* dating back to early January of '23. I wasn't sure what I was looking for or what relevance Powell's death might have to Esther's kidnapping. Probably none. But too much had happened around Mrs. Goodfellowe not to raise the question. An hour later, I had neat stacks of newspapers to one side. In short, this is the story they told:

On January 1, 1923, Mrs. G, then in her mid-fifties, marries Eric Alan Powell, age thirty-two. No one quite knows where the young man came from. They only know where he's landed: in Mrs. G's bed. There are stories about gambling and tales of criminal involvements. The tongues wag. The busybodies fuss. Mrs. G silences them quickly. Her new darling is handsome, apparently refined and profoundly witty. If people have been expecting to see a young man who wastes her money, one who insists that she invest in various ridiculous if not nefarious schemes, then they're disappointed. Powell conducts himself as a man worthy of the woman he's married and the status he's attained. After a while people simply accept it: Mrs. G and her new husband are one of those unlikely pairings that nature springs on decent society: unusual but not unnatural. She has clearly never recovered from the double blow of losing her husband and her daughter, and now Fate has given her a genuine second chance at love. Her good friends sincerely rejoice at her newfound luck.

But Mrs. G's new happiness is short-lived.

At 6 a.m. on the morning of October 6, 1923, a middle-aged Brooklyn secretary named Francine Baker takes her terrier, Snookums, for a walk along Surf Avenue, the main street of Coney Island's amusement park. She treasures these walks, when the street is still quiet, well before visitors, even in autumn, fill it to capacity. She turns onto the boardwalk and takes a deep breath of salty ocean air. She holds her face to the wind, enjoying how it sweeps off the Atlantic. The beach is just the way she likes it—empty and peaceful.

Mrs. Baker resumes her stroll, but takes only a few steps before slowing to a halt. A car is parked to one side of the boardwalk, a brand new black Packard. Mrs. Baker automatically tightens her hold on Snookums' leash. What's such an expensive car doing there, at this time of morning? She glances around, but sees no one else. Snookums barks and strains at the leash. She eases up on it and he drags her forward, tail wagging. As she comes abreast of the car, she can see that she's mistaken. The car is occupied. There's the top of a man's head. He's in the driver's seat, his head thrown back on the headrest. No doubt, he got drunk the night before and passed out.

The window on the driver's side is rolled down. Mrs. Baker's better instincts tell her to take a wide berth around the car, but curiosity and Snookums get the best of her. So she goes up to the window and gets an eyeful.

It's a sight she'll remember for the rest of her days.

With a piercing scream, she stumbles backward and falls flat on her butt. Snookums is hopping and yelping around her. After a moment's shock, the woman scrambles to her feet and scurries home, the short-legged dog racing ahead of her. Her husband, Fred, can't fully grasp what she's babbling about. But he understands enough to call the cops.

Police find the body of a white male slumped behind the steering wheel. The dead man is of slender build. He's wearing a black full-length cashmere coat over a dark blue suit with a white shirt and a gray-and-white checked silk tie with a rare black pearl tiepin. He's also wearing a gold wedding band on his left hand and a diamond pinkie ring on his right. The fingers of his right hand pinch a blood-spattered cigarette stub and his left hand grips a dark gray hat. His Colt .380 is still in his shoulder holster. From the smoothness of the skin on his hands, one would say he's in his twenties or thirties. It's impossible to tell from his face.

He doesn't have one.

Someone has used a Remington pump-action shotgun to great effect. The nose is gone and so are both eyes. The rest of the face is a pulp of splintered bone and raw meat.

The medical examiner estimates that the victim has been dead two to four hours. He deems the shooting too vicious for it to have been professional. The killer's blowing the man's face away gives the crime a touch of the personal.

The dead man is carrying no formal identification. His wallet and billfold are gone. But his car and clothes indicate someone from the upper echelons of society. One of the uniforms suggests organized crime, but the detective on the scene nixes that. The Packard is not the car of mobsters. It's grand, all right, but it moves too slowly. No, this guy wasn't a mobster. Just some poor rich slob who got himself into trouble, maybe with an angry husband who paid someone to off him.

The hat's inner band contains the initials E.A.P. A check of the car registration shows it to belong to one Katherine Goodfellowe. The dead man is tentatively identified as Eric Alan Powell, her husband of nine months.

The widow is devastasted, but she's in for more bad news.

A check into Powell's background unearths wanteds in Chicago for marriage fraud. Investigators also turn up rumors about gambling debts. They learn that Powell was a familiar face in the demi-monde of secret, affluent gamblers. Gossip has it that he owed fifty to a hundred thousand dollars. Investigators theorize that Powell made the fatal mistake of crossing a loan shark. They begin to push the loan shark theory hot and heavy, but soon run into trouble. No one is willing to admit to having lent Powell money. This isn't surprising, of course. No one wants to concede anything self-incriminating. But not even the snitches the cops depend on can supply a single name or firm figure to the amount of money Powell supposedly owed.

They do, however, turn up something else.

Word has it that Powell had a terrible argument with his best friend, a guy by the name of Bobby Kelly. Powell and Kelly had been pals since childhood. Kelly is a convicted thief, albeit a small-time one. The argument is said to have been bitter and violent, and it took place only three days before the shooting.

Police reconstruct the crime as follows: The two men meet to supposedly work out their differences. They're sitting talking in Powell's car when Kelly makes an excuse to get out. Maybe he says he has to take a leak. He walks off, does his thing. He comes back and sees Powell relaxing behind the wheel, taking a smoke. Something clicks in Kelly's head—or maybe this has been his plan all along. He takes out his shooter and holds it down low. He approaches the car and signals for Powell to roll down the window. Powell does and Kelly gives it to him—right in the kisser.

Police fan out, searching high and low for Bobby Kelly, but he's nowhere to be found.

Despite all the rumors and information unearthed about Powell, no other viable suspects are developed. The investigation stalls, and then cranks to a halt. No one is ever arrested.

Good story. Did it have anything to do with Esther? Or her affair with Sexton Whitefield? Was there a connection between Whitefield, Powell and Kelly? Or was I just mixing apples with oranges?

The same photo of Powell accompanied each article. He sat cross-legged on a wooden chair next to a small writing desk in a gaudily furnished room, full of stuffed chairs with plaid throws and mincing tables with lace doilies. The gas lamp on the wall threw odd shadows, but you could see his face clearly enough, perceive the deep-set dark eyes, the smooth chin and arched cheekbones.

One small line in a *Times* report especially caught my eye. An unnamed source was quoted as having told police that he'd seen Kelly a week prior to Powell's death and that Kelly had hinted he was on to "something big." I found this interesting, but according to the news reports, investigators failed to find any use for this information.

Was Kelly's "something big" the Goodfellowe heist?

Police suspected that Esther's disappearance was tied to the heist because of the proximity of the two incidents. Couldn't the same logic be applied to Powell's death? Investigators had never confirmed the motive behind his murder. Could it have been related to the heist?

The more I thought about it, the more likely it seemed.

Had he somehow fallen victim to the scheme? Perhaps stumbled upon it and had to be silenced? Or might he have been a knowing accomplice? Given the fact that Powell's circle of acquaintances had apparently included criminal elements, and that his best friend and suspected murderer was a thief, it seemed much more likely that Powell's involvement would've been active rather than accidental. Was Powell's death the result of a falling out among thieves? If so, then what, if anything, did it have to do with Esther?

## *42.*

I needed to talk to Katherine Goodfellowe again, but instinct said to wait. I had to be prepared before seeing her. I had to have as much information as possible.

Despite all the hoopla and hype as the hunt for Kelly heated up, the articles contained very little real information beyond the fact that Powell and Kelly had been childhood friends. They did mention, however, that Kelly had an older sister, Katie Jones, and she was adamant about her brother's innocence.

She lived in a five-flight walkup on Larchmont Avenue in the Bronx. The next day, I climbed the stairs to a dusky hallway, located Apartment 29 and rang the bell. A petite blonde answered. She opened the door without even asking me to identify myself. Amazing. In a city with as much crime as New York City, most people, not just women, exercise caution before opening the door to the unknown. Yet here she was, looking at me with open curiosity.

But all that changed seconds later.

When I identified myself and explained that I wanted to ask about her brother, her face closed and she nearly slammed the door shut. I put a hand out to stop her.

"Please. I'm not here to write anything bad about him."

She looked me up and down. "What's a spade doing writing anything about him at all?"

"I'm actually doing a piece on Esther Sue Todd."

"Who's she?"

"Name doesn't sound familiar? About three years ago, she disappeared."

"Yeah? And what's that got to do with Bobby?"

"Don't know that does. But it might."

For a moment, perplexity overtook suspicion, but then suspicion surged back.

"You trying to make Bobby responsible for something else that happened?" She didn't wait for an answer. "You reporters—you disgust me." She made to to swing the door shut.

"Listen, I'm giving you a chance, fair and square, to set the record straight. Nobody else did that before, did they?"

Her blue eyes narrowed. "What paper did you say you were working for? I ain't never heard of no Negro reporters."

"I work for a colored paper. The *Harlem Chronicle*."

"Never heard of it. Who reads it?"

"Quite a few people."

"Folks that matter?"

"White folks, you mean?"

"Ain't that the only kind worth mentioning?"

I made an effort to check my temper. "All I can say is this: Once something gets into print, good or bad, it has a way of finding readers ... and influencing belief. It doesn't always matter whether the folks who did the writing were black or white. What does matter is that it gets written down in black and white."

She gave me two seconds of a cool appraisal. Then she stepped back and gestured for me to enter.

I stepped into a small, square vestibule with a chipped green-and-white-checked tile floor, dingy wallpaper and a painted tin ceiling. Nothing of Christmas cheer here. A beat-up table with playing cards sat to one side. There was a chair, too, and a pencil and pad. The setup reminded me of a hotel. One article had mentioned that Katie Jones worked at the Sunset Arms, a small lower East Side establishment that catered to the one-hour trade. She led me to a tiny living room. It was boxy, with cheap furniture and a scratched dirty wood floor.

I smelled the cat before I saw it. I like cats, but this one made me nervous. Torn ear, one eye sealed shut with dried yellow pus, the other a baleful green. Tattered dirty white fur and about the size of a small terrier.

The cat was taking up the one halfway comfortable looking seat in the room and Jones shooed the animal away.

The beast sprang down with an angry yowl. Jones kicked it. The cat hissed and raised a paw to strike. Jones gave the animal a look that would've frozen a snake. The cat dropped its paw, flicked its tail with what dignity it could muster and stalked out. At the door, it paused, favored each of us with one evil last look and then exited.

"Don't take Lucifer seriously," Jones said.

"Lucifer? His name is Lucifer?"

"It's a she."

All right.

She sat down in the chair and motioned for me to take a seat on the sofa. The sofa was covered with animal hair. It was also low and slumped in the middle. I perched on the edge, knowing that if I relaxed and slid backward I'd have a heck of a time getting up.

"Now you say you're writing about somebody else—not Bobby?"

"I'm working on a column about a woman named Esther Todd. She was a pianist, a protégée of Mrs. Katherine Goodfellowe. I was wondering if your brother knew her."

"I don't know if he did or didn't."

"You never heard him mention her name?"

"She a spade?"

"Yes," I said, bristling but trying to keep the irritation out of my voice. "She's a dark-skinned individual."

Jones shook her head. "My brother don't have no truck with spades. Me, I ain't got nothing against you people. But my brother can't stand your kind."

That might've been true. He might've avoided blacks in the light of day. But that didn't mean he avoided them under cover of night.

"Did Mr. Powell or your brother ever speak of a man named Sexton Whitefield?"

"Nope. Who is he?"

"Never mind. Do you have a picture of him?"

"My brother? Wait a minute."

The only picture I'd seen of Bobby Kelly was a newspaper photo at the library. That photo was grainy and shadowed. I hoped Jones's photo would be of better quality. I also hoped that by asking her for it and showing a bit of sympathetic interest, I'd soften her up.

She was back in a minute. The photo was no bigger than the palm of my hand, but it was clear and crisp. Bobby Kelly was in his early thirties, but had a baby face, dark curly hair, broad shoulders and the face of a youngster, with a dimpled chin.

"Nice looking," I said and handed back the photo.

"Thanks. I keep thinking about him out there alone, scared. Too scared to even call me."

"He got anybody other than you?"

She shook her head, gazed at the photograph for a moment, and then eyed me. "You one of them people say my brother had something to do with Eric's death?"

"Did he?"

"'Course not. Bobby and Eric were friends from way back. We grew up together. Bobby worshipped Eric. Followed him around like a puppy. Did everything Eric ever told him to do."

She dropped the photo on the coffee table and grabbed up her pack of cigarettes. "One time, Eric stole a box of cigs from Jimmy Lean's grocery store. He took Bobby behind the woodshed to smoke them. Bobby had asthma. He knew he shouldn't been smoking. Eric knew it too, but it didn't matter."

She lit herself a cigarette, shook out the match and inhaled deeply. "Bobby got real sick. Had to be taken to the hospital. Cops showed up, wanted to know where they got those cigarettes. Eric must've told Bobby to lie and Bobby did. Said he took him. Bobby was only nine. Sheriff knew he was lying, but he couldn't do nothing. So they both got off scot-free. Bobby hurt Eric? Hmph, he wouldna never laid a hand on him. Would've died for him first."

She exhaled a stream of smoke. "The cops keep asking me if I know where he is—like I'd really tell if I did." She squared her shoulders. "I don't know nothing 'bout where he is. I just hope he stays there till they find out who did it. Or at least, till they know he didn't."

"Did Bobby ever tell you about Eric having enemies?"

She gave a short humorless laugh. "He didn't have to. Everybody knew about Eric, everybody but that high-siddity wife of his. I told Bobby to get away from Eric. I warned him, 'Eric's dangerous. He's crossed the wrong people.' But Bobby wouldn't listen. And when Eric got blown away, some folks made sure Bobby got the blame."

"You're saying it was a setup?"

"I know you don't believe me. Nobody does." She paused. "Well, one person did. Or made out like he did. But maybe he was lying, too. He came here, just like you, with promises about clearing Bobby's name. Got me to talk to him. Then he left and never looked back."

I frowned. "Who was this?"

She shrugged. "Some writer. Not like you, though."

"What does that mean?"

"He was a writer, not a reporter." She tapped her foot. "Look, I think this was a bad idea talking to you."

"Could you give me his name, the writer?"

"Why?"

"Maybe we can put our heads together. Come up with something."

She was suspicious, but then shrugged. "Fine. I think I got his card somewhere. You stay right here. Don't start snooping."

"I wouldn't dream of it."

I put my steno book away and she left the room. The minute she walked out, Lucifer skulked back in. Made me wonder whether the cat had been lurking just outside the door. The beast saw me and stopped in its tracks. I didn't move, just watched it. The cat bared its two little fangs, gave a hiss and walked in an arc around me toward the chair.

"Coward," I said.

Lucifer gave me one of her evil looks. I thumbed my nose at her, no longer impressed. Jones returned and handed me a little white calling card.

"Tellman Carter," the card said. "Writer." There was a phone number.

Carter. The name rang a bell.

"What exactly did he want to talk to you about?"

"Said he was writing a book. He wasn't really interested in Bobby, though. It was Bobby's relationship with Eric. He said he was talking to a lot of people who'd known Eric or handled the case: the cops, the medical examiner. I don't think he got to talk to Mrs. Goodfellowe. He wanted to, but she turned him down flat."

But he *had* spoken to her. I remembered now. She'd mentioned him. He'd made charges, she said. Asked questions—apparently, the kind she found highly insulting.

"Anyway, he's the only one who said he didn't believe Bobby did it."

"Did he say why?"

She shook her head. "All I know is, he said he'd get back to me and never did."

"You didn't try to contact him?"

"I tried to put a call through, but the operator said the number had been changed and she couldn't give me the new one. For all I know, he could've been lying about everything—just like you." She folded her arms across her chest. "I think you should go now."

I thought so, too.

I was halfway down the stairs when I heard her call me. I looked back over my shoulder.

"Yes?"

She was standing at the top of the stairs. "If you find this Carter fellow, would you ask him why?"

"Why what?"

"Why he gave me hope, and then took it away."

## 48.

Was there a connection between the Powell-Kelly case and the heist or Esther's disappearance? I still didn't know after talking to Katie Jones. Was I barking up the wrong tree again? For some reason, I sensed a tie. But I couldn't figure out what it was.

Who was Tellman Carter? Had he just been feeding Kelly's sister a line when he said he believed in Kelly's innocence? Or had he actually found a new angle on the Powell killing? And, by extension, the heist and the Todd kidnapping? Maybe his reasoning had nothing to do with Esther's case, but suppose it did?

The Gotham High Bookstore on 48th Street and Sixth Avenue had one of the most comprehensive book collections in Manhattan. I went there right after seeing Katie Jones.

A salesgirl who looked as though she couldn't have been more than fifteen was standing behind the information counter. When I asked her where I might find the works of Tellman Carter, she pointed to the back of the store, the psychology section.

"He's a doctor?"

"No, I don't think so. An alienist is what they call him. You know, someone who studies criminals. Tries to figure out how they think."

Interesting. I followed the girl's pointing finger and headed to the rear of the store. I walked past the travel section, the true crime section, the zoology and cookbook sections, to arrive at the psychology area. It wasn't big, so it was easy to find Tellman Carter's works. I took down a copy of each one and went to a small, nearby table.

Carter had three titles—*The Delinquent Son, The Criminal Family* and *Criminal Friendships*. Nice titles, surprisingly poetic for books about killers, thieves and con artists of the worst kind. Carter had a solid, straightforward style of writing, too. In the preface to *Delinquent Son*, Carter said he believed society could reduce crime through prevention if it only understood what made people "turn bad" to begin with. He also thought we could predict who was likely to react in a criminal manner, what kinds of personalities indulged in crime once and which tended to be repeaters— repeat offenders, he called them. Interesting term.

What interested me most about Carter's books, though, was the frontispiece. I was looking for the book Katie Jones said Carter told her he was writing when he came to see her. When had that visit taken place? These three books were done earlier. *Delinquent Son* came out in 1919, *Criminal Family* in 1921 and *Criminal Friendships* in 1923. The books appeared every two years, like clockwork. *Criminal Friendships* could've been the book Katie Jones was talking about, but I doubted it. The timing was too close. Powell died in October of '23. It was highly unlikely that Carter would've been able to do research, finish writing the book and have the publisher put it out within two months. Of course, there was an easy way to check. See if *Criminal Friendships* mentioned the Powell killing.

Several minutes of scrutiny disclosed that it didn't.

I started to reshelf the books, then thought better of it. Carter's books looked as though they could be good reading. Furthermore, it might be easier to talk to the man if I knew something about his methodology beforehand. I took the books up to the counter. The slip of a girl who'd been standing behind the information desk was now working the cash register.

"Say, you wouldn't have a copy of his newer work, would you?"

She frowned. "What work?"

"Well, I see that he puts out a book every two years. The last title came out in '23. I'm assuming there was one last year, too."

"No," she shook her head. "I don't think so. He put out *Criminal Friendships* and he hasn't brought out another one since."

"All right, thanks."

I paid for my purchases and left.

Someone had been in my house. I sensed it the moment I walked in the door. At first, I couldn't pinpoint the difference, but then it came to me. There was no Arctic breeze sweeping through the place. I climbed the stairs and looked up. Sure enough the skylight had been fixed. I was astounded. Sam was a miracle worker.

Despite my concern that he'd keep me on the line, I called to thank him. "How'd you manage to get that done so fast?"

"Called in a couple of favors. It was no big deal. Now, tell me. What're you up to?"

"Nothing." I crossed my fingers behind my back. "I'm just planning on doing some reading."

"Reading?"

"Yeah, reading. There's nothing wrong with that, is there?"

"No, but ..." He struggled to find words. "Lanie," he said finally. "Just please stay out of trouble."

"Why, of course I will. Why'd you even feel the need to ask?"

Despite the repaired skylight, the house was cold. It would take time for it to warm up. I curled up on the sofa in a thick sweater under two blankets and read Carter's books. With the exception of pauses to eat or use the bathroom, I read his books one right after the other.

His idea was to explore relationships among criminals and analyze qualities that society would normally see as positive in a human relationship, i.e., loyalty, trust, cooperation, and teamwork, when applied to organized crime. He also wanted to see how these qualities could evaporate in ways that seemed inexplicable to outsiders, to explore and possibly understand how mobsters who'd covered each other's backs for years, sometimes decades, could turn on one another and slaughter each other in a bloody frenzy.

It was two o'clock in the morning when I finished, edified, exhausted and very, very thoughtful.

## 44.

Early the next morning, at exactly five minutes after nine, I put in a call to Carter's publisher, Reinhold-Whitaker. I explained to the company operator that I wanted to contact one of its writers. I told her which one and she put me through to his editor. Joe Blue it was.

It took quite a bit of wrangling, but I finally got him to tell me why Carter never contacted Katie Jones again. It was a reason she would've accepted.

"May I come in and talk to you?"

After a moment's hesitation he agreed.

The snow was melting. The pristine winter wonderland had transmogrified into a landscape of dirty slush. I actually wasted time dithering over whether to wear my nice, sexy shoes in order to dazzle Blue in the hopes of getting more info out of him. Then reality set in and I grabbed my ugly, but warm, winter boots.

Carter's publisher had offices in a skyscraper on East 42nd, a few minutes' walk from Grand Central Station. It was a quarter past ten when I got there. The receptionist, a woman in her early twenties, spent a lot of time batting her eyelashes and making friendly with the guy in the three-piece suit before me. When it was my turn, she said pointedly, "This is not where you apply to join our cleaning staff."

"Then I'm in the right place," I said.

Joe Blue was a tall skinny man in his mid-thirties wearing a pale blue shirt with a cheap bowtie. When he saw me, the usual look of surprise flickered across his face, but he recovered quickly and extended his hand to shake mine.

"Excuse me for saying so, but I didn't think a person like you would be interested in Carter's books."

"Well, I guess he has a wider readership than you realized."

"Yes ... I suppose." He glanced at his watch. "I really don't think I can tell you any more than I said on the phone."

"Tellman was traveling, doing research, when it happened?"

He nodded.

"Do they know who did it?" I asked.

"No, just that he was shot. Robbed, apparently. He was found in an alleyway in Chicago."

Bobby Kelly's childhood city: Had Carter found Kelly? Dug too deep, come too close to the truth?

"What was Mr. Carter doing there?"

He shifted uncomfortably. "You know, I really don't think I'm free to go into detail here. I mean, it's an ongoing investigation, and I don't know you or anything about your, uh ... newspaper."

"You know enough."

"Excuse me?"

"You wouldn't have agreed to meet me if you didn't."

He picked up a pencil, tapped his desk with it. "Maybe seeing you was a mistake."

"Look, I respect your wanting to protect Mr. Carter's memory. But aren't you even more interested in finding his killer?"

"Don't tell me you're investigating his death?"

"No, but I'm working on a case that could be related."

He was thoughtful. "Do the police know about you?"

"Does it matter?"

He leaned back in his chair, weighing his options. From outside came the sound of garbage trucks, of men yelling instructions to one another. We were on the second floor, too low to escape the sounds of the city.

"I didn't know that Carter meant to go there at all. He hadn't said anything about having to do more research. In fact, he'd told me that all of his out-of-town research was done."

"Was the Powell-Kelly case to be part of this book?"

"Why do you ask?"

"I just finished speaking to Kelly's sister. She said Carter stopped by to see her."

Blue nodded. "Carter was excited after that visit. He wouldn't tell me why, though."

"Did he finish the book?"

"No. He'd written about a third of it when it happened. I never even got to see sample chapters."

"Who's got the manuscript?"

"His widow."

"I'd like to read it—"

"Not possible."

"That's for Mrs. Carter to decide."

"She refuses every request."

"Try."

He considered it. "I'd have to give her a reason. Clearer than the one you've given me."

"Tell her..." I reflected. "Tell her it might mean the fulfillment of a mother's dying wish."

The Carter residence was at the Normandy, an imposing building of impeccable pedigree at a ritzy location, 86th Street and Riverside Drive. Mrs. Carter turned out to be a frail-looking woman in her late fifties, small-boned, like a bird, with sharp features and a halo of thin blonde hair. Well-dressed in a black tweed suit and very pretty, she wore a gold bracelet that was thick with charms and looked uncomfortably heavy on her thin, liver-spotted wrists. She was pale, her pallor underscored by her dark clothing.

"I don't see many people these days," she said.

"Thank you so much for seeing me at such short notice." I'd sat in the office as Blue made the call and seen his surprise when she agreed to meet me within the hour.

"I usually don't see people so quickly, but I had space in my schedule this morning—and well, you sounded so interesting. I was curious. Would you like some coffee?"

Pictures of her and Carter decorated the walls of the hallway. They showed a big bear of a man in his sixties, given to wearing khaki safari suits.

She showed me into the living room. The exposure was north, but caught the rays of the afternoon sun. The room had little furniture, mostly comfortable reading chairs. Three of the walls had been given over to hardcover books. Books, books and more books—all protected in glass-covered bookshelves. The remaining wall was a frieze of Thai shadow puppets and African tribal masks. More pictures of the Carters stood on the fireplace mantel, photos of him among the Aborigines of Australia and the tribal hunters of New Guinea. Noticeably missing were safari photos and animal trophies. The emphasis was on people, not objects, and getting to know humanity in all its diversity.

I spied pictures of two people in their twenties, the Carters' children probably, and a group photo that included three generations—the Carters, their children and grandchildren. It was the comfortable home of affluent bohemians: intellectual, worldly, tasteful.

She offered me a place on the sofa and took a seat in the armchair nearby. Her posture was upright, her legs crossed at the ankles, her hands held in her lap. She had clear blue eyes and they were bright with curiosity.

"Mr. Blue said you're a writer?" She made the statement a question. "Also specializing in crime?"

"I'm very interested in one of the cases your husband researched. The Eric Alan Powell killing. Remember it? October of '23? The headlines were everywhere." I outlined a newspaper headline with my hands. "'Young Husband of Fifth Avenue Socialite Found Shot in His Car?' Police thought Powell's Chicago buddy did him in, a petty thief by the name of Bobby Kelly. Kelly skipped town and has been on the lam every since. Your husband spoke to Kelly's sister, Katie Jones. She says he told her he believed her brother didn't do it. He was the first person, she said, who believed in Kelly's innocence as much as she did. She said he was very clear about that. He gave her reason to hope that her brother could be cleared."

"Yes, and?"

"Miss Jones said your husband told her he'd get back to her, but never did. And now she's wondering whether he lied to her just to get her to open up and talk."

Sophie Carter was indignant. "My husband would've never done that! He'd never take advantage of someone. If he said he believed her brother was innocent, then he did. He didn't get back to her because—because of what happened. Surely she knows that."

"No, Mrs. Carter, she doesn't. Apparently, she's totally unaware of the fact that your husband's gone."

"I'm sorry to hear that, but I still don't understand what all this has to do with you. Are you working on her behalf?"

"No. I'm doing research for my column. Your husband's activities might be very relevant to my topic."

"Which is?"

For some reason, I'd been reluctant to talk to her about Esther Todd's disappearance, but now I did.

"Esther's family is desperate to know what happened to her. I'm wondering whether Powell's killer kidnapped her, too. If your husband got a new bead on him, then what he found out might be germane to Esther's case."

"Or it might have nothing to do with it?"

"I need to look at your husband's papers. Not just the manuscript but the notes, too. I need to know who he talked to and what they said."

She thought it out. Her expression said she'd reached the other conclusion I had, the one I'd left for her to see for herself.

"You know, of course, that Tellman was found in Chicago?"

I nodded, knowing where this was leading.

"They never found my husband's killer. Someone shot him down and left him to die in an alleyway. Police said it was a botched robbery, but that didn't make sense. Tellman went to some rough places to conduct research. But he was never foolish. And he never said anything about an appointment with anyone in the neighborhood where he was found."

"Did you let the police see his papers?"

"They showed no interest in them. After all, Tellman mostly researched solved crimes. Cases where the guilty parties were behind bars. The Powell case was the only one in which the killer was still at large." She frowned. "But why would Kelly shoot Tellman, the man who believed in him?"

A good question.

"Maybe your husband learned something that changed his opinion. Did he tell you he was going to Chicago?"

"No. In fact, I thought he'd gone to Boston. That's what got me so worried. I tried to call him at his usual hotel in Cambridge, but they said he wasn't there. He'd come in, then checked out hurriedly. I called everyone we knew in the Boston area. No one had seen him. So I called the police. Two days later, an officer came by. He said they'd found someone answering Tellman's description—and they'd found him in Chicago."

Her expression was pained and perplexed. "These crimes—the Powell killing, that poor woman's kidnapping, the Goodfellowe robbery and now my husband's murder—

they may have nothing to do with one another. But you think they do."

"Yes, I do."

She was thoughtful. After several seconds, she went to the fireplace mantel. Her gaze rested on a large, silver-framed photo of her husband. He stood in what looked like a prison courtyard, prisoners gathered behind him. She picked up the photo and studied it.

"My husband had a big heart," she said. "He expected to find the best in someone if he looked hard enough, dug deep enough. He wasn't naïve, exactly, but what I liked to call a determined optimist."

She sighed and set the photo down, then turned to me, her hands clasped together.

"I usually refuse requests to see Tellman's unpublished work. Several university libraries want his manuscripts for their research libraries. A number of alienists and students have asked to see his notes. I'm considering the university requests, but I've turned down all the individuals. It's important that Tellman's ideas are preserved and presented properly. I won't allow them to be dissected, distorted or outright stolen. That's what I told the others and that's what I'm telling you."

I was deeply disappointed. "Mrs. Carter, I—"

"Having said that, I've decided to let you see the papers—but only under certain conditions."

I was so relieved I would've agreed to just about anything.

"You may only view the sections relating to the Powell case, and you'll have to read them here, in my presence. Understand?"

"Yes. That would be fine."

"Come back in two hours. I'll have everything ready."

## 45.

Reading under Sophie Carter's watchful eye didn't turn out to be as bad as I thought it would be. Actually, she was of great help. Her husband had been a prodigious writer. He'd managed to write only five chapters of a projected twelve, but those five were plenty. They consisted of roughly seventy-five pages each, bringing the unfinished manuscript to a hefty 375 pages.

"He would write and write and try to get everything down as fast as he could," she said. "Then he'd hand it to Joe. Joe's a genius. He'd rework the manuscript until it shone. Sometimes he'd take out material and advise Tellman to save it for another book. So every book contained the seeds for the next one." She smiled wistfully. Those days were gone now. The good times were gone.

I could understand why she'd limited me to the Powell notes. Carter had been a voluminous note taker, one who had his own idiosyncratic way of jotting things down and cross-referencing information. Going through it all would have meant hours of work. I would've gotten through it on my own, but I got through it faster thanks to Sophie Carter.

Her husband might well have been a visionary when it came to crime and criminal behavior. That I couldn't say. But after reading those three books, I knew that he was a talented true crime writer of the first degree. His unedited chapter on Powell and the copious notes he'd made of his interviews only served to strengthen that opinion.

The Powell case fascinated Carter because what little was known of Bobby Kelly indicated an almost blind loyalty to Powell. Carter's research had borne out Jones's statement that her brother had worshiped Powell since childhood. Kelly even imagined himself as Powell's "lost" brother. What made Kelly's sudden vicious attack on Powell even more incredible was the fact that Kelly had no record of violence, armed or otherwise. He was a petty thief who always made sure his victims were nowhere near home when he broke in. Had Kelly carried a hidden rage against Powell for all those years? If so then over what? And what had brought it to the surface? Why had he killed his best friend, as the newspapers said, "in an explosion of anger?"

Carter couldn't figure out Kelly's motive. It bothered him. It also bothered him that as far as he could tell, Powell's killing was premeditated. It had not occurred spontaneously, in any "explosion of anger." It was not a murder of hot-blooded rage, but cold-blooded precision. Too many aspects of the crime scene underscored that point to ignore it, not the least of which were the out-of-the way setting and the fact that Powell had made no defensive moves. There were no wounds to his hands—scratches, bullet holes or otherwise—to indicate that he'd raised them in a useless but instinctive effort to protect himself.

Carter's papers also raised questions about Powell's personality. Powell was a slick con artist who liked "weak" victims: lonely widows he could easily manipulate. Like Kelly, he had no history of physical violence. So on the face of it, it seemed unlikely that Powell would've helped plan a murderous armed heist. Nevertheless, something told me he'd done just that. In the months before he died, something had persuaded him to move on to a higher, more complicated level of crime than he'd ever attempted before.

Something or some*one*. Powell would've been part of a team, never the team leader.

I rubbed my eyes and Sophie Carter gave me a sympathetic smile.

"Would you like a cup of tea?"

"Yes, please."

She soon laid out a warm pot and some scones. I gratefully accepted the tea, but didn't touch the pastry. If I ate, I'd get distracted. The tea would fill me without waking up my stomach. I sagged back in the chair, sipping my tea, and studied the stack of Carter's notes.

Was I following another fascinating, but ultimately useless path? No, this had to be right. Too much violent crime had taken place around Katherine Goodfellowe for it all to be coincidental. Somewhere, somehow, an organizing intelligence was at work.

And I had to find it.

Setting aside my cup, I resumed my examination of the papers.

Carter's notes told how he'd repeatedly asked Katherine Goodfellowe for an interview, but been met with a stone wall of silence. There were no notes about the questions he planned to ask or from the interview he finally had with her.

"I see here," I said, "that he was highly interested in the morgue photos. Why? He didn't strike me as the kind of man given to morbid curiosity. Did he want to use them in his book?"

"Highly unlikely." Sophie Carter shook her head. She refilled my cup. "Tellman was an intellectual, not a sensationalist. Such photos would be graphic, and any book that had them would be a very different product than the one his readers were used to."

A closer read showed that he'd pestered the cops for the pictures and when that didn't work, he'd turned to the medical examiner himself. It wasn't clear how far he'd gotten, if at all, in obtaining the photos, but he had turned up one interesting tidbit: Katherine had refused to go to the morgue and identify the corpse. She said she didn't want to be forced to remember Powell that way, so the law had to find another way to formally identify the remains.

Powell had a record in Chicago. NYPD sent for it. That record included information about Powell's physical appearance, not only his height, but also such theoretically immutable details as the circumference of his head, size of his feet, length of his arms, his fingerprints, etc. A former cop working as a bounty hunter out of the Windy City acted as a courier and brought a copy of the file, which Carter said did not include fingerprints, to New York.

"Must talk to B.H.," Carter wrote. The initials probably referred to bounty hunter. And then I saw that Carter had made an appointment to see one "Denver Sutton (BH), at 1 pm on August 7, 1924." Sutton … Sutton. Where had I heard that name before? With a frown, I remembered. Wasn't that the name of Mrs. Goodfellowe's security chief?

It sure was.

*All roads lead to Goodfellowe House.*

"Just when did your husband go to Chicago, Mrs. Carter?"

"It was in August, early August."

I looked back at Carter's handwritten notes. Had he gone to Chicago instead of going to see Sutton, or right afterward?

"Excuse me, Mrs. Carter. I hate to ask this, but on what date was your husband killed?"

"August fifth."

So he died before he could talk to Sutton. What would he have asked him? I could think of one question right off the bat. Why hadn't the record included fingerprints? Different police departments followed different standards and levels of inclusion when it came to deciding which information to keep for their records, but one would've thought that fingerprints would be one of the standards. There was still some resistance to using them, but every forward-thinking police department had instituted the maintenance of fingerprint files if not as part of a permanent program, then at least on a trial basis.

The notation for Sutton listed a phone number, but no address. Not that it mattered. I knew where to find him.

Carter had made one other appointment. It was with "J. Finnegan & Sons." His notes didn't indicate what line of business the company was in, but he must've thought it important. He'd underlined the August 1 appointment three times. There was neither an address nor a telephone number.

However, that was nothing to worry about. It shouldn't be difficult to track down a company with that name.

"Mrs. Carter, could I use your telephone, please?"

I had the operator put in a call to Sutton, but received no answer. I had better luck with the other number: The owner turned out to be a merchant of the dead.

Heading across town, I thought of the war widow in the *Times* story. Unlike that woman, Sophie Carter knew what had happened to her husband, but she didn't know the who or why of it. In that sense, she was like Katherine Goodfellowe. Despite Mrs. G's outer coldness, no doubt she, too, grieved for her husband and wished deep in her heart for an explanation. Then there was Ruth Todd and Kathy Jones. Neither of them even knew what had happened to their loved ones, much less why. Sophie Carter, Ruth Todd, Katie Jones and even Katherine Goodfellowe: They formed a sisterhood of uncertainty. They were as different as any four people can be, except for that one unenviable tie.

J. Finnegan & Sons turned out to be a funeral parlor on the corner of 66th Street and Park Avenue. It seems they did a fine business in laying away the carriage trade.

Despite the grandiose title, the sole owner and proprietor turned out to be one Jules Finnegan, Jr. Apparently, Jules Finnegan, Sr. had already passed to the other side. Finnegan, Jr. was a short, stout man in a pinstripe suit. He had a bald pate, bushy gray eyebrows and incredibly small feet for a man of his girth.

"Mr. Finnegan, thank you for seeing me at such short notice."

"Well, you said it was urgent."

Not only did Finnegan resemble a banker, his office looked as though it belonged to one. That made sense. It was important to make the customer feel comfortable and right at home. Where would a rich customer feel more at ease than in a banker's office?

"So, what can I do for you?"

"Do you recall a Mr. Tellman Carter having phoned you and set up an appointment? It would've been for August 1, 1924."

He frowned. "That was more than two years ago."

"Yes, I understand, but is there a possibility that you kept records of appointments, maybe made a notation of what Mr. Carter wanted?"

"Just what is this all about?"

I explained about Esther and her family's request that I write about her. "In retracing her footsteps, I came across Mr. Carter's name."

"You're not saying he was involved in her disappearance?"

"No, but he may have dug up some information that would help solve it." I explained about the research that Carter was doing. A light went on in Finnegan's eyes.

"The Powell's case?" Finnegan raised a pudgy finger and wagged it thoughtfully. "Now I remember. There was this fellow who said he was a writer. Wanted to know if I'd handled the embalming. He knew we had, of course. It was right there in the paper. We specialize in restorations, you see. If the deceased has suffered extensive damage—as sometimes happens in a motor vehicle accident—then we're often called in to repair the body and make it ready for burial. We're able to do extensive cosmetic repairs."

"So you did the work to restore Powell's face?"

"I had to rebuild it. It required delicacy, fine feeling. He'd been a beautiful young man. When I saw what they brought in, it was hard to believe it was even him."

"How so?"

"The bullets had not only ripped away the soft tissue, but done extensive damage to the skull. It's the skull that gives a face its distinctive shape, you know, the distance of the eyes to the nose, the height of the cheekbones, the breadth of the nose. Well, the bullets fired into Mr. Powell's face had fractured much of the frontal skull. It took hours to piece it together. We used putty to fill in the holes, then laid a new kind of skin over it."

"You can do that?"

His smile was smug. "We can do anything."

"Did Mr. Carter want to talk to you about the restorative work, or did he mention something else?"

"He wanted pictures of the body. Before and after."

Of course. Carter had struck out in trying to get pictures from police sources. So he'd done the next best thing. But why were the photos so important to him? What did he hope, or *expect*, to see?

"And you have such photos?"

"Yes, but they're not for the general public. They were made to provide guidance. Keep track of the work."

"Did you agree to let Mr. Carter see these photos?"

"We were ... shall we say, still in the midst of a negotiation when ..."

"I see. And what were the terms of this suspended negotiation?"

He inclined his head, as if to say, "Why would they interest you?"

I inclined mine with a partial smile, as if to say, "Try me."

He raised his hand, open palmed, in a little gesture that said, "Okay, I will."

He withdrew a notepad from his desk, took a pen and wrote a figure on it, then pushed the notepad across the desk to me. It was a four-digit sum. I could forget about getting the newspaper to pony up the money for that one.

"What was Mr. Carter's counter offer?"

"There was none. We never heard from him again."

No, of course not. Carter was off in Chicago, being killed.

"So there's no way for me to see the photos without ..." I gestured toward the sum on the notepad.

"I'm afraid not." He stood. "Now if that's all, then—"

"How do you suppose Mrs. Goodfellowe would take it if she were to learn that photos of her husband in his damaged state were on file somewhere, available for sale to the right price? How would others in her circle of friends feel if they were to learn that photos of their loved ones, might also be available for the right sum?"

He sat down heavily and was silent for one very long minute. His expression was full of resentment, his eyes full of appraisal. Then he drew back the notepad and ripped the top page away. He tore the page into bits and dropped them into the wastepaper basket.

"I could do the same to the photos," he said.

"Word about the pictures being for sale would do the same to your reputation."

He understood. Jaw set, he went to the next room. I heard him rifling through a file cabinet. A minute later he was back with a file. He sat down and opened the file on his desk. The photos were in a separate envelope within the file. He took them out and slid them across the desk, one by one.

I've seen some gruesome and battered remains in my time. Back when I was a crime reporter, I saw bodies ripped open by machinegun fire, mangled by speeding trains, bloated and rotting after being pulled from the river. None of it was pretty. But none of it was as ugly as this.

"The first bullet was not fatal," Finnegan said. "It pierced his left cheek, bored a diagonal path and exited the back of his neck, on the right. The second bullet shattered his nose. He was still alive then."

"But debilitated by pain and shock, no doubt."

"It was most likely the third or fourth shot that killed him. The third penetrated his left eye socket. The fourth went through his temple, also on the left. The subsequent shots simply served to rip his face apart. There were ten shots in all."

The first three photos showed Powell after he'd been washed and autopsied. The bullet holes were evident. As Finnegan said, the gunshots had battered Powell's face into a bloody pulp of soft tissue and fragmented bone. The only distinguishing features left untouched were his hairline, his ears and his chin. The dead man had a broad forehead and smooth hairline, softly rounded ears and dimpled chin.

I shook my head. No wonder they killed Carter.

The second set of photos, about four in number, showed Finnegan's progress as he systematically put Powell's face back together. The last photo showed the finished results.

"Here," said Finnegan, handing me another picture. It was the same shot I'd seen at the public library.

"Very handsome," I murmured.

"That's what she wanted me to make him look like again."

"She, being Mrs. Goodfellowe?"

He nodded. "I told her it would be a miracle, but I could do it."

I compared the last shot of the restored Powell to the studio portrait. "You do excellent work," I murmured.

Finnegan beamed with pride.

I laid aside Finnegan's photo and concentrated on the photo of Powell alive. The room he was sitting in bothered me. I couldn't imagine Mrs. Goodfellowe having such a horribly furnished room in her house. I brought the photo closer, studying it intently.

"What is it?" Finnegan asked.

I shook my head. "Probably nothing."

## 46.

The guard booth outside Goodfellowe House was empty. Sutton must've taken off for the day. Before showing me in, Roland whispered an anxious question:

"Did you get to see her?"

"Yeah," I whispered back. "We can talk about it later."

He wanted to say more but we were at the open parlor door by then and Mrs. Goodfellowe could see us.

"Well," she said, "looking me up and down. To what do I owe the pleasure—again?"

"I'm here about a Mr. Carter, Mr. Tellman Carter—"

"Him!" She rolled her eyes. "But why in the world would you ask about him? I thought you were working on Esther's case."

"I believe that Mr. Carter uncovered information that might be relevant. —"

"You're mistaken."

"Perhaps. But could you tell me what he wanted to see you about?"

"I could. But I won't. It seems to me you're on a fishing expedition. Nosing about in affairs that don't concern you."

"I know that Mr. Carter was very interested in your second husband, and that he wanted to see photos of his remains. Do you know why? Did he tell you?"

"No, he didn't. But it's really no business of yours."

"Did Mr. Carter ask whether you'd met Bobby Kelly or seen him around your husband?"

Her lips pressed together. "How dare you mention that name, that—"

"Mr. Carter's dead, by the way. Shot to death in your husband's hometown."

"I'm sorry to hear that, but—"

"Did you know that he told Kelly's sister he thought Kelly was innocent?"

"I know no such thing. It's no—"

"Don't you want to know why Mr. Carter said that? Aren't you curious as to why he wanted to see the postmortem photos?"

"He was—his questions were unacceptable."

"I'll tell you what I think he suspected—and what I now suspect, too: that the dead man wasn't your husband. It was Kelly."

"You're crazy," she whispered.

"The killer obliterated his victim's face. Why?"

"Anger," she said, her voice shaking. "Anger and jealousy. Eric once told me how Robert envied him."

"The photos show that Powell had a smooth chin; Kelly had a dimpled one—"

"Ridiculous."

"Your husband killed his friend and switched identities. And he did it to create an alibi."

"A what? What for?"

"To cover his part in the heist."

Her lips parted in shock. "Oh no, you won't. You are not going write that. I won't let you." She rang her little bell. "Roland! I won't listen anymore. Get out."

She was the picture of aristocratic, blue-blooded stubbornness. Despite her fall from social grace, she had power and she knew how to use it.

But power has its limits.

"No matter who we are," I said, "we can't change reality by simply wishing it wasn't so. We can deny the truth; even try to conceal it. But sooner or later, the truth wins out. So think about it. Reflect on everything I've said. Because I'm not finished. With or without the paper's approval, I will continue to dig."

"You're worse than the others. You say you want to help, but you just want to—"

"Think about it. One has to wonder. About them. About *you*."

"What do you mean?"

I didn't answer. Her eyes showed sudden understanding.

"Oh, no," she gasped. "You think that I ..."

Roland appeared in the doorway. Seeing her agitation, he touched my forearm. "I'm sorry, miss, but you'd better go."

"You're wrong," Mrs. Goodfellowe said in a horrified whisper. "Terribly, terribly wrong. How could you think that I'd--?"

"Your husband dead, a faceless corpse; your protégé kidnapped and your home robbed——"

"Esther? You think I hurt Esther." She sounded hurt and bewildered. "Oh, no," she said again.

I waited, hoping she'd say more, but all she did was murmur, words, phrases that were barely sensible.

"You don't understand. I've got to make you understand. You can't go out there, thinking that ... I can't let you ... I—"

Her gaze went to Elizabeth's photograph and she stilled. An unutterable sadness touched her face.

"Did you know that Esther was the same age as my daughter when she died? They were both taken from me so ... so suddenly. I had no time to prepare. I never thought about them dying. They were so young. I never..."

Her eyes glittered wetly. I was transfixed, and I think Roland was, too. I'd never seen her this way or imagined such vulnerability. The transformation from haughty socialite to grieving mother had happened so quickly. Perhaps, it was always there, just below the surface. Perhaps, it had merely taken the shock of my unspoken accusation to bring it out.

"Maybe Elizabeth's death was a curse to humble me," she said. "I was—am—a proud woman. Born of a proud family. Maybe the Lord thought I needed a lesson."

Her right hand gripped her handkerchief, working it into a ball. "After Elizabeth died, I buried myself in this house. I wanted nothing to do with anything." A tear escaped her iron control. She dabbed at it.

"Then I heard about Esther. I felt compelled to hear her play. It was at a small church. Music like I'd never heard before. I can't tell you how it affected me. I wanted to do everything for her. Everything I'd been too thoughtless, too selfish to do for my daughter. I even thought, stupidly, that God was giving me a second chance."

There was another tear. "Hurt my friends? Maybe. But Esther? Never. She was my heart, my Elizabeth, come back to me. Don't you see? She was my last chance to live."

## 47.

I must admit. Her tears got to me. Tough Lanie Price. Sure, sure. I felt like a cad when I left Mrs. Goodfellowe's house. Trying to fulfill my promises to a little boy, I'd gotten a man killed, nearly cost Sam his job and now I was even beating up on an old widow woman in a desperate, pathetic search for a solution that would fix everything.

Cold sunlight streamed through the glass doors to the newspaper building's main entrance and dappled the brown marble vestibule floor with a flat, hard light. How many more days would I get to witness that particular play of sunlight? I felt a surge of nostalgia, already anticipating that my days with the paper were numbered.

I was about to write what could be my last column for the *Chronicle*. It might not even be that if Sam refused to print it. I would talk to him about it beforehand, of course, sort of lay the groundwork. That would be simpler, and more diplomatic, than my usual approach, which was to write the piece and then battle him over it.

It had been two minutes since I'd pushed the button for the elevator and there was no sign of it coming. I glanced at my watch. It was after six. Johnny had probably taken off for the day. He usually didn't wait around for Lewiston, his replacement. The evening operator was a nice enough guy, but he was always late. There was no telling when he'd show.

I headed for the stairs. Thank goodness, we weren't high up.

One floor away from the office, the sound of a male voice floated down.

"Selena..."

My ears perked up. The voice was familiar.

"Sam, you know she's gone off the edge. You need me. You need what I have to offer."

"Now why would you think that?"

A pause. The sound of movement. A new intimacy in Selena's voice.

"Aren't you ready for something new? Something hot and sassy?"

My face grew warm. My hand tightened on the railing. I couldn't clearly hear Sam's answer. I continued up the stairs, treading lightly.

"You're an excellent reporter, but the column belongs to Lanie."

"Now, you and I both know I'm not just talking about that."

I leaned over the railing and peered upward. Sam and Selena stood on the stairway, two floors above. He was holding copy. She was holding him. Her arms were linked around his neck, her pretty, overdone face turned up to his.

I turned the corner on the stairway. She saw me. An evil smile flickered over her lips. Seeing her gaze, he started to turn around, but she caught him by the chin.

"Now, Sam, dear Sam. Don't be difficult."

Stroking his chest and puckering her lips, she stood on tiptoe and kissed him. It wasn't a long kiss, but to me it lasted an eternity.

He unlinked her arms from around his neck. "Thanks, but no thanks."

"Really?" she said. "But you liked it. I could tell."

"Yes, I liked it—I'll admit that—but not enough to want more. Now, let go."

She leaned into him, purring. "C'mon, I can lay it out just as well as she can. Do it double-time, baby, and with half the hassle."

"Look, you're a very attractive lady, but you're—"

"What? Not good enough?"

"Hello." It was time to make my presence known.

He whirled around, stunned. "Lanie, I—"

I shook my head. What was there to say? I climbed the last steps between us and pushed past him. He grabbed me by the elbow. I couldn't bear to look at him.

"Selena," he said, "Maybe, you want to leave us alone."

"No," I said. "No need to break up the meeting."

"Lanie," he said. "We have to talk."

I nodded. "But not right now. I have business to attend to." I forced myself to look at him. "And it looks as though you do, too."

Selena must've read the pain in my eyes. I sure read the triumph in hers. Images of Sam and Selena, and the sound of her insidious whispers, followed me up the stairs. I moved with leaden feet, gripping the banister. By the time I reached the newsroom, I felt dizzy.

Normally, the place was half-empty by then. Most folks came in as early at six or seven a.m., so they went home at four. But it was late Monday, deadline time, so a whole lot of people were working late, trying to beat the clock. A bunch of folks looked up when I came in. At the look I gave them, several dropped their gaze again.

I plunked down in my chair, leaned on my desk and covered my face with my hands. Then I counted from one to thirty, my heart thudding like a long-distance runner.

It was my fault that he was out there with her. I'd pushed him away again and again. What did I expect?

I glanced at the wall clock. Were they still in the stairwell or had they gone off somewhere else, where they could be alone? I wanted to go back and check. But I had something more important to do.

A column to write.

I straightened up and willed myself to concentrate. As I rolled a fresh sheet of paper into the typewriter, Selena breezed in. She was smiling from ear to ear, glowing with guilty pleasure, patting her hair and smoothing her skirt. Eyes followed her as she trotted back to her desk. Heads swiveled back to the door as Sam entered. He strode over to my desk, bent down and spoke in an intense whisper.

"I want you in my office. Now."

# 48.

Mrs. Goodfellowe had filed another complaint. Sam was embarrassed about the scene on the stairwell, but he was way more upset about Mrs. Goodfellowe's call.

"Lanie, she could shut us down. Actually, she wouldn't have to. Canfield and his crowd would do it for her. What were you thinking?"

"Sam, please—"

"I thought you understood. You could lose this column. Hell, you could lose your career. One call from Canfield and you wouldn't be able to get a job at any paper of standing."

"I do understand—"

"Do you? Goodfellowe talked to Canfield; Canfield talked to Ramsey. If you don't change tracks, I'll have to give your column to Selena. I won't have a choice. She's already done a draft copy—and it's a damn fine one. It's bright, cheerful, Christmassy."

Give my column to—? I flashed on the scene in the stairwell. "I should've seen it coming."

"I'm sorry, Lanie. I'll have to do it."

"Oh, yeah. Tell me how they're forcing you."

His expression hardened. "They're not forcing me. You are."

I half-rose. "What're you tal—"

"You're leaving me little choice. You insist upon doing things your way, and you don't tell me what's going on—not till it's too damn late."

"This should not be about covering your ass. It should be about the Todd case."

"No, it should be about the paper—and the fact that I'm responsible, not just for you, but for every soul who works for me. You're worried about one family; I'm worried about fifty."

He was right. But so was I. I had to make him see things differently or we'd both lose. For once I decided to be diplomatic and concede a point or two.

"All right. You're angry and you have a right to be. I should've told you about my being attacked. I should've dug deeper before going with Whitefield. But please, believe me. This time I'm dead on."

He shook his head in bewilderment. "You don't know when to stop, do you? We've taken a huge blow to our credibility. This paper is practically on its knees, and you're still pushing."

That temper of mine surged back. I stood up, trembling. "I'll stop when Esther Todd is found—dead or alive. I'll stop when I know who took her from her family, who robbed her of all she had. I'll stop," I said, "when I've kept my promise to her son."

He gave me a long look of frustration. "Do you think you're the only one who cares about Esther? I could've blocked you from writing that column to begin with. I almost wish I had, 'cause you don't appreciate what anybody does for you. You keep demanding more and more. Nobody's sacrifice counts but your own."

I was speechless. Did he really see me that way? As self-righteous and obsessed? "Sam, listen—"

"No, you listen. Esther Todd is probably dead. You know it and I know it. Hell, the whole world knows it. Every one of those people out in that newsroom wishes it wasn't so. Every one of them would love to see her found, and her killer caught. But none of them is willing to lose their job to bring up the bones of a dead woman—and I won't ask them to."

"That's not what I want—"

"Isn't it?"

"No, it isn't." I sank back down in the chair, all anger gone. "You're right, Sam, right about so many things. About me being so pigheaded. And how I've gone about this whole thing. But please don't let outsiders force you to make a choice you don't have to make. Don't let them pit us against one another."

I spoke from my heart, reaching for the compassion in his, the compassion that was being used against him. "It's not the Todd family versus the families in the newsroom. It's the truth versus lies and darkness and the ugliness it hides. Please, let me file this last column."

His expression told me nothing, so I played my last card.

"If it turns out I'm wrong, you won't have to fire me. I'll quit."

That got him. Sadness flitted across his face. He cleared his throat in the way of a man choosing his words carefully.

"Lanie," he began, "you know that to me, you're irreplaceable, but to the world, and that includes this paper, you're not." He paused. "So if you make that kind of offer, I'll to have to take you up on it."

Though spoken softly and expected, his words were a blow. Heart in my throat, I nodded. "I know."

There was a long silence.

"All right," he said. "Tell me what you plan to write."

Terrified of saying the wrong thing, I took a few seconds to collect my thoughts. Then I began, watching his face for reaction.

The structure of the column would be simple, I said. I would review Esther's kidnapping and bracket it with descriptions of Eric Alan Powell's murder and the Goodfellowe heist, stringing them together like pearls in a necklace of crime. I explained my theory that whoever killed Powell might've kidnapped Esther, most likely because she knew something she shouldn't have.

"The only official suspect in the Powell killing was Kelly, but he makes a weak one. He had no apparent reason to shoot

Powell. But Powell would've had an excellent reason to shoot him, if he wanted to fake his own death as a prelude to robbing his rich wife."

"Humph," Sam said.

He was clearly intrigued. Leaning back in his chair, his arms folded across his chest, he reflected. Fifteen long seconds went by. Finally, in agitation, he ran his hands over his face, sighed and sat up.

"It sounds good, Lanie. Real good. Crazy as it is, it could even be right. But you know I can't print it. We'd be endangering the paper."

"We'd damage it more by not printing it."

"Tell you what: I'll give you twenty-four hours to give me something that would justify every word. This time tomorrow, be here to show me what you've got. It has to be airtight, or else."

He didn't have to say more. I took a deep breath. Twenty-four hours. It was better than nothing, but was it enough?

"Thanks." I started to leave.

"Lanie?"

"Yes?" I paused in the doorway.

"Be careful. Watch your back."

I nodded and went out.

Selena sauntered over and whispered in my ear. "So much for your chances of screwing your way to the top."

The next sound was of my hand meeting her flesh. She stumbled back into George's desk. There were snickers and giggles. Sam had come out to lay an edited piece on George's desk. Stunned and holding her cheek, Selena turned to him, pointed at me and pouted.

"Did you see what she—"

"Shut up," he snapped.

Back at my desk, I put in a call to the Chicago police department, the criminal records division. It took a bit of doing, but I finally got someone on the line who knew about the Powell case, one Lieutenant Daniel Ramsey. His voice was gruff, but he seemed all right.

"What d'you need?"

"Do you have Powell's fingerprints on file?"

Ramsey thought about it for a second. "Yeah, we should."

"Could you check, please?"

"Lady, that's gonna take time."

"I'd appreciate it. It's important."

"Why?"

"I'm working on a story angle, an old case. And I'm wondering if Powell had something to do with it."

Ramsey took a moment. "Okay. I tell you what. You call me back in a couple of hours and I'll see what I can do for you."

"Thanks."

After hanging up, I took out my notepad and found the telephone number for Denver Sutton.

"So, what can I do for you?" he said when I identified myself.

"I'd like to meet with you and have a talk, about Eric Alan Powell."

He paused. "Powell, huh? Well, that's a name I haven't heard in a while. And you want to talk about him? May I ask why?"

"It has to do with a story I'm working on."

"The same story you were doing when you came by today? Mrs. Goodfellowe was mighty upset after that. I don't think she'd appreciate my talking to you."

I paused. "Put it like this: Given what I'm preparing to write, Mrs. Goodfellowe would be upset if you didn't talk to me."

"What does that mean?"

"It means meet with me."

"Okay," he said, still cautious. "But when?"

"In an hour."

He paused and I held my breath.

"Where?" he asked.

I thought fast. I didn't want to meet in a fancy club, just a nice anonymous dive. I gave him an address. He hesitated.

"Is that one of them Harlem speakeasies?"

"It sure is. You scared to come up here?"

He gave a chuckle. "Hell, no."

# 49.

Biggie's Manor House was a basement dive on the east side of Fifth Avenue and 132$^{nd}$ Street. Pimps, prostitutes, gamblers and queens made the bulk of the clientele. Biggie's had replaced Edmond's Cellar, which had stood at the same spot. Ethel Waters once described Edmond's as "the last stop on the way down." Some might've said Biggie's was a rung below that.

It wasn't much more than a dank hole, but I liked it. The decor was simple and the entertainment fine. Some of the better musicians dropped in after hours. On a lucky night, you might've even catch "Jazzlips" Richardson or the Bon Ton Buddies strutting their stuff.

The bad thing about Biggie's was the hootch. That was some nasty liquor. The nice thing was that everybody minded his or her own business. By midnight, the place would be hopping. By three in the morning, it would be packed. But this was still early in the evening. The place was half empty and there was no entertainment, but that was okay. I didn't want crowds or music, just privacy.

Sutton was waiting when I arrived, his back to the wall, at a table in the corner lit by a single low candle. He greeted me with a nod. Again, I had the feeling that I'd met him before.

The cellar was cold, so I kept on my coat. He took a brown leather pouch from an inner jacket pocket, produced some rolling papers and rolled himself a cigarette.

"So how long have you been with Mrs. Goodfellowe?" I asked.

"A few years."

"Since before the heist?"

"Since after."

"How'd you come to work for her?"

"C'mon. You know the answers to these questions."

"Maybe," I shrugged. "It's always good to double-check."

"That it is," he nodded. "Well, as I'm sure you already know, Mrs. Goodfellowe's second husband got himself all shot up. They couldn't identify him the regular way, so they needed someone to bring in—well, let's just call them identifiers—and the file was in Chicago. I brought it and when I did, I met the widow. We kept in touch. After the heist, she contacted me and requested my services."

"That's like closing the barn door after the horse is out, isn't it?"

He shrugged. "Better late than never."

The waiter brought our drinks.

"So why did they pick you?" I continued. "To bring the identifiers, I mean? Was it just the luck of the draw?"

"Not quite. I was sort of their Powell expert. But, of course, I probably know more about criminals in general and how they think than your average cop."

"How so?"

"I was a bounty hunter, and a good one. I spent time studying my prey. Which reminds me. Why would a pretty little lady like you be interested in a rat like Powell?"

"Actually, it's more like I'm following up on a friend's interest."

He tilted his head in a question.

"Tellman Carter," I said. "You remember him?"

He sealed the cigarette and stuck one end between his lips. "Tellman … Tellman Carter. A writer, right?"

"He had an appointment with you."

"That was a while ago. He never showed up."

"You're sure?"

He lit his cigarette and nodded. "Why're you asking?"

"He's dead—murdered."

"All right," Sutton said slowly, exhaling smoke. "This is beginning to sound interesting."

"Did Carter say why he wanted to see you?"

"Not that I recall. He just said he was writing a book on crooks, and that he wanted to talk to me because I was a bounty hunter."

"Did that strike you as unusual?"

He shrugged. "Not really. I mean, yeah, he's the first writer who ever called me. But if you want to talk to an expert, then I'm your man."

"I believe Carter wanted to see you about Powell."

"He didn't say, but I would've been the right person to see."

"What could you have told him?"

"Just about anything he needed to know." He looked at me. "What do you want?"

"For you to fill in the blanks. Right now, all I know is that Powell was a pretty boy who turned an older woman's head."

"He was a swindler. He married Mrs. Goodfellowe fully intending to bilk her—and he might've done it if he'd lived."

"I take it she wasn't the first dowager to fall for him?"

"Not by a long shot. Most of the others were too embarrassed to say anything. They were glad to pay and get rid of him."

"How did he get them to pay up?"

"Pictures. He'd get them to do things that no decent lady, especially of a certain age, would do, not even for her husband."

"He drugged them?"

"Probably. And then it was just a matter of blackmail, pure and greedy. A threat to send a copy of a embarrassing picture to a local paper and that would be that."

"How often did he get away with this?"

"At least four times that I know of. The third woman, also a widow—well, they were all widows—with large inheritances—she balked. She managed to get hold of the pictures, and the plates, and she turned him in. He jumped bail and hit the road."

"That's when you came in?"

"Not quite. You see, these ladies were widows, but that didn't mean they were entirely alone. In two cases, grown children were involved. They suspected what Powell was up to, but couldn't get their mothers to believe them."

"Until it was too late."

"Yup. Powell was gone and the money was gone with him. The widows didn't want to go after him. They were too scared. But the kids weren't. It was the children of the third widow who contacted me. Then the fourth heard about me and got in touch, but by then Powell had touched his new mark and scooted off again.

"Powell was smooth. He didn't just change states; he changed names. He'd stay with a woman for a few months, work on her, and get her to trust him. He'd cut her off from her friends and family, make her so hungry for him she'd do anything to keep him.

"I tracked Powell for more 'n a year, gathering evidence. I was making plans, hoping to spring a trap when it happened."

"Somebody else caught up with him first."

"Yup." He raised his hands and shrugged. "And that was that."

I shook my head. "I don't think so, Mr. Sutton. There's more to Powell's story."

"Is that so?" He leaned forward. "Why don't you lay your cards on the table? Tell me what you're shooting for. Maybe I can provide a little guidance, straighten your aim."

"You know that I've been writing about Esther Todd." I paused, realizing that the Todd disappearance predated his arrival, so he might not know about it—though it became part and parcel of the heist lore, which he did know. Just to be safe,

I briefed him on her case and how her disappearance got tied into the robbery.

"It's all too much of a coincidence," I said. "I think the murder, the kidnapping and the robbery are all connected." And then I told him the connection I saw. "I've seen photographs of Eric alive and Eric dead. They're different."

"Yeah, one's bloody and one's not."

"I'm serious. It's the chins. The photos clearly show that Eric Alan Powell had a dimple. Bobby Kelly did not."

"Hmph," he said. "You certainly picked up on something that everybody else missed. You've got sharp eyes, you do." He drew deeply on his cigarette. "Was there more?"

"The overkill," I said, ignoring his mocking tone. "Obviously, Powell wanted to make Kelly's corpse unidentifiable—so that when they found it in the car, they'd think it was him."

"As I recall, Powell was not only found in his car, he was found in his own clothes. You telling me that Powell forced Kelly to swap clothes with him, sit quietly in the car and let Powell shoot him?"

"Powell could've given him the clothes as a gift. Kelly would've been happy to get them. He would've worn them in a minute. Powell could've done any number of things to get Kelly to do what he needed him to."

He gave a skeptical shake of his head. "And you base this theory on just a pair of photos?"

"Even without the pictures, the case for Kelly doing the killing is pretty damn weak. Kelly was a petty thief. He wasn't even an armed robber. Furthermore, he adored Powell. He was subservient to him. Why would he turn on him? Where would he find the strength to kill him so viciously? The cops never even came up with a motive."

Sutton sighed. "Well, it's an interesting theory, real interesting. Too bad it's all wrong."

He crushed out the remnants of his cigarette in the glass ashtray on the table, and started making himself a new one.

I've never seen anyone make a cigarette as fast as he did. With a few flicks, he had it rolled and stuck in his mouth.

"When you spend as much time tracking a man as I did, you get to know him. In some ways, you know him better than he knows himself. I certainly knew Powell better than any of the women he married. And I can tell you the one thing none of them ever guessed."

"And what's that?"

"He loved men."

He smiled at my astonishment and lit his cigarette.

"You're telling me that he and Kelly were lovers?"

"Long-time. Big-time. Since childhood."

The statement hung in the air, as heavy as the smoke floating upward from his cigarette. I was surprised all right, stunned is more like it.

"It started when they were boys on Chicago's South Side. Didn't many people out there know about it."

"So this Mr. Loverman business ... Powell was just playing ..."

"A role."

"And Kelly went along with it?"

"He had to. He never did take a fancy to the scam, but I guess he always believed that none of those old women meant a thing to Powell."

"You telling me that Powell felt differently about Katherine Goodfellowe?"

"No, I'm saying that something about that setup made Kelly snap."

"Jealousy?"

"Greed. I think they had a falling-out over the money. Y'see, Mrs. Goodfellowe was the richest of all of Powell's wives. I think he decided to stick with her. Maybe he was getting tired. He was getting older, too, and there are only so many rich old widows you can swindle and get away with it."

I saw his point. "So you think Kelly got upset because Powell decided to stay married?"

"Yup. If you want to know why he shot his life-long friend, then look no further."

I turned this new angle over, aware of him watching me. "Why didn't you take this information to the police?"

"They didn't need it. Powell was dead and they knew who did it. Who cares if they had the wrong motive, as long as they had the right guy?"

Smoke wafted over his face. His slanted eyes studied me, as I studied him.

"If you feel that way, then why are you telling me?" I asked.

He had a disarming smile. "I like to help people. And I see that you do, too. This column you've told me about. And your trying to find this woman, help her family: You done put a lot of work into it. I can respect that. I'm listening to you and thinking, 'Good cause, but bad start.'"

"Excuse me?"

"Bad start, I said. You're going off in the wrong direction. You won't come up with any new leads this way, by claiming something so totally wrong—very imaginative and gutsy, mind you—but still wrong." He gave a deep laugh. "If you go on this way, no one will help you. I want to prevent that."

I felt faintly insulted. "How nice of you."

"You really think you're hard-boiled, huh?"

"I'm no sob-sister."

He gave another deep-throated chuckle. "Okay ... okay. So, you're good at your job. But yours is different from mine. You're a good writer, not an investigator."

I stirred my coffee. "So what's your pitch?"

He pretended not to understand. "S'cuse me?"

"You're working hard to convince me that I need you. When somebody does that, it usually means they need me. What do you want?"

His lips drew back in a lazy smile that revealed no teeth, just turned his mouth into a wide, curved slit. Smoke came out in little puffs as he spoke.

"I like you," he said slowly. "I really do."

"Nice to know it."

"You know, it was dang hard for me to lose Powell like that. He meant years of work, time I can't get back, can't get paid for. But there's another reward—for Bobby Kelly. And that I can be paid for."

"You'd like me to inform you if I get any information on Kelly."

"We could split the reward, fifty-fifty."

I shook my head. "Kelly's dead. But even if he wasn't— thanks, but no thanks."

I started to get up. His hand shot out and grabbed me by the wrist. He was quick, all right. It was easy to imagine him as the quickest draw in the West. His grip was firm, confident and very warm.

"Let me go," I said.

He released me and held his hands up in an attitude of surrender. "Hey, sorry. I just want you to know that I didn't mean to insult you. I just thought we could help each other out."

"I'm not interested in a bounty. I want information on Esther."

"All right, then I'll take the bounty and you'll get the information."

"If you're so sure Kelly killed Powell, then why are you still in New York? Everyone else, including his sister, seems to think he's skipped town. And it makes sense, considering how many cops were after him."

"Yeah, it makes sense. Some." He stood, pushing back his chair. "Look, why don't you think about my offer? It can't hurt. And you never know. It might just get us both closer to our goals. The cops aren't interested anymore. It's just you and me. You help me find Kelly and I'll help you find your missing piano player."

"All right," I said. "I'll think about it."

Sutton surprised me with an offer to drive me back uptown. By the time I got to the newsroom, everyone had left. Even Sam. Was he with Selena? I shook myself free of the thought, reached for the telephone and called Ramsey in Chicago.

"Oh, Mrs. Price. How ya doin'?"

"Fine, thank you. You have that information I need?"

"Sure do. The answer is yes. We have the prints. Or I should say we did."

"Why the past tense?"

"He's dead, isn't he? No need to have 'em cluttering up the files. His records have been archived. I had to go downstairs to the basement to dig 'em out."

"What I need to know is whether they were in the files that were used to identify his remains."

"I wasn't in this division then. But I heard about the case. The prints? Yeah, normally they woulda been there."

I paused. "Listen, do you know Denver Sutton?"

A guffaw. "'Course I do. Who doesn't? Sort of a legend around here. Got a thing for the cowboy look. A great guy. Good bounty hunter."

"So you think highly of him?"

"If I needed someone backing me up, he'd be the one I'd choose."

I was thoughtful.

"Anything else?" Ramsey asked.

"No ... nothing." I thanked him and signed off.

## 50.

I'd found most of my answers. I had my story. There were a few gaps, but I had a fairly clear idea of who could fill them. I hailed a taxi and gave the driver a Park Avenue address. I told the driver to pull up across the street from Goodfellowe mansion and wait. I handed him a bill.

"Will that cover you for an hour?"

"Oh, yeah. It sure will."

I didn't have any more of that particular denomination, so I hoped we wouldn't have to wait too long. It was already nine at night. Theoretically dinner was over and all domestic chores done.

Park Avenue is an elegant block. Even the shadows are elegant. Long dark cars moved up and down the street, pausing before doormen buildings to discharge gents in top hats and ladies in fur. I watched them for a while, but soon I got bored. Park Avenue didn't have the action I was used to. It was nice, but it wasn't Lenox.

Minutes dragged by. The cabbie tried to gab, but after a few of my monosyllabic responses, he got the message and lapsed into silence. More minutes crawled by. It was getting close to the hour mark and I was beginning to wonder whether this was such a good idea, when the door to servants' entrance opened and he come out, a tall thin man with a sense of natural grace. His gray hat was tilted to one side; his immaculate dark overcoat hung straight and true.

"Pick him up," I said.

The driver started the engine, rolled across the street and drew alongside the curb. I lowered the window and called out, "Roland!"

He jumped back. "Who's there?"

"It's me."

"Miss Lanie?" His relief was palpable.

"Get in, Roland. Let's go someplace and have a coffee."

"Well, I ... I had plans for this evening."

"This won't take long. I'd really like to have a talk."

"About Beth? Did you see her?"

I pushed opened the door and slid over. He hesitated, but then got in. We drove uptown to a blues bar near the Cotton Club. Outside, a billboard advertised Bessie Smith.

The club was in a half-basement. It was a crowded, narrow room with a small podium at one end. It sounded like Bessie had the mike. We squeezed up to the bar, just inside the door.

"It's a dive," I said, "but a comfortable one."

"Yeah," he said, looking around, taking off his leather gloves. "Looks okay."

The bartender appeared, a woman in her forties with a thick waist and tired expression. "What'll it be?"

"Just coffee for me," I said.

She raised an eyebrow, but then shrugged and turned to Roland.

"The same."

"All right, then. Coffee it is," she said, waddling away.

Somebody left, opening the door and a blast of frigid December air came in. I repressed a shiver. Roland looked at me and smiled.

He was around sixty, old enough to be Beth's father, but attractive. How did he feel about her? Had he given me her address so I could spy on her for him? Was he jealous of her and her relationship with her baby's father? Could he have been the father himself?

"How long have you been with Mrs. Goodfellowe?"

"Nigh on twenty years."

"You like working for her?"

He shrugged. "It's a job."

"So you were there before Beth came?"

He nodded. "I helped train her. She ... she was a good child."

"Was?"

He put down his cup, encircled it with his hands. "Things changed after Mr. Eric arrived. You know, Miss Katherine's second husband?"

"Changed how?"

"Well ... I think he gave Beth ideas, the kind that no colored girl should have."

"Such as?"

He had such a hangdog expression that I felt a surge of pity. It seemed obvious what he was getting at. But experience had taught me the danger of making assumptions. So I asked him straight out:

"Did he make love to her?"

The hands on the cup tightened. "He talked to her and I'm sure he got her to meet with him. To go places with him, and yes, maybe even let him ... you know."

I spoke gently. "Were you in love with her?"

He gave a bitter chuckle. "Now what would I be doing, a man of my age, in love with a little bitty girl like that?"

"Why not? You're a good-looking man. Elegant. Well-mannered. A lot of young women I know would..."

He shook his head. "You're awful nice to tell an old man that. But I know better."

"What a man knows, or thinks he knows, and what he feels are two different things. So, tell me, were you or aren't you?"

He nodded. "Okay, yeah. I guess I was soft on her." He smiled sheepishly. "Heck, I was crazy 'bout her."

After that, it was easy to get him to talk. He wanted to get it out.

Following the robbery, everyone was so preoccupied by the investigation that no one noticed the changes in Beth. One day it hit Roland that her waistline had expanded.

"It was like there was nothing there one day and she was showing the next. By the time we noticed, it was too late. I was gonna talk to her, but Miss Katherine sent for her that same day. It happened so fast. One minute she was on staff, the next she was out on the street. I tried to talk to her, but she shrugged me off, told me not to worry. 'I'll be fine,' she said. 'I'm gonna be well taken care of.'"

"What did you think she meant by that?"

"Well, I suppose I believed—or wanted to believe—that maybe her baby's father hadn't walked off after all. You know, that's what we'd all supposed, but how were we to know?"

"Had you ever heard her mention anybody? Seen her with someone?" I had a specific person in mind, but I wanted him to be the one to mention him.

He reflected. "No ... I didn't."

"Did you think she was just talking to reassure you?"

"Yes ... and no. I mean, I'd always sensed a certain steel in her, deep down beneath all that softness. I'd always suspected something tough as nails. But the way she talked to me when she left that day, there was something more, something that, well ... that bothered me."

The bartender reappeared. "Want anything more?"

Roland and I both shook our heads, no. He tipped his cup up, looking into it, but seeing something else entirely.

"Weeks went by. I thought about her. I admit it. I couldn't get her out of my mind. We didn't have an address for her, but we knew nobody had hired her, nobody worth mentioning."

"You mean nobody in Miss Katherine's rank and file."

"That's right. We would've heard about it."

He took a sip of his coffee and grimaced. I watched him set his cup back down and asked my next question.

"So how did you find out where she was living?"

"I followed her."

He'd seen her on 125th Street. It was about a month after she'd been dismissed. He nearly went up to her, to ask her how she was doing, but something stopped him. At first he didn't know what it was, but then it him that she looked incredibly slim. Her stomach was flat. She wasn't pregnant.

Had she lost the child? Now he wasn't sure what to do. What would he say? If she had lost the child, then would she be interested in getting her old job back? Maybe he could talk to her about that.

But even that idea failed to put him at ease. There was something about the quick smile she gave the vegetable dealer and something else in the snazzy way she was dressed. It was all wrong.

He was a widower. He and his wife had never been able to have children, but they had tried. His wife had endured three miscarriages before giving up. So he knew a little bit about how women reacted to losing a child, especially so late in the pregnancy. His wife had been torn up about it. He'd heard other men talking about their girlfriends and wives who'd miscarried, saying their women had gone through the same thing. He told himself that different women reacted differently, but couldn't help wondering just how well he knew Beth after all.

He followed her home. He didn't have the nerve to go up to her apartment and talk to her, so he took down the address and went away wondering. More than wondering. Worried.

And perplexed.

He took a deep breath, rubbed his face with his hands. "You must think I'm a sick, dirty old man, chasing after a child like that."

"I don't think that at all."

"You'll change your mind when you hear what else I'm thinking."

"I don't think so, but go ahead and tell me."

He rested his elbows on the bar. "It's this way. I told you that I never heard her talk about a man one way or another. And it drove me crazy. She got a bit sassy after Mr. Eric took an interest in her. Naturally, she got real quiet after he died."

I could imagine.

"If it hadn't been for the fact that Mr. Eric was dead," Roland said, "I would've wondered whether he fathered her child. I'm ashamed to admit it, but it would be a lie to deny it."

"No reason to deny it. Those things have been known to happen."

"But she never said nothing about nobody else, and now I don't know what to think." He paused. "Well, I do know what I think, but it's not pretty."

"And what's that?"

"I don't think she was pregnant at all." He bit his lower lip. I couldn't tell whether he was trying to hold the words in or to force them out. "I think—it sounds crazy to say it—but I think she wanted to be fired."

"Why would she want that?"

He scratched his head. "I don't know."

I was about to ask another question when the bartender appeared. She slapped her check on the bar. Roland reached for his wallet.

"It's on me." I picked up the bill, and then stared at it. "*Seventy cents?* For just two cups of coffee?"

"No, miss. It's twenty cents. That's a two, not a seven."

"Oh," I said, relieved. Then I had a thought. Frowning, I asked her, "Do you have a telephone?"

"In back. By the ladies' room."

I paid the bill and added a nice tip that sent her away with a smile. Then I pushed away from the bar.

"Roland, could you excuse me for a second?"

"Okay." He looked bewildered.

It took two minutes to cut through the crowd. Once I at the telephone, I dug out Sophie Carter's number.

"Mrs. Carter? It's Lanie. Sorry to disturb you so late, but I need you to check on something."

"What is it?"

"Tellman's appointment book. Could you double-check when he was supposed to have met with Denver Sutton?"

"Is it important?"

"Could be."

"Well, all right. Wait a second."

She put down the receiver. I heard her moving about. The telephone was in the room Carter had used as an office. She was back within a minute.

"I found the appointment book," she said. "Hold on." The light sound of her ruffling pages came down the line. "Oh, here, yes. Here it is." A pause. "It was for the second of August."

My heart thumped. "I was sure it was for the seventh."

"Tellman's two has a short tail. Many people take it for a seven."

"Thanks." I hung up and just stood there for a second.

A seven. It was a seven. The seventh of August.

I remembered Roland. I had to get back to him. I pushed my way through the crowd and was relieved to see him still sitting there.

"Wow," he said. "You look like you got good news."

"Yeah. Sort of like an early Christmas present. Feels like it, anyway."

"Is it about Beth?"

My smile faded and I shook my head. "No. It has nothing to do with her."

"So, how is she?" he asked, his voice tentative.

"Doing well," I said, thinking how he wouldn't recognize his little friend in her anymore. "You know, it's funny … how you said she might not have had a baby. When I was in her apartment, I didn't see any sign of a child, so I asked her about it. She told me she'd sent him down South to stay with her mother."

He frowned. "Her mother? But that can't be."

"Why not?"

"Her mother's dead. Been dead. For more'n twenty years."

*"Are you sure?"*

"Sure I'm sure. Beth grew up in an orphanage. And she's not from down South neither. The orphanage is up there on 125th Street. You know the one, St. Jude's Orphan Asylum. It's run by a convent."

"Beth, in a convent orphanage?"

"I went up there with her one day. She wanted to visit 'em, take a cake to the kids."

"And the nuns knew her?"

"Oh, they knew her, all right. They sure did."

## *51.*

I had the taxi drop Roland off, then take me over 410 St. Nicholas Avenue. The front door was open. The lock had been jimmied. I went inside and had to walk around a drunk sleeping in the lobby. I went upstairs, anticipating the look on Beth's face when she saw me. She didn't disappoint me.

"What the hell are you doing here?"

"We need to talk."

"Well, come back tomorrow."

"It can't wait." I pushed past her.

"You can't bust in on a person like this." She slammed the door and turned to me. "I never did like you."

"That's too bad, 'cause I sure liked you."

Her mouth dropped open, but nothing came out. She didn't know how to answer.

"Beth, I need the truth."

"About what?"

"About you ... and Eric and what happened to Esther."

She was wary. "I don't know what you mean."

"Beth, it's over. This is your chance to save yourself."

"Go away."

"Don't make me do this the hard way. I don't want to call the cops on you. Not yet."

She swallowed. "I got nothing to say to you."

"All right. Let's try it this way. Esther disappeared on a hard, cold night, a night as cold and lonely as this one. Either she went away by herself, or she was kidnapped. Well, we know she didn't just go away, don't we? She was taken. It's just a question of who did it. Was it a crazy boyfriend? If so, then it was a one-man show. But it wasn't, was it? The kidnapper had help: somebody who posed as Esther when Mrs. Goodfellowe's Packard was sold, somebody who faked Esther's scar, wore Esther's clothes and made believe she was Esther."

"You're nuts."

"Would a crazy boyfriend enlist a woman's help? He wouldn't—but thieves would."

She didn't answer and I knew that Roland was right.

"You never were pregnant, were you? It was just a ruse to get Mrs. Goodfellowe to fire you."

Defiant. "Why the hell would I want to get myself fired?"

"'Cause it would've been too dangerous to walk out on your own. If you'd quit within months of the heist, the cops would've been suspicious. Ruth said you were scared. Of course you were. You thought that if they suspected Esther, they'd suspect you—and they would've been right."

"You get outta here."

She went to the apartment door and yanked it open. I stood my ground. I wouldn't have been doing her any favors by leaving.

"You'd better close that door and listen. You're on the losing team, baby. What has Eric done for you? All this time, what has he done? Has he bought you fine clothes? Or paid for a nice place? He hasn't and he won't. He's left you like a sitting duck."

"Shut up!"

"Talk now or forever hold your peace—'cause the clock is ticking."

"Get outta here!"

"I can help you. I can help you find a good attorney. But if you don't speak up—"

"I don't need your help. You hear me? Now get out! Get out!"

"It's over, Beth. Don't you understand? I'm going to make it over."

We locked eyes. She saw my resolve and I saw her fear. Her bravado wilted. She looked out her open door as though it was her last vision of freedom, then sighed, closed the door and leaned against it.

"Nobody's gonna believe you," she said in a monotone without conviction. "You got no proof."

"It doesn't matter. Once I tell them what happened, they'll start digging. They'll pull you in and make you talk. And there'll be no negotiating. The time for that is now. Come on, come with me. I'm sure we can make a deal."

"I'm not talking to no cops." She shook her head. "They'd kill me."

"We'll go to my office. Talk to my boss. Write up your story. I'll call a lawyer."

"I don't know," she whispered. "It's too late."

"It's not too late. Come with me."

She thumbed the tears away, smearing her eye makeup. Hugging herself, she came back down the hall and collapsed in her sole chair.

"What am I going to do?" she moaned. "What am I going to do?"

I told myself not to feel sorry for her, but I did. "Esther told you about her problems with Whitefield, didn't she?"

Beth nodded.

"So you did know his name," I said.

"I was too scared to give it to you."

"Maybe," I studied her. "But I think you were just doing what you were told to do."

She straightened up. Fear flashed across her eyes. "What did you say?"

"You were given instructions, weren't you?"

"How did you know?"

"Lots of little things. I don't want to go into it right now. What I want to hear about is Esther."

She was quiet, finally realizing that the game was up. "It was my fault," she said in a small voice. "What happened to Esther, it was my doing. She told me about Whitefield, and I told Mr. Eric. Next thing I knew, he was telling me to make sure Esther got to the hospital that night. He didn't say why. I wouldna never done it if I'd known why."

"What did he do to her?"

"I don't know. He didn't tell me. Really. He never told me."

"And you didn't ask?"

She looked down. "I was afraid to."

"Do you know where he's hiding?"

"He's gone. Been gone."

"Where? Don't protect him anymore."

"Protect him? Oh, please, no. You think I'm here 'cause he left me? They killed him. Said it was too dangerous to have him walking around. Someone might recognize him. And that if I ratted, they'd kill me too." She gazed at me. "Look at you. You ain't nobody. How you going to protect me?"

Before I could answer, she shook her head. "I'm not saying nothing more. They'll kill me if I talk."

"You'll go to jail if you don't."

Thick tears spilled down her face. "Please, give me time to think."

I let out a deep sigh. She'd had three years to think. Three years more than she'd given Esther.

A sound came from the hallway. She and I exchanged looks. She got up and went down the hall. I heard her open the door.

When she reappeared seconds later, she wasn't alone.

## 52.

He shoved her into the room and stood next to the closet, just on the edge of the room.

"How you doing?" he asked me.

"Fine, Bellamy, just fine," I said. "But maybe not as well as you."

He wore a long gray coat, the bulky kind, and had both hands stuffed in his pockets.

"Where's your cane?" I asked.

"Left it at home."

"You don't really need it, do you?"

"Nah. But this," he said, "this I need." He withdrew his right hand and showed his heater. "I never leave home without it."

Beth quailed. "Please. Please, don't."

"Get your coat," he snapped.

"I won't tell. I—"

"Get your fucking coat. Or I swear I'll do you right here, right now."

Beth threw me a terrified glance.

"Get it!" he barked.

Beth jumped and grabbed the thin coat that lay at the foot of the bed.

"How'd you know I was here?" I asked.

"I started keeping tabs on you after that last phone call, the one where you asked me if I'd spred Whitefield's name around. That's when I knew, dealing with you wasn't going to be so easy."

His threw a lustful glance at Beth, then said to me, "You know, you almost caught me, that last time you were here. I was on my way over, for my regular appointment, you might say. If you'd stayed a minute longer, you would've seen me."

No wonder Beth had been such a hurry to make us leave. I didn't want to think about how much time and effort might've been saved.

"Well, I guess some people have all the luck," I said.

"You'd better believe it." He motioned toward the hall. "Let's go."

"Where're you taking us?" Beth asked.

"You'll find out when you get there. Now move."

He shoved the gun back in his pocket and we went downstairs, with me in front. He had parked his car at the corner, he said.

It was freezing outside. A frigid wind whipped us as we walked. Street lamps threw weak circles of light across the deserted street and created pools of blackness in between.

Bellamy gripped Beth by the elbow and held her close to cover the gun. When we reached the car, he tossed me the keys and told me to do the driving. He made Beth sit in the back with him.

"One false move and I'll blow her heart out of her chest."

I started the car.

"Head downtown. A hundred and twenty-fifth."

"What's down there?"

"The dock."

Our eyes met in the rearview mirror, Beth's and mine: stark terror in hers; fear battling reason in mine. I had to keep my wits.

Two minutes of silence. Traffic thin going both ways. Cold sweat on my hands. A surreal conversation from the back seat.

"Please," Beth moaned. "What you going to kill me for? I didn't tell her nothing."

"Which is why I got to do it now, before it's too late." A pause. "C'mon baby, don't cry. You knew what you were getting into."

"No, I didn't."

"Maybe not. You're pretty, but dumb." A thoughtful sigh. "On the other hand, you did do a damn good job of telling our lady reporter here about Whitefield."

I met his gaze in the rearview mirror. "So you're the one who told her to tell me about Whitefield?"

"Called her right after you left my house. I didn't think you'd actually find him, though. It took me for a loop when you did. Had to do some quick thinking. But I'm good at that."

That last self-serving compliment I ignored. "Why did you guys hang around? Why didn't you clear out?"

"Why should we? I like this city. After the heist, I felt like I ruled it. Furthermore, I liked the idea of sitting it out. I liked the idea that while everybody was running around—thinking about how the robbers must've burned rubber down to Mexico, they were all right here. Anyway, it was the best place for me to be. I could keep an eye out in case any smart alecks came along … and I was right. One did."

Pausing for the light at 135th and Broadway, I glanced up at the rearview mirror and saw the grille of a familiar car in the distance. I picked up the conversation where I'd left it when we got into the car.

"Ritchie was in on it, too, wasn't he? He must've been. You couldn't have done it without him. You guys worked together for more than thirty years. You were that close."

I kept my eyes on the road, but took my right hand off the steering wheel and held my index finger and thumb half an inch apart. My eyes flicked up at the rearview mirror. The grille was still back there.

"Keep your eyes on the road," he said. "We wouldn't want to have an accident, would we?"

I shrugged. "According to you, we're dead women, anyway. An accident now would just take you with us."

Uncertainty flickered in his eyes. "You wouldn't dare."

"Please—" said Beth.

"I would, if I wanted to. But I don't. Not anymore."

"What does that mean?"

I forced my gaze away and trained it on a point up ahead. He didn't need to know how many times I'd thought of ending it since Hamp's death. He didn't need to know anything about me.

"So why'd you kill him?" I asked.

A muscle moved in his jaw. Otherwise, he was as still and hard as stone. Behind him, the grille had disappeared. I'd been mistaken. There was no one back there. No one ahead. Just darkness and the devil behind me.

"Did Ritchie get cold feet?" I persisted. "Was he gonna gab? Or did you guys have a falling out over how to split the proceeds?"

"You're mighty curious for a woman who's about to die."

"I risked my life for this information. I deserve to have it."

"All right, then. Yeah, he chickened out. The sweetest deal we'd ever made and he was gonna mess it up." He made a sound of disgust.

"Were you guys part of the original plan?"

"No, we figured it out. When I confronted them, they offered us a cut. Why not? But Ritchie wouldn't have nothing to do with it."

"He threatened to turn you in?"

"Nah. Me and Ritchie, we went way back. He said he wouldn't."

"Obviously, you didn't believe him."

Bellamy stared ahead. "Well, let's just put it this way: he was a good cop."

"Who knew too much. So you set him up. Did you pay that prisoner?"

"Didn't have to. Just gave him the opportunity."

"And then you shot him, too."

"Yeah, just like any good cop would."

He spoke without irony. He meant it. He was crazy and he was going to kill us. I should've been scared. Instead I was numb, so numb I couldn't even feel my hands on the steering wheel. It was as if they belonged to somebody else. None of this seemed real. Not even the sound of my voice.

"So was it worth it? Betraying the badge, and all that?"

"Yeah, I'd say so."

We were at 125th Street, sitting under the elevated tracks of the Broadway local. I debated the wisdom of taking instructions from a killer. Once we were at the dock, we'd be alone with him.

Of course, sitting in a car on an empty, icy street in the dead of the night, we were already pretty far from help. If I tried something—

"Whatever you're thinking, don't do it. She'd be dead in a second. And you a second after."

I turned the wheel, passing under the pylons and arches of interlaced steel of the Riverside Drive viaduct, and headed down toward the dock, the river and a darkness deeper than night.

## *53.*

The Manhattanville dock was a popular point of departure for crossing the Hudson River to get to the Palisades Amusement Park. Folks referred to it as the "Fort Lee" Ferry Dock after the service that carried people across the water to Fort Lee, New Jersey. The pier was bustling during the day, but it was desolate at night. And right then, the only light came from the moon, gleaming fat and hazy in the black sky.

Bellamy pushed and shoved us to go ahead. He might not have needed his cane to walk, but he did have some kind of mobility problem. Propelled by fear of the gun at our backs, Beth and I stumbled forward, moving faster than Bellamy, leaving him a little ways behind.

"Hey, slow down!" he barked.

The tracks of the New York Central Railroad bisected the dock area. Beth tripped over a rail covered by snow. I caught her as she fell and saw a rusty railroad spike. It was short enough to conceal in my hand, and sharp enough to do damage. I scooped it up. Beth stared at me, terrified and shaking her head no. I put my finger to my lips.

"What're you two up to?" Bellamy said, coming up behind us.

"N-nothing," Beth said, dragging her gaze away from me.

Trudging through ankle-deep powder, we covered the last yards to the ferry terminal building in silence. It was a wide, squat structure. Dark now. A good place to do dark work.

"Is this where you brought Esther?" I asked.

He shot the lock off the door and pushed it open. "Get inside."

"No!" Beth cried. "Oh, please no!"

It must've hit her that this was it. We had reached the killing ground. It wasn't so much that she planted her feet as that she froze. She couldn't go in. He put his hand to the flat of her back and shoved her inside. She stumbled forward and fell. I went in and helped her up, glancing around.

Moonlight filtered through soot-covered windows, giving just enough light to make out details. We were in the main ticketing area. A thin wood sign leaned against the near wall, waiting to be mounted. A large waiting room, full of long wood benches, was to the right.

We were just inside the doorway. Bellamy gave us each another push. Beth fell back a step, but this time she sprang back fighting. Driven by terror, she threw herself at him, pounded his chest with her fists and clawed his face with her nails. For some reason, he'd didn't just shoot her. I guess he was too shocked at her sudden rebellion. Instead, he tried to get hold of her. But she kicked and screamed like the madwoman fear had made her.

I jumped on his back and drove in the spike. Hard. It went into his shoulder. It drew blood. But it didn't stop him. All he did was grit his teeth and fling me away. I could've been a feather.

Beth broke free and bolted. She was out the door. Bellamy ran after her. He paused just outside the entryway, took quick aim and fired. There was a sharp scream and then nothing.

I grabbed the sign.

It was heavier than it looked, so I didn't wield it as well as I wanted to. Still, I swung it with all my might. The sign caught Bellamy in his knees just as he got off his second shot. His legs buckled and he went down with a grunt.

I jumped past him to go after Beth, but he caught hold of my ankle and pulled me down. I kicked at him, but he managed to get on top of me. He got his hands on my throat. He must've lost the gun in the fall, because he was using both hands to strangle me. I tried to pry his hands away, but he was too strong for me. My right hand shot out and hit his nose with the base of my palm. It hurt him, but not enough. That man was a bear. He grabbed my right wrist and brought it down to my chest, and he leaned forward, so far forward I could feel his breath on my ear.

"You should've left it alone," he whispered. "You should've let it be."

I twisted around and sank my teeth into his left earlobe. He cried out, his left hand going to his bloodied ear. Then he slapped me. My left hand flailed around in the snow, searching for something, anything—and found the butt of his gun. He choked me, pressing down, putting his weight behind it. My fingers grabbed for purchase on the gun, slipped over it, then curled around it and took hold. He was suddenly aware that I had something in my hand. I could see it in his eyes. But it was too late. I turned the gun and fired.

The flash illuminated a face frozen in shock. He grabbed at his throat; blood bubbled out between his fingers. His eyes were horrified. Warm blood spattered my face. His mouth parted as though he wanted to say something. But no words emerged—just an unintelligible grunt. Then he slumped down, heavy and still. I push his upper half off me and squirmed out from beneath his legs.

My hands and face, and the collar of my coat, were wet with his blood. My ears rang from the report. Trembling, I scrambled to my feet. For ten seconds, I stood bent over, my hands on my knees, catching my breath. Then I straightened up, the gun in my hand. Bellamy's eyes were open, his features slack.

Beth and now Bellamy: They were gone and any information they'd had about Esther was gone with them. I had one chance left to find out what I needed to know.

Only one chance left to play it right.

Beth hadn't managed to get far. She lay a few feet from the door, at the entrance to the pier. I ran to her and dropped down on my knees beside her.

Good God, she was alive. Hurt bad, but still breathing. The bullet had caught her in the thigh and clipped a main blood vessel. There was a lot of blood, but the cold and the snow were helping, making the blood pump slower. Even so, she needed help. Fast.

"Lanie?" a voice called in surprise.

I looked up to see the driver of the car with the familiar grille. "Sutton?"

He rushed the last few yards. "Are you all right? I was following you, but I lost you. I—"

Beth opened her eyes, saw him and moaned. Working her lips, she tried to talk. But I shushed her.

"It's okay," I said. "You're going to be fine."

He quickly assessed her condition and registered the gun in my hand. "You shot her?"

"Of course not." I untied my scarf and cinched it around Beth's thigh, improvising a tourniquet. "It was Bellamy. He's back there."

I jerked a thumb toward the ferry building. Sutton went to the terminal, stopping at the sight of Bellamy. I stood up, watching him, then glanced down at Beth. I needed to get help, but I couldn't leave her. Not now.

He came back. The skin around his eyes was tight. He gestured toward the gun. "You'd better let me take that."

"No, I don't think so."

He frowned. "C'mon, it's dangerous for you to have that thing. You know that." His frown melted into a reassuring smile. "I don't know why you did it, but it must've been in self-defense, right? But you're colored, and when a ..."

"You don't need to tell me what happens when a colored shoots a white, especially when the dead man's an ex-cop."

His smile lost some of its charm. "So give me the gun."

"Why? Are you going to tell them you did it?"

"Something like that. Yeah."

"Why? You don't even know me." I gave him a hard stare.

"Lanie, what's the matter with you?"

"I'm curious. That's all."

"About what?"

"About why you were following us."

He tried to play it off with a little shrug. "Well, I, uh ..."

"Make it good, now."

He didn't answer, not that I expected him to.

"You know what else I'm wondering? Why you didn't seem surprised when I said it was Bellamy who shot her. You didn't even ask who he is. Why is that?"

"Well, I ... I remember the name. That's all. One of the cops working the heist had that name."

"Yes, he did. Now, wouldn't you want to know why a cop would shoot her down?"

Silence.

"Sutton, what were you hoping for? That Bellamy would kill me—and then you could kill him?"

Something moved in his eyes, something ugly. "Come on. Give me the gun."

He took a step forward. I raised the gun and pointed it at him. He stopped. His face showed irritation, but no sign of fear.

I'd have to change that.

His gaze flicked from me to the gun and back, calculating.

"Don't even try it," I said.

"What's going on, Lanie?"

"You're surprised, aren't you, to find me alive?"

"I don't know what you're talking about." He took another step forward and held out his hand. "Why don't you just give it to me?"

I raised the gun an inch higher. "Don't tempt me."

His expression hardened. "Why would you want to shoot me?"

"I don't *want* to. But I will if I have to. Now unbuckle your holster—don't touch your gun—just unbuckle your belt and let slide on down to the ground."

He opened his mouth to speak.

I cut him off. "Do it!"

He raised open palms. "Okay … okay."

His hand went toward the gun. I pressed the trigger and snow powder exploded an inch away from his right toe. He started and then gave me an admiring nod. I raised my chin. Without further argument, he quickly unhitched the belt. He let it dangle in his right hand, and then slowly lowered the belt and holster to the ground, keeping the left hand in the air.

"Now what?" he asked.

"Kick it toward me."

He nudged the belt aside with his foot.

"I said kick it!"

He kicked it. I was tempted to pick it up, but he would've lunged at me, so I gestured for him to move back. I was scared, but trying hard not to show it, and wondering how long I'd have to hold him before the police showed up—and wondering who they'd arrest—him or me—once they did.

"How'd you know?" he asked.

"Powell's identification had to be made based on a file containing his description. That file had to be brought in. From Chicago. And that file was brought in by you."

"So?"

"So when it left Chicago, it had contained fingerprints. When it arrived, it didn't. Somebody, somewhere, at some time lost those prints. And most likely that somebody was you."

He thought about that, about what it meant. "Then you knew when you met me?"

"I was suspicious, yes. Then you fed me that line about Powell and Kelly being lovers. It was titillating, but it wasn't really relevant."

"You being a gossip columnist and all, I figured …"

"You thought I'd be distracted. Well, I was … for all of two seconds."

I tried to hold the gun steady, with both hands, all the time wondering how many bullets I had left. I couldn't run. I couldn't leave him with Beth. I gestured with the gun and he fell back a step. Another realization hit me.

"You were the Remington Man."

"The what?"

"That's what you carried. A Remington. At the Goodfellowe heist. And it was a Remington that took Bobby Kelly's face off."

He showed grudging appreciation. "Guess I underestimated you."

"I guess you did. You lied about meeting Carter. He had an appointment with you right before he was killed. And he kept it. Whatever he told you got him killed. Who did it? You or Powell?"

He smiled with false modesty, admitting responsibility.

"And Whitefield?"

Another smile of useless charm.

"And after I told Bellamy I still had doubts, you moved in to convince me, didn't you?"

No response.

I cocked the hammer. "Answer me!"

He shoved his hands out. "All right, all right. What if I did?"

"What if I shot you, right here, right now? Just dropped you in your tracks?" I looked him dead in the eye. "You attacked me."

"Well … yes. But," he raised an index finger. "It proves I never meant to hurt you. I could've killed you then and there. Instead, I—"

"You needed me to write a story that would frame Whitefield."

He gave an eloquent shrug.

"Who masterminded the caper?" I asked. "You or Powell?"

"What do you think?"

"That it was you. Powell just wasn't that bright."

"Powell was a small-time operator. When he married Mrs. Goodfellowe, he was planning on taking her for a few grand, then moving on. But it was like I told you, he started liking her and he decided to go straight."

"And that's what got him in trouble. It gave you time to find him."

"When I did ... well, I have to say, I was impressed with the setup."

"You guys killed seven people: Bobby Kelly, Esther Todd, Mrs. Gray, the guard, Jack Ritchie, Sexton Whitefield, and Tellman Carter ... and then Powell, too, of course. All those lives ... destroyed. For greed." I tilted my head. "Why Esther? With the others, I can sort of see what you were thinking—but Esther? What did she have to do with any of it?"

"Powell had his cover. I needed mine. Esther told Beth about her man troubles. Beth told Powell. He told me. The idea to kidnap Esther—make it look like she was part of it—it came to me, just like that." He snapped his fingers.

"Just like that, huh?"

"Yeah, just like that."

My face felt hot with anger. It took all of my self-control not to press that trigger.

"So tell me pretty lady, what're we gonna do now?"

"You're going to tell me what you did with Esther."

"You must be dreaming."

He lunged and I pulled the trigger. The gun gave a loud click and nothing else. It was empty. For a hair's breadth of a second, I was stunned. Then I chucked the pistol at him and he knocked it away. I turned to run and he dove after me. We wrestled on the pier. He had me pressed up against the low wooden guardrail, his hands around my throat. I tumbled backward over the railing and he went with me.

The fall knocked the wind out of both of us. But fear cleared my head fast. I scrambled to my feet and ran. The ice wasn't smooth; it had a rough, almost pebbly surface. I turned around the corner of the terminal, hoping to reach the riverbank, but slipped and slid to a stop.

The Hudson glowed in the light of the full moon. Its surface was not completely frozen. Where we'd landed, the ice was hard and blue. But other areas were a mottled black and gray. Chunks of broken ice floated just below the surface. Some were as wide as a kitchen table, others as narrow and sharp as spears. I scanned the expanse, hoping for an unbroken stretch of blue ice to the water's edge.

"Come here," Sutton yelled. "You can't get away."

He was back on his feet and coming after me. I took off again, but my feet slipped wildly and I fell. I got up and tried again. But he was right behind me and got a handful of my coat. I squirmed out of it. I was almost free, when he slipped. His feet went out from under him and he landed hard, bringing me down, too.

I wrenched my arm free. Then it came, a sound one never forgets, the dull explosive crack of breaking ice.

He lay flat on his stomach, staring at the fissure beneath us. Then he looked at me. We both knew what was going to happen. In that second, I rolled away, the ice broke and he fell through. Where he'd been, for several seconds was nothing but black water. Then he shot up, flailing, gasping and spitting water.

"Help me," he sputtered. "Please."

Frozen with fear, I hesitated.

"Please!"

I couldn't let him die. For every reason from the humane to the practical, I had to save him. My coat was lying half on, half off the ice. I took hold of the sleeves and flung the bottom of the coat toward him.

"Grab hold of it!"

I anchored the toes of my shoes in the ice as best I could, but that was less than a little and he was heavier than a boulder. For a few seconds it was a toss-up as to whether he'd pull himself out before he pulled me in. Kicking his feet as though swimming, he managed to get his elbows on the ice. For a moment his upper torso was up, over the edge. Then he slipped back, pulling the coat with him and yanking it out of my hand. I thought he was a goner, but he came up again, spitting water.

I took off my belt and tossed him the buckle end. But the belt was too short to reach him, so I inched forward and threw it again. He was able to grab hold of it and pull. But this time I couldn't anchor myself. Instead of pulling himself out, he was dragging me forward.

There was no way I could save him.

And he knew it.

The whites of his eyes were gone. From lid to lid, they were bottomless black pits, the eyes of the damned and the doomed.

"Esther," I whispered. "Tell me about Esther."

That lethal grin came back. "Don't know what you mean."

"C'mon man, you're gonna die."

He pulled on the belt again.

I tried to dig my toes in, but slipped forward. "Tell me what you did with her."

"Never." His voice was ragged, his face bluish white. His gaze went over my face as if searching for an explanation and he shook his head. "I just never thought," he whispered, "that it would be you…"

Then he gave me a ghost of that deadly smile, let go and dropped under. One minute he was there; the next he was gone.

And the secret of Esther's fate was gone with him.

## *54.*

The wide beam of a flashlight shot across the ice, moved up my body and hit me full in the face.

"POLICE! Stay where you are."

Someone in the neighborhood had heard the shots and called the cops. They didn't let me go with Beth to the hospital, especially not after the tally was taken: one dead cop, one dead security chief and a gunshot victim who was rapidly going into shock.

Soon, I was back at the Harlem station house, facing interrogation. They did let me change into dry clothes: a prisoner's uniform. I never thought I'd be glad to don those particular glad rags, but they were more than acceptable that night. The uniform was dry and warm, something that couldn't be said of my clothes.

But there the feeling of warmth ended.

I had a lot of explaining to do.

With all those pale faces staring at me, I knew I couldn't go it alone and I was suddenly tired of being strong all on my own. I asked to make a phone call.

Sam answered on the first ring.

Those were a long two hours we spent at the station. If it weren't for Sam, and input from Blackie, they wouldn't have allowed me to go home. Sam brought me to my door.

"You need me to stay, Lanie?"

I nearly said no, but caught myself.

He set off to run a bath of hot water. I went to my bedroom and undressed, dropping the clothes in a heap on the floor. I took a good look at myself in the mirror and grimaced at the sight. My forehead and cheeks were scratched and bandaged. My jaw was bruised and swollen. There was a knock at the door. I slipped into my bathrobe.

"Come in."

Sam entered. "Your bath's ready."

We were both aware of my nudity under the bathrobe. I put a hand up to cover my battered face. He reached out and took it away. Lacing his fingers with mine, he led me down the hall to the bathroom. He'd lit candles and set them on the floor around the tub. The light was soft and warm. He gave me a kiss, gentle and protective. "I'll be downstairs," he said, then went out and closed the door.

I slipped out of my robe and eased down into the water. It felt good. I leaned back, closed my eyes and tried to expunge all thoughts of the struggle on the ice. But I couldn't forget Sutton's dark eyes, windows into a soul condemned, just before he let go of my hand.

I shuddered. The water's warmth—welcome as it was—couldn't lessen my inner chill and failed to ease my sense of guilt.

What could I say to Ruth? That I now knew why Esther had disappeared, but didn't know what had been done to her or where she was? I felt deeply saddened and couldn't relax, so I reached for my towel and got out.

Sam put me to bed. He tucked me in as though I were a child. He started to leave, but I asked him to hold me. He stretched out next to me and wrapped his arms around me.

"You've got to get some sleep," he whispered.

"I can't. I keep seeing Sutton's face right before he went under."

"First time you've seen a man die?"

I nodded. "It was horrible, but..." I rubbed my forehead, "that's not all of it. I failed. I didn't find out where Esther is. Ruth and her mother still don't have her back. I wanted to do that for them, Sam."

He drew a deep breath. "Lanie, you tried—"

"That's not good enough. I went in like a bull in a china shop. Now's everything's broken."

He was thoughtful. "You know ... from everything you've told me, the answer's there, among those pieces."

"If it is, I can't see it. I've wracked my brains for something, anything. I went over my notes. Came up with the Powell angle, but…" I sighed.

"You did well, real well. Now, get some rest."

I nodded and closed my eyes. He started to get up.

"Don't go," I whispered.

"Are you sure?"

I knew I could trust him. "Yes, very sure."

That was not the night for discovering each other. We fell into an exhausted sleep, but not for long. I woke up in the dark. Sam, still fully clothed, was sleeping with his arm flung across my waist. I listened to his regular breathing. It was nice to have him there. I hadn't let any other man get this close— emotionally or physically—since Hamp died. It was nowhere near as frightening as I'd thought it would be. Instead of feeling threatened, I felt protected. I felt Sam's goodness and strength and warmth. I wanted to reach out and wake him, to touch him and get even closer, but one thought stopped me.

One worry I couldn't put aside.

Easing out from under his arm and the blanket, I got out of bed and threw on my robe. Sam slept on. I blew him a kiss and went out, softly closing the door behind me.

Downstairs, in the living room, I took out my notes and sat down to study them. Twenty minutes later, I sensed another presence and looked up. Sam stood in the doorway.

"Lanie, you should be sleeping."

"I've found something."

He sat down next to me and we put our heads together. He'd been right. The answer had been in front of me all the time. It was right there, in the notes from Bellamy's interview.

*"He might've been one of the ones who sat across from us and talked about what a wonderful person she was … all the time knowing he was the sick fuck who took her, and maybe even still had her,* buried in his basement…"

We called the Harlem station house and left a message for Blackie.

"There's nothing more we can do now," Sam said. He glanced at his watch. "It's nearly three. Try to get some sleep."

I didn't think I could, but I must've. Next thing I knew, the telephone was ringing and Sam was gently nudging me. I'd fallen asleep, curled up next to him on the sofa. He handed me the phone.

Blackie listened intently. After a short exchange, we hung up. I told Sam: "Time to get going."

I put on work clothes—an old pair of pants, a large man's shirt—and grabbed some heavy gloves. Then we set out for Bayside—Bellamy's place.

Blackie and two patrolmen were already there. He'd just ordered his men to go to work on the front door. One officer stepped forward with an axe. Sam raised his hand.

"Whoa. You don't have to destroy it. Let me have a go at it."

"Be my guest," Blackie said.

Sam pulled out a small set of tools, selected one—a thin metal rod-like tool—and inserted it into the keyhole. A few sensitive twists to the left and right and the door popped open.

"I didn't know you could do that," I said.

"Where'd you learn it?" Blackie wanted to know.

"Just one of my many talents," Sam said. He pushed the door open and made a sweeping gesture toward the inside. "Shall we?"

We all trooped inside.

"You're thinking the basement?" Blackie asked and I nodded.

We found her buried behind a wall. Her body was wedged into a narrow space between the stone foundation wall and a newer brick one. He had wrapped her in red carpet and propped her up in a standing position.

"Bring her out," Blackie said. "But be gentle about it."

The men used pick axes to remove more of the wall encasing her, and then slowly, painstakingly, set her free. They laid her on the ground and unwrapped her, then stepped back, struck with surprise, horror and dismay.

"God, she's like a mummy," said one. "Like one of them people they talk about finding in an Egyptian tomb or something."

Her face was sunken, the skin stretched over her skull, but her features were still recognizable. One could see the rippling scar. The corner of a dark and rotted cloth protruded from her mouth. Her killer had bound her wrists with an electrical cord. There were no signs of apparent injury.

"I wonder what killed her," said the second patrolman.

Blackie knelt beside her. With infinite care, he gave the cloth a little tug. It didn't come out. "It's wedged fast."

He reached for it again, but then stopped. "It's better if the coroner does it. I'm guessing he'll say she choked to death. That the guy stuffed this rag down her throat to keep her quiet and stuffed it too far."

"This wasn't an accident," I said. "From what Sutton told me, I'd say it was planned from the beginning."

"But you said Bellamy wasn't in on it at first. That he came later."

"Maybe they moved her body here later. Maybe agreeing to keep her was Bellamy's way of proving that he'd keep his mouth shut."

"Or of making sure Sutton didn't betray him," Sam said.

"Either way ..." Blackie said. "It would've been kinder if they'd just put a bullet in her head. Dying like this, and in the dark," he shook his head. "It must've felt like forever."

## 55.

Later that morning found me knocking on Mrs. Goodfellowe's door.

Roland shook his head. "I'm sorry, Miss Lanie, but I can't let you in. Miss Katherine says she don't want to see you no more."

"Well, she's going to have to. She's got bad news coming and it's better if it comes from me."

His forehead creased with deep worry lines. "What bad news?"

"Bad news for you, too."

Fear touched his eyes. He let me in and closed the door. "What's happened?" His voice was a whisper.

"Beth's been shot."

"My God, no! But wha—"

"I can't tell you when or why or how—not yet."

"Roland! Who's that at the door?"

Katherine Goodfellowe's querulous voice rang out from the living room. The sliding French doors to the room were slightly parted.

"I have to see her." I said, leaving him in the entryway, frightened and horrified.

Mrs. Goodfellowe sat in her wheelchair by the fireplace. Except for her change of clothes, she looked much as I'd left her.

"What are you doing here?" she asked.

As I neared her, she used her good hand to back her chair away from me. Despite her outer show of imperiousness, she was good and scared. She had reason to be.

"Roland!" she cried out.

He came to the doorway.

"You don't want him to hear what I have to say," I said.

Her eyes flicked from me to him, her fear battling her pride. Finally, she nicked her head at him. "You can go."

Her gaze followed him. As soon as he was gone and the parlor doors were slid shut, she turned on me. "You're on thin ice."

I almost laughed, thinking of the evening before. "Ma'am, you have no idea."

"What do you want?"

How would she take the news?

"We've found her," I said.

"Who?"

"Esther."

Her eyes registered shock. A moment passed. A heartbeat. Her voice was tight as she asked, "Where was she?"

"In a most obvious place."

Her eyes searched mine, uncertainty added to the mix. "You're sure it's her?"

"Yes."

"And she's?"

"Dead, Mrs. Goodfellowe. Been dead, for a long time."

She fell silent. The only sound was of the flames crackling in the fireplace, and the tick of the clock on the mantelpiece.

"I've always known," she said. "I just hoped..." She blinked back a tear. "If the family will let me, then I'd like to help make the arrangements." She paused. "Do they know what happened? Why or who?"

"Why?" I repeated. "That's a good question. As a matter of fact, it's exactly what I wanted to ask you. Why?"

Waxen mask or not, her eyes were a dead giveaway. They were dark with fear. Using her good hand, she half turned her wheelchair away.

I gripped the arms, swung her back and made her look me in the eye. "Bellamy's dead, Mrs. Goodfellowe. I shot him."

"You wh—"

"As for Sutton, he's on ice, too. Literally. The whole rotten scheme's fallen apart. Do you understand? It's been shot to smithereens."

She drew herself up. Her heavy-lidded eyes grew narrow and her lips pressed into a tense pink line.

"Get your filthy hands off me. And get out."

Cold anger chilled my spine. This lady wasn't getting the message. She needed me to drive it home.

"You'd better stop thinking about my hands and start worrying about my lips, 'cause they're about to spread the word––about you and your husband and how he killed his best friend 'cause he needed a corpse to hide behind."

"No––"

"Your man Sutton helped him do it and then kidnapped Esther. He did it right before the heist to make it look as though she was in on it. Then Bellamy and Ritchie entered the scene. They weren't as clumsy as the papers made them out to be. They actually figured it out. Sutton offered a payoff and Bellamy went for it, but Ritchie didn't, so Bellamy nailed him."

"I don't––"

"And you were the puppet mistress, pulling all the strings."

She was rattled to her blue-blooded core, but her pride gave her strength. "You're a fool."

"Yes, I am," I sighed, straightening up. "Because I didn't want to suspect you. Not for your sake, but for Esther's. Her family trusted you. They believed in you and, for their sake, I wanted to believe, too. Even when you told me straight to my face that Esther was dead––"

"I never told you that."

"But you did. You said it, sitting right here, trying to convince me of how much Esther meant to you. *'Esther was the same age as my daughter when she died.'* Those were your exact words."

"I was talking about my daughter."

"That's what I told myself, too. But you weren't. At best, it was what Freud would call a 'slip of the tongue.' At worst, it was arrogance talking. You knew that Esther was dead, not just disappeared. Now, I want to know why. Why did you do it?"

Her eyes were as cold as a mama crocodile studying its young. We were discussing Esther, but Mrs. Goodfellowe's eyes showed no remorse, none.

"Why not tell you? You can't do anything. You never could." Her lopsided smile was arrogant. "Why?" Her gaze moved over the grand room, and returned to me. "Isn't it obvious? It takes money to maintain all this, to uphold an image. I didn't have it."

"But your husband—"

"My first husband spent as much as he earned. I used a good part of my inheritance just to keep up appearances. And then I went and married Eric. When I found out what kind of man he was, I realized just how foolish I'd been. I was always weak for scoundrels, men who didn't think the law applied to them. I should've known better."

She was quiet for a moment, nostalgic but bitter. "When Mr. Sutton told me what sort of man I'd married, I decided to make the most of it. Eric had married me for my money. Soon he'd learn that I didn't have any. I decided to use him before he could leave me. We'd become partners in a way he'd never foreseen."

"So the heist was your idea."

"Mine and mine alone."

"Sutton tried to say it was his."

She smiled wistfully. "I liked him. If I'd been younger ..." Her smile faltered. "He was trying to protect me. But the idea was mine. Sutton and I forced Eric to go along. If he refused, we said we'd turn him in. He told me he didn't believe me. That there was no way I'd face that embarrassment. I told him he was right. If I couldn't turn him in, then I'd kill him—or have him killed. That he believed."

"But what about Esther? How could you have done that to her?"

Her expression changed. It softened, and then almost as quickly hardened. A shrug. A dismissal. "I gave her a place in history. Something she wouldn't have achieved on her own."

My fingers itched to get around her scrawny neck. But I resisted. I don't know how, but I did.

Her lips sloped in that lopsided curve that passed for a smile. "You're shocked?"

"By your hypocrisy? God no, I wish I were."

She reddened as though I'd slapped her.

I had everything I needed, so I turned to leave. Her needling voice followed me.

"I hope you don't think you can peddle your little story to the police. With everyone dead, they'll never believe you."

I paused and turned. "Everyone dead? Where'd you get that idea? *Beth* isn't. You aren't."

She blanched with shock. "But you said—you said Beth was sh—"

"Exactly. I said 'shot.' I never said 'dead.' That, I'm afraid, was you expressing an expectation."

The parlor doors opened and Roland came in. Sam, Blackie and Reed were right behind him. Her gaze returned to me.

"I should've had you killed," she hissed. "I should've let Bellamy and Sutton move against you sooner."

"Yeah," I nodded. "You should have."

## *56.*

I made time to phone Katie Jones and tell her the truth. She argued, called me a liar and every other name in the book, then slammed the phone down, but not fast enough to keep me from hearing the sobs break through.

Sophie Carter received a phone call, too.

Esther's funeral was held December 23rd. She had indeed been brought home in time for Christmas. Her fans filled the small Baptist church of Christ, the Redeemer. They spilled onto the church steps on 123rd and Third Avenue. I gave the eulogy. Dianne Todd gathered enough strength to attend. She would live long enough to mark Christmas with Ruth and Job, and then pass away in her sleep on Christmas night. By New Year's Day, she would be resting in the ground alongside her long lost child.

Sam and I attended Esther's funeral in the morning and the Agamemnon Awards dinner that evening. Byron Canfield, of all people, presented Esther with a posthumous award, naming her the Best Young Talent of 1923. His eyes met mine across the room as he announced the award and explained why she was chosen. It was a deeply satisfying moment. Job, dignified and grave, received the honor in his mother's name. His acceptance speech was brief and poignant.

"My mama was a great pianist," he said, "but she was an even greater mama. And I miss her. I miss hearing her voice but I still got her songs. I got them on paper, all written down for me. And one day I'm going to sing them for you. Then you'll know just how great my mama was. In the meantime, thank you. On behalf of my mama, my Aunt Ruth and Grandma Dee, I thank you for this award. But most of all, I want to thank Miss Lanie there. She had faith. And she kept her promise."

His eyes met mine and I wanted to thank *him*, to bless him and his family for giving me a chance to feel relevant again. In helping them, I'd helped myself.

My Christmas column, detailing Esther's fate, turned out to be the best piece I wrote that year.

Sam and I had a long talk. I would keep my job—but with a twist. I would report on crime among the smart set. After all, they had their troubles, too. And it was a subject that nobody was covering—at least, not regularly.

Christmas Eve found Sam in my kitchen. He had taken his shirt off, revealing a lean, muscled torso. He was down on one knee, covered with a fine layer of dust. I paused in the kitchen doorway to watch as he hammered two planks of wood together to make another cabinet. He'd already made one and done a good job of it. His work was so skilled I wondered if he hadn't at some point done carpentry for a living. I'd asked him, but all he'd said was "Baby, I've done a lot of things. This isn't the least of them."

It was hard to recognize my boss in the half-naked man standing in my kitchen. Covered in sweat and dust, he bore no resemblance to the straight-laced, buttoned up persona he presented at work.

Which was as it should be.

His hands were not large, but capable and square. They gripped the wood with a familiarity born of practice. The muscles in his back rippled as he swung the hammer and drove in the nails.

He looked up, saw me and gave a smile that made my heart flip. I wasn't quite ready to let go of my sadness over Hamp, but I wasn't holding on to it as tightly either. It was no longer a shield between the world and me.

"Lunch is ready," I said. "All spread out upstairs, on the dining room table."

He raised an eyebrow and I realized how my words could be interpreted.

"Don't," I said, "don't even go there."

"But you make it so hard not to."

He gave a mischievous smile and then returned his attention to the wood. "Just let me get the back of this one together and I'll be right with you."

"You've been working down here for hours. You need a break."

"In a minute."

He placed a nail and hit it with his hammer. The hammerhead popped loose and flew up. It would've hit him in the eye, if he hadn't ducked in time. The hammerhead landed on the floor with a clunk.

"Shit," he said through clenched teeth. He grabbed up the hammerhead and stuck it back on, but the piece wouldn't stay. He was disgusted. "This is a piece of junk. My neighbor borrowed my hammer last week, said he'd return it. Now he won't answer the door."

"Why don't you stop for now?"

He looked over at me. "'Cause I told you I'd do this for you and I keep my word."

"But you don't have to do it all at once. Take a break. Lunch is getting cold."

I so wanted him to eat and enjoy himself. I'd even gone out of my way to make 'normal' lunch for once. No funny breakfast food, this time. What I was serving was warm and healthy. Furthermore, our Christmas tree was waiting for us to decorate. It was a fine thick pine. Sam had bought it.

"All right, all right." He arched his back and worked his shoulders to loosen his muscles.

I had a sudden image of my hands on his back, massaging his shoulders—and maybe even going lower to massage something else, too. I saw myself working hard, doing all I could to ease his tension.

Then it hit me what I was thinking. It hit me so hard I blinked and averted my gaze.

"What?" he asked.

"Nothing."

"You sure?"

"Hm-hmm."

I swallowed and forced myself to smile at him, hoping that he wouldn't see my embarrassment.

Apparently, he didn't.

"Just let me clean up," he said, yanking a plaid red kerchief from his back pocket.

Blissfully unaware of how he was affecting me, he mopped his brow and all around his throat, the muscles in his arms and chest rippling with every move. I found myself staring, and my thoughts running away again, conjuring up images no decent woman would ever entertain.

"Mind if I use the bathroom?" he asked.

"Of course not."

He put down the broken tool, grabbed his shirt off the back of the chair, and set off toward the back. There was a bathroom just before the backyard door. Soon, I heard water running. I picked up the broken hammer. It looked irreparable. Worse, it looked dangerous. If the hammer's head had hit him, it could've done serious damage.

Fifteen minutes later, Sam came back, buttoning his cuffs. "Hope I wasn't too long."

"Not at all. Here."

In my hand was Hamp's leather tool kit. Surprised, Sam made no move to take it.

"Please," I said, offering it to him.

Still hesitant, he accepted it. "You're letting me use these?"

"No, I'm letting you have them."

His eyes widened. "Are you sure?"

"Hamp wouldn't have wanted them to go to waste." After a moment, I added. "I know I'll never use them."

He nodded. "Thank you."

He went to the kitchen table and unrolled the kit. I stood next to them, feeling the pain but knowing it was bearable. Believing too that I'd made the right decision.

Sam's hands moved over the tools with the sureness of an expert. He picked up each implement and studied it, murmuring words of admiration.

Finally, he looked up at me. "Beautiful," he said.

"Yeah, I know. They were—"

"Not them. You." He took me in his arms.

That last kiss had been gentle and polite and shy. This one was deep and hungry. The grip on my lower back was sturdy and firm.

I leaned into him, closed my eyes and gladly felt the earth slip away.

❤

BLACK ORCHID BLUES

A LANIE PRICE MYSTERY

ॐ৹

AN EXCERPT

Queenie Lovetree. What a name! What a performer! When she opened her mouth to sing, you closed yours to listen. You couldn't help yourself. You knew you were going to end up with tears in your eyes. Whether they were tears of joy or tears of laughter, it didn't matter. You just knew you were in for one hell of a ride.

Folks used to talk about her gravely voice, her bawdy banter and how she could make up new, sexy lyrics — or give new meaning to old ones. Queenie captured you. She got inside your mind, claimed her spot and refused to give it up. Once you heard her sing a song, you'd always think of her when you heard it. No matter who was singing it, it was her voice that came to mind.

Sure, she was moody and volatile. And yes, whatever she was feeling, she made you feel it, too. But that was good. That's what could've made her great — *could've* being the operative word.

I first met Queenie at a movie premiere at the Renaissance Ballroom, over on West 138th Street. The movie I'd soon forget – it was some ill-conceived melodrama – but Queenie I would always remember.

It was a cold day in early February, with patches of dirty ice on the ground and leaden skies overhead. It was late afternoon, an odd time for a premiere, so the event drew few fans and, except for Queenie, mostly B-level talent.

It was a party of gray pigeons and Queenie stood out like a peacock. For a moment, I wondered why she was even there. She was vivid. She was vibrant. And when she found out that I was Lanie Price, *the Lanie Price,* the society columnist, she went from frosty to friendly and pestered me to see her perform.

"I'm at the Cinnamon Club. You must've heard of me."

Well, I had, actually. Queenie's name was on a lot of lips and I'd heard some interesting things about her. I could see for myself that she was bold and bodacious. I decided on the spot that I liked her, but I couldn't resist having a little fun with her, so I shrugged and agreed that, yeah, I'd heard of ... the *Cinnamon Club*.

Queenie caught the shift in emphasis and was none too pleased. She raised her chin like miffed royalty, pointed one coral-tipped fingernail at me and, in her most magisterial voice, said, "You will appear."

I smiled and said I'd think about it. I finally found time to stop by one night two weeks later. I called in advance and Queenie said she'd make sure I had a good table, which she did. It was excellent, in fact, right up front.

To the cynic, the Cinnamon Club was little more than a speakeasy dressed up as supper club, but it was one of Harlem's most popular nightspots and it topped all the other hot clubs on that hottest of streets, West 133rd, between Seventh and Lenox Avenues, what the white folks referred to as "Jungle Alley."

The place was small, but plush. The lighting was dim, the chairs cushioned and the tables round and tiny, set for two. All in all, the Cinnamon Club seemed luxurious as well as intimate.

It was packed every night and most of the comers were high hats, folks from downtown who had come uptown to shake it out. They liked the place because it was classy, smoky and dark. For once, they could misbehave in the shadows and let someone else posture in the light. That place had only one spotlight and it always shone on Queenie.

Rumor had it that she was out of Chicago. But back at that movie premiere, she'd mentioned St. Louis. All anybody really knew was that she'd appeared out of nowhere. That was late last summer. It was mid-winter now and she had a following.

You had to give it to her: Queenie Lovetree commanded that stage the moment she stepped foot on it. Every soul in the place turned toward her and stayed that way, flat out mesmerized and a bit intimidated, too. Only a fool would risk Queenie's ire by talking when she had the mic.

A six-piece orchestra, one that included jazz violinist Max

Bearden and cornetist Joe Mascarpone, backed her up. Her musicians were good — you had to be to play with Queenie — but not too good. She shared center stage with no one.

At six-foot-three, Queenie Lovetree was the tallest badass chanteuse most folks had ever seen. There was a toughness about her, a ferocity that kept fools in check. And yes, she was beautiful. She billed herself as the "Black Orchid." The name fit. She was powerful, mythic and rare.

Men were going crazy over her. They showered her with jewels and furs and offers to buy her cars or take her on cruises. In all the madness, many seemed to forget or stubbornly chose to ignore a most salient fact, the one secret that Queenie's beauty, no matter how artful, failed to hide:

Queenie Lovetree wasn't a woman at all, but a man in drag.

When Queenie appeared on stage, sheathed in one of his tight, glittering gowns, he presented a near-perfect illusion of femininity. He could swish better than Mae West. His smile was dirtier, his curves firmer and his repartee deadlier than a switchblade. From head to toe, he was a vision of feminine pulchritude that gave many a man an itch he ached to scratch.

That night, Queenie wore a dress with a slit that went high on his right thigh. Rumor had it that he packed a pistol between his thighs, the .22-caliber kind. He took the mike and launched into some down and dirty blues.

During the set, Lucien Fawkes, the club's owner, stopped by my table. He was a short, wiry Parisian, with hound dog eyes, thin lips and deep creases that lined his cheeks.

"Always good to see you, Lanie. You enjoying the show?"

"I'm enjoying it just fine."

"Good to know. I'll tell the boys, anything you want, you get."

After Queenie finished his set, the offers of champagne, the invitations to join tables poured in. He took exuberant pleasure in accepting them, going from table to table. But that night, they weren't his priority. He air-kissed a few cheeks, exchanged a few greetings and then slunk over to join me.

"The suckers love me," he said. "What about you?"

"I'm not a sucker."

"Well, I know that, Slim. That's why you're having drinks on the house and they're not."

He sat down and turned to the serious business of wooing a reporter.

"So what do you think? Am I fantastic or am I fantastic?"

"I'd say you've got a good thing going."

"You make it sound like I'm running a scam."

I hadn't meant it that way, but given his fake hair, fake eyelashes and fake bosom, I could see why he thought I had.

"I'm just saying you're perfect for this place and it's perfect for you. Everybody's happy."

"It's okay," he said. "For now."

"So you have plans for bigger and better things?"

"What if I do? There's nothing wrong with that."

"Nope, not a thing. I've always admired ambitious, hard-working people."

"Honey, I ain't nothing if not that. You got a ciggy?"

I shook my head. "Never took to 'em."

He faintly arched an eyebrow, then turned and tapped a man sitting at the next table. When the guy turned around, Queenie said, "Butt me, baby."

"Sure."

He produced a cigarette and lit it for him. Queenie thanked him with a dazzling smile and a husky-voiced, "Thanks, Bill." Then he turned his back before the fellow could make a play. I made mental note, with an amused smile. Bill arrived with our champagne. We raised our glasses in a toast.

"To success," Queenie said.

We each took a sip, then he leaned in toward me.

"People say you're the one to know. That you are 'the one' to get close to if somebody's interested in breaking out, climbing up. Because of that column of yours. What's it called?"

*"Lanie's World."*

"That's right. *Lanie's World.*" He savored the words. "And you write for the *Harlem Chronicle?*"

"Hm-hmm."

"So you think you can write a nice piece on me?"

"Well," I hesitated. "There *is* some small amount of interest in you, but—"

"*Small?* People are crazy about me. The letters I get, the questions. They want to know all about me. Where I came from, what I like, what I don't. What I eat before going to bed."

I shrugged. "But they've heard so many different stories that—"

"I promise to tell you the whole truth and nothing but."

I resisted the urge to raise a skeptical eyebrow. I'd been in the journalism game for more than ten years. I'd worked as a crime reporter, interviewing victims and thugs, cops and dirty judges. Then I'd moved to society reporting, where I wrote about cotillions and teas, parties and premieres. It seemed like a different crowd, but the one constant was the mendacity. People lied. Sometimes for no apparent reason, they obfuscated, omitted, or outright obliterated the truth. And often the first sign of an intention to lie was an unsolicited promise to tell the truth, "the whole truth and nothing but."

There were areas, of course, in which I was sure Queenie would be factual, but there were others ... It didn't matter. I'd decided to interview him. I was sure to get a good column out of him. I just wasn't sure that this was the place to do it.

People kept stopping by the table, shaking his hand, complimenting him and inviting him to join them. Men sent drinks, flowers and suggestive notes. But they were out of luck that night. After every set, he'd rejoin me; tell me a little here, a little there.

"I like action," he said, "lots of action, diamond studs and rhinestone heels. I love caviar and chocolate, sequins and velvet. Most times, I'm a lady. But I can smoke like an engine and cuss like a lumberjack. The men all love me cause I call them all Bill."

During one of the longer set breaks, Queenie invited me back to his dressing room, where he could talk without interruption. He described how at age fourteen, he'd fallen in love with a sailor, who smuggled him on board ship and took him to Ankara.

"He was the greatest love of my life, but that bastard sold me."

*"Sold you?"*

"Yeah. To a guy in a bar." He saw my expression and said, "But seriously. I'm not lying. And that guy turned around and sold me, again — to a sultan for his harem."

Believable or not, Queenie's tales were certainly fascinating.

He described corrupting wealth and murderous intrigues in which the sultan's wives poisoned each other and one another's children in a never-ending struggle for power.

"For a while there, it was touch and go. I didn't eat or drink nothing without my taster."

"How terrible," I said, with appropriate horror and sympathy.

When he was nineteen, he said, the sultan sent him off to an elite finishing school near Lake Geneva, in Switzerland.

"Honey, I couldn't take that place. I made tracks the first minute they weren't looking. Went to Paris. Got me a nice hookup, performed at the Moulin Rouge. Would've stayed there, too, but a rich uncle came and found me."

"A rich uncle?"

"Hm-hmmm," he said, with a perfectly straight face. "He's dead now. But that's okay, 'cause now I've got lots of rich uncles." He gave a wicked wink. "A girl can't have too many, you know."

At the look on my face, he threw his head back and his shoulders rocked with deep, raunchy laughter. He laughed so hard, tears rolled down his cheeks.

"Oh, shit," he said, trying to regain control of himself. "I'm ruining my makeup."

I didn't consider myself a prude. I'd seen and heard

enough to be well beyond what shocked most people. So it wasn't Queenie's stories in themselves that got me; it was the obvious pride and conviction with which he told them.

Queenie, I decided, was that rare individual who really was bigger than life. Most of what he was saying was hokum. That was obvious, but it was okay. It was more than okay because it would make rip-roaringly good copy.

Back out on in the club room, watching him onstage, I mused about his real history. No doubt it was like hundreds of others. He'd been a touring vaudevillian, had grown up singing gospel in some church down South, then either run away from home or been kicked out. He spent years in smaller clubs, dark and dirty. There had been underworld characters who had smoothed his path and maybe even a wealthy man or two who had taught him to love the finer things in life, men who lived double lives, who loved women during the day and other men at night.

Queenie liked to flash a big diamond ring. When he sang, the ring caught the light. It was a lovely yellow diamond, set in yellow gold, surrounded by small white diamonds. I had a good eye for jewelry, but at that distance I couldn't say whether it was fake. If it *was* real, then it was worth ten times a poor man's salary. If it wasn't, then it was a darn good imitation and even imitations like that cost a pretty penny.

"That got a history?" I indicated it when he rejoined me.

He glanced at it, smiled. "Honey, everything about me has a history."

"Care to tell me this one?"

He fluttered his large hand daintily and held up the ring for a long, loving look. Then he smiled. His golden eyes were very feline and his soft voice just about purred.

"Not this time, sugar. But I will, if you do a good piece on me. If you do it right, then I'll give you exclusive access to Queenie Lovetree. You'll be my one and only and I won't share my shit with anyone but y—"

Gunfire exploded behind us. I started and Queenie's eyes widened. Heads swiveled and the music shredded to a discordant halt. Then someone gasped, another screamed and people nearby us started diving under tables.

At first, I couldn't see why.

But as people scrambled to get out of the way, I could see the club's bouncer, a man named Charlie Spooner and the coat check girl, Sissy Ralston, unsteadily emerge from the area of the entrance. They were winding their way past the tables, coming toward the stage area, their hands held high. Directly behind them was a dark shadow. It clarified itself into a man wearing a black broad-brimmed hat, a long, black coat and black gloves.

He had the business end of a Thompson submachine gun pressed against Spooner's spine.

The bouncer was a good guy, a war veteran, married with a kid on the way. He'd been on the job six months, had taken it he told me because he couldn't find anything else. Now his olive-toned skin had turned an ashen gray; his usually jovial face was tight with fear.

I knew the Ralston girl, too. That child couldn't have been more than sixteen. She was just a kid trying to earn money for her family. Her father had died the year before and her mother was a drinker.

Death march. I flashed on stories my deceased husband had told me about the war, stories of both soldiers and civilians being marched to their execution and a chill went through me.

The gunman shoved Spooner and Ralston ahead of him to the small open space just before the stage and had them stand side-by-side.

"Everybody, up! Take your seats and show your hands."

People were too scared to move.

"I will count to three and then start shooting — for real. One ... two ..."

My heartbeat was pounding a hot ninety miles a minute, but my hands and feet felt cold. From the corner of my eye, I saw Queenie slip his right hand under the table. The gunman caught the movement and swiveled his gun at us.

"Bring it out," he said. "Nice and slow."

Queenie gave him an insolent look and mouthed the word, "No."

The gunman's lips twitched. He looked Queenie in the eye, jammed his chopper into Spooner's back and pulled the trigger. *Ratta-tatta-tat.* Blood exploded from Spooner's chest. The bouncer arched with a cry and dropped to the floor. Ralston crumpled in a dead faint. Screams erupted throughout the crowded room.

"You!" the gunman pointed at Queenie. "You made me do that! Now, everyone get up," he yelled to the rest of the room. "Get back in your seats and show your hands or I'll start shooting. And I won't stop till the job's done."

Folks scrambled to get back in place.

He turned back to Queenie and me. "Come over here, the both of you, where I can see you."

We edged out from around the table, but kept our distance.

The gunman was taller than me, but not by much, which made him short for a man. The coat seemed to have padded shoulders, but I had the feeling that he would've appeared broad, anyway, that he was built like a quarterback, muscular and stocky.

For the most part, he'd successfully masked his face. However, given his height and proximity, I could see under the brim of his hat. He had a distinctive almond shape to his eyes and they were light-colored: blue or gray, I couldn't be sure. And the band of skin showing over the bridge of his nose was light, too. In other words, this was a white guy. Last, but not least, I thought I detected an accent. European, northern European, perhaps. So, not just any white guy, but a *European* white guy. He'd sure traveled a long way to cause trouble.

"Now, you," he told Queenie, "take the heater out or she's next." He pointed the gun at me. Predictable, but effective. I was scared. Sure I was. But I knew how to control it. It wasn't the first time a killer had trained his sights on me, and with my luck it wouldn't be the last.

Queenie slipped his hand through the slit of his dress and eased out a small black handgun. Cute. The gunman laughed at the sight of it, but then his smile turned ugly.

"Put it on the floor and kick it over here."

Queenie did as told.

"Get over here." The gunman indicated the space right before him.

Queenie glanced at me and, for all of his bravura, I saw the fear in his eyes.

"Come on," the gunman growled.

Queenie's gaze returned to the gunman. Stone-faced, he held up his gown to step delicately and ladylike over Spooner's body. He stood before the gunman, chest heaving, eyes narrowed and said with tremulous bravado, "Well?"

The gunman slapped him. He was half a head shorter than Queenie, but wide and solid. Queenie swayed under the blow but didn't stumble. He seemed more stunned than hurt. His hand went to his lip and came back bloodied. His jaw dropped in alarm.

"My face! You piece of shit! You hurt my face!"

The gunman slapped him again. This time Queenie went down, tripping over Spooner's body, to land in a spreading pool of blood. Queenie scrambled away from the corpse with a horrified cry, his hands and dress smeared in blood. The gunman stepped over Spooner's body, took a step toward Queenie and the singer cringed.

"Please, no—don't hurt me again!"

"Get up. Get up and shut up."

Queenie got to his feet, all resistance knocked out of him.

The gunman looked over at me. "You. Come here."

I took a step forward. He produced handcuffs from his pocket and tossed them at me. I caught them instinctively.

"Cuff up the songbird," he said. "You," he told Queenie. "Hands behind your back."

"Who are you?" I asked.

"And what do you want?" Queenie added.

The gunman cocked his head and looked down at Queenie. "Why, I want you, my love. I want you." He chuckled. Then he straightened up and aimed the gun at me. "Go ahead. What are you waiting for? Cuff him up and do it right."

I cinched Queenie's hands behind his back. When the gunman ordered me to step back, I did. He bade Queenie to stand next to him. He checked the cuffs and nodded. "Good."

He grabbed Queenie by the yoke around his wrists and started backing out, winding his way to the corridor back stage left. "Don't move anyone. I warn you, don't move."

He kept Queenie in front of him, using him as a shield.

Queenie panicked. "Oh come on now, people! Y'all ain't gonna let him take me like this, are you? Somebody do something. Please!"

People stayed frozen to their seats. No one was willing to play hero. Not in the face of that weapon.

Queenie's eyes met mine. "You! Slim, you—!"

The whine of police sirens rent the air. I suspected that the cops were headed to another emergency, but the kidnapper imagined the worst. He pushed Queenie aside and panned the room with a furious spray of gunfire. The bullets took out the wall sconces and the room fell dark.

Like everyone else, I dove under a table and covered my head. I couldn't believe it when a spray of bullets ripped up the floor two inches away from my face, but didn't touch me.

"Motherfucker! Get your hands off me!" Queenie cried.

The back door banged open. There was the sound of a scuffle and a scream. Then the door slammed shut and all I could hear was the heavy beat of my own terrified heart.

❤

# ABOUT THE AUTHOR

*"Just the facts, ma'am. Just the facts."*

Once upon a time, Persia studied drama at the High School of Performing Arts and all kinds of good stuff at Swarthmore College. She spent a year at Columbia University's Graduate School of Journalism to emerge with a master's degree.

She has worked for The Associated Press in Arkansas; Washington, DC; and New York. She has also written for Radio Free Europe/Radio Liberty, Inc., (RFE) in Munich, worked as a freelance book editor, done cultural reporting and voice work for European publications.

A native New Yorker, she's fluent in German, breathtakingly disorganized, and sporadically inspired to cook. She enjoys Indian and Thai food for dining, romantic thrillers and detective stories for reading, movies about superheroes, and television programs about desperate housewives and true crime. Her perfect Sunday morning includes a lengthy and lazy browse through the *New York Times* online.

She loves afternoons at the Met and dreams of weekends in the Hamptons, but is in fact is a real homebody. There's almost always some suitcase standing around half-packed in her home, but it's from her last trip and not in anticipation of any new one. As a writer, she's a monumentally undisciplined procrastinator who growls at her friends when they distract her, but then busily distracts herself.

For more damaging information, you'll have to visit her online at *www.persiawalker.com*.

CPSIA information can be obtained at www.ICGtesting.com

224671LV00001B/25/P